Bound in Darkness

The Legend of Mortem | Book Two

J.L. Weir

Trigger Warnings

Bound in Darkness contains content which may trigger some readers. If you are bothered by torture, kidnapping, self-harm, or mentions of rape, and domestic violence, please consider carefully before reading this book.

CHAPTER 1

Silas and Jadis were in their master suite dressing for the upcoming party, but Silas had been dressed for an hour. He wandered around the house elated; his exuberance overshadowed his normally calm and controlled demeanor. It was obvious he couldn't wait to reveal her change to their clan. Jadis, however, was dawning and discarding multiple outfits, all the while trying to motivate herself for what laid ahead. Mag and Limi playfully romped around the room, and their boisterous roughhousing had Silas fully entertained. He sat in his chair next to the large floor-to-ceiling windows, waiting for Jadis to finish 'primping,' as he called it.

"I think I like you better naked," he joked, with a coy smile as he watched her failed attempts to pick an outfit.

"I thought you wanted me to get dressed?" She tossed a discarded camisole at his face, which he caught with a light hearted smile. She slowly strolled over to where he sat and placed her hands on either side of the chair, climbed into his lap, and straddled him.

This was more than a soiree for Silas. Her reveal taking place later in the evening was his pièce de résistance, and she was his newly *turned* hidden gem. Jadis, however, was a mixture of anxious emotions; the mere thought of telling their clans she was Nosferatu sent her mind spiraling into an abyss of self-doubt. She felt like she was choking on her untold truth, and was fixated on their worst-case reactions. The visions seemed to go off in her head like a carousel of slides, slowly clicking one after the other like scenes flickering onto a blank wall in a darkened room, an animated movie without sound or color.

"Baby," Silas gently whispered as his eyes met hers. "Calm yourself; your mind is besieged with unnecessary thoughts and worry." His words were absolute and provided her a sense of tranquility. She wrapped her arms around him and placed her face in the crook of his neck.

"This is an evening we've been anticipating, for two and a half weeks to be precise." He wrapped his arms a bit tighter around her, and his devotion, his confidence were unwavering. She knew this was a fate they could no longer conceal. She let out an exasperated sigh, much to Silas's amusement.

The effervescent sounds of the staff preparing for the hundred or so guests arriving within the hour, was as abrasive as a single cricket hiding under a floorboard while one tried to sleep. She mentally closed the bedroom door to put some distance between herself and the racket endlessly pounding in her head. Once she had *turned*, all her senses were heightened ten-fold. It had only been seventeen days since her conversion, and Silas had been grooming her, helping her to cultivate, refine, and control all her newfound abilities. However, there were hours when certain sounds would suddenly turn into the equivalent of a screaming siren, and her auditory range seemed endless. Silas, on more than one occasion, had to help her drown out the noises when she couldn't control it herself.

"Now stop dilly dallying, and get ready, baby. We don't have a lot of time," Silas playfully stated, along with a kiss.

"*Dilly dallying*? Really?" she replied in a mocking tone. She finally got up from his lap and walked over to the antique dresser, looking into the mirror deep in thought. She studied her features and the uniqueness of her eyes—Silas's eyes. *Damn.* She was still trying to get used to her *new* look. She studied the changes to see if they were noticeable enough for anyone to pick up on before disclosing the truth.

She raised her hands to her ears to muffle the noise the closed door couldn't. *What I need is to calm down. I have Silas by my side; everything will be fine,* she told herself.

"You worry too much. Nothing is going to happen." He felt her trepidation, not to mention she was covering her ears, so naturally, he knew the noise was once again getting the better of her. "Here, let me," he offered.

She dropped her hands, turned around to face him, and clung to him. He hugged her back and enveloped her body with his. He laid a gentle kiss to the top of her head, cupped her face in his hands, and lifted her head so her eyes met his. "It's going to be fine; you don't need to worry about this. I'll be with you the entire time."

He bent down and parted her lips with his. Once again, Silas took control, and a hush of silence washed over her. She gently pulled away and looked up at him. "Thank you, baby. As always, my knight in shining armor," she joked.

"I'm not sure about that. The armor's a bit tainted and blood stained, and I think your knight is more of an assassin."

"*Blood*, huh?" She looked up at him with one raised eyebrow. In an instant, she nipped his bottom lip with her canines and licked the droplet of blood with her tongue. "You taste amazing, *assassin*."

Silas grabbed her and tossed her onto her back on the bed. She let out a yelp and laughed as her body bounced on the mattress. He hovered over the top of her and pinned her arms above her head. "Feeding time, is it?" he asked coyly.

"Maybe, or maybe it's time for something else?" She winked as she wrapped her legs around his waist and pulled him down on top of her. She felt his arousal rising beneath his jeans as he settled between her legs.

"I'll take the *something else*," he said, already aroused. He gently rocked back and forth, rubbing his hardened muscle on her crotch. Her body was alive with desire and hunger—hunger for not only his blood but his sex.

"Our guests will be here in about forty-five minutes, baby—" Silas rumbled.

She cut him off. "I only need forty-four." She winked.

He quickly unlatched her bra and tossed it to the floor. "All right then." He straddled her waist, pulled his shirt over his head, and tossed it aside, revealing his perfect body and mesmerizing tattoos.

She was always enamored with Silas. *He's gorgeous, perfect, and mine.* She ran her hands over his shoulders, down his muscular chest, and slowly traced his tattoos and battle scars with her fingers. They were like poetry intertwined, portraying centuries of life well lived. *The battle scars, however, told more about his hardships, the wars fought and won, his bravery, and courage than the tattoos did.*

She moved her hands further down and unbuttoned his jeans, freeing his erection. He quickly repositioned their bodies and slipped off her panties as well as his jeans.

He rested his hard body on hers, and the soft warmth of her tongue welcomed his. Her eyes became the cat-like slits mirroring his own.

"I can never get enough of you," she whispered.

He kissed his way down her neck and slid his mouth across her vein. He paused and listened to the heightened beat of her pulse. He gently kissed his way across her collarbone, to the other side of her neck, and back up to claim her mouth. "I think I'm hungry as well," he murmured.

She writhed beneath him. She craved him in every way, from blood to bone. She let out a low, animalistic growl, and it was clear to Silas, she was no longer mortal in the slightest.

She was a now a complex labyrinthine, an ornately designed mythical being. She had ascended into a mixture of her semi-mortal coil as a bruja and Silas' vampirism. They just hadn't figured out what she was capable of, although she had a feeling Silas already had an idea.

He parted her legs and thrust himself inside. *Exactly what I want, need. God, he feels amazing.* As he rocked back and forth, she grabbed the back of his neck and pulled him to her, needing to feed.

He turned his head and aligned his neck for her, so she could take his vein. "Let me help you out a bit. Your aim is mediocre at best," he joked.

She was still a bit awkward being newly turned. At times, she struck his vein with her canines; other times, she missed and had to try again. She wasn't sure which entertained him more.

She sank all eight canines into his musky, tanned skin. The blood flowed over her tongue and her body consumed every drop. Her appetite was insatiable when it came to him; his blood was like an aphrodisiac. Feeding and fucking simultaneously turned her on more than she had anticipated.

As soon as he felt the sting of her bite, a low growl rose up from his chest. He rocked with greater force, trying not to move his neck, until she took her fill.

His blood flowed over her tongue and seared through her veins. With each hungry pull, she felt the orgasm coil up. He shoved so hard, she released his throat, pressed her head back into the pillow, and let out a chesty moan.

He licked the blood from the tips of her canines and took her mouth to his once again. He didn't think he would ever get used to the way his own blood tasted on her tongue. "Shit, that's intoxicating," he mumbled.

He gently turned her head to the side, exposing her neck. He felt her pulse thumping beneath his mouth as he pierced her tender flesh with a lust filled hunger.

The painful pricks sent a jolt through her body. "Damn, that catches me off guard every time," she moaned.

As her blood pooled into his mouth, he let out a low, deep-throated rumble that vibrated her body.

"Oh—shit," she cried out as a crack of sensations rocked her body.

Each grind of his hips, and the feeling of her core throbbing against his shaft, brought about his own release. He removed his canines from her neck and rested his face next to hers. "Damn, that hits hard."

He lay on top of her for a short time before slowly pulling out.

"There's no better feeling than lying in your arms," she stated.

"I couldn't agree more," he replied.

She lay there sated and listened to his heavy breathing as their chests rose and fell together.

He rolled over and pinned her body beneath his. "I finally have every-thing I've ever wanted—the perfect mate."

"Me too, baby. You have no idea how much I cherish you. I believe I'm obsessed with you, assassin."

"And you're all mine—say it. I want to hear it with your new voice," Silas purred.

"Yes, baby. I'm yours and don't you ever forget it," Jadis replied.

"Good to hear." He playfully tangled her body in his.

"Silas, let go—I can't breathe." She laughed.

He playfully rolled over a couple of times with her in his arms and slapped her naked ass. "Let's go, mon chéri. We have a party to attend, not to mention a little announcement," Silas said, beaming.

"Great, you just had to go there." She jumped out of bed and playfully smacked his chest. He grabbed her hand and pulled her body firmly into his.

"I can't wait to see the looks on their faces. I have a feeling Eden and Aiden's expressions will be worth every penny. Now get dressed; everyone's already arriving," He said along with a pat on her ass.

"I know, I hear them." She heard the nervousness in her own voice as she answered him.

They put their jeans back on, along with matching bluish-grey shirts, which Silas had picked out. His was a button-up, collared dress shirt, and hers was a flowing silk tank. They matched perfectly. It was apparent her indecision about what to wear took too much time. *Not sure what is with Silas dressing us alike; it's just his thing. It's pretty charming.* She chuckled, not realizing she was doing so aloud.

"You find it amusing?" he asked.

"Yes. The fact you, this big, bad, blood-thirsty assassin picked out matching outfits for us." She waved her hand up and down his body and gently tugged at the front of his shirt. "It's adorable and charming."

He raised his eyebrow. "*Adorable and charming*, huh? I'll show you *adorable and charming*." His tone was playfully menacing.

She laughed and poked him in the chest with her finger. "You'd be scarier if we didn't match," she teased.

He grabbed her finger and pulled her in for a kiss. "Let's go. We need to greet our guests. Being fashionably late is becoming a habit. No pun intended," he quipped, with a wink and a half-cocked smile. "Just one more thing."

"What?" she asked.

"We need to conceal you. If any of them see you looking like this, they'll know you've fed. Your eyes speak for themselves. They're sated like a leopard's after a kill."

"Really?" She looked back into the mirror. *Yep, they'll know, the transformation is plain as day. Not only do our shirts match, but our eyes are also an exact mirror of each other.*

"Let me." He quickly showed her how to conceal them, having adding a little of his own energy to make sure they didn't betray her before it was time. "There, you look just like you did when they last saw you in the Valley of the Old Gods."

She turned and looked into the mirror. *Sure enough.* As she gazed into her 'normal eyes,' her only thought was they seemed to have lost their essence. *I love having Silas's eyes; these are just mundane and nondescript, another pebble in the sand.*

Silas gently rubbed her shoulders. "There is, was, nothing *mundane* about you, and you've never been a *pebble*. You've always been stunning; now it's just an enhanced version."

He bent over, kissed her cheek, and traced her jawline with his fingers. "You're enticing, my love, regardless of which set of eyes we're looking at."

She reached up and placed her hand on the side of his face. "I'd rather have your eyes." She smiled.

"Agreed, and the sooner you get them back, the better. Now let's go."

"Wait—what about your eyes?"

"I'll mask them as well." He interlaced their fingers together and led her out the door with Mag and Limi in tow. They walked out to the hallway and headed toward the top of the expansive staircase. Beautiful hand-carved railings lined the upper hallway and stairs, while the dark-oak flooring stood out from beneath the edges of the decorative oriental rugs. The parlor was large, with floor-to-ceiling windows offering a panoramic view of the Jungle outside. Deep-red velvet curtains adorned the windows, gracefully cascading in soft, pleated piles upon the dark wood floor.

The bartenders were quietly waiting for the guests to arrive, and the wall behind them was lined with every hue of amber liquid in their ostentatious bottles. The caterers were busy making their final preparations for the guests who would be dining with a mortal palate, while the Nosferatu would be feeding from amenable hosts throughout the duration of the party. There were two rooms, one on either side of the main parlor that would serve as a more private dining area for the vampires. There were always plenty of beautiful women who were willing blood hosts, all longing to be suitable bedmates.

Jadis knew her sisters were about to enter, and she looked up at Silas for reassurance. Once again, he squeezed her hand in response. "Relax, baby, it'll be fine."

As soon as they made it to the top of the stairs, Skye and Ivory entered through two large, ornate front doors, having been opened by two impeccably dressed doormen. They walked in hand in hand with Syth and Agaeus. The moment Jadis saw them, she pulled from Silas's grip and hurried down the stairs.

Skye and Ivory looked up and saw Jadis trotting down the steps toward them. They let out squeals of excitement and ran to her. They embraced each other like they hadn't seen each other in months.

Silas and his brothers greeted each other as well before turning their attention to their mates. They greeted Jadis, Skye, and Ivory with a kiss on either cheek and a tight embrace. They hadn't seen or spoken to each other since they left the Valley two weeks ago. Silas and Jadis were too busy enjoying each other, not to mention hiding the fact she had *turned*. Their allusiveness went unquestioned; It wasn't uncommon for Nosferatu to retreat for a period of time after mating.

"Jesus, Jadis, you look amazing! We never thought being mated to Silas would look so good on you," Ivory teased.

Skye looked at Silas and laughed in jest. "You've been good for my sister. What have you done or dare I ask?" She held Jadis's hands out in front of her, and she knew right away she looked different but couldn't quite put her finger on it.

Ivory grabbed Jadis's hand and spun her around. "What the hell? Did Silas also build you a gym?"

As Jadis laughed nervously, she heard Silas in her head. "Shhh, calm, baby, they don't know."

"What and speechless? What the hell is up with you?" Ivory exclaimed, in a joking manner.

Jadis let out a sigh, releasing some of the nervous tension she had been holding in. She felt like she had been holding her breath since the moment they had entered.

Ivory grabbed her hand. "Come, we need a drink."

"I couldn't agree more," Jadis replied as they headed straight to the bar.

Ivory ordered their drinks, and the bartender politely set them down. As Jadis gulped down the entire drink Skye and Ivory were a bit taken aback.

"Damn, Jadis. I've never seen you drink so fast." Skye laughed.

"Everything okay?" Ivory asked telepathically.

"Yes, I couldn't be happier." Jadis answered aloud. *Which is the honest truth.* "It's good to see you both. It's only been a couple of weeks, but it feels like it's been months."

"Agreed." Ivory held her glass up, and Skye and Jadis returned the gesture.

"Here's to being newly mated and a lifetime of happiness," Ivory said.

"Cheers to that," Jadis and Skye replied in unison.

As they gently clinked their glasses together, a crack of thunder captured Jadis' attention and pulled her gaze to the expansive windows. *I'm nervous enough as it is, and now there's a storm heading our way.* She watched the bolts of lightning snake their way through the windows, lighting up the room. The colors had her hypnotized. *I can feel the static in the air with each flicker.* She lifted her hand out in front of her, feeling the gentle, energetic buzz.

Skye noticed Jadis reaching her hand out as if hypnotized. "You okay? You seem distracted," Skye asked, as she Ivory side-eyed each other, trying to see what she was so taken with.

As soon as Jadis noticed her sister's eyes on her, she quickly snapped her hand back.

"Okay, why are you being so weird?" Ivory demanded.

"Beautiful, isn't it?" Silas offered telepathically, having noticed Jadis watching the storm. She looked in his direction and smiled.

"Are you even listening to us, Jadis?" Ivory questioned.

"What? Yes, Ivory, I heard you. I was looking at my mate," she replied, keeping her eyes fixed on Silas.

Skye playfully shoved Jadis's shoulder. "Bullshit! Something's up with you, we can feel it."

Silas, Syth, and Agaeus joined the girls and ordered a couple of drinks for themselves.

"Jadis is fine," Silas offered.

Silas stood behind Jadis and wrapped one arm around her waist. She rested her hand on his forearm with a tight grasp, trying to maintain her sense of composure. As she looked up at him, his smile lit up the room. *He also looks like a fox in the henhouse,* she thought, which brought her back to her heightened state of mind. *The party is just beginning, and I feel like a fly stuck in a web, waiting for the inevitable.*

Silas heard her and laughed aloud, interrupting her train of thought.

"What's up with the two of you?" Syth asked as he raised a questioning eyebrow.

"No doubt about it, somethings off," Agaeus agreed.

"What's with the evasive answers, brother? Do tell," Syth demanded.

Jadis was so engrossed with the noise and the feel of the energetic buzz, Silas had to mentally take hold of her thoughts before she *turned* with the storm's intensity.

"We have a little announcement to make," Silas replied.

Silas' words broke her fixation, and she glared at him.

"We want details and now," Skye demanded.

Ivory waved her hand at Silas and Jadis to give up the goods. "Out with it."

"Oh my God! Are you pregnant?" Ivory's booming voice attracted the attention of everyone nearby, causing them to turn and stare at Silas and Jadis.

Jadis nearly lost it once again. *It isn't the announcement we planned, although I would prefer it,* she thought, along with a burst of laughter.

"No, we're not pregnant. Not yet anyway." Silas laughed.

A voice broke in from behind. "I see the party's already started without us?"

Jadis spun around. "Aiden!" she exclaimed. She jumped right into his arms, and he swept her up and spun her around.

Silas went as rigid as an iron coffin nail. No matter how well he and Aiden were getting along, he still struggled with his affection for Jadis.

Aiden set her down and held her hands out in front of her. "You look amazing—happy." Aiden was at a loss for words staring at her. *There's definitely something different about her.* "Fresh?" was all that came to mind.

"*Fresh*? Well, that's the first time I've ever been told I look *fresh*. Usually, someone's referring to me as a pain in the ass."

Aiden laughed as well and let go of her hands to greet Silas. "Cousin, good to see you again. It's been awhile. Being mated looks good on you," he said, acknowledging that Jadis belonged to him.

Silas grasped his forearm. "Good to see you too, cousin."

Another voice broke in from behind. "You still can't keep your hands off each other, I see?"

"Aria, you actually showed up? I thought you had dignity," Jadis replied in jest.

"And I thought you'd look better," Aria quipped back, along with a tight embrace.

We've come a long way since having met a month ago in the Valley. Our initial meeting was more of a knife to the throat kind of introduction, Jadis thought.

Aria took her place next to Aiden, who wrapped his arm around her shoulders. She in return wrapped one arm around his waist. Silas proceeded to hand a drink to everyone, and they all held up their glasses to one another and took a drink.

"What, no crack knives?" Jabari laughed as he sauntered over to give Jadis a hug, having walked in with Aiden and Aria.

"Not yet anyway," Jadis replied.

"Give us a couple hours," Aria joked, as she gently nudged Jadis with her shoulder.

"I see you were able to keep her locked down for a couple of weeks?" Dante announced.

"Dante, welcome. Good to see you again, brother." Silas said as he grasped Dante's forearm. They gave each other a quick hug, along with a couple of hard pats on each other's backs.

Dante looked at Jadis and winked. "I see my brother's in one piece and sane? I'm a bit surprised."

"There's that funny vampire. I thought I missed you, Dante. I was wrong," Jadis teased.

He picked her up and gave her a suffocating squeeze. He finally set her back down and looked her over, not once but twice, with a curious expression.

Bain strolled up, grabbed Jadis's hand, and spun her around. "Since you're both standing here and we haven't been summoned, I'm assuming Silas has you wearing a certain anklet?" Bain offered, looking down at her foot.

"Missing your nannying duties? I thought you would have moved up the ranks," she joked.

"Yep, that's the smartass I know." Bain laughed.

Jadis heard the squeals coming from Maddie and Chloe, who walked in with Eden.

She moved from the current crowd at the bar and headed toward them. She suddenly realized Silas caught her and slowed her down. She hadn't realize how swiftly she moved. *Thank God for Silas.*

"What's up with Jadis?" Bain asked, looking to Silas.

"What do you mean?" Silas asked, like he knew nothing.

"Come now, Silas. I can see it. I felt it picking her up. There was something different. Is she okay?" Dante asked, truly concerned. He cared for her in ways he continuously tried to deny to himself. After everything that had taken place between them all back on the yacht, he was genuinely concerned. The 'little possession' was no joking matter.

Silas gave him a hard pat on the shoulder. "Trust me, she's better than okay." He smirked.

"Apparently, they have some sort of announcement," Agaeus offered. The curiosity piqued once again in everyone standing around.

"Oh, hell," Bain rumbled. "Jadis and anything secret can't be a good thing. I believe this party will be interesting, to say the least. So how much should we drink before your little *announcement*?" He tilted his glass toward Silas, who again laughed aloud.

"Have the bottle," Silas suggested.

A flash of curiosity flashed across everyone's face. Eyebrows raised, heads tilted to the side, all trying to decipher what Silas wasn't telling them. The way Silas was acting was completely out of the ordinary; he was never upbeat in such a manner.

Dante turned toward Bain. "A very familiar feeling is rushing over me. Something is a foot as we speak."

"I agree, this feels all too familiar. You still have that double-headed coin?" Bain joked.

"What I *have* is the need for another drink," Dante rumbled..

"As Silas said, you should grab the bottle," Bain added, causing them both to laugh.

Dante materialized a coin in his hand and tossed it into the air toward Bain.

"I call heads this time," Dante declared.

Bain snatched the coin out of midair and as soon as he opened his palm, it was on tails.

"I'll remember this later. I had my turn once already," Dante reminded him.

"Sorry, wizard, tails is tails." Bain smirked back, shrugging his shoulders.

Jadis was busy greeting Maddie and Chloe, while Silas moved in to greet Eden.

"You both look amazing. I've missed the two of you." Jadis was truly happy to see them again. *They were there during one of my most trying and confusing moments,* she thought. *More like a beacon of light, softening the darkness that seemed to embrace me. Not to mention Maddie running interference between Eden and myself on multiple occasions.*

"You look so different. We thought you might look a little rough after everything Eden and Aiden had shared with us. Seriously, Silas must be taking good care of you. You look amazing, yet different somehow?" Maddie politely looked her up and down with a warm smile.

"It's really good to see you so happy," Chloe offered.

Jadis ran her hand up and down Chloe's arm. "I'm really happy you're both here."

Jadis caught the way Maddie and Chloe subtly glanced at each other and then back at her. *"They're noticing. What if I do something stupid again, like I did when I almost materialized next to them?"* Jadis said to Silas telepathically.

"They don't know, my love. Just enjoy yourself. Everyone is truly happy to be here. At the end of the day, we're all family. There's no judgement."

"Really, Silas? 'No judgement'?" She looked over at him and raised an eyebrow.

"Well, you do give them plenty of reason, if we're going there." The statement cracked them both up. *He's right. After all, I am my own worst enemy.*

"What's so funny?" a voice asked.

Jadis turned, only to see Eden standing inches from her.

Silas was there in an instant, saving her from herself. *Even after everything we've been through, Eden still intimidates me,* she thought, while staring at him blankly.

As Silas and Eden grasped each other's forearms, and hugged each other, Jadis took the opportunity to gather her composure.

Eden moved to Jadis and gave her a genuine hug. "It seems you've finally been behaving yourself, and you look great," he offered.

Jadis didn't like how Eden was looking at her. *Even though he sounds lighthearted, I can tell he's curious. Once again, his subtle keenness to seek information is unnerving. If anyone is going to sniff out my turning, it will be Eden.*

"Thank you. You look good too. How are the headaches, or should we say migraines?" Jadis raised a curious eyebrow, doing her best to act nonchalant.

"I found a cure. It's called a little distance and this. "Eden pulled a bottle of pills from his pocket.

"You didn't," Maddie exclaimed. "You're as incorrigible as ever!"

"That was a smart move on your part Eden, I believe you'll need those later," Silas joked, raising his glass to him.

Jadis slapped Silas on the stomach, giving him a look of death, which he of course brushed off.

Eden, however, was taking it all in and studying Jadis's appearance. His curiosity when it came to her, was cynical. On more than one occasion bedlam had followed her to his doorstep.

Jadis practically pulled Silas back to the bar trying to escape Eden's unrelenting, curiosity.

CHAPTER 2

The party was in full swing, and the cacophony of music and voices drifted through the busy atmosphere. Everyone had arrived hours ago, and the food was being served for the guests who did eat, while the blood hosts were being escorted to the private rooms for those with other appetites. The boisterous laughter radiated from the rowdy crowd and all business was left at the door; tonight was a night for celebration.

Eden quietly turned to Aiden. "Something's a-miss, I can feel it."

"I agree." Aiden nodded.

It had been hours since Jadis thought about their announcement, and she was hoping they could wait for another time. She felt guilty their admittance of her turning would potentially ruin the festivities. *Leave it to me to,* she thought before Silas interjected.

"Stop baby, this is a good thing. As usual you're over thinking it."

"Silas I turned without the clan's permission, much less a single lord's, how is this a good thing? Eden will lose his shit and you know it."

"So what's this little announcement the two of you aren't sharing?" Lars blurted out.

Leave it to fucking Lars to bring it up! Jadis thought as she looked at him and glared.

"Fess up, we want to know," he demanded.

"*Announcement? What announcement?*" Eden asked as he looked straight to Jadis with his head cocked.

Great! All eyes are now focused on me, and I feel like they're searing into my very soul, she thought, before trying to get out of Eden's way.

Silas caught Jadis; she moved so quickly trying to get away from Eden, he took immediate control. He knew if she materialized elsewhere in front everyone the cat was out of the bag.

"I guess it's time, come." Silas motioned to the staff to clear one of the rooms off the parlor. He took Jadis' trembling hand in his and chuckled.

All the worst-case scenarios Jadis had conjured up earlier were now in the forefront of her mind once again. They made their way to one of the smaller rooms, and one of the female attendants closed the door behind them, shutting out everyone but immediate family and a few of the vetted waitstaff.

Jadis was hoping Aria would be able to calm Aiden when he heard the news. *It is anyone's guess as to how this is going to go at this point,* she thought.

"Enjoy each other's company, it's well deserved. We'll make the announcement shortly," Silas offered.

Silas now sounds like the 'all business' vampire I'm used to, there's no escaping this now, she thought.

Jadis's sisters' could always be counted on to break the tension with their laughter and jokes, and Maddie of course, could always be counted on to add a bit of reassuring support.

Maddie walked over to Jadis and squeezed her hand. "Whatever it is, I'm sure it will be fine. Relax, I can see the tension all over your face." She smiled. "Let's get another drink."

Jadis walked to the bar with her and joined her sisters, as well as Chloe and Aria. All the while she could feel Eden watching her every move.

"I think a bomb is about to drop," Dante said to Bain.

"Yep. I can't even imagine what we're about to find out."

Eden saw the looks on Dante and Bains faces, and joined the private conversation. *"I already feel a migraine coming on."* He tilted his glass toward them and took a large swig.

"I believe something worse than the portal is about to unleash itself," Aiden added, also having joined the conversation.

Silas was watching Jadis from across the room and as soon as she looked at him, he winked at her, and smiled like it was time.

She shook her head, as if to say no. *"Not yet,"* she replied telepathically.

"You can't put this off all night, my dear."

One of the barmaids walked over to Silas, rubbed her hand up his arm, and gently squeezed his bicep. "Can I get you another drink, milord?" She placed her other hand on his lower back before tilting her head to the side, exposing her neck. She looked up at him and pulled her hair to the side. She seemed to care less he was mated and was offering up more than an alcoholic drink.

Did she really touch my mate? Not only that, but she's also offering to feed him, as well as spread her fucking legs, As soon as the thought crossed Jadis' mind, she lunged at her. In an instant she had the barmaid pinned to the ground, with her throat in her mouth.

Maddie and Chloe let out a short, gasp filled scream; Skye and Ivory grabbed each other's arms and Ivory exclaimed, "Holy shit!"

Aria, however, didn't make a sound. She didn't dare move from Aiden's side as she stood with her mouth gaping open; she didn't know how to react.

Silas didn't bother trying to stop Jadis, he was completely in awe, he was captivated, not to mention turned on at the sight of his mate attacking and feeding from the barmaid.

The girl was not merely consumed by Jadis, but every cell in her body was drained. The waitress's mouth gaped open, releasing her last breath as she curled up on the floor in a fetal position, transforming into the likeness of solid ash. She took on the appearance mummified body, ancient and preserved for thousands of years.

Silas stood protectively, making sure no one intervened.

Jadis gracefully stood and glanced at everyone in the room, all of whom were standing as still as inanimate objects. Their expressions ranged somewhere between stunned, to shock, to amusement. She wiped the blood off the corner of her mouth with her thumb, and gently sucked it off. She then casually stepped over the mummified body as if it was nothing. As soon as she turned around to face everyone it was clear; she was Nosferatu, she had been *turned*.

Silas held his hand out to Jadis, and let his eyes resume their *new normal*.

Aria was in shock as she looked at their eyes; *they're the same cat-like-slits, swirling with color. They look like an exact replica of each other's,* she thought.

Dante, Bain, Aden, and Eden were mortified. Lars, Jabari, Agaeus, and Syth stood in quiet amazement.

"And we just thought they had matching shirts," Lars announced as each chuckle grew with intensity.

Dante snapped his wrist and silenced the few remaining barmaids, quickly putting them in a comatose state of mind to keep them still.

Jadis had her back to Silas, who had protectively wrapped his arms around her chest. She latched onto his forearms and looked up at him.

He bent down, smiling from ear to ear, beaming with pride before he took her mouth to his.

"I think I'm in big trouble," she said silently, looking to him for comfort.

"You're in trouble all right," he whispered.

She pulled her head back. "What? Are you mad at me?" *If Silas is mad, that's it. I'll completely fall apart.*

He looked at her with a coy grin. "Once I get your ass back to the bedroom, you're going to be in trouble, big trouble. I think you need to be punished, and I have a few ideas."

She could feel his arousal against her butt, and she released a huge sigh of relief. *At least something feels normal right now; Silas is turned on.*

Eden cautiously stepped forward and cleared his throat. "I hate to interrupt the two of you love birds, but what the everlasting hell was that?"

As Jadis and Silas stood facing the crowd, they also looked at Silas in shock; the transformation in his eyes was undeniable.

"Holy shit," Skye exclaimed, to the amusement of Ivory and Aria who laughed so hard, they were crying.

"Silas, have you lost your goddamn mind? What were you thinking, turning Jadis?" Eden hollered.

"I didn't turn her, Eden," Silas said it sternly, but he looked amused. Jadis, however, wasn't amused at all. She practically crawled inside Silas to hide from Eden's wrath.

"Look at her," Eden snapped, as he stepped forward again. He grasped her jaw in his hand, and slowly turned her head from side to side. He studied her as if he couldn't believe what he was seeing with his own eyes. A rumble of warning rose from Silas, which Eden ignored.

His eyes snapped up to meet Silas'. "Jadis, of all people. You turned the biggest pain in my ass into a newborn vampire? Shit!" Eden let go of her face and rubbed his forehead. "Not to mention, she has eight, count them, eight fucking canines. This'll be an unmitigated disaster."

"I promise you, Eden, I didn't turn her, not the way you're thinking. This is all Jadis. She turned the night I took her as my mate," Silas insisted, with a proud shrug of his shoulders.

"And you, Silas, look at your eyes. What the ever-loving hell did she do?" Eden questioned.

"Me? I didn't do any of this, I swear!" Eden didn't bother to acknowledge Jadis.

"Silas, you know goddamn well what it takes to turn someone. Jadis didn't do this on her own," Eden barked, not believing it for a minute. He couldn't fathom the idea she was capable of turning without Silas's help.

Dante looked at Bain. "Turning Jadis? Well, tonight has taken an unexpected turn of events. Pun intended." He laughed. "Remember what we said on the yacht that night, about dining on rats?"

"I do." Bain nodded. "This is bad, can you imagine? Look at her, she looks like Silas. She just put that girl to her death without hesitation. On top of it, look at her body. She mummified her!"

Dante was truly at a loss. "I have no idea, However, I have a daunting feeling this will turn out worse than her portal bullshit."

"Cheers to that, this is beyond the realm of reason," Bain uttered as the two of them clinked their glasses. Unable to ignore the laughter all around them, they too succumbed to Lars and the girls' amusement. Eden, however, wasn't laughing at any of it. He was outraged.

Lars looked over to Aiden, who was in shock. "Aiden, you thought she was a pain in the ass before, what do you think now?"

"I bet you're happy she belongs to Silas now," Bain joked.

"Laugh it up. It's all fun and games until there's nothing left to eat," Dante added.

"Jadis, of all witches, or should we say originals. Not only can she call upon the Old Gods, but now she possesses the powers of Nosferatu," Aiden stated to no one in particular.

Jabari placed a strong hand on Aiden's shoulder. "Is it always this entertaining? No one will ever go to their grave tired around your family. Had I known it would be this much fun, I would have joined clans with you all years ago." Jabari let out a belly laugh, grabbed another drink, and watched as the show continued. He took a seat on the solid mahogany bar stool, looking to Aiden for an answer, or not.

"Until lately, no. This is all classic Jadis, pulling some fucked-up shit. She was uncontrollable as it was; now I can't even imagine the shit this will bring on." Aiden couldn't help himself either; he laughed at the shitstorm they were all in at the hands of Jadis, once again. However, he was completely enthralled with her looks; he couldn't take his eyes off her. The same feelings he had pushed down reared their ugly head.

Dante re-filled his glass and took another drink. "At least we to to experience a few weeks of peace and calm."

"Hey, Eden," Jabari called out.

Eden turned his head ever so slightly and side-eyed Jabari.

"This is one hell of a party so far," Jabari announced as he raised his glass to him and laughed all the more.

Eden ignored his comment and glanced around the room; not only were the girls laughing, Dante and Bain had joined in, and now he had lost Jabari and Aiden.

"Am I the only one here who hasn't lost my goddamn mind?" Eden was exasperated with everyone. "She isn't the newborn Nosferatu you want to be in charge of!"

"You thought an anklet and chains were needed before, can you imagine now?" Bain said in jest to Silas.

"You're seriously out of your mind, cousin," Aiden announced as he shook his head.

"Still being an ass, I see," Jadis snapped at Aiden. However, it was more of a rumble with her new voice. Everyone reacted to the tone of her voice in one way or another.

Aria turned to Aiden. "Have I lost my mind, or did she sound like Silas?"

"I think we're all about to lose our minds," he joked. "And yes, she sounded exactly like him."

Silas turned his attention back to Eden. "Eden, she did indeed turn on her own. I was as shocked as all of you are now."

"Silas didn't turn me, Eden. It just happened," Jadis offered, trying to help.

Dante raised an accusatory eyebrow at her. "The hell if Silas didn't turn you. Look at yourself, it's undeniable. You're clearly Nosferatu now. It didn't just happen—not unless you did something to make Silas turn you?"

Everyone looked in Jadis's direction with that statement. *Wonderful, it's as if they're waiting for an admittance of guilt, and now I'm completely under scrutiny with nowhere to run.*

"So, if that's the case, why haven't Skye and Ivory turned? Hell, they mated Syth and Agaeus. Unless the two of you have an *announcement* as well?" Eden snarled toward the four of them.

"No," Agaeus replied. "They didn't turn."

"I didn't make Silas do anything! Seriously, it's not like I wanted to become one of you. I just woke up a vampire." She tried her best to defend Silas and herself.

"Let me get this straight—you want us to believe you just woke up after having turned while sleeping? You went to sleep that night and bam, you *turned*," Eden said, as he snapped his fingers. "Just like that! Well, there you have it then. Makes perfect sense to me." Eden threw his hands up in the air. "It's not like I'm six hundred and seventy-plus years old and have never seen this happen." Eden looked to everyone else. "Makes sense, doesn't it? Jadis turned, just like that!" He snapped his fingers in her face this time.

His anger and sarcasm are pissing me off. "I wouldn't do that if I were you." She growled in Eden's face and bared her canines—all of eight them.

Silas grabbed onto her as soon as she moved toward Eden, knowing she couldn't control the sudden onset of anger that was unfamiliar to her. The room went still, and a wave of shock crossed everyone's face at the same time.

"Yep, this is where Jadis dies," Lars offered to the hushed, gaping crowd.

Silas tenderly stroked her cheek. "Control it, baby. The smallest of threats right now will challenge you, forcing you to turn."

Maddie stood to walk to Eden, but he held his hand up, stopping her in her tracks. "Not now. I got this," he stated, never taking his eyes off Jadis.

She quickly sat back down, not knowing what Eden was about to do. She truly was a bit concerned for Jadis right now.

"You've got to be kidding me? Did you just challenge me?" Eden growled. His canines dropped from his gums as he stepped toward her.

Silas let out a cautionary rumble of warning, vibrating from his chest. "Back up, Eden."

Eden ignored the warning. He was solely focused on Jadis having challenged and threatened him. He couldn't believe what he was seeing, much less hearing.

Lars took another drink before breaking the awkward silence and the tension once again. "She just called your ass out!" He enjoyed taunting the situation for his own amusement, as usual.

Aria played bartender now that the few remaining staff were currently comatose, not wanting to stop the party. She thoroughly enjoyed the show as much as everyone else.

Dante silently addressed Bain and Aiden, *"Oh, shit! This is about to turn into a three-way brawl."*

The three of them decided it best to step forward in case there needed to be an intervention. Aiden placed a hand on Eden's shoulder. Dante placed his hand on Silas', and Bain stood halfway in the middle, staring at Jadis, who was currently wrapped in Silas's arms as he held her back.

Bain shook his head at her. "Don't do it, darling, you'll be on the losing end of this fight." He tried to bring her down a notch or two, as the shit became all too serious.

Eden was determined to make his position in their hierarchy clear. He would put Jadis in her place regardless of how new she was, or where Silas stood on the matter. The only problem he had to contend with, was Silas; he would protect Jadis at all costs. Despite his anger, he knew Jadis had no control over her newly acquired, instinctual responses. Even so,

Eden was not going to back down and he put his finger in her face. "Take it down. I'm not playing with you right now, baby girl."

In response to Eden's threat, she released a low, guttural snarl, curled her lip, and slapped his finger out of her face.

"Oh shit!" Maddie gasped.

A few more hushed phrases came from the other members of their clan, as well.

Silas snatched her hands and folded her arms across her chest. He tilted his head and looked at Eden, waiting for him to make his move.

Fuck, I have no idea how to control the change. Hell, I don't even know what's happening to me, Jadis thought.

"Eden, she doesn't know what she's doing. It's instinctual at this point, and we both know that."

Eden didn't disagree with Silas, and he looked back to Jadis, who raised a defiant eyebrow at him.

"Oh no, you didn't," Eden growled as he leaned forward in her direction. "Do—not—provoke—me—again, Jadis," he stated, enunciating every word. He suddenly laughed aloud, sending a wave of caution throughout the room.

Dante side-eyed Bain and Aiden. "I think Eden just lost his mind. Jadis has finally pushed him over the edge."

"I think my migraine has returned full force," Eden barked in her face. "Until we figure this shit out, no one's leaving this room. Dante—Bain, seal it."

Eden proceeded to walk over to the body still lying on the floor and kneeled down to study it. "Silas, want to explain this?" He asked as he waved his hand back and forth over her corpse.

Maddie cautiously approached Eden and handed him a full glass, which he didn't hesitate to take. She remained at his side, resting a soft hand on his shoulder. She then looked at Jadis and winked.

Jadis flashed a half-turned-up smile resembling Silas' and Maddie's eyebrows shot up in bewilderment.

"Unfortunately, I can't. This is her first kill," Silas said it as if it were the most normal thing in the world.

"*First kill?*" Bain repeated to Dante. "I feel a nanny position opening. Don't forget we flipped the coin already; again, you lost," Bain added as the laughter between the two grew once again.

"What's that supposed to mean, *flipping a coin?*" Jadis asked, as she cocked her head; even her movements were different—acute, animalistic.

"Just an inside joke, darling," Dante replied.

"I suppose I'm at the center of your and Bain's jokes again?"

"Yes!" they replied without hesitation.

Jadis looked at Skye, who cautiously brought her a drink. She handed it to her from behind Silas's back, trying to stay as far away from Eden as she could get.

Eden looked from the corpse, to Jadis, back to the corpse, and finally to Silas. "So, what you're telling me, you did nothing that could have changed her. She didn't make you do something by using her powers while you were a bit distracted by *other* things." He handed his empty glass to Maddie, who quickly had Aria refill it.

"I didn't turn her, and yes, I've been a *bit distracted*." Silas winked, looking to Jadis. "But neither of us did anything. The night I took her as my mate, nothing out of the ordinary took place other than her having a rough, restless night, more than I had expected."

"Tell me every detail." Eden held up his hand. "Well, almost every detail. I feel like you aren't speaking the truth in its entirety."

Silas ignored the last statement. "There isn't anything to tell. It wasn't until we finally awoke the next morning I noticed the change in her. As soon as she rolled over and looked at me, it was clear she had turned. After studying her for a few minutes, we realized I had also changed."

"I have no words right now." Eden once again rubbed his forehead. "Silas, do you feel any different?"

"I feel as though we've morphed so to speak; otherwise, I'm fine," he responded.

"Right now, we don't know if either of you are truly *fine*, as you so casually put it."

"Relax, Eden. I would know if Jadis or I were in danger, or a danger to anyone else. I've tolerated your interrogation up to this point as your questions aren't without merit, but do not question my intelligence," he warned.

Not wanting to challenge Silas or his abilities, Eden changed the subject. "Why did you wait so long to tell us what happened? What have the two of you been doing for the last three days that was so important, you couldn't make a call? You've never had a problem reaching out to us before where she's concerned," Eden reminded him.

"Exactly *what we've been doing*?" Silas smirked.

"You know what I'm talking about." Eden finally stood back up, looking at Jadis for an answer. "Jadis?"

She shrugged her shoulders. "I'm sorry, I didn't mean for this to happen. It just did."

"That's rich coming from you. None of us has ever known you to not mean everything you do," Eden replied..

She furrowed her eyebrows at him. "Don't be snarky."

"*Snarky*? You're really trying my patience right now." Eden's icy tone as the words left his mouth were so calmly menacing, it held her still.

Aiden finally stepped in. "Look, the situation is what it is right now. There's nothing we can do about it. We can't turn her back to just being a plain ole pain in the ass," he said, with a wink and a smirk.

"Well, maybe, just maybe, this has to do with my possession. Silas did say I had turned more than once, although he only shared the basics with me, so who knows?" Jadis offered. All eyes shot in her direction, followed by a hushed pause.

"Well, I'll be dammed, Jadis. I never thought you would be the one to come up with the most logical explanation of the evening," Aiden replied, half-joking.

She subtly flipped him off to his amusement, while everyone else seemed to contemplate what she had said.

"It would make sense," Silas agreed.

"Surprisingly, it does sound logical. We need to figure out our next steps. We also need to figure out what Jadis is before some real shit happens," Eden stated.

Jadis' only response to Eden's subtle jab was to squint her eyes at him.

"We need to keep Jadis to ourselves. This doesn't leave this room, understand?" Eden demanded of everyone currently sealed in together. Everyone nodded in agreement.

"If this gets out, Jadis, there'll be a huge target on your back. Silas, you know who I'm talking about—yes?"

Once again, it seems as if everyone but me is privy to what Eden's talking about.

"You've said enough, Eden," Silas grumbled. He was annoyed Eden would say something that would pique her curiosity.

"Want to fill me in?" Jadis asked, looking between Silas, Aiden, and Eden, who were clearly not going to tell her anything.

Silas kissed her cheek. "Later, my love."

She still intently watched Eden and Aiden, and she could tell they were speaking to each other privately.

"Dante—Bain, we need to contain this situation," Eden stated calmly.

"So, now I'm just a *situation*?" she asked, addressing them all.

"When are you ever not a *situation* to contend with, darling?" Dante joked.

"I see you're amused as usual at my expense."

"You give us plenty to be amused with," Bain teased.

Silas turned Jadis to face him. "Don't worry about them," he said with a dismissive wave. "We knew they would be in shock; neither of us expected anything less." He picked her up in his arms, and she wrapped her legs around his waist.

Clearly, Silas won't be any help whatsoever, Eden thought. *He has a newly turned mate, and that's all he'll focus on. I'm more concerned about Jadis's blood lust and hunger; it's inevitable. I'm not at all confident he Silas will control her. More than likely, he'll end up joining her. If that happens, there won't be a mortal alive who's safe from the two of them. Jadis was completely unpredictable before. Now that her humanity, what little she had to begin with, is gone, there's no telling what's going to happen.*

Eden motioned everyone over to the bar, letting Silas do whatever he was going to do with Jadis.

"This is bad." Eden said as he nodded toward Dante, Bain, and Aiden. "Silas will be useless to us, I'm afraid." Everyone agreed in one way or another.

"If Silas reverts—" Bain began.

Agaeus cut him off, defending his brother. "He's in full control; when is he ever not? I don't know what you're all so worried about."

"Remember who you're talking about. No one's in more control of themselves than Silas," Syth added.

"Let's hope the last four hundred years has calmed him down." Aiden truly dreaded the alternative.

The girls joined Silas and Jadis.

"This is crazy!" Ivory stated. "You'll have to give us all the dirty details."

"There are no dirty details." Jadis shrugged. "It just happened."

"Apparently, I'll need more than a couple of little crack knives now," Aria quipped.

The lightning strikes shooting through the windows, along with the sounds of the crackling thunder outside, captured Jadis's attention once again. She stared out the windows, enthralled with the storm's menacing beauty.

Ivory looked at Jadis and how easily she seemed to become distracted. "Jadis, you okay?"

"I just want a drink." She let out an exasperated sigh of relief now that Eden and the rest of the group were at the bar, and the secret was out in the open. *They may all be at the bar drinking, but they keep glancing at me.*

"I'm going to leave you to your girls while I go talk with Eden." Silas cupped her face in his hands and gave her a hard kiss. "I can't wait to get your ass back to bed," he said, along with a playful smack to her ass.

Chloe stepped back, and Jadis snatched her before she knew what happened, keeping her on her feet.

"What the hell was that about?" Chloe asked.

"The body." Jadis motioned to it as if it were nothing but a turned-up rug. "You almost fell over it."

"Oh, damn! That's awful. Shouldn't we do something about that?" Chloe asked.

"Do what you will. She got what she deserved," Jadis said, with a cold, inhuman rumble, one that her sisters had never heard from her before.

"Jadis!" Skye exclaimed. "What the fuck?" She wasn't quite sure how to reply to Jadis's coldness. *Hell, I know she hates mortals, but even this is beyond her.*

Maddie and Chloe were still in shock at the entire situation and had no idea how to respond.

"Come." Aria shuffled all of them away from the corpse laying in the middle of the room. "I'm so glad I didn't miss this. I can't remember the last time I was this entertained."

They made their way over to a couple of large loveseats on the opposite side of the room facing the expansive picture windows. Jadis flicked her wrist like Silas had taught her, and the music began playing in the background, to the amusement of all the girls.

"What the hell else can you do?" Aria questioned.

"I have no idea? it's only been a couple of weeks. Silas has been teaching me, but there's so much to know. It's overwhelming, to be honest."

The girls chose to ignore the conversation being had at the bar. *At least my girls aren't taking this seriously, which is exactly what I need,* Jadis thought.

Eden looked at Silas as he joined them at the bar. "You do realize you'll have to control her?"

"Yes," Silas replied dismissively.

Eden poured himself another drink. "Silas, you did stand there as she drained that girl in front of everyone. You obviously did nothing to stop her."

Silas glared at Eden. "I'm aware. I was curious, I wanted to see what she would do. It's not like this is the first time any of us has had to dispose of a dead body. Hell, I've seen how far you've gone yourself, Eden."

Syth, Agaeus, and Dante tilted their glasses to Silas in agreement.

"Silas, as I said earlier, we have to contain this situation. We all know this can't end well if she's not monitored at all times. Hell, we don't even fully know the extent of her powers or what she truly is—"

"Stop," Silas interrupted Eden and tilted his glass at him. "I agree with you. I have no idea what has happened either. What I do know is she's mine, so whatever takes place will be my decision and mine alone."

"Silas, it won't work that way this time. This concerns and involves all of us. She's our family, and it's our sworn duty to protect her."

They heard the sudden burst of laughter from the girls sitting across the room, distracting their attention away from the conversation at hand.

"Damn, she looks amazing." Dante tossed back another drink, hiding his true feelings and not wanting to come to terms with the fact she was now Nosferatu. *"The girls are playing with fire, and they have no idea. Jadis is more dangerous than ever. She has clearly crossed the devil's threshold."* Dante said to Bain telepathically.

"Look at her, we thought she was something to look at back on the yacht. I can barely contain myself, and Silas is two feet from me," Bain admitted.

With a wicked smirk, Dante tilted his glass to Bain. *"You and I both, cousin, Silas is one lucky bastard. I would take her to bed without hesitation. Shit, I'd take her here, there, everywhere."*

"You speak the truth. The only problem is I'd have to put a blindfold on her to cover her eyes. Can you imagine looking down, only to have Silas looking back?" Bain laughed aloud as did Dante, who practically choked on his drink.

"She may be heaven on the eyes, but she's hell for the soul," Dante added.

"Silas has always been a glutton for punishment," Bain replied.

Dante and Bain diverted their eyes the moment Silas looked at the two of them, having caught them staring at Jadis. He hadn't been paying attention to what they were talking about, but he knew it was regarding Jadis; the look of warning he gave them was undeniably clear.

"You thought you had problems before, Eden," Lars stated. *That girl is going to put them all over the edge,* he thought.

Eden and Aiden stared at Silas, and the excitement, desire, and pride were written all over his face. They knew based on his dismissive attitude, this wouldn't end well.

Silas is most definitely going to follow her down the rabbit's hole, Eden thought.

"Silas?" Eden stated, trying to bring his attention back to the conversation.

"Yes, Eden, I'm still listening," he replied. However, he didn't bother to look at him.

He's leaning against the bar, watching his mate like it's a fucking casual night on the town. His placid attitude alone is enough to know she's going nowhere.

"What do you have in mind, cousin?" Silas asked, with a voice of warning.

"I think we should all head back to our compound. It's safe, has state of the art security, it's secluded, and most of all, it can be locked down," Eden suggested.

"Remind me again about it being *locked down*?" Silas questioned in jest, as he looked Aiden's way.

"Touché." Aiden chuckled.

"Good luck. She'll never agree and we aren't leaving our home. We're staying right here," Silas firmly stated.

"Silas, it's not safe for either of you. If word somehow gets out, she's in danger, and you know as well as the rest of us, they won't hesitate to come for you to get to her. How secure is this place in the grand scheme of things?" Eden argued.

"Trust me, there's more to this place than meets the eye. Security here is state of the art as well. She's my one and only concern. You don't think I haven't thought it through? A few of my Mortem Warriors have been here since leaving the valley, unbeknownst to her."

"No one has ever dared to doubt Silas when he said he had taken care of a situation. If he said it's handled, it's handled—no questions asked," Syth stated in defense of his brother.

"Goddamn it." *It always comes down to what Silas ultimately decides. He has, however, earned the very honor.* Despite Eden's frustration with Silas's unwillingness to compromise, he would never question Silas's capabilities, dedication, or loyalty to the family, nor his skill in handling whatever comes his way. However, he also knew the potential consequences of Jadis being discovered.

"Bain—Dante," Eden said aloud.

"What the hell did I tell you about the nanny position," Dante said to Bain.

"Tell me this isn't happening right now." Bain grabbed a bottle of bourbon off the shelf from behind the bar. He had to step around the still-comatose bar maidens in order to refill his and Dante's glasses. "Here it comes." They fake clapped their glasses together and took a drink.

"I know where this is going, Eden, so get it over with," Bain replied.

"Silas, I would appreciate it if you would at least allow Bain and Dante to stay here with you and Jadis if you insist on staying," Eden suggested.

"No. I can take care of the affairs of my own home," Silas stated.

"Anyone else want to chime in here instead of standing there, like this is all fun and games? This is serious shit right now, so stop all the joking bullshit and back me up!" Eden demanded.

"We're talking about Silas right now. What more would you expect? I'll snatch her ass right out of this house if I have to," Aiden threatened.

"I suggest you don't even try." Silas moved so closely to Aiden they were now chest to chest.

Lars, Eden, Dante, and Bain quickly intervened and in an instant, Jadis materialized next to Silas. He felt her rush to him, lifted his arm up, and she protectively wrapped her arms around his waist.

"What's wrong?" She had felt the threat to Silas as soon as he and Aiden faced off.

"Nothing, my love," Silas replied.

"Then why are you and Aiden acting crazy?"

"It's just a disagreement, nothing more. Go back to join your girls." Silas smiled down at her and patted her butt.

She rolled her eyes in response. "I assume the disagreement is about me. What's going on now?"

"Well, she should know, Eden. Why don't you go ahead and fill her in?" Silas leaned back against the bar with Jadis wrapped in his arms and waited for him to tell her.

"This ought to be good," Aiden stated, along with an eye roll of his own.

Eden took a moment before he spoke, contemplating his words. "Bottom line, you can't be trusted. Not to mention you need protection more than ever. We think it's best for you and Silas to come back to the compound and stay with us for the time being, at least until we figure this all out—"

Jadis stopped him midsentence. "Oh, hell no, I'm not leaving here." She squeezed Silas's forearms and looked up for reassurance. "You better not have agreed to this bullshit."

"I haven't agreed, baby. I already told them we were staying put." He then looked at Eden. "You heard her, we're staying in our own home." He then glanced around to see who was going to challenge him.

"Well, let's go all the way then, Silas. I can, and I will pull rank on you. When one of us is in a situation we all deem dangerous, we can make a unanimous decision to put either you or me in charge. Right now, I'm more than confident everyone will agree, your sole focus is on Jadis, as it should be, but it's clouding your judgment."

Silas set his glass on the bar and turned his body, so he faced Eden. He gently moved Jadis to the side. "Don't think you can pull rank on me, Eden," he warned.

Eden held up his hands in a gesture of peace. "I'm not here to fight with you, but we have to come to some sort of reasonable agreement. We need to make a pragmatic decision. That's all I'm saying. If you refuse to come with us to the compound, then I suggest Dante and Bain stay here with you as well," Eden offered.

"Not this shit again. Don't I get a vote in this?" she asked.

She was cut off by a unanimous, resounding, "No," coming from everyone standing there, except for Silas.

Eden laughed aloud. "You're the last person making any decisions right now."

She cocked her head at him, thinking about what he was saying. Just as she began to argue with him, he held up his hand and stared at Silas, and cocked his head.

Jadis glared at Eden and then looked up at Silas. "There is more to this than any of you are letting on."

"Silas, Dante and Bain are the best alternative," Eden stated as he continued looking at Jadis. He too, was more or less fascinated with her new look as much as he hated to admit it.

"Well, what's it going to be?" Bain asked with a heavy sigh as he took another drink. He looked over at Dante, who had the same unenthusiastic expression. They then looked to Silas to see what he would decide.

After a few moments of silent contemplation, Silas spoke, "Eden speaks the truth. I can't argue his logic. Dante, Bain, you'll stay here for the duration."

"Let the games begin," Dante huffed. "This will be one hell of an assignment this time." Dante was more frustrated that once again, he had to be in her presence on a consistent basis, especially now that she had turned.

"Cheers to that," Bain stated.

"Silas! If you think I'll allow them to babysit me again you're sadly mistaken!"

"My love, it's just a precaution. Eden is correct in his assessment. There will be a target on your back, and we can't leave anything to chance. I won't now, nor will I ever jeopardize your safety, much less your life. Been there, done that."

He tried to pull her into him, but she fluently moved out of his reach. He had moved just as quickly and stood face to face with her.

"This will be good," Aria said to the girls. "I can't wait to see her tell Silas what's up."

"I won't stay here with them so the three of you can laugh at my expense. *Been there, done that.* I'm assuming next I'll be wearing a golden anklet?"

"No one is laughing at you, mon chéri, least of all me. This is temporary and no, unless you challenge me, you won't be wearing the anklet." He winked, trying to calm her heightened state.

"Why don't one of you tell me the truth then? Who's target hunting? Eden? Aiden? Anyone? Are one of you going to tell me what's up?" She waited a minute, but no one so much as spoke a word.

"Baby, I'll tell you everything later. Right now, this is how it's going to be."

Silas is serious right now, and he looks worried. This is just perfect, Jadis thought.

The threat to Jadis brought up abysmal memories from not so long ago. Mistakes Silas vowed would never be made again. Eden had spoken the truth, pulling Silas from the temporary, peaceful solitude he had been enjoying with her; reality struck a vein. He knew they would have to face the truth at some point, he just hoped it wouldn't happen so soon. He had been avoiding the inevitable.

"Well, then you can BE here with them," she seethed. "I'm leaving!" She made it to the door before the words finished leaving her mouth. Silas, however, was right behind her, holding it shut with the palm of his hand.

Eden turned to Bain; his concern clear. "It's sealed; she's not getting out, not to mention she's no match for Silas, Nosferatu or not," Bain stated.

"I wouldn't be so sure," Aiden chimed in. "It's not like she hasn't shocked the shit out of all of us on more than one occasion."

"I can't argue that," Lars agreed.

"Silas, back off! I'm not asking you," she threatened.

"Calm, baby, this isn't what I had imagined either. I would love to stay here locked up in our home, keeping you naked, just the two of us and our pups," he said as he gently stroked her cheek. "Unfortunately, it's not the reality we live in. It's not the world our clans have ever known."

He was still leaning over her with one hand on the door. The compassion in his voice and on his face was undeniable. *Shit, there's no way for me to be mad at him. He's speaking from his heart, no doubt about it. He does want to ignore the world and its darkness for me—with me.*

"Yes, baby, I would. I would give anything to live like we've been, but the darkness surrounds us. It always has, always will because of who, what we are. We are Nosferatu, and we cannot run, nor can we hide from the threats it brings upon us. I won't dismiss the threat, nor will I continue to pretend it doesn't exist."

"Why? I don't understand." She replied, genuinely confused and a bit scared from his sudden admission. "We killed the Baskales and the Segans. What can be worse than that?" she asked, even though she wasn't fully sure she wanted to hear the answer.

"Baby, there are always monsters lurking in the dark. We can't be careless, we haven't lived as long as we have by being weak, naïve, or delusional. We're alive and as you put it, *on top of the food chain* for a reason."

They both chuckled at the inside joke. She reached around to the back of his head and pulled him in for a kiss.

"*Top of the food chain*?" Jabari looked to Aiden for an explanation.

"We probably don't even want to know." Aiden said as he subtly shook his head.

"Always my assassin in bloody armor," she replied.

Their eyes swirled as the burning desire and hunger rose to the surface.

"Dante, Bain, since you're staying here, Eden can clean up the mess. Jadis and I'll continue this in private."

He reached for her hand and pulled her away from the door. "Let's say our goodbyes. It's time for bed."

Silas, of course, let everyone know they could see themselves out when he opened an obscure door on the other side of the room.

"Limi—Mag, idvam," Silas called as he held the door for them.

Once Silas and Jadis were out of sight, Eden spoke up, "Keep the body. We need to know what Jadis did to her. Aiden, get it to the lab when we get home."

"I got it." Aiden was as curious as the rest of them, and was already kneeling over the dried-up corpse and studying it in amazement.

Everyone saw themselves out as Dante and Bain took a seat on the loveseats. They put their feet up on the coffee table and settled in.

Dante tossed Bain his own bottle of Suntori Hibiki. "Our party is just beginning, I'm afraid."

"Eden, on your way out, send the two brunettes our way. Get rid of everyone else." Bain didn't want to deal with the staff himself at this point, they had bigger problems.

Eden nodded. "Whatever the two of you need to get through this, you've got."

"I believe you volunteered us for this; you should be staying here as well." Bain's aggravation was clear.

"Not a chance in hell," Eden shot back. "By the way, don't let Jadis find those two in her house in the morning. I don't need any more mummified bodies back at the lab."

Dante and Bain rolled their eyes, a little something they too had picked up from Jadis.

Dante tilted his glass to Bain. "I've got a dreadful feeling we're heading down the rabbit's hole with Silas."

"You and me both," Bain agreed.

"I might need you to do me a favor," Dante suggested.

"Dare I ask?"

"You remember that little bit of sorcery you placed on Aiden to keep him from slipping it to Jadis? I need you to triple dose me."

Having been caught off guard by the off handed remark, Bain nearly spit out his drink. "Fuck, we're in trouble."

CHAPTER 3

It had been a week since the party, and Jadis, Silas, Dante, and Bain had since settled into a comfortable routine.

Silas and Eden decided to meet to discuss some upcoming business, and Eden wasn't happy when he found out Silas was bringing Jadis, not that he was surprised. He chose to bring Chloe and Maddie along to hopefully distract Jadis and keep her from killing someone.

Eden and Maddie were getting ready for what he hoped would be an uneventful evening. He couldn't help but feel a sense of dread wash over him as he sat in the large, hand-carved, antique chair sitting in his and Maddie's master suite. He contemplated everything that could go wrong while putting on his black and brown, Alexia leather oxfords.

"Calm, vampire," a silky-smooth voice said. Maddie lifted his chin to meet her gaze as she crawled into his lap. "It's going to be fine, my love."

Eden sat back and pulled her closer to him, admiring her low-cut silk top. She again lifted his chin to look at her eyes, not her cleavage.

"I wish I could believe that, darlin, but you know as well as I do, Jadis has little to no control over herself right now." He moved a strand of hair off her chest and gently placed it behind her shoulder. "I have a gut-wrenching feeling taking her out in public will go sideways and fast. You saw Silas at the party, he won't do a damn thing where she's concerned, other than let her get away with whatever she does, not to mention revel in every moment."

"It'll be okay, baby. You're always overthinking everything." Maddie winked. "There'll be plenty of us there to distract her. Not to mention, we haven't had a night out in a long time with all the crazy drama that has taken place lately."

"Exactly, Jadis drama."

"Let's be fair, you all brought her here. You pulled her from her home, from everything she knew. You threw her into a whole new world, one with real monsters, least you forget. One could venture to say you all brought the drama to her." Maddie raised her eyebrow, waiting for a response.

"There's a reason I took you as my mate, darling." He grabbed the back of her head and pulled her in for a kiss. "I love that big heart of yours, you know that, right?"

"Yes, baby. Now let's get going before we don't make it at all." She kissed him again and stood.

They were escorted to a private booth overlooking the entire club. It sat about fifteen feet above the dance floor, allowing a panoramic view of the club's activities. It was large, easily seating at least twenty-five guests, but quite private. *It's sophisticated and classy, just like Silas and his brothers,* Jadis thought.

There were heavy, gold-velour curtains hanging from the hand-carved, wood pedestals. The dark, blood-red, leather cushions stood out from the dark wood, timber lounges themselves. The tables were also intricately carved from the same dark-timber wood.

As soon as they made their way to the booth, the bouncer opened a black velvet rope which kept the rest of the patrons out of the area. A half-dozen personal waiters and waitresses greeted them. One of the blonde bottle girls set her sights on Silas, ignoring the fact he walked in with his arm tightly wrapped around another.

*What the hell? At least Silas didn't acknowledge he*r. Jadis suddenly felt a strange sensation; she wanted to see her draw her last breath. Another unfamiliar onset of anger and jealousy shocked her. *I mean, I've wanted to kill people before, but this is bad.* She brushed it off as soon as Ivory's annoying laughter broke the silence, as well as her fixation. She figured Silas was too busy chatting with Eden and the rest of their group to notice her reaction.

"You *figured* wrong. I notice everything, baby." Silas looked at her, cupped her face in his hands, and pulled her mouth to his. He patted her butt and smiled warmly. "She's nothing, my love."

Silas sat back in the plush, leather bench, and Jadis had her hand resting on his thigh as she leaned into him. She was practically sitting in his lap, claiming what was hers. He laid his arm across the back of the bench behind Jadis and stroked her shoulder and neck with his fingers.

The bottle girl walked over to place a forty-year-old bottle of Mikonas Scotch Whiskey on the table. She purposely bent over in front of Silas allowing her breasts partially slip out of the tight, low-cut, spaghetti-strap top.

Jadis was fixated on her as she watched her every move. She felt her desire for Silas as well as read her every thought. She knew exactly what the girl wanted to do with him, what she wanted him to do with her. *First off, she wants me out of the way. She's also making a plan. As soon as the gold-digging slut, meaning me, sitting next to that gorgeous man goes to the bathroom or the dance floor, she'll make her move.*

Eden was troubled, having a dreadful feeling he knew where this was heading. He looked around, only to notice no one else was paying any attention to the altercation slowly brewing beneath Jadis's hardened expression. *Shit! Dante and Bain are too busy with a couple of their own 'hosts' to notice. Agaeus, Syth, Ivory, and Skye are also too distracted with each other to notice anything or anyone. Trying to control Jadis is tantamount to trying to pin down a hurricane with a coffin nail.* He decided to take matters into his own hands, so he psychically sent the waitress to the main bar, as far away from Jadis as he could.

Maddie knew Eden was already stressed out. "What's wrong, darling?"

"I don't trust Jadis and Silas to save my life. The blonde, let's just say it's a damn good thing she got out of here alive."

"Why?" Maddie was a bit confused by the statement.

"Did you not notice Jadis's fixation on her? The waitres's thoughts about Silas weren't what Jadis needed to pick up on."

Maddie playfully squeezed his thigh. "Darling, anyone who knew what another girl was thinking about their mate would feel the same way, myself included. If some random girl touched you, I'd want to kill her too."

Her words and touch always seemed to calm him. He grabbed her by the back of the head and pulled her in for kiss. "I don't know, sweetness. Jadis isn't trustworthy in the least, especially lately."

"Baby, Jadis isn't a cold-blooded killer."

Eden pulled back, cocked his head, and raised both eyebrows. "She's not? Are you forgetting how easily she killed the barmaid a week ago?

Not only that, but she also has every ounce of Silas's support, *lest you forget*." He winked.

"I can't argue that, baby, but we're all here tonight. You've got all of us. What is she going to do?" She handed him a drink off the table. "Relax, baby, as you say, right now, the situation is contained." She smiled.

They had all moved about over the last few hours, allowing their mates to conduct whatever business the girls weren't privy to, not that they cared. The girls were drinking, laughing, and joking around with each other about the events that had taken place over the last few months, as well as Jadis's new abilities when they overheard their mates talking. They were speaking about the incident in the cave and the fact they had sensed another vampire while there. Every time Jadis picked up on it, they quickly changed the subject. She couldn't remember much of what had happened after the events unfolded, but something definitely didn't sit right. Deep down, she knew another threat was looming on the horizon, or so she thought. For all she knew, it was just the paranoia she still suffered from on occasion.

"Where's that fucking mate of mine?" Maddie demanded aloud.

The girls cracked up; it wasn't like her to cuss, much less to drop the F-bomb in public.

"Maddie!" Jadis yelled. "Did you seriously just say *fucking*?"

Maddie covered her mouth with both hands, as the rest of the girls continued to mock her.

"*Fucking* mates, get your asses over here," Skye yelled.

"Skye," Jadis snapped. "What the hell have you all been drinking?"

"Ohhh—just cause you're a big bad vamp now and can't get drunk, doesn't mean the rest of us can't," Ivory said, mocking her.

Jadis winked at Skye and raised her eyebrows at Ivory. She let her canines drop from her gums and let out a deep, guttural snarl.

Ivory shrieked at the sight and shoved Jadis's shoulder. They hadn't even realized all eyes had been on them for the last ten minutes.

"Jadis, stop! What are you doing? Skye, make her stop right now," Ivory demanded as Skye, Maddie, and Aria lost it.

"That's not funny, Jadis! I'm not used to you doing that shit yet," Ivory exclaimed.

"Oh lord, I believe we should be joining our mates before shit gets out of hand," Eden stated.

They had all been fully amused by the girls' drunken state.

"Well, shit, I thought I've heard it all," Lars announced. "I believe Maddie wants your *fucking ass* at the table straightaway!" Eden looked at him and couldn't help but laugh along.

Silas's eyes caught Jadis', and he gave her a come-hither look and a coy grin that touched her very core. Her eyes became slit-like. She stood and sauntered toward him.

"Well, that's enough business for the night. I believe I'd rather join the party," Silas stated, agreeing with Eden.

Aiden set his tablet on the table and stood, heading Aria's way. Everyone else followed suit.

"I believe I was summoned?" Eden bent over Maddie and took her mouth to his.

Jadis made it part of the way to Silas before leaping into his arms. He walked back to the booth, plopped down with Jadis on her back, and fell on top of her.

"Stop, you two." Ivory pushed Silas's shoulder since they had practically landed in her lap.

"Excuse us, lass. We didn't see you sitting there," he joked.

The look on Ivory's face, having never heard Silas joke around, is priceless, Jadis thought as she Silas laughed and repositioned themselves.

The laughter went on, the drinking commenced, and business was concluded for the night. It had been a couple more hours before the bottle girl was back, and from what Eden could pick up on, she was on a mission, and Silas was it. He noticed Jadis tracking her every move.

"Shit," Eden mumbled under his breath.

"What, baby?" Maddie asked.

"I should have made her absence permanent." Eden sighed as he and Maddie stared at the blonde.

Jadis felt Eden watching her as she fixed her sights on the bottle girl. However, she chose to ignore him as usual. There was a greater pull calling her name; *Death,* she thought.

A familiar feeling suddenly washed over Eden. After what had happened at the party, he knew the shit was about to hit the fan.

"Silas," Eden hollered, trying to get him to grab hold of Jadis.

Silas ignored Eden and continued stroking Jadis's hair, letting the chips fall where they may. He had also blocked Eden from sending the bottle girl away again, for no other reason than his own entertainment.

Everyone turned their attention to Silas and Jadis, knowing he wouldn't stop Jadis, nor would he let anyone else. Jadis's killing thrilled him, not to mention it was a complete turn on.

The girl walked around the booth, bent over, laid her hand on Silas's bicep, and whispered in his ear, "Anything else you need, just let me know." She stood, winked, and flipped her hair at Jadis.

Lars laughed aloud as usual. "She just had to go there!"

Eden stood next to the booth, while Dante and Bain made their way around the back to stand behind Silas and Jadis.

"Did she seriously just touch Silas like that and flip her hair at me?" she snarled to Skye, who sat to her right.

"She did, but I don't think she meant it the way you're thinking." Skye wasn't laughing now. She wasn't quite sure what Jadis would do.

"Bullshit," Jadis quietly hissed.

Silas grabbed the back of her head and rested his forehead on hers. "Calm, baby. She's nothing. Ignore it—for the moment."

That statement just gave the rest of the group the false assumption he would stop her from whatever she was about to do.

Jadis let out a low-pitched growl. "She just rubbed your arm, Silas."

"I get that. Hell, if some bastard touched you, he would already be dead." Silas winked.

That was his subtle way of giving her the go ahead. Jadis let her get three steps away to make everyone circling them from behind think she would let her go.

As soon as she walked around the table to pick up a glass, she used the opportunity to give Silas another clear view of her cleavage. Jadis lunged over the table and snatched her up. She lifted her off her feet with one hand and body slammed her to the floor. The girl screamed and tried to fight her off, but Jadis grasped a fistful of her hair in one hand and grabbed her throat with the other, muffling her screams. She snarled in her face. "He's mine!" She wrenched her head to the side, exposing her neck, and sank her canines deep into her pulsing, mortified vein.

Silas held up his hand to everyone ready to intervene, stopping them. He didn't so much as look in their direction as he was solely focused on his mate.

Eden nodded to Bain, who cloaked their entire area. Dante followed suit without having to be told. He wiped the minds from everyone who had just witnessed her attacking the waitress, essentially zombifying the entire club.

Aiden had moved Aria to the side and stood next to Eden. "You weren't wrong, brother," Aiden agreed.

Dante looked at Bain. "What did I tell you about that fucking rat farm? Now seems like as good a time as any to breed them."

"Maybe we can genetically modify them to taste mortal?" Bain suggested.

"What the hell are the two of you rambling on about? Can at least one of you focus on the shit right in front of us for two fucking minutes?" Eden demanded.

"That's what we're doing," Bain answered, motioning his hand between Jadis and Silas. "This—those two—that's what we're talking about."

Maddie, Skye, and Ivory let out an initial scream, only to cover their mouths with their hands in total shock. It didn't take long though. Moments later, they were rolling in laughter. Agaeus and Syth also joined in on their mates' amusement, offering no help at all.

Eden was once again exasperated with the entire group not taking any of this seriously.

Maddie looked at him and couldn't help but to be amused. *He's lost all patience, not that he has any to begin with. Jadis saw to that a few days after we had taken her in.*

Silas sat motionless with one leg bent, and the other out straight, while his arm still rested on the back of the bench. He watched every move Jadis made, desire overtaking logic.

Jadis stood and looked at the corpse laying at her feet in the same mummified, fetal position. She took two steps back toward Silas before looking at Eden.

"What? She deserved it. She was all over Silas, and he's mine," she snarled.

"That she did. I don't know, Eden—Jadis is right, the waitress was coming onto Silas. That was a mistake—big mistake!" Lars announced.

"Do not defend her! She needs to control that shit," Eden snapped.

Jadis ignored Eden and proceeded to grab a white linen napkin off the table that had been wrapped around a champagne bottle. She wiped the blood from her hands and tossed it toward the mummified body. It landed on her face, partially covering it. She strolled over to Silas and crawled onto his lap.

Silas moved his hips to reposition them under her, grabbed both sides of her butt, and pulled her in, taking her mouth to his.

"You're mine," she mumbled.

"Get a room. You two need to take that shit somewhere else." Ivory jokingly shoved Jadis's shoulder trying to push her out of the booth.

No one in the club mattered at this point; it was again just Silas and Jadis. *Screw Eden's attitude*, Jadis thought. "Eden you would have done the same thing had some guy come on to Maddie, much less touched her."

"She's right," Silas agreed, looking up at Eden. "I've seen you kill over Maddie before, *least you forget*. Especially right after the two of you were mated—need I remind you?"

Screw the club full of zombies, I was protecting what was mine and only mine, Jadis thought.

"And *you're mine and only mine*," Silas replied.

"I am yours, assassin."

Silas stood and picked her up in his arms, and she wrapped her legs around his waist. He headed straight for his private office just around the corner from the VIP area. He entered through a hidden door, leaving the mess, well—body, for his brothers to clean up once again.

Eden rubbed his temples, contemplating everything going on and the direction it was all headed in. *Jadis is dangerous, the girls are drunk, Silas is too enthralled with Jadis to do anything.* He finally looked at Aiden, who stood in silence next to him. "This will never end," he snarled.

"I think your headaches are contagious. And here I thought she was hard to handle before."

"Dante, Bain, we need to meet, this can't continue. Her little killing spree is over." Eden was now pulling rank, regardless of what Silas would have to say.

"Agreed," they replied.

"Killing like this will raise the suspicions of the wrong clan." Bain's searing words of warning weighed heavy on them all.

"We need to get this shit cleaned up again, but right now, I need a goddamn drink." Eden grabbed his glass off the table and plopped down, trying to decipher the direction Jadis and Silas were heading in, taking them all along for the ride.

Maddie scooted in next to him and placed her legs over his. "It will be fine. We'll figure this out together. This burden isn't yours alone to carry."

"Maddie speaks the truth." Aiden gave Eden a couple of pats on the shoulder. "Our biggest issue will be contending with Silas."

"Getting Jadis to obey is like trying to pull blood from a stone," Eden rumbled.

No one spoke as they all sat back down and grabbed a bottle off the table, regardless of what it was.

"Apparently, it's self-serve again." Aria stated, to Lars's amusement.

"I like her, Aiden; someone else with a sense of humor."

Ivory and Skye were no better and continued laughing with Lars. They had known Jadis their entire lives, and this was nothing more than a ramped-up version. They were no longer surprised in the least.

Aria tilted her glass toward the girls. "This shit is crazy. I didn't know drinking with dead, mummified bodies was a thing, and I live near the fucking temples."

Aiden laughed aloud. After all, he didn't disagree. *This shit is crazy. And sure enough, the mummified body is still on the floor.*

The office door opened and closed behind them, with nothing more than a thought from Silas. He fell onto the black-leather couch sitting in his office with her still wrapped in his arms. They laughed as they bounced off the couch and almost landed on the floor. Silas caught them, having placed a hand on the dark, stone tiles.

"I think Eden's pissed," Jadis joked, to Silas's amusement.

He lay on top of her, staring into her freshly fed eyes. "He's more than pissed right now." He chuckled.

"Well, you did sort of leave a mess for them to clean up—not a mess, just a body," Jadis said as she furrowed her eyebrows at him in jest.

"My mess? I believe that was all you."

Jadis stared back at Silas, and his arousal was clear. *His eyes say it all. My killing, my feeding is his dirty little pleasure.*

He bent down and took her mouth to his. As loving and gentle as his kiss was, she loved how powerful his body felt consuming hers.

The taste of the blood from her latest victim was still lingering on her tongue, which only ratcheted up his arousal. "The taste of fresh kill," he moaned as he pulled her leg up, settling himself firmly against her crotch.

Jadis moved with purpose and took them both to the floor. She rolled Silas onto his back, pinned his hands above his head, and straddled him. She rubbed her crotch across his and slowly rocked back and forth. *He's well-endowed to say the least.* She brought one hand down, slid open his zipper, and undid the top button, freeing all of him. She ran her tongue up his throat, along his jawline, and playfully nipped the skin above his pulse.

He could taste the scent of her thoughts, and it spiraled right into his dick. He sat straight up, pulled her shirt and bra off, and tossed them to the side. He then flipped her over and pinned her on her back beneath him. He trailed his fingers down the center of her chest, over her breast, and gently kneaded it in the palm of his hand.

"Have I told you lately how intoxicatingly dangerous you are?" he whispered.

"And you've set me free," she replied.

"That I did," he rumbled.

He slid his body down just enough to pull her nipple into the heat of his mouth. He twirled his tongue over the plump, pink bud. He kept her arms pinned above her head in a vice-like grip as she arched her back, moaning for more. The loud thumping of her heartbeat against his chest brought about a hungry desire to claim her all the more.

"My God, you always feel so amazing," she moaned.

He glanced up at her with a heartfelt smile. "As do you, my love."

He kissed the side of her neck again and lingered just under her jawline; feeling and listening to the increased, rhythmic beat of her heightened pulse beneath his lips.

"I can see the blood coursing through your veins." He let out an animalistic growl, ran his hand down her stomach, and unbuttoned her pants. He slid his hand beneath her jeans and rubbed her sex with his fingers.

Her desire increased with every touch, and she moaned as each finger slid inside, while his thumb rubbed her nub.

"You're so hot, so wet for me." He repositioned himself and ripped off her jeans. He crawled back over her and spread her legs with his knees. He then bent down, and his mouth fell to hers.

She moved her hands around his back and shoulders, feeling the muscles flex and soften with each erotic movement of his body. She reached down, cupped her fist around his erection, and rubbed it up and down his shaft.

"I want to hear you begging." His voice was barely a whisper. "Tell me what you desire most, mon chéri."

"You, nothing more—now give it to me." She moved her hips, urging him to give her what she desired, and pulled him in for a deeper kiss.

He responded with a hard thrust and a guttural moan. Her hips quickly matched the rhythm of his.

Ahhh, shit—it feels as good as it hurts. He was rough, and she wanted it hard.

"I possess all of you," he whispered. He dominated her, owned her, and she was powerless against him. He rotated his hips and thrust them more forcefully.

"I need to taste you," she whispered.

He positioned his head, and she cupped her lips around his neck. She let out a deep-throated growl as his blood satiated her thirst. Every drop sent a multitude of sensations through her body. *Never have I tasted something so powerful, so enticing, I taste Silas, my mate.*

He continued to rock his hips, driving himself further in, which sent her mind into a frenzy of emotions as the orgasm rose to the surface. She slid her hand down his back and grabbed his ass, pulling him deeper.

Not only did her thoughts, feelings, and desire hit her, his did as well.

She dug her nails into his ass and gently dragged them over his body. She let go of his throat and tossed her head back.

As she pulled away, he felt the warmth of the liquid trickle down his neck and she slid the tip of her tongue over the punctures as they healed, greedily taking every last drop.

He looked to his beautiful mate and took her mouth; the taste of himself on her tongue nearly undid him. He released a guttural moan, grabbed her jaw, and exposed her neck.

The harsh pricks searing through her body finished her orgasm. "Shitt—" she moaned.

He felt her body give in, and his own release rose to the surface. He lifted his head and let out a guttural growl as his seed filled her core. She lay quietly beneath him, reveling in the power she felt radiate from his body, as his dick pulsed inside her.

"This room is soundproof, isn't it?" she teased, after their bodies had a chance to come down.

He gently pulled out and rested on top of her. "And if it isn't?"

"Then I assume we just woke the dead—I might have to kill the bitch again."

Silas cracked up. "Do you have any idea how lucky I am you're all mine?"

He looked into her eyes and slid his thumb across her bottom lip. He licked a bit of the blood from the corner of her mouth with a coy, cocky smile.

She pulled his mouth to hers and tasted her own blood on his tongue; it was an affirmation she alone owned him.

CHAPTER 4

Silas set his glass down on the nightstand and slipped out of bed. "Come, darling, let's get out of here for a while. I want you to scc something." He walked over to the bureau, opened the drawer, and tossed Jadis her bikini bottoms.

"You want to go for a midnight swim?" she asked as she put the suit on. "Don't I need the top?"

He sauntered over and pulled her mouth to his. "No, I like you topless," he said coyly. "But if you want to go for a swim, I'm in. I just have something to show you first."

"That sounds intriguing. You're always full of surprises." She smiled. "Where is everyone else? Not sure I want to walk around topless."

He interlaced her fingers with his and led her out of the bedroom. "No one's downstairs, you're fine." He winked.

Jadis stopped and looked up at him. "You do know how much I love and appreciate everything you do for me— yes?"

"I do, baby. I see it reflected in your eyes every time you look at me."

He moved a few strands of hair off her face, gently placed it behind her ear, and cupped her jaw in his hand. "We're mated. I know exactly what you feel and think. I've never been so happy as I am with you." Silas gleamed with adoration. *She's a single flower in a thorny, begrimed bush.*

She has lit up the darkness that has engulfed the majority of my life. He bent down and kissed her as he pulled her body to his.

She wrapped her arms around his neck and held on tight as he lifted her up and embraced her tightly. After a few minutes, he set her back down. "Let's go, baby. The darkness awaits. I want to show you a new world. When you look into the night, it'll be different, but you'll be able to see as well as you do during the day. The colors, however, will be illuminated, it'll seem as if you're looking through a green lens."

Silas loved every second teaching her how to use her newborn skills. He reveled in it. With every new skill she mastered, his heart swelled with pride. His favorite pastime became teaching her how to use and control her new abilities. He also spent hours cultivating her skills in hand-to-hand combat, as well as teaching her how to use the weapons he kept in his massive cache.

"Do I have to do anything? What's so different about tonight? I've been in the dark before," she questioned as she looked up into his beautiful, adoring eyes.

"You look around like you would any other time. The difference tonight is I can see your eyes have fully morphed, their change is complete. If you need to see the tiniest of detail, look in its direction with your mind. Your eyes will automatically focus on whatever it is you're looking to." He lifted her hand and kissed the back of it.

Once they made it out the front door and stepped into the darkness, the blackest of landscape jumped to life before her very eyes.

"Damn, it's incredible." She looked up at him in awe. *It's like discovering a whole new world; best of all, I'm discovering all of it with Silas.*

Silas was as excited and as thrilled as she was. He felt as though he too was re-discovering the world for himself, through her eyes. It brought him back to life again, filled with wonder and amazement, something he hadn't felt in hundreds of years.

As they continued their walk down the sandy jungle path leading to the lagoon, he coached her on how to use her new night vision, what to see, and what to look for. The darkness morphed with color; different tones and greenish hues consumed the landscape, and she could see with eagle-eyed acuity. She could see the creatures scurrying around as easily as they could see her. It was magical, and she found herself grinning from ear to ear, as was Silas.

She could decipher a droplet of water falling from the tip of a leaf a block away, an ant scurrying underneath a rotting leaf laying on the jungle floor. She felt like a fledgling in an undiscovered world. Each time she giggled with delight and asked Silas if he could see what she was seeing, he chuckled in response, answering with a simple yes.

He taught her the difference between the shadows that subtly moved with the air like leaves, flowers, or trees, versus the shadows that moved with life. Creatures moving in the night cast different tones due to their body heat; they were surrounded in subtle red hues that warped around their figures.

They made it down to the lagoon and stood in the sand at the edge of the water, hand in hand. *Hell, I can see all the way to the bottom. Every living creature in the lagoon is as clear to me as the fish in a glass tank.*

"Silas, look, do you see them? Look at the seahorses sleeping in the sea grass. There's a couple of blue crab. I can even see the little pink shrimp. This is crazy." She beamed.

Silas was next to her, only he was looking at her, not the lagoon. She reached up, grabbed the back of his head, and pulled him in for a deep kiss. His tongue met hers with a slow, intertwining welcome, offering up that delicious, old-world taste.

Even kissing Silas is different now; it feels more passionate. It always brought about a ravenous desire. Since they were mated, and she had turned, all her senses had been enhanced a hundred times over. She was already turned on, as was Silas, evident by the large bulge in his swim trunks.

He pulled back and stared at her, still captivated by her looks when she changed. He hadn't yet gotten used to her eyes mirroring his own, not to mention her double set of canines. *Only the rarest, purest breed of Nosferatu has eight canines, yet here she is with all eight of them gleaming in the dark, peering out from behind her perfect, full, rosy lips,* he thought.

He let out a guttural moan. "Look at you, baby. I'm at a loss for words."

He picked her up in his arms and jumped into the center of the lagoon. She let out a yelp, and they came crashing down into the water, sending it splashing onto the volcanic rocks rising straight up the back of the lagoon. He held her in his arms, and she had her legs wrapped around his waist as they slowly rose out of the water. He gently spun her in circles, wrapped in his arms. They tousled around in the lagoon, swimming, laughing, and splashing each other.

He chased her around to see how swiftly she could move in the water, and he could match her speed with ease. *Hell—everything Silas does is fluid, graceful, and effortless,* she thought.

She would swim to the bottom, and he would follow. She could now hold her breath as long as a siren does stalking a sailor from the depths of the sea.

Silas stood at the bottom of the lagoon, staring at his vampire. He watched her hair flowing, gently around her face and above her head. The beautiful, mahogany hues reflected off the silvery beams of moonlight that stretched to the bottom of the lagoon. Her strands looked like soft waves, gently flowing with the water. Her eyes swirled and lit up the water around her face. *There's nothing more stunning or memorizing,* he thought.

Every time they rose back out of the water, he was face-to-face with her. She would swim in circles around him, only to dive back down. He reached out and grabbed ahold of her, wrapped his arm around her waist, and pulled her to the surface. His hands gently rested on her lower back before he slowly felt his way around her waist and up her ribs, before stopping at the underside of her breast. His mouth was still planted on hers, and their tongues seductively pulled out a hungry desire in them both.

His massaged her breast and ran his thumb over her hardened nipple. He pulled back slightly and ran the tip of his tongue across the points of her canines before he pierced the tip of it, allowing them to savor the droplets together.

Silas now stood in the shallows with the water up to his shoulders as the waves gently washed over their bodies. She used her new powers to remove their swimsuits. With a flick of her wrist, she ripped them off and tossed them to the other side of the lagoon, where they gently floated down onto the small sandy beach.

"Impressive! You're getting strong. Your control is getting better every day," he whispered, before trailing his lips up and down her throat, which pulled out a hungry, lustful growl from her.

"You're what's impressive, sire," she said with a low moan.

"I like how that sounds and I believe your *sire* needs to be deep inside you," he groaned.

He lowered her onto his hard shaft and with a hard push of her hips downward, he penetrated further into the soft, tight opening.

She moved her body up and down on his vein as he held her hips. "I need you to throw me down and take it," she whispered.

"Your wish is my command."

His hungry, amber eyes captured her gaze as he made his way onto the beach and laid her down. He moved his hand between her legs and slipped his fingers in, her carnal moans calling to him, desperate for more. He slowly pulled his fingers out and pushed her thigh to the side before sliding what she was truly desperate for, into the heat of her body.

The harsh rotation of his hips took her breath away; the pressure rose with each ravenous movement of his body.

"Silas—" she muttered.

He knew what she wanted and re-positioned his neck against her mouth. His blood pooled into her mouth as she fed, which only seemed to ramp up his lusty moans from deep within his chest, his rhythm intensifying, moving harder, faster.

Wanting to come at the same time he fed from her, he pulled her head back, forcing her to release the grip she had on his neck. He turned her head to the side, exposing her tanned, velvety skin.

The razor-sharp points of his canines sank deep, sending painful electric jolts throughout her body. Her orgasm surfaced and cracked open with waves of pleasure.

"Oh, damn," he moaned, feeling her release.

She let out a wordless, growl mimicking the sounds of his own moans. He released her throat and shoved his tongue into her mouth, allowing the warmth of his liquid pulse into her slick, throbbing core.

He let out a guttural moan, and the vibrations rumbled through her body as well as the ground beneath them. He rested on top of her, and she kept her legs wrapped around his waist as he continued to gently rock back and forth as he came down. He lifted his head and gently kissed her lips.

She smiled up at her gorgeous mate and stroked his cheek with the back of her hand, admiring every inch of his perfect, stubble-laden face.

"I waited so long to find you. My brothers and I told each other we were fools, waiting for something that would never come back to us. I still can't believe we're mated. At times, I think I'll will wake up, and this will have just been a dream—"

She pinched his chest unexpectedly.

"What the hell?"

"Just letting you know this isn't a dream," she joked.

He rolled over, pinned her legs with his, and slapped her ass, forcing her to yelp.

"Tit for tat, baby," he jokingly replied, with another hard smack.

"Dammit—*tit for tat*? I barely pinched you, and you left your hand-print on my ass." She grabbed his wrist and tried to pin it down.

"Just leaving my mark, darlin," he said, looking down at her with that familiar wicked grin.

He playfully rolled over, wrestling his wrist from her grip, and pinned her beneath his large body.

"Sooo—baby, I have a question," she said nervously.

"Well, based on your tone, I'm almost afraid to ask what you want." He raised his eyebrow, waiting for her question.

"I was just thinking we could go somewhere for a while?" She didn't know how he would react, especially after what had happened at the party, not to mention the club. She saw the contemplation in his eyes, and he was clearly thinking it through.

"Well? Stop looking at me like that and just say no already," she replied, knowing Eden wouldn't allow it for one minute.

"After careful consideration, the answer is no," he stated matter-of-factly.

"No? Why? What could go wrong if I'm with you?"

"Let's see, you killed the servant at the party without hesitation, did you not? And how about the club?"

He sounds serious. "You sound like Eden right now, what the hell?"

"I have to agree with him. You're grounded to this house with Dante, Bain, and me until further notice."

"Mmkay, whatever you and Eden want."

She moved instantaneously and stood on the beach, putting her swimsuit bottoms back on.

"Don't be mad, baby. You heard Eden; you aren't to leave the house," Silas replied as he moved directly in front of her

"Since when do you ever listen to Eden?" she snarked. Her annoyance clear. *The moment Silas becomes Eden's puppet, boy, my life is over.*

"I don't find this funny at all, assassin. Why are you laughing like that? It annoys me, even though I get it," she said, trying to be understanding.

"Baby, when are you going to learn?"

"Learn what? Stop being so coy, it's not amusing."

"No, but you are, my dear."

"Well, I'm happy to be amusing you so." Jadis began to walk away when Silas grabbed her hands, pulled her into him, and pinned her arms behind her back.

"I'm not angry with you, I'm just disappointed." She stood on her tiptoes and kissed his perfect lips.

"Let's get a couple things straight. First off, I'm not Eden's *puppet boy*. Second, I have to agree, a vacation sounds amazing." His eyes lit up the night as he winked at her and smiled down with that shit-eating grin she loved so much.

"Fine—wait? What did you say? Are you messing with me right now?" she asked, realizing he had been joking the entire time.

"Yes and no. Teasing you is thoroughly entertaining no matter how it happens. Plus, you do sort of deserve it. You're always putting everyone else through the ringer, myself included."

He's fully amused with himself right now. "Whatever, but you said yes?" she asked, making sure she heard him correctly.

"Yes, baby, there's nothing I would deny you. Have you not figured that out yet?"

She jumped into his arms. "Where should we go?"

Silas's laughter rumbled in his chest. "I figured since you were asking, you already had a place in mind."

"Not really. I thought you were going to *deny* me."

"Don't worry, mon chéri. I know exactly where I'm going to take you," he said coyly.

"Where are we going?"

He threw her over his shoulder and headed back to the house. "You'll find out soon enough."

She slapped his ass, stinging her own hand in the process. "Shit, that hurt my hand." She laughed.

"I'll remember that later," he said with that sexy, velvety rumble. "We need to pack. We can head out tomorrow—well, this afternoon, I should say. Right now, it's time to take you back to bed."

They awoke late that afternoon and packed. Silas told Jadis what to bring since she had no idea where they were heading. The staff was downstairs, preparing for their departure. They had four regular staff members who had worked for Silas and his family for generations. They knew just about everything there was to know about Silas and his brothers. They were as loyal to him and his family as anyone could be. LaLaurie's family had been employed by his clan as long as Silas and his brothers' could remember. She was in her seventies now and was Jadis's favorite. She was more like a grandmother to her, even though Jadis was about ninety years older.

Silas and Jadis spent some of their evenings together with her sitting outside on the veranda, watching the sun set beyond the palms. Jadis mostly pestered her to tell her stories about Silas and his brothers, to his dismay. He always tried to divert her attention to another topic, but LaLaurie wouldn't have it. She loved to tell the tales as much as Jadis loved hearing them.

LaLaurie was in the room, helping Jadis pull out her clothes from the expansive walk-in closet. "Here, my love," LaLaurie stated as she handed Jadis a velvet jewelry case she had filled.

Jadis didn't need to look at what she had packed. *She has amazing taste and is always impeccably dressed,* Jadis thought as she tucked it into her suitcase.

"Who's telling Dante and Bain we're going on vacation? I assume they're going with us?" She raised an eyebrow at Silas, hoping he would tell her they were headed out alone.

LaLaurie casually looked at Silas as well and chuckled.

"We'll go tell them together, and since you're wondering, yes, they'll be accompanying us." Silas quietly waited for her to protest.

"Whatever. I'm just happy we're going somewhere." She gave a dismissive wave. *It isn't worth the fight.*

"What? Has hell frozen over? I believe this is the first time you haven't pitched a fit where they're concerned. Maybe I should take you on vacation more often." He slowly approached her and tossed his duffel bag to the side. He grabbed the small of her back and pulled her in for a long, passion-filled kiss.

"Come, let's go fill them in. I'm sure they'll be thrilled." He was thoroughly entertained knowing how they would react.

"I think I would like to see this for myself," LaLaurie admitted. Silas politely held the door for her.

They found Dante and Bain sitting out back, drinks in hand.

"What's up with the two of you?" Dante asked as he raised his eyebrows.

"Ah fuck, this can't be good," Bain huffed under his breath.

"You want to tell them, or should I?" Silas looked at Jadis, not asking.

"Well, since I don't even know where we're going, you tell them."

She peered at Dante and Bain with the same smirk they had sent her way on more than one occasion.

"We're all going on a vacation." Silas waited for their reactions or their protests.

Bain's expression changed from confusion to dread. "Vacation? What the hell does that mean?"

"Just what I said, we leave in an hour. Be ready," Silas stated.

Silas and Jadis sauntered out of the room, leaving the two of them to stew in their annoyance.

They looked to LaLaurie for an answer. "Don't ask me, my loves." She laughed before walking away.

"By the way, since you're wondering, we're heading to Fréyonne, *but Jadis doesn't know,"* Silas added, telepathically.

Jadis looked back at the two of them, who hadn't so much as flinched, and couldn't help but to laugh at their unenthusiastic expressions.

Jadis looked up at Silas. "Well, wherever we're going, it must be good based on how Dante and Bain look right now." She then turned to Dante and Bain. "What, cat got your tongues?" she joked as they walked away.

"Since it's your brother, I guess that means you're calling him to tell him what's up now." Dante leaned forward and re-filled his glass, waiting for the fireworks on the other end of the line when Eden received Bain's call.

The private line rang in the command center, sending a wave of ominous silence throughout the room.

"Well, this can't be good. You going to get that, or let it ring all night?" Lars sat back, waiting for Eden's face to turn three shades of crimson.

"Bain, this better be nothing more than an update," Eden groaned.

"Yes, it's just an update, brother. No need to worry," Bain snarked sarcastically.

"What the hell now?" Eden leaned back in his chair, waiting for the unwanted news.

"They've decided to go on a little vacation." Bain's voice told Eden there was more, even though he didn't say it.

"*Vacation*?"

Eden looked at Aiden, who shook his head and rapped his fingers on the desk.

"Yes, you know, you pack a bag and head out for a few days or a few weeks. Apparently, Jadis is bored," Bain replied.

"You've got to be kidding me? Can't they just stay put for five goddamn minutes?" Eden snapped.

"It gets better," Bain said, half-joking. The silence on the other end of the line spoke volumes.

After a momentary pause, Eden spoke, "Do I even want to know—" Eden interrupted himself. "Ahhh shit, don't even tell me."

"Yep, you guessed it."

"What you're not telling me is that Silas is taking her to Fréyonne? This is just fabulous. There's only one reason he's taking her there; he has every intention of teaching her to hunt and feed. It's only been a week since she killed the waitress in the club. I knew that would bring it out of him; the look behind his eyes that night said it all. Son of a bitch!"

"You do know where he's going to take her once they get there—yes?" Bain asked.

"Yes, his old killing fields, his hunting grounds." Eden was more than concerned; the apprehension was all over his face and clear in his tone.

"So, how big should the clean-up crew be?" Lars joked.

"Big—looks like we're headed down the ole rabbit hole with Silas," Bain sighed.

Eden had no words; he was at a complete loss. He had no idea how to contend with Jadis, much less Silas.

"Go—and don't let those two out of your sight for a moment. We'll figure out what to do from here."

Eden leaned back, put his feet up on the desk, interlaced his fingers behind his head, and stared at the ceiling.

No one knew what to do. They could contain Jadis if needed, but not Silas; he outranked every one of them except for Eden, and that was sketchy at best.

"I might have to make a call myself," Eden admitted after what seemed like an hour.

The stunned silence, not to mention the looks on the faces of everyone sitting there, brought about the realization of how serious the situation had become.

Aiden's mind spiraled back to another time altogether. As long as Jadis had Silas's unwavering support, she could pillage whatever village the two of them happened upon.

CHAPTER 5

As soon as they stepped out of the private jet, Jadis knew where they were. "Fréyonne, really?"

"Yes, it's one of my favorite places." Silas smiled.

They were escorted off the tarmac and hopped into a limousine that had been waiting for their arrival. After a short drive, it pulled to a stop and parked in front of a palatial estate.

Silas stepped out of the limo and reached back to offer Jadis his hand. "I assume by your expression this is a pleasant surprise?" Silas hoped that would be her reaction.

"Yes! Do you know how powerful and old this place is? I've always wanted to go here, I just never did. I don't even know why—I can feel it already."

She leaned her head back, let go of Silas's hand, and stretched her arms out, taking in the energy surrounding them.

"Not sure I want to know," Bain said, making Dante chuckle.

"Funny," she replied as she rolled her eyes at them. She turned back around to admire the home they stood in front of. The estate was beautiful, and the property spanned for blocks.

Jadis looked back at Silas, who stood behind her, resting his hands on her shoulders. "Do you own this?"

"Yes, well, our clan does. It's known as The la Couvent du Monde, it's the oldest structure in the la de Martiseau River Valley," he replied proudly.

"I assume it's been in your family for generations?"

"Yes, but how we came about it is a story for another time." He smirked, looking at Dante and Bain.

Jadis caught that familiar expression. *Here we go, they have a secret I know nothing about.*

Three well-dressed men waited for them at the entrance gate. "Good evening, m'lords. Welcome home." The eldest greeted them politely with a thick Southern drawl.

"Good evening, Bishop," Silas replied.

Dante and Bain also greeted him informally, with a forearm grasp and a pat on the shoulder.

"Good to see you again," Dante stated politely.

"It's good to see you, m'lord."

"Jadis, this is Bishop. His family has been with us for as long as I can remember," Silas offered.

"Good evening," she stated politely.

"Good evening, miss. Welcome home." He smiled warmly and kissed the back of her hand.

He snapped his fingers, and the two other staff members quickly picked up their bags. Silas took Jadis's hand and led her in the direction of the home.

They walked down what she assumed was the original red-cobblestone path. Mag and Limi ran ahead, smelling and exploring their new surroundings. The cobblestone walk was lined with perfectly pruned hedges weaving their way around what appeared to be a formal Fréy garden. There was an enormous cast-iron fountain in the center of it all. The ornamental plants and flowers were stunning; their sweet scent drifted throughout the gardens, having been carried by a warm, gentle breeze. The walk led straight to the antique-white front doors adorned with multiple glass panels. The rest of the doors and windows were simple, while a pediment underscored the main entrance. The entire home was lined with doors and windows available and across from each other. They allowed the air to easily flow between them when opened on hot, muggy summer nights before the days of air conditioning.

As they walked in, the expansive solid-wood staircase stood forefront and reminded Jadis of the one back home. *I wonder if this is where Silas got the idea from for the staircase in our home; they certainly have a thing for staircases. It's just like the one back at Aidens as well.*

There were a dozen staff members who stood in a line and greeted them with a slight nod of their heads as they passed. Jadis smiled at each of them, although none of them spoke. Dante, Bain, and Silas simply greeted them by returning the nod. Jadis almost laughed aloud, solely based on the way the staff members shifted their stance and nervously side-eyed each other as soon as Mag and Limi ran through the doors behind Dante and Bain.

She looked at the stairs that made their way up the three floors. *The wood steps showed the wear and tear of almost three centuries.* She glanced around, admiring the antique furniture and various statues decorating the foyer and hallways.

Silas and Jadis made their way up to the third-floor master suite. He opened the door for her and as soon as they walked in, a large, antique bed became the focal point of the entire room. An expansive, multi-colored, antique Persian rug covered the gleaming cherrywood floors.

Silas took their bags from the gentleman who had carried them up and set them on a chaise lounge sitting catty-corner to the ornate bed.

She noticed a massive oil painting hanging on the opposite wall. It was a semi-erotic scene depicting a couple wrapped up in one another's arms. The animals and plants were a bit more indistinct than the lovers, who were at the forefront of the picture. The lovers were naked, and their bodies were intertwined on the ground with the forest surrounding them. Off in the distance was what appeared to be gravestones, covered in vines, surrounded by a decrepit iron fence.

"You like it?" Silas asked as he pulled her from the bedpost she held onto while admiring the painting.

"Yes, very much so. It's hauntingly beautiful."

"As are you, my love."

She pulled away from Silas and plopped backwards onto the bed, admiring what seemed to be the original bed curtains, tied back with fat, braided, velvet ropes.

Silas crawled over the top of her. "You look amazing in my bed, mon chéri."

The smooth, velvety rumble of his always turned her on. She pulled him down for a kiss before the questions ran through her mind. "*Your bed*? So, this was, is, originally your room?" The realization he must have spent many of his days and nights there also brought up an uncomfortable feeling.

"Yes, and you should have been lying in it for the last one hundred and fifty years," he rumbled as he looked down at her and winked.

I wonder how many women over the last hundreds of years he has shared this bed with—his bed. She couldn't help but let the thought cross her mind, making her stomach churn at the very notion. She cocked her head at Silas, waiting for an answer. "Since you're reading my mind, how many?" she demanded, not wanting to know.

"It's not like I'm a puritan."

He said it so casually, the pang of jealousy she felt was more like a punch in the gut. His laughter grew as he rolled onto his back, taking her with him. She sat up on top of him, staring down into those gorgeous, magnificent eyes, and straddled his hips. She slapped his chest, and he quickly grabbed her arms and pinned them behind her back. She couldn't help but smile even though she was truly seething with envy.

"How many? I want to know, well, maybe I don't, hundreds of years is a lot of women. Well shit—I can't even." *Once again, I'm my own worst enemy, letting my thoughts run wild. All the while, Silas is just lying here, looking amused.*

"If you must know, I don't take lovers, at least not the kind you're thinking of, and if I'm being honest, the majority of them didn't make it through the night alive."

It didn't bother him one bit, knowing how many mortals he has killed over the centuries.

He moved his hips under her, letting her know he had more on his mind than a bunch of dead feeders. His eyes were already changing, reflecting his sudden desire, not to mention the bulge slowly rising in his jeans between her legs.

"Well, *if I'm being honest,* IF we happen to run into any of your old lovers who did happen to make it through the night, I promise you I will kill them—just so you know." She raised an eyebrow at him, letting him know she was serious.

He rolled back over, pinning her beneath him.

"I assume you at least changed the sheets—yes?" she asked.

Silas laughed aloud. "You're crazy. I've never been one to allow strange females in my personal space, much less my bed. That's something we all hold sacred. So, in reality, you're the only female who's ever been in my bed."

"Well then, maybe we should break the virgin in?" She was now as ready as Silas.

He let out a low moan. "Hell yes, a mate after my own heart."

He bent down and claimed her mouth, and the warmth of his tongue meeting hers had her melting in his arms. They most definitely broke the bed in, for at least an hour or so before taking a quick nap.

Jadis rolled over and laid her head on Silas's chest. "I want to go out. Can we go downtown?"

"I was thinking the same thing. I have a lot I want to show you. Let's get dressed. It's only nine; the streets are just coming to life."

They jumped up, excited as two kids heading out on their first date. She couldn't wait to see Fréyonne with Silas. He'd known the city since before it became what it was today. *To think Silas is three hundred-plus years older than* Fréyonne *is hard to comprehend,* she thought, while getting dressed.

Silas put on a pair of dark-grey dress slacks, along with a black-leather vintage Herlane belt and a white button-down shirt that he had tucked in perfectly. He left the top two buttons on his shirt undone, exposing a hint of his tattoo-adorned, perfect chest.

Jadis wore a matching light-grey, knee-high, form-fitting wrap dress. The bottom was slightly longer on one side than the other, exposing the majority of her thigh. She pulled her hair into a messy, partial updo held up with a couple of gold, antique, Ipheanorian hair pins Silas had given her. They sat in opposite chairs, putting their shoes on, both of which were black and grey. His were a pair of Sagalatore Fingano leather oxfords, and hers were Bolenta Veniata stilettos.

He stood, walked over to her, and held out his hand. She looked up, and he was stunning. She had never seen him dressed up before, and it took her a minute to regain her focus. He was coyly smiling with the corner of his mouth turned up, as he looked down at her.

"Shall we?" he offered.

As Jadis stood, he held her in place and walked in a circle around her. He stopped behind her and gently slid his hands around her waist.

"You're a vision to behold. I'm not sure I want to take you out looking like this," he whispered before kissing the crook of her neck.

She wrapped her hands around his forearms and tilted her head to the side to look up at him. "You keep that up, we're not leaving," she murmured back.

Jadis knew he was contemplating his next move, so she quickly decided for him. "Take me out, baby. I want to see your Fréyonne. We can finish this later. I need to recover anyway. I don't think I could take you again right now if I wanted to." *I'm a bit sore from breaking in his bed*

"Whatever your heart desires, my love." He took her hand in his, and they headed downstairs. They walked into the main parlor where Dante and Bain had been waiting for them.

They looked at Jadis and Silas and focused their attention on Jadis, which made her feel self-conscious. She hated any attention being focused on her, much less the attention Dante and Bain staring at her with wide eyes and frozen expressions.

"Wow! The two of you look amazing," she politely offered. *Hell, I've never seen them dressed up either, they're flawless.*

"You're stunning, darling. Well—should we get going?" Dante offered, fumbling for words. He was taken aback by the vampiress standing before him. His secret, unrequited love was more than stunning, she's perfection.

Trying to sound normal, Bain cleared his throat, took another drink, and set it on the table. "I've never seen you all dressed up. Normally, you're a hot mess." He winked.

She rolled her eyes and smiled, but it was apparent they were gathering their composure. *For whatever reason, I can't pick up on their thoughts, it's more like subtle impression—it's strange.*

"Ready, baby? The car's waiting." Silas smiled.

Dante and Bain reluctantly followed, and she assumed they weren't ready for whatever Silas had planned, hence their strange behavior.

"What, no words?" she asked in jest.

They stepped out of the limo and were in front of Labady's Blacksmith Shop. The sounds of laughter filled the streets, lit by the flickering neon lights hanging from almost every venue on the strip. Street performers were out and about, greeting tourists, and it was decorated with balconies, beads, and hundreds of people. The loud music thumped from somewhere about a block or so away.

Jadis had forgotten about her new hearing, and the sounds were instantly overwhelming. Silas looked down at her and smiled.

"Control it, baby. You know what you're doing now, drown it out." He lifted her chin and gently placed a kiss on her lips.

"I don't know what I would do without you. You do realize I'm obsessed."

"I believe I'm just as *obsessed* with you. Shall we? I need a drink"

He placed his hand on her lower back and escorted her into the old Cretion tavern. The host escorted them to a private table set in the back corner, three steps above the dance floor which allowed a perfect view of the entire room. It wasn't the typical crowd one would see in an old tavern; everyone was dressed to the nines.

"Do you always travel like this?" She made more of a statement, she already knew Silas only accepted the best.

"Only when the company's worth it."

One of the waiters, who was also impeccably dressed, set a bottle of Glendeon MaCru on the table, along with four highball glasses. He then carefully poured the Glendeon over a single, round ice cube sitting in the center of each glass.

"It's amazing; how old is this place?" She looked all around the tavern, absorbing every detail. Her mind was like a mini computer now, and she catalogued an entire room in mere seconds.

"It was built in 1773 and is said to be where the Landry brothers opened their blacksmith shop as a façade, so they could carry out their privateer efforts." Silas looked at Dante and Bain, all of whom had a mischievous smile on their faces.

"I'm assuming there's more to this story?" She waited for Silas to continue.

"Well, yes, sort of."

She took a moment to read each of their expressions. "Landry brothers? Ahhh—I assume by the looks you all are giving each other, you're the Landry brothers, in the flesh?" She tilted her head, trying to read their expressions. *They look as if they're reliving some very fond memories.*

"Yes, darling, we are them, in the *flesh* as you put it. Only the brothers were me, Dante, Syth, and Agaeus. Everyone else joined us from time to time, for the entertainment," Silas explained.

Silas appeared to be amused as he twirled the glass in his hand, letting the ice cube clink against the sides, smiling at no one in particular.

"Well, now I have to know. Fess up, I want stories." She waited for one of them to begin. They again looked at each other coyly and casually took another drink.

"So, it's safe to assume feeding was the *privateer efforts*?" she guessed.

"Yes, it's a long and complicated story, but that's the gist of it," Silas replied, cutting to the chase as always.

"*Long and complicated*, you can say that again," Dante offered, as he tilted his glass toward Silas. "We used our blacksmith shop to hide what we were truly doing. We weren't out in the open in those days like we are now. Nosferatu, in general, had family-run businesses all over the world that we used to conceal our true identities. This was no different. However, this place holds very fond memories for us all."

Silas scanned the room as if he were seeing it as it was in the 1700s. She could read his thoughts and see his memories. *It looked much different then but still the same as it does now somehow.*

"Come on, I want to know." She squeezed Silas's thigh and moved it from side to side, urging him to tell her the story.

"Okay—okay." Silas chuckled. "We were just four hundred and thirty-three years old when we commissioned this place to be built. Fréyonne was much different then, it wasn't a nice place for the most part, at least for the mortals. They were sold in the middle of the business district for whatever reason. They were sold on boats, in the bustling area known as Vieux Levatou, and in the most sumptuous room of the most luxurious hotel in the South—the Mon Tre` Hotel. We didn't use mortals the way they used each other. We fed, and we killed, but we've never enslaved anyone; we are hunters by nature after all. This area was especially seedy; we were able to go undetected and carry on as we chose. Not that our existence is, was a secret, we just chose to keep our identities concealed for many reasons as you know. No one ever tied us to the missing, we were very careful, meticulous you might say, in destroying the bodies and any evidence. The riffraff all came to this area looking for an escape with booze, courtesans, or whatever else they could get a hold of. It made for the perfect hunting grounds; the mortals who went missing from this area never caused much of a stir. If we fed uptown, there would be more of an investigation into the missing, so we kept our tastes simple for the most part, and released them after having erased their memories."

"Please, Silas, you never kept your taste simple. There were plenty of occasions when we had to clean up your *uptown* messes," Dante stated.

"Well, maybe," Silas agreed, lightheartedly. "I always did want more of an affluent meal."

"*An affluent meal*? Maybe you can show me the difference?" Jadis tilted her head toward Silas and winked.

"Baby, I have every intention of *showing* you."

Dante and Bain gave each other a look Silas and Jadis ignored.

"Here we go," Dante said to Bain privately.

Bain didn't answer, he looked to Dante and took another drink.

"I suppose I did choose to feed uptown more than I should have. However, I have no regrets, nothing but fond memories of a past long ago," Silas admitted.

Of course, Silas never regrets anything he does.

"Tell her the story of the Broussard family. If you want to know your mate's taste, that family is the perfect example," Dante offered, sounding amused.

"Who? I assume you killed him, his family?" Jadis asked.

"Silas, Agaeus, and Syth almost took out the entire family," Dante added, as their laughter grew with the memory.

Silas raised his eyebrows and looked at Dante. "We? Is that right, Dante?"

Jadis chuckled with the thought. *Silas seems to be accusing Dante of having something to do with their deaths.*

Bain re-filled his glass, and tilted it toward Dante. "Shall we talk about Dante's tastes?"

Dante took a drink without speaking; however the smile radiating across his face let her know what he wasn't saying.

"Go on, tell her," Silas urged.

"I think she wants to know about the family," Dante replied, trying to divert the attention away from him.

"Come on—I want to hear this," she begged.

"Yes, baby, we were their demise. I was tired of feeding on the riffraff of the inner ghetto. I could never stand the smell of body odor covered in cheap perfume, much less the taste. At least they bathed in their uptown residences. It was the year 1767 when we happened to run into Mr. Broussard down on the docks. His actual name was LeBlanc Le Cormier de Broussard. He was an original colonist of Franoix Périrault territories at the time. He helped to establish the first settlement, the Périrault colony in 1697, now known as Veiux Borleon. He had twelve children and a mistress. He was a bastard by today's standards, however, it was an entirely different time and place. It was late in the evening, the air thick with the humidity and sweltering heat. He was awaiting another shipment of Casquette girls, originally known as a Fille a' la Cassette. Essentially, they were young virgins being brought here from Franoix. Mr. Broussard enjoyed his fair share, allowing them to be housed in his home under the care of his housekeeper, a Franoix-Casidean woman known as Madame Guillory."

"He sold young girls as courtesans?" Jadis questioned.

"Yes, he assumed of course, Agaeus and I were as affluent as he and offered to sell each of us two of the soon-to-arrive virgins. We saw it as an insult, we didn't have to pay for anything or anyone. Not to mention, there wasn't much that could entice us into a financial arrangement with a mortal. Agaeus and I decided we would go ahead and make the deal. We offered enough for each virgin to ensure we were invited to his home to finalize the arrangement. We insisted that we wouldn't conduct our business at the docks like the paupers did, it was generally an unhygienic place covered in lice and vermin. He agreed, and it was obvious he was already counting the money."

Jadis could see, feel, and sense the entire scene simply by reading Silas's thoughts as he spoke; another well-developed ability she had recently acquired.

Silas continued, "We met him the following evening and arrived at his plantation just after sunset. A dozen servants greeted us, holding onto our horse's reins in the half-round, dirt driveway. They escorted us into his home where both Mr. Broussard and his mistress were awaiting our arrival. We made our way into the parlor, and his mistress saw herself out. Most of the conversation consisted of grandiose stories of his accomplishments and finances, of course we were unimpressed and had other ideas. We smelled the money, the children, his mistress, and the virgins. Their smell wafted throughout the home, pulling our desire to hunt and feed to the surface. Bored of the conversation already, Agaeus decided he didn't want to entertain the bastard any longer. He cloaked himself, leaving his imprint in Mr. Broussard's mind. He was none the wiser and had no idea Agaeus had slipped out while I stayed back. I would rather toy with my prey for a-while for the sheer enjoyment of it." Silas chuckled.

"Of course you would." Jadis laughed.

Silas winked and continued. "Agaeus made his way to his mistress' room, leaving Mr. Broussard to me. I smelled the blood and laughed, and Mr. Broussard stared at me as if I were crazy. I set my drink down and circled him. As I *turned*, he tried calling for help, but I silenced him before he had the chance to call out. His eyes were terrified, his pupils dilated from the shock, and the fear emanated from his body, which only served to ramp up my hunger."

"*Toy with your prey*?" she teased as Silas paused to take a drink.

"You know I like to play before I feed." He winked.

Her face flushed at the sexual undertone as soon as Dante and Bain laughed at the comment.

Silas continued, "Dante and Syth finally joined us and proceeded to meet Agaeus upstairs. I kept Mr. Broussard pinned in his chair as I looked around his office, genuinely curious as to his business dealings. I ran my hand across the wall, feeling the velvet wallpaper concealing the uneven plaster, before finding a wall safe hidden behind a large candelabra. I thumbed through his desk, pulling out anything that might be of use to us later on. He was rich for the time, and I took note of his finances and business arrangements while Agaeus, Syth, and Dante moved amongst the bedrooms on the third floor. Once I made a mental note of the information I found in his bookkeeping records, I pulled him out of the chair and fed."

"Unless my thoughts deceive me, that's not exactly how it went." Dante tilted his head, waiting for Silas to respond. Silas's sole response to the accusation was a mischievous smile.

"Okay—I'll finish for you," Dante offered. "Silas didn't let him sit for a few minutes as he so casually put it. He left him sitting there for hours as the four of us came and went from his office. We always returned for another drink between feedings. I believe at one point, Silas did more than feed from one of the virgins on his red-velvet settee as Mr. Broussard watched from his paralyzed state of mind." Dante laughed.

"Holy shit, Silas—did you really do that to the poor bastard and the virgin?" Jadis asked amused, at least until the thought hit her. *He had sex with another! It's a good thing he isn't allowing me to see that.*

"Yes, I'm afraid so. Like I said, we were young, it was a different time and place," Silas offered, justifying their actions.

Silas looked at her and smiled warmly. "There's no one but you, my love," he added in response to her sudden onset of jealousy.

She dismissed the thought, not wanting to see or think about her mate with another. "Were you all upstairs killing his mistress and their kids?" She was taken aback by how easily they told the story. *It's as if they had just gone to dinner at a local restaurant.*

"Well, yes," Silas answered. "We made our way through the entire home that night, so don't let Dante sit over there like he had nothing to do with it. If I'm not mistaken, you headed straight for the virgins. Am I wrong, brother? Not to mention you didn't just feed from them either, now did you?" Silas brought his so-called uninvolved absence to light.

"No—no, you're not wrong in the least. But let me be clear, I did not take the kid's innocence sexually, anyway." Dante admitted. "I have certain tastes myself," he said with a smirk and a quick sideways glance at Jadis.

She cocked her head in response to the strange look as he held her gaze for only a moment.

"Had?" Bain now called his statement into question.

"Not that I need all the gory details, but did anyone survive that night?" Jadis asked. *I'm almost afraid to know the truth. It should bother me, but it doesn't.* It was a strange feeling, and she found herself struggling with her coldness.

"You're Nosferatu, my dear. The death, the feeding, it won't bother you for long. It's normal. The little pangs of guilt you have now will dissipate with time. Soon enough, you too will kill without regard," Silas offered.

Silas tried to put her conscience at ease, but she wasn't sure *killing without regard* was what she wanted to hear. However, she found his sincerity endearing as always. "So, how long did you let him sit there while you killed and fed from them?" she asked as she found herself more amused with the story than upset by it.

"All night, I saved him for last. I tend to savor my meals." Silas winked as he looked at Jadis with that smooth, upturned grin of his. "I ended his misery shortly before the sun rose."

"Wait—the four of you drained fourteen people plus the virgins in one night?" She was a bit shocked by the admission. "How could you all possibly feed on so much blood?"

"No, we only fed on eleven between us. Which in reality is only about two each," Silas replied, correcting her mathematical calculations.

"Oh, okay." She laughed. "Only *two each*, got it," she repeated as she took a couple of sips.

"We were young, but a child's body to a full-grown vampire isn't all that much," Dante explained.

"So, off the subject, you said his mistress. Where was his wife, the mother of his twelve children?" Jadis asked.

"Rumor had it the mistress was the mother of his children, well most of them anyway. He refused to marry her for whatever reason," Silas replied.

Silas seems to pity her, just a bit anyway, not that it saved her life.

"No, I had no intention of *saving* anyone, they were just our entertainment that night, nothing more. But yes, you're correct. I did *pity her, just a bit.*"

Silas emphasizing the just a bit part. God forbid he has a heart, she thought, making herself chuckle.

"Unless it comes to you, don't think I have a heart or a conscience, darling." Silas grabbed her face and pulled her in for a kiss. "My heart and conscience belong to only one," he whispered.

The warmth of his breath tickled her ear, forcing a giggle from her.

"Enough of the story already. I'm feeling a bit hungry reliving all of that." Silas tossed a couple of one-hundred-dollar bills on the table for their waiter.

"Come, my love, let me to show you how to dine in Vieux Levatou." He was already standing, holding one hand out to her.

"God, yes. I'm hungry too. I think my stomach is growling," she admitted before thinking it through. "Umm— feeding? From each other or—?" She wasn't sure where this was heading since they had Dante and Bain in tow. Silas didn't answer, he just proceeded to lead her out of the tavern into the bustling streets.

"And here it begins," Bain rumbled to Dante, knowing where they headed. They finished their drinks and followed Silas and Jadis.

As they walked the strip, Jadis kept her arm wrapped in Silas', listening intently to his every word. There was a story in every alley, hotel, bar, or street corner. *He's a walking history book. He knows things about the city no one else could possibly know.* She was fascinated as he recalled every detail, making the stories and history lessons all the more entertaining. Dante and Bain chimed in often as well. The place was clearly near and dear to their hearts. They too had as many stories and history lessons as Silas. She loved every second of their moonlit walk. They passed through the crowds of tourists and locals as if they were invisible. It looked like the waters parted as they walked. She wasn't sure if it was by Silas' doing or Dante or Bain's.

"It's each of us, darling. I want you to see how easy it is to disappear into a crowd. Think yourself invisible, and you'll essentially cloak yourself. Dante, let her take over."

"Wait—how?" she questioned.

As soon as the words left her mouth, the crowds closed in. A couple of girls who appeared to have been having quite the time bumped into her shoulder, which pushed her partly behind Silas, who stopped her from *turning*.

"Hold steady, baby. You can take whatever revenge you want later. Remember her, remember her smell, remember her essence, pin her in your thoughts."

She did as instructed and felt the girl's imprint in her mind. The look of shock that suddenly crossed her face forced the three of them to chuckle.

"It's that simple. You have more control over the world and its inhabitants than you realize," Silas offered.

They walked a bit further into the city as the three of them continued giving her *cloaking* lessons, which she picked up on right away. *It seems like everything I do, everything they tell me to do, comes with ease.*

"You're a quick learner." Silas nodded, his pride clear.

Dante and Bain were also impressed at the ease in which she picked up on their lessons. They also enjoyed teaching her as much as Silas.

They continued to walk uninterrupted once again, as she took over. They were now headed out of town, and the streets were getting a bit darker the further away they got from all of the neon lights. The drunken hollers, laughter, and music all seemed to be fading into the distance.

As they rounded a corner, they were suddenly in an upper-class part of the city. The clubs were larger, the streets clean, well-lit, and without the glare or sounds of the buzzing neon lights. The luxury cars were picked up and delivered back to the upper-class clientele by valet. The music became that of a traditional band; the trumpets, trombones, clarinets, and drums seeped through the night air.

"Lesson one, feeding in public, let them see us," Silas instructed.

"Why do we want them to see us?" She was now confused.

"So you can toy with them, let them interact with you, and then take your pick. Let your appetite show you what you want. It can be done in the shadows, but I think it's more appealing this way."

Silas, my scholar, indeed. Okay—just toy with my victim, no big deal. I can do this. It's like a cat playing with a mouse, she thought to herself, which brought about another chuckle from Silas who listened intently.

"Just how quickly do you think this will go south?" Bain asked Dante telepathically.

"I give it twenty minutes, tops. Hell, reliving all this is making me feel the pull. It's not what I needed at all," Dante admitted as he proceeded to pull a flask from his pocket.

"I'm right there with you. I'm feeling it myself," Bain admitted, taking out his own flask.

"Here goes nothing." Jadis sighed.

She looked to Silas for reassurance, and he squeezed her hand, acknowledging her trepidation. She let down the veil, and they were once again visible to the mortal eye.

As they strolled down the vibrant street, passing by the luxurious clubs, the women couldn't help but notice the captivating presence of her three companions, which made Jadis uncomfortable. The valets nodded in their direction as they passed by; Silas, Dante, and Bain politely retuned the gesture. She felt awkward searching for a victim. *It doesn't feel authentic, it feels forced. Not to mention all eyes are on me as well. I don't even fully understand what I want. The last two times I killed was indiscriminate, it was natural and felt right.*

They had stopped in front of a busy club, and the patrons were clearly inebriated. They were surrounded by laughter, exuberant chatter, and people moved about from all directions. She didn't know what to do at this point.

"You're overthinking it, baby. Your body will know what you want as soon as the feeder presents itself. Just relax, there's no pressure. If you don't want to feed, don't feed. If you do, then feed."

She looked up at Silas. *God, how I love him.*

"And I you, my love." Silas lifted her chin and gently kissed her on the lips.

They were suddenly approached by a group of girls who were happily intoxicated and most likely in their twenties. They slowed as they got closer to them to take in the sight that was Silas, Dante, and Bain.

"Here we go, get ready for the cleanup," Bain uttered to Dante.

Dante looked at him with a troubled expression, having more than the *cleanup* job on his mind, and he wasn't thinking about feeding or the approaching crowd.

"My God, look at the three of you!" one of the girls exclaimed as they drunkenly made their way to them.

The need to satiate her hunger hit Jadis like a freight train, just as intensely as it had during her previous encounters. Only this time, she was able to control it.

"Not yet. Hold it, baby," Silas instructed.

She did as he instructed after taking a deep breath to calm herself. *Their annoying laughter and squeals of excitement looking at the vampires in my presence are as annoying as hell.*

"I think I get it. I do want to play with them. You were right, this will be fun." Jadis side-eyed Silas with a smirk.

"That's it, baby. Let's play—shall we?" Silas squeezed her hand, ready to let her do her thing.

They stopped and faced the drunken quartet, and Jadis heard Silas telling Dante and Bain not to interfere.

"Damn, girl! How the hell did you get so lucky?" the brunette hollered as she approached Dante.

Jadis stared at her, and her head instinctually cocked to the side.

"Jesus, look at you, a tall drink of water," the second blonde added, who now gently held onto Bain, lifting his hand up in the process. "Mind if we borrow these two for the rest of the evening?" she asked, her words slightly slurred.

The last two of their drunken friends also sauntered toward Dante and Bain.

"*A tall drink of water*? That's rich. You can't come up with anything better?" Jadis clapped back.

Silas let her hand go and stood slightly behind her.

The leader of the pack stepped forward, having decided she would be the one to challenge Jadis. "What did you say? Who the fuck are you?"

She moved right around Jadis to Silas and rubbed her hand up and down his arm, stopping at his bicep, and copping a feel. "How about you drop the skinny bitch and come with us for a real party." She looked directly at Jadis when she made the statement.

"Apparently, I'm the lucky one, and you're just a washed-up whore." Jadis moved into her body and slowly slid her face up the girls; starting at her chin and stopping at her ear. "I can still smell them between your legs," she snarled.

"What did you just say to me, you little bitch?" The girl tried to push Jadis away to no avail.

As soon as Jadis captured the girls attention, it was apparent, she was Nosferatu. Her gleaming white canines had fully protruded from her gums, her eyes were glowing amber, slits, and her pupils were coal black.

The girl let out a high-pitched scream, and Jadis grabbed her by the throat, muffling the sounds.

Her friends took a bit longer to figure out what was going on. One of them came from behind her and as soon as she saw Jadis, she too let out a deafening scream. Jadis took her by the throat with her other hand; the other two, she simply silenced with her mind and held them in place like she had seen Silas and his brothers do so many times before.

Jadis dragged the smooth tips of her canines along the girls vein before sinking them into the pack leader's friend first. She wanted to let the one who touched Silas watch her drain her girlfriend. She released her grip and the girl's mummified body fell sideways. As she looked to the other girls, they were a mixture of shock, disbelief, and horror as the tears streamed down their frozen faces. Jadis stepped over the lifeless body and focused on her next victim—their leader. She grabbed a fistful of her hair and wrenched her head back, exposing her neck.

"I could forgive the bitch part, but you touching what's mine was a—mistake—a big mistake," she snarled into her face, slowly annunciating every word.

She moved the hair off her cheek and wiped away a tear with her thumb. She softly placed her thumb into her mouth and sucked it off as she walked the girl backwards into a large bush concealing the sidewalk.

Fuck me. Dante thought to himself, watching Jadis. *Her actions are velvety smooth, deadly, and more than enticing.*

Jadis read her every thought, every emotion; her fear, her anxiety, as well as the shock and horror knowing she was about to die. She took it all in, and the gratification was overwhelming. She watched her pulse thumping under her soft, perfume-laden, skin, and she could see the blood coursing through her veins. Her ears picked up on the sounds, tu tump— tu tump—tu tump— She latched onto her neck and let the blood flow over her tongue. She fed a bit slower this time, savoring her meal. She tossed her body to the ground next to her friend and turned back toward Silas.

"You weren't kidding, baby. That was a hell of a lot of fun!" She felt their blood coursing through her body, tingling all her nerve endings.

"Damn, darling, that was amazing!" Silas stated. He grabbed the back of her head and pulled her in for a deep, blood-ridden kiss, savoring the taste. He slid his tongue across the tips of her canines, reveling in the sharp sensation and iron taste.

Dante and Bain felt their own excitement growing, their need to hunt becoming ravenous.

Once Silas let Jadis go, she nodded in agreement to what he had said telepathically. She turned to Dante and Bain and sauntered toward them. She wiped the blood from the corner of her mouth and rubbed her thumb across Dante's face, leaving a small trail of blood down his cheek. She then slid her thumb over his bottom lip before doing the same to Bain.

Jadis cracked up at the look on their faces, and Silas wrapped her in his arms from behind and stared blankly at Dante and Bain.

Dante and Bain stood stagnant, feeling as if their life depended on it. They had no idea how Silas would react to Jadis touching them like that.

Assuming they would bear the brunt of his jealousy neither Dante or Bain so much as flinched.

"I saved those two for you. You seem to be—I don't know—hungry?" She put her thumb in her mouth and seductively sucked off the remainder of the blood.

Dante's and Bain's eyes widened, which forced Silas to laugh aloud. That was the last thing they expected from Jadis, not to mention Silas.

The four of them stood in front of one of the busiest, high-end clubs in the district with two dead bodies, two comatose girls, and a trail of blood down Dante's and Bain's cheek, yet no one on the streets appeared to have noticed, which piqued Jadis's curiosity.

"Silas, did I forget something?"

"Sort of. Rule number two, when you kill in public, make sure you cloak the area." He winked.

"Oh, shit. That would have been smart," she replied, feeling stupid.

"You're not *stupid*. I'm proud of you. You were perfect. How does it feel to kill, feed, and toy with your meal for the fun of it?"

"I had my doubts, but you were right. It's fucking amazing!"

Jadis was feeling tipsy but not from the alcohol; she was feeling the effects of her rising blood lust. She finally and fully understood what Silas was trying to explain. She spun around and pressed her body against Silas' and placed her hands on his chest.

"You feel incredible, vampire," she growled, the desire clear in her tone.

"As do you." He turned his attention to Dante and Bain. "I think she left you both an offering, it would be rude to not accept it."

Silas was well aware their desire to hunt and feed matched his own, so he decided to give them what they wanted and essentially released them from the unwritten covenants prohibiting such behavior.

They stood as still as marble statues, trying to figure out how to handle their current predicament.

Dante finally wiped the blood from his cheek with his thumb and sucked it off, looking straight at Silas and Jadis. After a few minutes, he spoke, "Well shit, if we can't beat them, we may as well join them. I'm thoroughly tired of babysitting anyway. This is just too enticing," he admitted as he looked directly at Bain.

"Let's do this," Bain agreed.

Silas, Jadis, Dante, and Bain were now in the middle of the vast open space behind away from the bustling streets of Vieux Levatou. Dante and Bain released the two girls from their catatonic state.

Jadis smelled the lush vegetation and the brackish water. The ghost-grey, moss-laden cypress trees became denser the further in they traveled. The noise from the nocturnal inhabitants echoed through the night air, disturbing the silence of the bayou. *It's eerie as hell, yet it's cryptically beautiful.*

As soon as the two girls were conscious again, they screamed at the sight of the Nosferatu staring at them. Dante and Bain had now fully *turned*. As Silas and Jadis stood in place, watching, he wrapped his arms around her.

He then pulled her tight and gently swayed to the music echoing from off in the distance. He softly sung the words of a haunting tune in only a whisper.

It's the same waltz he was humming to me the first night we met, Jadis thought.

"I've got their blood on my hands.

I've got their blood in my veins.

I guess that's the price they pay.

We shall sing songs of living, my dear.

We shall dance amongst their graves.

A heart that's dark and true, a waltz of lovers—"

Dante's voice suddenly rang out when he yelled, "Better run!"

The girls had already taken off running in the opposite direction and as soon as they heard Dante yell to them, they began screaming.

One of the girls was so terrified, her body moved faster than her feet. She tripped and fell, causing Jadis to laugh. Her friend clumsily gathered her up and they headed further into the density of the bayou.

"Why didn't Dante or Bain silence them, keep them from screaming like that? Someone's going to hear." *Shit, their screaming will attract unwanted attention, a murder trial, and probably a prison sentence.*

"The thoughts popping into that head of yours are nothing short of entertaining. No one's going to prison. They're just hunting and probably a bit more than that before they feed." Hinting to the fact they would be having sex first. "They'll control the situation."

Silas said it so nonchalantly, the concern left her. As soon as Dante and Bain casually gave chase, Silas pinned her on her back in a small clearing, on the cool, moist ground, surrounded by the lush vegetation.

The moment he had her undressed, he shoved himself inside her tight, slick core.

The blood lust ran heavy through them both. Even though he hadn't fed, the taste on her tongue, watching her hunt and feed was all he needed, not to mention he felt everything she did.

She rolled them both over and pulled him up into a sitting position, so she could straddle him. She then slipped herself back down on his full, hard shaft again.

"It feels amazing, sex after hunting and feeding is intoxicating," Jadis whispered.

"I couldn't agree more." He held onto her hips, moving her up and down. Before she knew it, the same familiar feeling rose as her nub rubbed up and down his crotch. The arousal hit quick and hard; her sex throbbed, and her body shuddered.

Silas quickly spun her around, so she remained sitting on top of him. Again, she gently moved up and down to the same hypnotic rhythm, with her back to his front.

"My God, you feel amazing, my love," he moaned.

She wrapped her arms around the back of his head and gently rested her face against his. He wrapped one hand around her waist and moved his other hand further down to rub her sex. She let out a guttural moan, drowning in the moment.

"I want to hear you moaning all night," he whispered, a bit breathless.

She couldn't speak. Between the feeding, the orgasm, and Silas still penetrating her, her mind was lost in many different ways.

"My love, feel it all. Take it all in. Sex after feeding is exhilarating. It will take you to the ground with desire," he stated, with a raspy whisper.

He read every thought swirling through her mind. The blood that was still coursing through her veins was a spiral of sensations. The one thing that was clear, was the sounds of his moans as his orgasm surfaced.

"Ahhh—fuck," he muttered.

He shoved her head and body toward the ground and lifted her hips with his other hand as he rose onto his knees. With each orgasmic thrust, he shoved harder, trying to get deeper inside of her.

"Silas—" was all she managed to growl as another heated swell rose.

He pulled out, flipped her onto her back, and entered again. He took all that was his, and he wanted it deep and hard. He lifted his head and let out a breathless, guttural roar into the moonlit night, allowing his own orgasm take flight with hers.

They lay breathless, hearts racing, pulses thumping, their bodies moist from the exertions of the last hour.

The sex was raw, aggressive, carnal. Silas was back in his old stomping grounds, and it showed in more ways than one. The sensations rocked her. *Silas never ceases to amaze me. The fresh blood seems to bring my body to life, arousing every nerve ending. Every touch is like electricity on the skin.*

Jadis was still half-asleep, wrapped in his arms when his voice broke the silence, not to mention the smack on her ass.

"We have company. Get up, darling, and you might want to put your clothes back on."

"Oww—dammit! You could have given me a head's up!" She put on her bra and underwear as fast as she could to Silas's amusement.

They watched as two shadowy figures appeared at the bend of the bayou, headed their way. Jadis was barely dressed by the time they reached them, and Silas had nothing more than his pants on and was still in the process of zipping them up, along with her dress.

Silas lifted his eyebrow, waiting for a response from one or both of them. Dante and Bain took a drink from their flasks but said nothing.

Jadis had seen their eyes change before, but not like this. It was altogether different, darker, more intense. There was a fury, intricately woven behind their coal-black irises. It shocked and scared her. *Poor girls. I can't imagine what Dante and Bain must have looked like right before feeding if they look like this now. The girls must have been terrified. I almost feel sorry for them.*

Silas cocked his head. "*Almost?*" She simply shrugged her shoulders and smiled.

"Wizards are more intense after feeding. It's normal," Silas offered.

"Well? Do tell," Jadis stated as they stood with anticipation. Silas, of course, was still putting the rest of his clothes on.

"So, Jadis, did you happen to know the ones you saved for us were virgins?" Dante asked.

"I have no idea what you're talking about."

Silas's eyebrows shot up. "Really? Shouldn't we all have smelled that from a mile away?" he questioned.

"That's very odd?" She cocked her head and purposefully gave Dante and Bain a shit-eating grin. *It's the same one they've given me many a day, or night, or morning, depending on the situation.*

"Well, I'll be dammed! Did you cloak that from the three of us?" Silas was directly facing her now.

"Sort of. I wanted to see if I could. You told me to cloak our surroundings," she said, trying to sound as innocent as possible.

Silas cocked his head toward Jadis. "Well shit, I'm going to have to pay closer attention to you."

"You don't play fair, do you? We'll remember that," Bain stated.

"Well, I must admit that was impressive as hell. We didn't even know until we caught them. We should have learned long ago to not underestimate anything you do." Dante thought it was almost a sweet gesture. *The only problem is that she does everything for a reason. She's more like Silas than they've given her credit for.* He was still trying to figure out how she stopped them from smelling the virgins. *At least it has sated my hunger for someone else, for a while*, he thought quietly.

"Well? Stop acting like nothing happened. How was it? You all haven't hunted in God knows how long, according to Silas. Was it worth it?" *He knew they would fall prey to the virgin card, given the chance*, Jadis thought.

"*It was fucking amazing*!" Bain joked, causing the four of them to laugh aloud.

Dante and Bain took the last drink from their flasks and tossed them aside, where they disappeared before hitting the ground.

"So, now what?" she asked, feeling like the party was just getting started.

"Well, I do believe it's my brother's turn to feed. Silas, I'm assuming you're next?" It was clear. Dante decided they were now all in this together.

"Silas isn't feeding from someone else. Oh, hell no!" she protested.

The three of them found her jealousy adorable.

"Baby, tonight, I'll take a man for your sake, but I generally prefer women. I'll let you get familiar with all of this first—okay?"

It took a minute to contemplate what he was saying before she finally agreed. "Fine, but no females!"

He pulled her to him and kissed her again. "Don't be jealous, you're the only one for me. Now let's go. I'm hungry too."

The sudden ring coming from Bain's pocket stopped them in their tracks. They stared at each other, knowing full well who was on the other end. Bain quickly silenced it, acting as if it didn't happen at all.

"What, you're not going to answer it?" Jadis squinted her eyes at him in jest. He didn't respond; he just continued walking.

"Come on, Bain, what if it's a hot date calling?" she joked, trying to get a rise out of him.

"Jadis, you're ridiculous. You do know that, right? Not to mention I believe I just ate my hot date." Bain winked. He stood quiet for a moment, to contemplate what they were bringing out in Jadis. *With Silas, Dante, and he having her back, teaching her all she needs to know, the fate of the world and all that resides in it are hers to control.*

Even though Bain shut the phone off, they knew Eden was still calling. Not only did they ignore the phone, but they also ignored his telepathic calls and headed back into town.

The gnawing hunger in Silas quickly took over; he needed to feed and now. *Not a moment to waste*, he thought. He grabbed the first gentleman who had been standing alone they came across. He pulled him into the alley just outside the club doors while Dante, Bain, and Jadis watched.

Silas became demonic; his irises coiled, blood red, and swirled around the ink-black, irises, which were now the shape of a diamond. *I think that just scared my soul into hiding! I've seen Silas enraged, happy, in love, and turned on, but this. This is on a whole other level.*

She found herself backing into Dante, and he placed his hands on her shoulders and gave her a gentle, reassuring squeeze. He slid one arm around her waist and placed his hand on her stomach. She held onto his forearm, afraid of what she was witnessing.

Silas had the man by his throat, so much so, the man's face turned blue. He bent over and sank his canines so deep into his neck, Jadis heard them scrape bone. *I'm going to throw up.* The animalistic growl he made was like nothing she had ever heard from him. She couldn't even describe the terrifying sounds as she stood there, digging her nails in Dante's forearm.

"I told you, you had no idea who you were dealing with," Dante whispered into her ear.

She stood in utter disbelief as Silas drained every cell. His victim turned ashen white and aged a thousand years in only a moment. *Now I understand the shock everyone felt the night I did that*, she thought.

She tried to speak but choked on her own words, to Dante and Bain's amusement.

"Well, holy shit, Jadis has nothing to say," Dante joked.

"So, now you understand, my dear, who Silas is. He is diabolic, Mortem through and through," Bain stated.

Silas let the body drop to the ground and turned it to ash at his feet. As he turned to Jadis, she almost let out a yelp. She had never seen the monster who now stood before her, sauntering toward her.

Silas saw the look on her face and let out low growl that now sounded demonic.

"My love, that was fucking amazing!" he said. "Do not fear me, my dear. I'm the monster you need. Remember me telling you that?" He cocked his head and held her gaze.

Ohhh shit, was all that came to her mind.

Silas took hold of her arms and pulled her into him. He reached around to the back of her head and pulled her mouth to his.

She felt the difference in his energy permeating her, scaring her. Even so, she was powerless wrapped in his arms.

Once he pulled back and looked into her eyes, he had become the vampire she knew, to her relief.

"Baby, hunting and feeding with you, with my brother, and cousin, is incredible. I haven't enjoyed myself this much in a demon's mile," he admitted.

Dante and Bain joined his amusement; however, Jadis was still too stunned to do anything but stare.

"Goddamn, that tasted fresh!" Silas announced.

"Holy shit!" was all she managed to say.

"Have you ever heard the old saying, *be careful what you ask for?*" Dante said to her in jest.

"Silas, we good?" That was the only thing she could come up with, which brought out another bout of laughter from them.

"We're better than good. Shall we show you a bit more of the city?" he suggested as he placed a kiss on her lips, soothing her terrified state of mind. That was the beginning of the four of them rampaging Fréyonne.

CHAPTER 6

Eden shot straight up in bed, waking Maddie in the process.

"Eden, what's wrong?"

"Ah shit, this is bad." Eden plopped back down and rolled over onto his side, so he could face her. "I think we have a problem and a big one, four big ones to be exact."

Maddie was a bit confused as she was still half-asleep. "Four problems, what do you mean?"

"They're all feeding, I can feel it. This will be the disaster I said it was." Eden rolled back over and rubbed his face with both hands. Maddie sat further up and rested her chin on her bent arm laying on his chest.

"What makes you think all four of them are feeding? I know you were concerned about Jadis and Silas. That was a given, but why do you think Bain and Dante would follow suit? They've never strayed before, or have they?" Maddie asked.

"I just know, baby, their energy is undeniable."

He picked up his phone from the nightstand and called Bain, but he didn't pick up, so he reached out telepathically, that too went unanswered. He stroked her hair and telepathically reached out to Aiden, since the foursome had shut him out. *"Aiden."*

"I'm here. What's up, Eden, or do I even want to know?"

"*It's bad, Aiden. Do you get the sense something's off with our band of brothers in Fréyonne? Have you heard from Bain at all?*"

"*No, but I've been a bit preoccupied, and it's not like him to check in constantly,*" he rumbled. "*What time is it anyway?*"

"*About 3 a.m.*" Eden looked back to Maddie, whose head was resting gently on his shoulder.

"*Well, maybe they're sleeping, or maybe you're suffering from a bit of paranoia?*" he replied. Aiden did know full well what was happening. It just didn't bother him like it did Eden.

"*No, it's been a week, and that same unrelenting feeling is washing over me.*"

"*The Jadis feeling, I assume.*" He couldn't help but find Eden's constant Jadis migraines a source of entertainment, as long as he wasn't affected in any way.

"*Yes, meet me in the command room with everyone else in twenty.*"

Aiden looked at Aria who was asleep in his arms. "*Make it an hour,*" he shot back, annoyed.

"*Make it ten, be there.*" Eden ordered. "I've got to get up, baby." He gently moved Maddie off him and kissed her forehead.

"No, stay, take care of this later." She snuggled her groggy head into his body, trying to keep him in bed as long as possible.

"I'm sorry, baby. This can't wait. You stay right here, naked, and I'll be back shortly."

"Your shortly usually ends up in an all-nighter," Maddie quipped back.

"Is that why you're so sleepy?" Eden joked.

"Actually, yes. Someone kept me up all night." Maddie pulled him in for a deep kiss as she slid her hand lower.

"Mmm, you're not playing fair, darling," Eden moaned as he slipped his tongue into her mouth.

A voice suddenly interrupted him, *"Where the fuck are you? You're supposed to be here. Let's go, Eden. It was so important, you had to pull me out of bed, and now you can't drag your own ass out of bed."*

"Relax, I was looking for my phone."

"Bullshit—just get your ass here."

"I have to go, baby. Business waits, but I want you here when I'm done." Eden was already getting up.

"Maybe, maybe not. Kiss me, and I'll think about it," she teased. He obliged and headed out the door.

"Ah hell, look what the cat dragged in." Lars had also been waiting, even though he had already been up working.

Eden ignored him as usual. "We have a situation on our hands."

"Yes, it's called Operation Sladis." Lars cracked himself up as usual.

"What? What the hell is Sladis, not that I have time for this?" Eden stated.

"Sladis, come on, you know— Silas—Jadis—Sladis!" Lars spelled it out to everyone but Eden's amusement.

"Really?" Eden replied, along with an eye roll. "I have a feeling we've lost Dante and Bain as well. It's time we check in again. They've been ignoring my calls and have shut us out telepathically. They won't do it again."

The entire clan was in the command center, working diligently on other business while Eden, Aiden, and Lars were tied up with their more pressing issue, *Sladis* as Lars put it.

Eden sat in his chair with his elbow on the desk. He rubbed his jawline and tapped his lips with two of his fingers deep in thought, trying to decide what the hell they would do about them feeding and hunting again. *More importantly, Silas is once again chasing the dragon. Not only have they followed Jadis down the rabbit's hole, but they've also fully crashed landed at the bottom. Silas, Dante, and Bain now share her blood lust. Since Jadis turned, it has been nothing but a blood bath. Silas is doing everything but stopping her. The four of them are on the hunt, leaving a trail of blood and ash wherever they go.* He also knew Silas would rationalize their behavior using the fact she needed to learn how to hunt, feed, protect, and control herself. However, there was no control where she was concerned. Everyone knew Silas was a cold-blooded, well-trained assassin. He enjoyed the thrill of the hunt and the kill more than anyone. Eden had also picked up on the subtle energetic nuances that Silas, Dante and Bain, were allowing, supporting, and protecting her. Back at Silas and Jadis's home, they let her to do what she wanted, when she wanted, and how she wanted, only now it would include killing and draining anyone she chose. Silas, of course would be right there, ready to stop anyone who dared to intervene. *He's most certainly turning her into a skilled, proficient, merciless killer. She's his mate, his lover, and his protege.*

Sometimes they chose to feed on the down trodden, the immoral wretches of the seedy lower ward, as Silas called them. When Jadis's taste required something different, they went uptown. No one was safe from the four of them, and Silas, Dante, and Bain indulged her like a spoiled bairn. Prior to returning to Fréyonne, feeding had become a boring need for survival. Feeding was now intoxicating to all of them; they no longer had any desire to control their blood lust. The thrill pulled Silas, Dante, and Bain back to the old days.

They slept all day, as usual and typically woke up late in the afternoon, drawn out of their sleep by the fading sunlight. Sometimes, Dante and Bain never came home at all but always met Silas and Jadis for drinks before they headed out. Their stories entertained the hell out of her. Staying up all night, drinking, feeding, and then sleeping during the day became a routine.

Jadis felt Silas rustle next to her. She had her back to his stomach, and their arms and legs were entangled together. "Good afternoon, baby. How did you sleep?"

"Amazing as usual, you?"

"Same. I had a strange dream though."

His statement woke her mind a bit, and she rolled to her side so she could look at him. "What do you mean? Is everything okay?"

"I don't know, it's unsettling. I'm not sure how to tell you."

"Okay, well, what the hell? Silas, you're freaking me out." She felt her pulse thump a little harder.

"I don't know, my love—I'm happy." He smiled.

"You're ridiculous! You had me thinking something was seriously wrong." She landed a playful smack on his chest.

He snatched her hand and rolled on top of her, squishing her into the mattress. He shoved her legs apart and settled in. She tried to fight him but even with her newfound strength, she was no match and found herself pinned beneath him.

"What's on the menu for dinner?" he asked.

"I don't know? I'm not even awake yet," she answered, still feeling groggy.

"And the sedated sleep begins. That too will subside with time."

"What's that?"

"When you're newly *turned*, the blood is like tryptophan. It'll have a sedative-like effect until your body adjusts. You just have to fight it off for the first few weeks. Let's get up and get ready. I'll choose our menu tonight, something special. And by the way, I'm so happy you're mine. Just when I thought a mate wasn't in my future, you walked into my club and right into my arms."

"I'm yours, assassin. Don't you ever forget it."

"I love how that sounds on your tongue." He winked. "Let's dress casual tonight and dine well," Silas suggested, having something new in mind for tonight's dinner.

She couldn't even guess what it might be. "That doesn't make sense, but I'm in." She just let Silas do his thing without question; he never disappointed.

"Well, first *thing's* first, I need an appetizer," he rumbled.

"Well then, what are you waiting for?" she replied coyly.

Once they were finished, they got out of bed, dressed, and made their way to the parlor where Dante and Bain were waiting as usual.

"It's about time the two of you showed up. What's on the menu tonight, darling?" Dante greeted her with a kiss on the cheek, ready to oblige her every whim.

She returned the gesture, squeezed his hand, and smiled. "Silas is choosing the menu for tonight."

"Well hell, this will be good," Bain replied, as he made sure they all had drinks.

Jadis tilted her head in Bain's direction, trying to get a sense of what he wasn't telling her. Silas took a seat in an antique loveseat, and she plopped down into his lap. She pulled his arm around her waist and gently held onto his forearm. Dante and Bain took their usual seats opposite them.

"Story time, what did the two of you do last night?" She felt like a kid waiting for her bedtime story.

Just before they told another tale, one of the staff members interrupted them, holding a phone. He proceeded to try to hand the phone out to Silas, who dismissed him as well as the call.

"M'lord, it's for you," he again stated, not sure what to do.

To his relief, Bain took the phone. He hit the speaker button so they could all listen in. "Eden, what's up?"

"*What's up*? You know exactly *what's up*. What precisely have the four of you been doing? You or Dante were supposed to check in three days ago. The four of you have been MIA for five. Not only did my initial calls go unanswered, but you've also blocked us out."

"I don't think we've *been MIA*, you know exactly where we are, but if you want to know what we were doing, ask Jadis." Bain tossed her the phone, which she caught without realizing it.

Everyone in the command center heard their laughter on the other end of the line; their amusement and failure to take anything seriously was undeniable.

"And there's your answer," Lars added, simply stating the facts.

They didn't need to hear from any of the four of them, their silence over the last five days said it all. Bain, tossing the phone to Jadis, said more than words ever could.

"Bain, you're an ass," she whispered. "Hi, Eden. Everything okay?" She raised her hand to all of them, looking for help, motioning between them and the phone. Not one of them spoke, but they sure as hell laughed, not caring whether Eden and the rest of them heard or not.

"So, baby girl, it seems we have a bit of an issue right now," Eden said.

"Really? Like what?" she asked, trying to play dumb, all the while her heart beat a bit faster.

"Other than Bain being an *ass*, it seems that he, as well as a couple of cousins and one mate, are MIA."

"Umm—no, we're all right here. I don't see anyone missing." She had no idea what to say to Eden, and her three amigos were of no help at all.

"Jadis, I'm not playing with you—" Eden began.

Jadis interrupted him, "Dante wants to talk to you." She threw the phone to Dante, who caught it mid-air.

"If you want to know, we began at Landry's." Nothing but silence on the other end of the line followed his statement. "Well, I guess that's that." Dante hung up the phone and set it on the table.

"That's it. We're leaving and now," Eden snarled.

By the time Eden returned, Maddie was up and getting ready for the evening.

"Baby, I have to go, they're all on the hunt." Eden was fuming, not to mention worried as hell. He knew he was taking himself and his brothers into the Devil's quarters, and the consequences were dire.

"Oh Eden, I'm so sorry. Is there anything I can do to help? I'll go with you to help with Jadis if you need," she offered.

"No, I need you here. I need you to do something for me and not say anything to anyone—understand?" Eden picked up her phone and entered a name and number.

"Eden, you're scaring me. I don't want you to go. Let someone else handle them."

The fear in her face and in her eyes tugged at his heart. "No, baby. I need to handle this myself. I should have stopped this before it got this serious. It'll be fine, rest assured. This is just a precaution, my love, but I need to rely on you. Promise me you'll do as I say. Call the number I just put into your phone if something happens. Once you call, he'll handle things. Tell him everything."

"Eden, please," she begged.

"I'll be back soon, I promise. It will be fine regardless of what happens in Fréyonne. I'll never stray from you, my love. I need you to know that first and foremost. You're my mate, my life's blood." He pulled her in and wrapped his arms around her, and she clung to him.

"Don't cry, darling. Look at me." Eden lifted her chin and looked directly into her watery eyes. "This is just another mission, nothing more, nothing less. You and I've been through this hundreds of times. Hell, Lars even nicknamed it Sladis." He chuckled, trying to lighten up the situation.

"Sladis? What does that mean?"

"You know Silas—Jadis—Sladis."

She couldn't help herself and she laughed aloud. "I guess that does pretty much sum it up. Promise me you'll be careful."

"I promise, baby. I have to go. The rest of the clan, along with Aria, will be staying here until I get back. If you need anything, you know you can rely on the family. Aiden is also filling Jabari in as we speak." He kissed her again and made his way out.

Maddie sat on the bed, tears streaming down her face when Chloe and Aria walked in to comfort her.

"They're feeding, and I have a terrible feeling they're going to pull Eden in," Maddie cried.

"Eden's too self-controlled to let that happen." Aria sat on the bed next to her, reached for her hand, and gave it a gentle squeeze. Maddie's sudden admission made her worry that if Eden started feeding, Aiden would surely follow suit.

"Don't think like that. He, Aiden, and Lars won't let that happen." Chloe tried her best to comfort Maddie as well, even though she too had the same dreadful feeling.

The front door blew open just as they finished the last of their drinks. In walked Eden, Aiden, Lars, and four warriors Jadis had never seen before, hell bent on stopping their party. She nearly jumped out of Silas's lap, but he easily held her steady.

"I see you all are about to head out?" Eden walked over to the bar and grabbed a drink for himself.

He is so casual. Thank the Gods I'm not alone to face him right now. The look, the tone in his voice, tells me we've pushed him too far.

"Soo—what do we have here, a party for four?" Aiden stated angrily. "What's for dinner, seeing how there are no blood hosts? Oh, that's right, the four of you are hunting."

"I think we just caught a dragon by the tail," Lars announced.

"I don't even know what that means," Jadis shot back.

Silas, Dante, and Bain all laughed as if they were privy to the meaning of the inner jab.

Eden tilted his glass toward Jadis. "Jadis, I'd like to hear from you, however I think I would get anything but a rational answer."

Here we go. Eden is once again scolding me as if this is my doing. She rolled her eyes at him as usual but didn't speak.

"I wouldn't do that if I were you. I'm in no mood, baby girl. You've somehow managed to pull these three right down the rabbit's hole with you," Eden scolded. "I'm curious? However did you manage to do it? What kind of magical pull do you fucking have?"

"You don't even make sense, Eden. How is any of this my fault?" she snapped back. "It's not like I'm Aradia in the wonder woods, and I certainly didn't slip them a magical little potion!"

The banter now brought about chuckles from everyone in the room.

"Jadis, you're correct. You aren't Aradia, but you're the Bewitching Queen of Blackened Hearts in the flesh," Eden snapped back.

"Careful, cousin," Silas warned.

"Well, that was a dig I wasn't expecting. Jesus, Eden, how am I supposed to be a vampire if I don't know how to be one in every way? What's the big deal? You all have been hunting and killing your entire existence." She raised one defiant eyebrow, waiting for an answer.

"Jadis, that's the lamest explanation for questionable behavior I've ever heard," Eden snapped back. "You know full well you can feed from Silas anytime you want or need. Clearly, there's nothing he would deny you. As for you, Silas, you know damn well you could have taught her to control that shit in ten minutes. You and I both know you brought out the huntress in her for your own pleasure."

She didn't move from Silas's lap, and he continued to sit back, ignoring Eden, all the while gently playing with her hair.

"Look, Jadis, we had no choice. The world worked differently. Like everything else, we've evolved with it," Eden explained. He tried to be rational as he was obviously getting nowhere fast, with the fab four. Not to mention the growing amusement was clearly not how he wanted this to go. *Although, if I'm being truthful with myself, I expected nothing less.*

"Dante, Bain, as for the two of you, what the hell happened? I knew she would pull Silas down with her, but I expected more out of you both. Care to explain?"

"She gifted us a couple of virgins, what could we do?" Dante answered.

Aiden and Lars let out a stunned, confused laugh, but Eden was unamused.

"Dante! Don't blame this on me, you all did this," she retorted.

"No, Dante's right. There was a swipe of blood and two virgins," Bain agreed.

She was now once again, the butt of their jokes and speechless. *Not sure how to worm my way out of this one, after all he isn't incorrect.*

"My God!" Eden stated, as he rubbed his temples. He reached for the two hundred year-old bottle of Glendeon MaCru at the same time. "I don't even know how to respond, and I'm sure I don't want to know."

"Holy shit. Only Jadis would find the kink in their armor. I would actually like to hear this. Aiden, how about you?" Lars questioned.

"I would indeed," Aiden replied, sounding amused.

"Eden, there's some migraine pills in kitchen," Jadis blurted out. She tried to be sincere, but it probably wasn't the best response she could have come up with. That was all it took, everyone in the room broke with laughter, and Eden's face flushed three shades of chartreuse.

"God, Eden, you're like an uptight father. Silas, can we go?" she asked, *"I need to get away from Eden's unrelenting scrutiny."* She added the last part telepathically to Silas, so she didn't offend or upset Eden any more than she already had—unintentionally of course.

"Yes, we'll leave in a few minutes." Silas quickly made a change of plans, unbeknownst to everyone else.

"Jadis, you will yield to me. You are now Nosferatu, and I am a lord." Eden's statement didn't sit well with Silas based on how stiff he went, and Jadis choked on her drink.

"Not to be disrespectful, Eden, but *yield*? What, did we travel back to the year 1400? Just because I'm a vampire now doesn't mean you control me. I won't now, nor will I ever *yield* to you."

Everyone in the room went wide eyed.

"Oh shit, here we go again." Lars took a seat at the bar, ready for the fireworks.

Eden took a few steps toward Jadis, and Silas moved her over, ready to stand up and confront Eden.

"Jadis, you will yield. Not only that, but you'll also bend the knee, and I won't tell you again," he demanded, with a calm, yet menacing voice.

Silas stood quietly, trying his best to let Eden take his place with Jadis. As hard at it was on him, he too had to abide by the laws regardless of his personal feelings. *Hell, after all, if someone refused to bend the knee to me, they would be put there one way or another.*

Bain turned to the group currently at the bar watching the show, all of whom were fully entertained. "This will be good. Jadis bending the knee and yielding, anyone ready to place a few bets?"

"Two hundred on Jadis not yielding or bending the knee." Aiden plopped it on the bar.

"I'll double down on Eden losing his shit." Dante slapped three hundred on the bar.

Lars also slapped a few hundred dollar bills down. "My money's on her not complying."

"*Bend the knee*? What the hell is that? You're not actually my maker. I'm sort of my own, so maybe I should *yield* to myself?" she offered, tilting her head to the side.

The laughter shattered the silence; no one could hold it back any longer. She was the only one to have ever challenged Eden like she did. As much of a pain in the ass as she was to him, the others found her utterly entertaining. There never seemed to be a dull moment with her around. Without a doubt, she brought flavor into their lives, as spicy as it was. Eden never took offense to anything she did or said; she was like a daughter to him, and he was just ill equipped to handle her.

"Baby girl, I've never tolerated disobedience, and I won't now. You will yield!"

"Careful, cousin, the only time she'll bend the knee is if I put her there," Silas stated.

"Silas, I'm pulling rank. It's already been decided by our clans as well as Lord Jabari. The four of you are done with your little feeding frenzy. We all know the dangers of pack feeding. It cannot, will not continue." Eden then turned to Dante and Bain. "The two of you couldn't even last twenty-four hours."

"She doesn't play fair, so we can all blame her for this one," Bain stated as he looked to Jadis and tilted his glass to her in jest.

"Bain! I didn't make you do this!" Although, she knew trying to defend herself was useless.

"Really?" Bain questioned. "Dante, did I forget anything?"

"No, only I'm pretty sure Silas had a little something to do with it if I'm not mistaken?" Dante looked to Silas, who ignored the remark, knowing full well he put Jadis up to it. *The virgins, however, are all on her*, Dante thought.

"You know what, I don't even want to know." Eden was already exhausted when Silas interrupted him, ending the altercation.

"Your timing is impeccable. You're going to have to pull rank tomorrow, the night is already planned. Let's head out and I'll stand back while you try and get Jadis to bend the knee." Silas chuckled.

Jadis glared at Silas who winked at her. *I assume Silas just decided he was still in charge of us, for the remainder of the night anyway. It seems this is his way of submitting to Eden without actually submitting*, she thought.

"We'll finish this before the sun sets tomorrow," Eden stated firmly.

Eden must be taking what he can get. I guess this is how they compromise. Shit, who knows.

As the four of them left, Silas held the door open. "Eden, you're welcome to join us. You may as well come along, rather than sitting here stewing."

Silas flashed a devious smile Jadis' way. *"Why did you invite them?"* she asked silently.

"You'll see. We just had a change of plans," Silas answered.

Of course, Silas always has a plan, or two, or three. She looked back, only to see the three of them reluctantly follow.

They made their way into town and arrived at the Old Absinthe House. They were escorted straight to a private seating area and Eden, and Aiden looked less than thrilled. Silas strolled up behind Eden, placed both hands on his shoulders, and gave him a couple of hard pats. He then proceeded to wrap one arm around his body and patted his chest.

"Remember this place, cousin? We sure as hell had fun here, not even you can deny that." Silas smiled in a manner that appeared to have ulterior motives. "Remember our old friend Cayetano Ferrer?"

Eden gave a half smile and what Jadis thought might have been a chuckle.

As they took their seats, the drinks were placed in front of them. They did their best to lighten Eden's mood, and it seemed to be working. It only took about two hours and a half-dozen drinks for him to finally relax.

"Want to hear a story?" Silas asked, looking at Jadis.

"You know I do. I love them. Who's it about this time?" *I assume it has something to do with Eden by the way in which Silas brought it up.*

"Eden, why don't you tell her about Cayetano Ferrer, his own absinthe, the crypt, and a granddaughter," Silas suggested.

Jadis watched as everyone side-eyed each other as if a secret was about to be revealed.

"Well—go ahead, tell her. We've been telling her stories all week. You may as well. Hell, we're all here. Enjoy yourself for a minute or two, cousin, shit's not that serious," Dante chided.

"Come on, Eden, I have to hear this one. If you tell me the story, I'll think about yielding." Jadis gave him a wink, bringing out a heap of laugher from their group.

"Jadis, I promise not only will you yield, but you'll also take a knee, story or not," he replied, with one raised eyebrow and a smirk. He took a drink and for a moment, seemed to be lost in thought. A look of amusement suddenly radiated across his face.

"This has to be good. Come on, Eden, don't make me beg," she demanded politely, not wanting to do or say anything that would anger him. *He's teetering on the edge of having a good time.*

"All right, I'll tell you, but when I'm done, I expect you on your knee," Eden replied, with a real chuckle.

Everyone, including Silas, laughed at the comment, knowing full well getting her to bend the knee would be a feat in and of itself. All attention was on Eden now as they waited for him to begin.

"The year was 1846. We were actually right here. Myself, Bain, Aiden, Silas, Dante, Agaeus, and Syth."

"Right here?" she repeated, contemplating exactly how old the place was.

"Yes, at this very table, as a matter of fact." He tapped the palm of his hand on the worn, wooden top. "Aesthetically, it was a bit different then. It's changed with time, not that it's important. We were dancing, drinking, and carousing with the rest of the drunken, rowdy patrons."

"Really, Eden, dancing? Like on a dance floor with women?"

"If you must know, we're all very good dancers," Eden offered with a demure tone. "We didn't have a dance floor, it was more like mayhem. You just danced anywhere you wanted. You could jump up on a table if you felt like it."

"Even if it wasn't your table," Bain interjected.

"Why are you all laughing?" Jadis asked.

Eden looked at her but didn't answer, so Aiden spoke up instead, "My brother loved nothing more than to hop on tables, causing a ruckus."

"No way! I cannot see you jumping on a table and dancing, much less doing anything else crazy." She cracked up at the mere thought.

"Don't let Eden fool you. He had no inhibitions," Aiden added.

"Eden—wild? I don't buy it."

"Yes, Eden was as carefree and reckless as they come," Aiden continued. "He loved snatching one of the courtesans from their client. He would leap onto their table, spilling his drink of choice, absinthe, in the process or not, depending on how many he'd had."

"Hence the name of the bar," she said. Silas nodded in agreement.

Bain placed a hand on Eden's shoulder in a joking manner. "Eden could always be counted on to provoke the pauperized crowd. He enjoyed baiting them and caused more than a few raucous fights."

Eden laughed along with the rest of them, to their delight. "Yes, I do recall a few fights," Eden admitted.

"Just a few, cousin?" Silas questioned with an amused tone.

Eden chuckled again before continuing, "The ladies clung to the men, sitting in their laps, paying amorous attention to them, all hoping to earn a pittance. The smell of sweat and body odor was pungent, and the laughter and hollers from the inebriated crowd caused quite the atmosphere. We only tolerated it long enough to take what we wanted, using them for our amusement and pleasure. A few of the more affluent patrons from the area decided to make their way in, with a half-dozen, high-end courtesans that night. They demanded we give up our table. Apparently, they decided it was the best seat in the house."

"That was their first mistake." Bain chuckled.

"Yes, I'm afraid it was," Eden agreed. "They and their ladies became our chosen for the rest of the evening. Silas and I influenced the group, who decided to take another table, next to ours of course, and Dante made sure the patrons currently occupying it left. After a couple hours, we decided it was time to leave. We headed to the outskirts of the city and made our way to the Saint Louie cemetery with our new friends in tow. The smell of smoke swirling up from a large bonfire hung heavy in the air. There was another group in the cemetery having a party of their own. Once we entered, it was clear we were intruding in on a voodoo ritual. Rhiamon Locasta, her three daughters, two granddaughters, and a dozen others were all there."

"Rhiamon Locasta herself?" she questioned in awe.

"Yes, I knew her very well," Eden admitted.

"Damn, I'm a bit jealous. I would never have guessed you of all people were friends with Rhiamon Locasta."

"There's a lot about us you've yet to know, baby girl," Eden teased. "You're just a babe in the woods in comparison," he added with a light-hearted chuckle.

That wasn't what she expected to hear from Eden tonight. "He jokes!" she said aloud.

Eden smiled, and took a drink before he continued with the story, "Tapered candles of every size, shape, and color illuminated the area. They were deliberately placed on certain headstones and every third crypt, and hung from some of the moss-covered tree branches. The flick-ering flames swaying in the breeze cast ghostly shadows that danced in and out of the tombstones. The area was quite secluded; it was raw, undeveloped, and wild. Snakes, spiders, and toads scurried all around, their sounds vibrating off the headstones. Bird feet hung from the branches, along with a number of other bones, plants, and various objects, none of which we paid much attention to. In the center of their circle a shirtless man was on his knees, barefoot, and wearing only tattered pants. His hands had been tied behind his back, and his lips had been sewn shut. He was about to either meet his fate or return as the walking dead, considering the freshly dug grave lying just beyond the circle of fire."

"Jesus, what did he do?" she asked.

Eden shrugged his shoulders. "Who knows, it could have been anything. Whatever it was, the poor bastard crossed the wrong path. The girls we brought with us were terrified, the men, however terrified or not, had been mentally incapacitated. They could see what was happening but were incapable of physically reacting. It wasn't the party any of them were expecting. We loved when they put up a good fight, but for the time being, Silas and his brothers held them steady until we were ready to hunt. We stood quietly, watching the ritual, hiding in the shadows. We were always fascinated by Rhiamon's ceremonies. Once their victim was lowered into the wooden casket and buried, we made our presence known. We greeted Rhiamon and ended up carousing with her, her daughters, granddaughter, and a few of her chosen followers. We finally released our prey, mentally sending them deeper into the bayou. We waited an hour or so, allowing them to hide before the hunt was on. Once we finished, we left their ashes for the bayou to consume. Shortly thereafter, we returned to Rhiamon, who was in the throes of inebriation, whilst dancing with the spirits.

"This is where Eden met the infamous Tituba Locasta," Aiden chimed in. "She was a beauty with the attitude of a demon. She was wicked, yet capable of intermittent sentimentality when it came to Eden. She had all the intentions of taking him as her lover, not to mention the father of her offspring.

"She wanted to have your bairns? And all this time, you have the audacity to judge me!" She had to wipe a few tears from her face as she practically fell into Silas's lap in a heap of laughter.

"Jadis, not even Tituba Locasta has anything on you." Eden laughed.

They calmed down as Aiden continued, "We drank the night away, absinthe and blood mixed together were always unpredictable. The effects were never the same and affected each of us differently. We stayed until dawn before we had to call it a night. Eden, however, decided he wasn't quite done with his party, so we left him with Rhiamon and headed home."

Bain then interjected, "Eden didn't come home that night, which wasn't unusual for any of us. After the second night without contact, we set out to find him. He had disappeared, we could sense him but were essentially cut off. Everywhere we thought he might be ended up vacant."

Eden swirled his glass and continued, "I ended up in a crypt that resided down in the old bayou. It was dug into the earth about thirty feet down. It was well hidden near the swamps and had been concealed by more than one powerful voodoo ceremony. The area went undisturbed by man; it was dangerous, unspoiled, and raw. Venomous snakes, alligators, poisonous spiders, bugs, and other creatures inundated the swampland. No one dared travel there without good reason, leaving Rhiamon and her followers to come and go as they pleased without raising anyone's suspicions. The chamber itself was well lit by candlelight. You had to walk down an old, brick stairway that wound its way down through the earth. Vines, and tree roots hung from the ceiling and grew across the uneven, dirt walls. It wasn't until you reached the main chamber that it became a solid stone room. Rhiamon, Tituba, and about a dozen other family members and friends headed there with us. Unbeknownst to myself or Rhiamon, Tituba, her granddaughter, had conjured up more than a few spells I was oblivious to, thanks to the ever-flowing absinthe."

Eden briefly paused as he lifted his glass and took another drink.

"Jesus, Eden." Jadis chuckled.

He smiled at her amusement and continued, "Rhiamon used the crypt for her consecrated ceremonies, it was the place of both life and death. The rituals were performed night and day, it was entertaining to say the least. There was a lot of dancing and ecstasy fueled by rum, drums, and sacrifices used as offerings to the spirits, both good and evil. I stayed in the crypt for three days as the party raged on. I was also given a throne." Eden laughed at the memory, as did the rest of the group.

"You sat in a *throne* like a king?" Jadis questioned, fully amused.

"Well, not really." Eden chuckled. "The throne was mostly an old, decorated, wooden chair sitting on a cement slab about five steps above the main dirt floor. Rhiamon didn't want to burn the hand that fed her so to speak. It was more of a gesture, letting everyone know my position. I was to be revered. Rhiamon's handmaids brought me whatever I wanted: virgins, upper class women, and high-end courtesans. Orgies weren't uncommon in the day, and I wasn't the only one partaking in the fornication."

"Oh, my lord," Jadis blurted out as everyone laughed at the pun. Her cheeks flushed at the mere thought of him participating in an orgy.

"Jadis, sex to us is nothing more than that. We have all participated with one or more partners. I do believe all of us has shared a woman at the same time, in the same bed at some point. Regardless of who else is there, sex with a woman is still sex. We don't shy away from it like mortals," Eden stated matter-of-factly.

"I don't even want to know." She scowled at Silas, thinking the worst.

Silas playfully cupped her jaw in his hand. "Always so jealous!"

She simply rolled her eyes as Eden continued, "Tituba, however, became more than jealous as I refused to feed from, or lay with, her. She wasn't getting the attention she wanted, so she decided to take matters into her own hands. She tainted the newest delivery of absinthe. Having added a bit of black magic, it made for a powerful concoction, and she tried using it to control me. It didn't work as far as turning me mindless; you can't kill what's already dead," he teased. "It had a psychedelic effect, and I wasn't sure what was going on."

"Eden was a mess when we eventually found him," Silas added as he shook his head.

"Tituba had buried a jar for two days which contained a sea worm and a toad. The toad would secrete more of its poison if it felt threatened, so by placing the creatures together in a jar and burying them, it created quite the toxin as they fought. She added a few more ingredients and poisoned the absinthe," Eden explained.

"How did you not sense it? You should have at least smelled it?" *I can't fathom how she got anything past Eden.*

"I didn't pay any attention to her, which was a mistake. I was more interested in fending off her advances."

"Please! Eden was as drunk as a sailor, between the blood, the alcohol, the party, the rituals, not to mention all his dilly dallying with the women. He didn't know if he was coming or going." Bain laughed. "It had been five days without a word from him."

"So that's why he's so worried about us supposedly being MIA for five days, as he put it," Jadis said to Silas telepathically.

"Precisely," Silas replied before taking over the story. "Tituba followed Eden out on the fourth night. She had prepared a crypt for the two of them and had planned on sealing him in with her until she got everything she wanted. She wasn't in her right mind. She liked to partake in the bottle a little more than most, not to mention a few medicinals as well, more specifically laudanum."

"Yes, it was on the fifth night I finally left the crypt, deciding I was ready to head home, having become thoroughly bored of the unrelenting mortal presence. Once I was outside, the sun was just an hour or so from rising. I was exhausted, and sleep was calling. I found an open crypt with an empty, large, cement coffin. The lid was partially askew, so I decided to sleep there for the day rather than going home. Unfortunately, Tituba made her way in at some point and sealed it shut. Unbeknownst to her, once we as Nosferatu are dormant as you know, there is no waking us. We don't function until our bodies recoup."

"She ended up sealing herself in with a hibernating corpse," Aiden added, laughing again.

"That's how we found Eden, in a graveyard, sealed in a cement crypt, with the screaming Tituba Locasta. We heard her yelling from a mile away. At that moment, we knew where he was," Silas explained.

"As soon as we popped open the lid, Tituba lunged, fell over the edge, and landed at Bain's feet," Dante added.

The sounds of genuine laughter from our group is exactly what everyone needed. Silas has managed to pull Eden to the dark side.

"'The dark side', huh?" Silas quietly re-stated.

"Eden was a goddamn mess. He didn't know if he was coming or going for another week. He was more than high from the absinthe and Tituba's poison," Bain explained.

"How I wish I could have been there," Jadis admitted.

"It was quite a sight to see," Aiden replied. "The original cemetery is long gone due to more than one hurricane. It's just swampland now, however, the memories will last a few lifetimes."

"That's not even the best part," Dante blurted out.

"How can it get any better?" Jadis asked.

Bain tilted his glass toward Eden. "As soon as we pulled him out, we got him up on his feet. As we walked out of the cemetery, he yelled, 'Oh, shit!' and grabbed his right leg. He kept yelling—"

"Oh, shit!" they all yelled out in unison, mocking Eden, interrupting Bain.

Bain calmed down enough to continue, "He kept grabbing a different body part and partially falling down more than once."

They again laughed hysterically. Eden included, and Jadis was well on her way to tears.

Aiden took over as the others were unable to finish the story. "We had to drag the two of them to Rhiamon and have her destroy the doll."

"Wait! Hold up—you mean she made a voodoo doll of you?" Jadis questioned.

Eden began again, "Rhiamon was scolding her granddaughter for putting them all in bad sorts with the creatures of the dark. We watched as she slapped the back of Tituba's head all the way to the back of the crypt, yelling the entire time that she could have angered the living dead who were capable of killing them all."

"A voodoo doll is all it takes?" she joked.

"Don't for one minute think about it, Jadis," Eden replied.

"It took another week for him to dry out and let the toxins leave his body. Dante and Bain sealed him in his room, in the house we're all staying at now. We monitored him for a week. No one left his side, and we saw to his every need," Silas added.

"Well, that sounds familiar," she stated, looking at each of them fondly and remembering how they saved her life and stood by her for a week. She saw an enduring look cross Eden's face; he smiled fondly and winked at her.

Silas pulled her in privately, *"Don't worry about it, baby. He knows you mean no ill will. He hasn't taken offense to anything you've said or done, for the most part,"* he teased. *"He would expect and want nothing less. He'll never admit it, but he actually admires your spirited nature. We all do."* Silas lifted her chin and gave her a gentle kiss.

Silas raised his hand and held up two fingers. A waiter appeared with a tray of green drinks in short, fat glasses. The phosphorescent, green alcohol swirled with translucent bubbles. A milky white, featureless, fog gently flowed over each of the rims, covering the tray as he walked. He set a glass down in front of each of them. Jadis looked over, only to notice Eden's was a bit different in color, and something in the liquid moved in a different direction.

Eden picked up his glass and swirled the liquid around the single triangular ice cube. He seemed to be contemplating drinking it or not. He shot a curious look Silas's way, and he offered the same look with a crooked, half-turned-up smile and one raised eyebrow, as if they were having their own conversation.

"What's this?" Jadis asked.

"Eden's drink of choice—absinthe, only his has a little more of a necromantic flavor, if you will," Silas answered. "I think a toast is in order," Silas announced. They all stood and held up their drink as Silas spoke, "If you cheat, cheat death. If you lie, lie on the bones of your enemies. If you feast, may you feast with the beast. If you steal, may you steal the heart of a woman. If you fight, may you fight for a brother. If you dine, may it be blood red wine. If you drink, may you drink with me!"

"May you drink with me!" Everyone repeated in unison as they tossed back their drink of choice.

Silas turned to Jadis, pulled her in for an embrace, and whispered in her ear, "Tonight, we feed together, brother to brother, cousin to cousin, and mate to mate."

Three hours later, their party was in full swing; not one of them was sober, and the jokes, the laughter, the banter flowed amongst them. They had moved from the table and now stood amongst the other patrons, genuinely enjoying themselves.

Silas had pulled Jadis to the dance floor, while the rest of them continued to carouse amongst themselves. She was surprised at how rowdy they were becoming, not that she paid much attention, but their boisterous voices were hard to ignore. They also had the girls swooning at their feet.

"Dante!" Silas yelled.

"What are you doing?" Jadis asked amused.

"I'm going to hang with Eden for a bit. I don't want you alone," Silas answered with a wink.

"What the hell do you want now?" Dante replied.

"Take my mate to the dance floor. I need to see Eden for a bit."

"You sure as hell pulled it off. Eden is back." Dante gave him a hard pat on his chest.

"Yes, yes, he is," Silas replied as he handed Dante Jadis's hand. "Watch my mate, brother."

"Will do." Dante smiled.

Dante turned to Jadis and placed one hand behind his back and bowed like it was the year 1800. "May I have this dance, lass?" he asked, with an enhanced Slavinian accent, as he held out his other hand out.

"You're ridiculous, wizard, but I would be honored," she agreed with a slight bow, joking with him. She took his hand, and he pulled her to the center of the floor and twirled her in circles.

Dante caught himself enjoying her a bit too much. Dancing with her took him back to a time long past. Conflicting emotions always clouded his thoughts when he thought about her or was in her presence. *His mind wandered back to the days when the women wore beautiful gowns with intricately laced corsets, the fabric twirling with each graceful step. The sputtering lamps and candles flickering on the stone walls of the Castle's Great Hall, casting ghostly shadows that danced to a waltz of their own. Entertainers, harpists, and minstrels entertained the royal guests during the most elaborate soirées.*

A crack of laughter from Jadis snapped him from the memory as he dipped her on the dance floor. He quickly realized he was dancing to the Devil's duet as he looked into her eyes, secretly yearning for more than a dance.

They had been on the floor for about an hour when she suddenly felt a tingle ripple through her like waves. They turned only to see some random girl next to Silas with her hand caressing his arm; her *turning* was immediate.

Dante pulled her in and held her in a tight embrace. He wrapped his arms around her, gently pulled the hair to the side, and rested his chin in the crook of her neck. They both caught Silas looking their way with a wicked grin, knowing exactly what she would do.

"Feeding time, my dear," Silas said telepathically.

Dante whispered in her ear as he ran the back of his fingers down her cheek and followed her jawline. "I think the lass is after your mate," he whispered.

He let go, and she lunged for the girl. She picked her up and slammed her onto her back on top of the table, in the middle of Silas, Eden, and Aiden. Her screams were quickly muffled when Jadis latched onto her neck.

"What the hell?" Eden barked, who was too drunk to care about anything other than enjoying himself.

Jadis quickly drained the girl and tossed her mummified body to the floor as she turned to Silas. Her freshly fed eyes blazed with both anger and desire.

Silas wrapped her in his arms and pulled her in for a heated kiss. He finally pulled away, clearly desiring to feed for himself.

Jadis realized the club was suddenly much quieter than it had been. She picked up on the fact there were two warriors at each exit, and the only ones left in the bar were fourteen beautiful call girls, whom she assumed were blood hosts.

Dante had sealed the club, keeping only the feeders to satisfy their needs, whatever they may be.

"If you can't beat them, you may as well join them." Eden's sudden admission shocked everyone but Silas. Eden suddenly grabbed a feeder and sank his canines into her neck.

He had turned into another, feeding Silas. *He has the same deathly look and is almost as terrifying as Silas had been when I watched him feed for the first time.* Jadis was shocked and once again, she heard the sound of ivory scraping bone.

Eden noticed her intently watching as he drained his victim. He then tossed her body onto the floor on top of Jadis's victim.

She stared at him, not knowing what to do or say. His irises became the same swirling blood-red embers, pooling around his sheer black, diamond-shaped pupils. *Even his eyes mirror Silas' when he feeds.*

He stared at her in an unfamiliar way, and she backed into Silas as close as she could get. Silas wrapped his arms a bit tighter around her.

Eden was suddenly face to face with her. He casually wiped the blood from the corner of his mouth with his thumb and sucked it off. He used his other thumb to wipe a trickle of blood on her bottom lip, which was accompanied by a burst of laughter.

"What's the matter, baby girl? You've never seen a vampire feed before? You're right, Silas. That was fucking amazing!"

Everyone but Jadis bellowed with laughter. She stood in shock, not knowing how to react. Silas bent over and gently licked the blood from her bottom lip.

Every one of them now had a feeder tucked under their arm, everyone but Silas. He was still holding Jadis and enjoying every damn minute of Eden having fed.

Eden placed a hard hand on Silas's shoulder. "Well, I think it's your turn to feed—yes?"

"Wait, not from one of them," Jadis protested.

"Baby girl, haven't you been feeding for weeks now?" Eden had turned the tables and now taunted her, using Silas as bait.

"That was different. I fed on women. I don't see any men here." She scanned the room for Silas's meal. *Nope, not a man to be seen.*

"Jadis, we feed, whether it be a man or a woman. It's all the same, so don't deny him." Eden knew he was doing a great job getting a rise out of her.

They all now standing in a half circle around Silas and Jadis, waiting for her to let Silas feed. *Nothing like group pressure,* she thought to herself. Unfortunately, they all read her thoughts and roared with drunken laughter.

"Oh, my God—fine." She waved her hand toward the feeder Eden held for him. Silas turned back into the monster she'd seen in the alley.

"Wait, you better not look at her like you do me when you feed," she growled, to everyone's continued amusement.

"Whatever your heart desires, my love," he snarled in that demonic voice she didn't recognize. He pulled the girl from Eden and spun her around, so she faced Jadis, so as to not look in her face, solely for Jadis's benefit.

He bit down, and Jadis gasped under her breath. *I don't think I'll ever get used to that sound.*

He tossed her body on top of her and Eden's victim and pulled her close. "You're the only one for my bed," he rumbled, darting his tongue into her mouth.

All she heard was the laughter and hollers; the blood bath now included a few more members of their family as each of them drained their feeders.

CHAPTER 7

They brought their next victims to the old Saint Louie Cemetery. "Its first body was laid to rest here in 1789," Silas explained as they passed through the locked, wrought-iron gates.

"She's here, isn't she?" Jadis smiled.

"Yes, mon chéri."

"You knew, didn't you?"

"I said I had something special planned for you for tonight. I just had to divert our plans a bit for Eden's sake."

"Did you know Rhiamon as well?"

"Yes, very much so."

"Don't tell me this is where Eden was found?" She was finally putting the pieces of the puzzle together.

He pointed to a cement crypt. "Sort of, this isn't the original cemetery. However, see that concrete coffin to the side of that burial vault? That's it."

Eden seemed to be both amused and annoyed with Silas for taking him back there.

"That's the actual coffin?" Jadis asked.

"Sure as hell is," Aiden announced as he stood behind Silas, holding him in a partial hug. He gave him a couple of hard pats on the chest. "Shall we show her how to hunt in the bayou?" Aiden suggested.

She looked to Silas, not quite sure what he meant.

"Release them!" Silas ordered.

All of them uncloaked the girls the brought with from the bar, sending them deep into the bayou, rather than away from it. The feeders let out wails as they frantically ran in different directions.

"When do we give chase?" Jadis asked.

"Give them about an hour or so to think they found a hiding place. They'll do nothing other than get lost out there. That's when the fun begins. The bayou will hide their scent, well slightly." Silas winked.

"What do we do until then?" she asked before she noticed that Eden had disappeared. "Where's Eden going?"

"He'll be back." He reached for her hand and took her for a stroll around the graveyard and surrounding swampland, while they waited for the hunt to begin. They stopped in front of a large, decorated, stone tomb.

"Is this Rhiamon Locasta? All this time, you never mentioned the fact you knew her."

"You never asked."

"We're back to that, are we?" she teased, along with a well-placed backhand on his stomach.

"You must want to be punished in front of everyone." Silas pinned her arms behind her back.

"Don't you dare, everyone is right here."

"I like it when you protest," he teased.

"Silas, stop. I want to hear about Rhiamon." She continued to squirm around playfully, trying to break free.

"If you insist, but we'll finish this." His statement was followed by a heady kiss.

"Rhiamon became a friend of our clan, one of the only mortals we tolerated and protected. Even though she was a mortal, she was entertaining, not to mention peculiar. She enjoyed our company, and we enjoyed hers—to a point. We met her shortly after she first arrived. The locals would commission her for her services. She was powerful in her own right. Stories about the *walking dead* living in the area scared all of the locals, and they craved her guidance on the matter."

"I assume you all were the *walking dead*?"

"Yes and no, superstitions ran wild in those days. She provided her customers the assistance they asked for as well as vengeance on the unfortunate souls who deserved it. We respected it. Many times, she turned the living into the dead, which essentially took the focus off us and placed it squarely on to herself and her rituals."

Jadis walked around her tomb, sliding her hand across the uneven, moist, whitewashed mausoleum. The only sounds, other than the chorus in the bayou behind them, were the crunching leaves beneath her feet as she slowly walked around the crypt, careful not to disturb the multitude of offerings laying at its base. The offerings included half-empty bottles of alcohol, flowers, burnt-out candles, and various coins.

She made her way back around to where Silas was still standing, patiently waiting on her.

He held out his hand. "Shall we go on a little hunt, my love? It's been long enough. They should be well hidden by now."

Silas 'turned' and she watched as his canines slowly appeared; she looked up at him and *turned* as well.

"May the hunt commence!" he announced.

The murky water kept everything from view, both dangerous and benign. Jadis and Silas swiftly navigated their way between the moss-laden trees with blackened trunks, rotting vegetation, and brackish water. As dense as it was, they could move seamlessly through the terrain. The thick, stagnant air and watery sludge mixed with the faint smell of sweat dripping from their prey, lead them in their direction. The bayou was alive with the sounds of frogs croaking, flies buzzing, as well as the screech of other animals and birds both hunting and being hunted.

"Just listen to the bayou, baby. You'll pick up on the mortal sounds. They'll stand out from the rest of the noises. Muffle out what you hear and listen for what you don't."

They stopped so she could do as Silas instructed. She suddenly heard the faint snap of a twig off in the distance.

"It's her, isn't it?" She smiled. "Two of them? You sent them together for us?"

"It sure is, and I did. Shall we?"

Not far from where they stood, Jadis heard the burp of trapped air releasing itself at the surface of the water, carrying with it the faint scent of perfume. In only seconds, they were hovering above their prey. The two girls hid in a murky spot at the water's edge, trying to conceal themselves under the rotten and broken branches leaning over, touching the saturated ground.

They looked up in shock and screamed. Jadis quickly silenced them and was able to hold them steady, using only her mind. Off in the distance, she heard the faint sounds of screaming. She looked to Silas, and they smiled at each other, knowing everyone else had located their prey as well.

"Shall we dine together?" Silas offered.

"Yes."

Silas snatched them up from their hiding spot and held his front and center. They bit down on either side of her neck and drank their fill together.

Jadis felt the victim's blood pull in two different directions. She could taste each other's energy, as well as their hunger, lust, and excitement for one another.

As soon as the first was drained, Jadis stared at Silas wide eyed. *The taste is altogether different, feeding as one.*

Silas tossed her ashen, mummified body into the deep water, allowing it to carry away what little of it remained.

He held the second feeder between their bodies, reached around, and firmly took hold of Jadis's lower back and pulled her closer as they fed. "Feeding with you at the same time is intoxicating," Silas crooned.

Jadis grabbed him by the back of his head and pulled his face toward hers. She licked a small trickle of blood with the tip of her tongue before she parted his mouth and slipped him her tongue. Her head reeled, her body was alive, and she craved him once again. She had fed with him before but never from the same victim, at the same time.

"I'm feeling a little something else, mon chéri. Shall we?" Silas's voice was just a raspy whisper.

"Yes," she mumbled against his lips. He reached for her hand, and they headed back to the cemetery, leaving the rest of their entourage to their meals.

Silas took her to a large mausoleum at the edge of the cemetery, tucked within in the cypress trees near the edge of the bayou. The large, old, wood door slowly opened with a creek and a loud scrape before shutting behind them. As they stepped into the darkened tomb, Silas waved his hand, and more than a dozen partially melted candles came to life. Their gentle, yellow flames flickering in the blackness, was barely able to relieve the darkness of the room.

It was eerie, and the energy sinister. The walls were lined with a dozen of the dead, their secrets and bodies lay entombed behind sealed walls. There was a large cement coffin in the center standing about 4' tall. Jadis's heart drummed against her breast; she was ready for something dead to rise from within the coffin. She then thought about herself and Silas. *We're actually the dead and have already risen.*

"Baby, you're right. We are the undead." His amusement forced a nervous smile out of her.

She wandered around the rather large room, hanging onto Silas, not letting him stray from her an inch. She ran her hands over the brass plaques, feeling the names and inscriptions that had been carved in old world script. "Did you know any of them?" she asked.

"Yes, we were friends or business associates. It was a dark period of time for some of our kind. Vampire's desiccated bodies showed up in the swamps, and we knew someone else had gotten to them. What we never knew for sure, however, they had all been drained. Rumor had it they had been put to the sword by another clan, one that resides underground in another country altogether. We laid them here out of respect. Their ashes are in the compartments, not their bodies."

Jadis looked up at him, not knowing what to say, but the questions about the other clan didn't set well for some reason. She cocked her head at him curiously. "Your story back on the Yacht—the third clan during the war, the ones who went to the underworld?" she questioned.

"We could only assume so without any other proof."

Silas picked her up in his arms, and she wrapped her legs around his waist. She heard a loud scraping sound, which startled her. She looked over to see the heavy cement lid had partially slid over, exposing the empty crypt sitting in the center of the room.

"Really? You want to—in there?" she asked nervously.

"Yes, in there." He smiled deviously. He removed their clothes, laid her in the coffin, and his body consumed hers in a claustrophobic, erotic entanglement.

He traced her throat with his perfect, sculpted lips. He slowly moved up her neck and whispered, "We shall dwell together in eternal darkness."

Her body was consumed with desire. *Just being in here feels dangerous, erotic, and forbidden.*

He moved one of his legs between hers and pushed them apart as he settled in. He traced the vein on her neck, and he felt the shivers running through her body as the cool tips caressed her skin. He slid his hand up her thigh and massaged it. He slowly rocked back and forth, rubbing his hardened erection against her sex.

She wrapped her arms tighter around his neck and repositioned her body beneath his, begging for him to slide his dick in. She let out a raspy moan, anxiously wanting all of him.

Silas let out a low, steady growl. "First, I have a need of my own."

She let out a gentle moan as he slid his tongue across her throat. "mon chéri, you're as enticing as they come."

He continued teasing her body with his hand as he trailed gentle kisses down her neck before he pierced her skin. *Damn, her blood tastes like my life. No one else will ever taste that faint hint of jasmine.* "You're mine. Say it," he moaned as he pulled his canines back.

She felt like she was in a sexual trance as he fed from her; her mind and body spiraled into a dizzying, heady need. "Yes, I belong only to you."

He forced his tongue into her mouth. "Taste what I taste, baby," he moaned.

"What I want is to taste you."

He positioned his neck for her, and the earthly liquid rushed in. "The way you taste," she muttered as she released her grip. "Now, Silas."

He responded to her desperation and moved his mouth to her breast, suckled her nipple, and twirled his tongue around the full bud. He then slid his hand between her legs and let his fingers find their way into the slickness of her body. She felt amazing beneath him, and he felt her tremble beneath his touch. He had never felt a desire so great. *I alone own her every beautiful inch, and I'll chain her to me for an eternity.*

She gasped and arched her back, needing, wanting more. He slowly circled her nub with his thumb and continued sliding his fingers in and out, calling her orgasm to the surface.

She let out another guttural groan as the unbounded sensation convulsed its way to the surface. Silas continued teasing her, reveling in each sensation rising from her body. She dug her nails into his back with one hand and reached for his erection with the other. She ran her cupped fist up and down his pulsing shaft.

"You keep that up, and I'm going to come in your hand," he mumbled as a wave of arousal grew with each tight stroke.

"By the Gods," she growled. She softly raised her hips, unable to hold back any longer.

He removed his fingers and with a hard thrust, he was deep inside. He rocked back and forth as her body stretched to take him all in. The more aggressive he became, the more the sounds of her moaning became a mixture of pleasure and pain. The intensity of her body tightly squeezing his shaft, brought about his orgasm. He dropped his head to hers and let out a deep, lung-filled growl, letting his seed fill her core. "Quod gaudens malum—sanctus cacas!" he exclaimed as he finished.

Her body responded in kind and rocked with another intense orgasm.

They lay in the cement coffin, enjoying the comfort of each other as well as the eerie peacefulness.

"You always have a way with words. What did you say this time?"

"That orgasm hurt, holy shit." Their chuckling turned into laughter.

"Maybe that's what I need to be saying."

"You're probably right," he replied.

He rolled onto his side and pulled her leg across his crotch. She rested her arm across his chest and watched as the flickering flames cast dancing, darkened shadows onto the ceiling of the cement tomb. It was mesmerizing, and her mind was caught in an emotional tug of war. *The crypt providing us such pleasure is built for whomever is beyond this world, beyond the realm of mortal comforts. However, as devoid of beauty as it seems to be, it surrounds us with a forbidden, comforting caress.*

"Your overthinking is always entertaining, my love." Silas's voice snapped her from her befuddled state of mind.

"Really? I believe you and the situations you put me in are the cause of my overthinking things. You do realize we're in a cement coffin, in the center of a crypt, in the middle of a cemetery?"

"*Situations*, huh? Shall we talk about the *situations* you've put me in?"

"No, we shall not," she teased.

"Well then, we should go see what the others are up to. Dawn shall be here soon."

He elevated them up and out of the crypt. They dressed and headed back into the graveyard, only to find Bain and Lars looking like they had just finished having sex with newly acquired feeders on top of a couple of cement crypts outside. The girls walked away fully dressed as if in a trance. Bain was shirtless, and Lars was still pulling up his pants. She felt her cheeks flush at the sight of Lar's naked ass. She turned head and looked up at Silas. "I will never un-see that."

Silas laughed aloud. "Where have you been all my life?"

Dante appeared from a smaller mausoleum; he was barefoot, his shirt was unbuttoned, and he held his leather oxfords in one hand and had a beautiful brunette following. Eden and Aiden sat atop another crypt, having a casual conversation. It was obvious they had just freshly fed again but hadn't had sex with anyone.

"Well, those are new faces?" Jadis joked, looking between them all, trying to ignore the fact they caught three of them in the middle of a sexual tryst. Jadis was still embarrassed; the heated flush of her cheeks obvious, even as she tried her best to divert her eyes.

"Well, the two of you disappeared, so we decided we needed a bedtime snack and maybe a good lay ourselves," Bain teased, laughing at her obvious embarrassment.

"Save your blushing, darling. It doesn't match the sting of your tongue." Dante winked.

"Really?" she stated, as she squinted her eyes at him.

They chose to release all the girls, wiping their minds in the process and sending them on their way. *They would escape death—tonight, anyway,* she thought. Jadis learned more from her clan than she ever thought possible. *They are amazing—the perfect killing machines. They do it with such finesse and dignity, who wouldn't be impressed,* she thought.

They headed home just as the sun peeked up from the horizon; gentle hues of blues and oranges crept their way through the dense tree line, forcing the darkness back into hiding.

It had been five days since Eden, Aiden, and Lars showed up at the mansion determined to put a stop to their nightly endeavors. Nosferatu living together generally took on each other's essence and behavior, so it wasn't unusual at all for a larger clan to pack feed once one started. It had only taken a few hours and two virgins to turn Dante and Bain, and it didn't take much longer for Silas to bring Eden and his brothers around. They hunted, partied, slept, and started all over again. Just as Eden was afraid, they did indeed follow Silas straight down the rabbit's hole, to Maddie's dismay.

Maddie sat with Chloe and Aria contemplating her next move. She knew without a doubt based on her last conversation with Eden, he was hunting as well.

"I just don't know." Maddie sat on the edge of their bed, staring at her cell phone.

"You do know they're all pack feeding. Eden was clear. He told you what to do if something like this happened," Chloe responded.

"Maybe we should go there ourselves?" Maddie was unsure of what to do at this point.

"And do what—exactly?" Aria asked. "It's not like any of us has the power to intervene. They're pack feeding. I knew the minute I spoke to Aiden as well."

"If Eden thought you could handle the situation, he wouldn't have put that number into your phone. This is serious; you need to call whomever it is," Chloe reasoned.

"It's Silas and his brother's father, Santiago," Maddie admitted. Chloe and Aria sat in stunned silence.

After few more minutes of careful consideration, Maddie reluctantly made the call.

"Yes, dear?" a voice answered from the other end of the line.

"Milord, it's Madolyn," she replied as the tears streamed down her face.

CHAPTER 8

They woke just as the sun set, and Silas and Jadis got dressed for the night's festivities. They headed downstairs, only to be greeted by Eden, Aiden, and Lars who were already waiting.

"I thought the two of you would sleep all night." Eden walked over and greeted Jadis with a kiss on the cheek. "What's for dinner tonight, baby girl?"

"I don't know? You choose," she replied, returning the gesture.

"I like that idea," agreed Silas. "Tonight, Eden, the choice is yours."

They took their usual seats just as Dante and Bain sauntered down the stairs to join them. They weren't alone and sent four beautiful redheads out the front door in a transfixed state of mind.

Jadis watched the girls leave before turning to Dante and Bain. "Really? Redheads this time? I think the two of you have now hit every color in the city."

"Not every color," Dante replied, with a coy grin and a wink, as he made his way to the bar. He brought Bain a drink and took a seat opposite Silas and Jadis.

"What's on the menu tonight, Jadis?" Bain asked.

"It's Eden's choice."

"Well, this will be good." Bain crossed one leg over the other and wiped a piece of lint off his Balai Santino oxford.

A look of amusement crossed Aiden's face. "Since my brother is choosing the menu tonight, I assume a good-old bar fight is inevitable."

Jadis got comfortable in Silas's lap. "A fight?" She chuckled. "Well, before we leave, it's story time. Who's telling the tale tonight?"

"By my count, I don't believe you've heard a story about Aiden. Seeing Dante and Bain come down with multiple partners brought up old memories," Silas replied.

"I thought story time was about Dante and Bain's exploitations?" Aiden stated, trying to divert the attention away from himself, since he knew what Silas was talking about.

"We know their story. They just sent them home." Silas motioned toward the door. "Eden, it's your brother. You tell Jadis about Aiden and the High Priest, Ubertino Veneziano."

Everyone in the room let out a fake cough or a chuckle from under their breath.

"This must be good. Come on, Eden. I've got to hear this one," Jadis replied.

"Well, if you want to hear a scandalous tale of a High Priest, sex, and drunken debauchery, Aiden's story is the one to tell," Eden replied, with an enhanced fake accent.

Aiden got comfortable in his chair with a smile that spread across his face. *Obviously, the memory is a fond one,* she thought.

Eden filled another glass and began, "It was the year 1500. Aiden, Bain, and I had traveled to Montefeltro out of sheer boredom and ended up staying in what is now known as Vanozzo City. We had heard stories of the parties, most of which are still legendary today. We decided to find out for ourselves if the stories were true. We were very young, roughly one hundred and fifty-nine years old at the time."

No matter how many stories they tell me, whenever they bring up dates and/or their ages, it never ceases to amaze me how old they all are, and how much life they've lived and experienced. Hell, I'd do anything to experience the world the way they have, she thought as she intently listened as Eden continued.

Eden suddenly paused and nodded at Jadis. "Well take you anywhere you want to go. Maddie loves to travel."

"Just name the place, mon chéri," Silas added.

"I appreciate that, Eden." She then smiled at Silas. "I'll think on it, but right now I want to hear the rest of the story."

"Very well." Eden nodded. "We had arrived a week before the High Priest, Ubertino Veneziano, held the craziest shindig in Vanozzo's history. The party became known as the Regale of Walnuts for a particularly scandalous trick performed by the sex workers hired to entertain the guests."

"Nooo—explain," Jadis said.

"It's not what you're thinking." Aiden smirked. "We may get freaky when it comes to sex, but no one's shoving a nut up my ass." His comment brought out a hearty laugh from everyone in the room, Jadis included.

Aiden continued, "The upcoming event was the talk of the surrounding villas, so we decided that was the party we needed to attend. We didn't need an invite, we just let ourselves in and influenced the guards and anyone else who dared question our presence. The High Priest's banquet featured a who's who of Vanozzo nobility and Carnege temple officials, as well as fifty of Vanozzo's finest ladies of the night. We wandered the entire palatial palace, making ourselves at home and mingling with the other guests. We also took our fair share of the female royalty upstairs to feed from. There was a lot of commotion, and nobody seemed to notice or question our actions. I assume they thought we were the royalty's sexual entertainment for the evening. Everyone turned a blind cheek."

Eden interjected and threw Bain's participation to the forefront of the story. "Go ahead, Bain. Tell her about Ubertino's wife Antonietta and her lady-in-waiting, Lucrezia , who was very much a virgin by the way."

"It's not just my story, Eden," Bain chuckled.

"What? The two of you had sex with the High Priest's wife and her lady-in-waiting?" Jadis questioned.

"Not only did Eden and Bain have sex and feed from them, but they did it in his personal quarters. I believe Bain left quite the bloodstain in his bed before dinner was even served," Aiden added.

"Well, well, well. I do believe the days of you all judging me are over," Jadis stated in jest.

"You give us one hundred and one reasons and then some to judge you. I don't believe those days will ever come to an end," Eden replied.

"Eden tells the truth." Dante chuckled.

"I did take Antonietta," Eden admitted. "However, she had quite the reputation. She was a beauty, no doubt about it. She was also notorious for the suspicious deaths and political intrigue surrounding her and her family at the time, which made her all the more enticing. Not to mention she was a very willing bedmate, even though we weren't in a bed." He smirked.

"Well, she was willing, at least until you bit down in the middle of your tryst, and she started screaming, having to be silenced," Bain added, looking fully amused. "We had to stop a half-dozen guards from breaking down the door."

"Yes, however the screams from Lucrezia, not to mention the sounds the brass bed curtain hangers made crashing against the stone floor, didn't help the situation at all," Eden retorted. "I believe she was putting up quite the fight before you even heard Antonietta scream."

Bain laughed, not disagreeing. "I can't deny a thing."

"Bain likes it rough," Dante joked, as he tilted his glass toward him.

"I have to admit, I do love it when they put up a good fight. The fear gives their blood a necromantic flavor," Bain admitted.

"Well, that sounds familiar." Jadis looked to Silas speaking telepathically, *"Eden's drink? A necromantic flavor?"*

"Yes, love, exactly." Silas gave her that crooked, coy smile of his.

"Seems it runs in the family, who knew?" She smiled.

"We made our way back downstairs where we released Antonietta and Lucrezia, who remembered nothing, well—almost nothing. After an elaborate feast of various fruits, breads, meat, and wine, what began as a carefully composed tango of manners soon evolved into a wild party with naked entertainers and sexual games. The fifty Vanozzo sex workers jumped on the table and performed a striptease," Eden explained.

"I can't believe you all got to witness that craziness." Jadis was feeling a bit jealous.

"They did more than witness it, my love," Silas stated.

"Yes, yes, we did," Aiden admitted as he playfully raised his glass to no one in particular.

Eden began again, "The lower-ranking courtesans danced seductively and undress while walnuts were strewn about. They crawled around on all fours, picking them up with their nether regions, if you will. Hence the regale of walnuts."

"No way! Did they really do that?" Jadis was slightly embarrassed since she was the only female at the table.

"They sure did." Aiden laughed, saying nothing more.

Eden continued, "A few hours later, Ubertino announced a new competition. The man who slept with the most sex workers during the party would win a prize, granted by the High Priest himself. There are no records of who won, however, the actual winner is sitting to your left."

"Aiden! Exactly how many did you sleep with? Never mind, scratch that. I don't think I want to know." Jadis held up her hand dismissively.

"Let's just say we didn't leave until dawn, and Aiden still has the prize," Bain added.

"Dare I ask what it is?" Jadis questioned.

"I don't know if you remember it or not, although I know it caught your eye. It's the solid marble statue of lovers sitting in the corner of our main foyer. You stood admiring it for a few minutes the first morning you spent with us," Aiden explained.

"Yes, I do remember it. It's beautiful, and I can't believe that's how you acquired it."

"Don't think Eden and Bain weren't partaking in the fornication downstairs as well. They probably had as many of the women as I did. We broke in just about every room in the Castle." Aiden laughed as he exposed Eden and Bain's so called *nonparticipation* in the contest.

"Well, I don't know about you all, but I'm ready to head into town. The story has made me hungry." Bain stood, ready to head out for the night.

Everyone else followed suit and moved around, filling their glasses for one last drink before heading out. As they reminisced about the story Eden had just shared, Jadis fully understood just how ancient they truly were; their knowledge and education spanning centuries. She turned to Silas and placed her hands on his waist and smiled.

"Have I told you lately how much I admire you?"

Before Silas could answer, Bain walked over and put a firm hand on his shoulder. "If you two of you are finished, can we leave? I need to feed."

"Yes, let's go," Eden stated as he headed for the door.

Eden took them to a tavern called The Spirits Barrel. It was a seedier bar just off the beaten path in the Lower Garden District. *Not exactly what I was expecting,* Jadis thought. It looked more like an old speakeasy than a modern bar. It rested on the edge of the bayou, surrounded by moss-laden cypress trees. The building was small, and the overhang sheltering the front walk was made of tin and didn't look entirely stable as it sloped down slightly on one side.

"What is this place?" Jadis asked Silas.

"Just wait, there's more to it than meets the eye," Silas replied.

"Coy as always." Jadis smiled.

They made their way up the uneven walkway toward the front door. The crowd lingering outside were carousing, smoking, and drinking. They looked intimidating and rugged, giving off the impression they were easily provoked. Their boisterous voices gradually subsided as they shifted their attention to Eden and the rest of their group, as they walked up. *I have an uneasy feeling they're sizing us up. If there's going to be a fight, as Aiden mentioned, this will be the place,* Jadis thought.

"Table for seven," Eden stated, winking at Jadis.

Jadis looked about to see who Eden was talking to since there wasn't a host or hostess in sight. "Who are you talking to?"

Eden smiled and nodded toward a large table whose current occupants suddenly gathered up their drinks and walked away.

Apparently, they've decided it's time to leave. "Of course, I should have known," she stated, looking up at Eden.

They headed to the table and took a seat. The tavern was a long, low-ceilinged, windowless room. The polished woods, aged tables, and rustic bar stools again confirmed her initial impression, but as soon as she looked behind the bar, it became obvious why Eden had chosen the place. It was a whiskey bar. There were hundreds of whiskeys, bourbons, ryes, and scotches. Bottles in every hue, shape, and size lined the expansive shelves. The selections ranged from your basic barroom drinks to rare Judanese imports, based on the labels Jadis quickly scanned.

One of the bartenders was at their table. "Did y'all come on ovah yah for drinks, what can I git cha?" he asked, with a thick Fréyonne drawl and a genuinely friendly smile.

"Ardbeg Special all around if you don't mind," Eden replied.

By the look on the waiter's face and his immediate reaction, it's clear Eden isn't ordering a ten-dollar shot, Jadis thought.

"Sir, ya," the bartender replied.

He quickly headed for the tavern and was back with a tray holding seven full highball glasses.

He set Jadis's down first. "Enjoy sha, ya?" he politely stated with a smile, before walking around the table and setting everyone else's drinks down

"Thank you," she replied.

"Pass a good time sha." He smiled.

Silas held up his glass. "To aged drink and young mates; to love without fear and life without regret; may the family that stands beside you be stronger than the fights before you; it's a bloody sure thing we're alive tonight; may you keep the dark ashen grave out of sight!"

"Aici, Aici!" Everyone shouted at once, along with two hard knocks on the table with their fists.

They stood around in a group, moving amongst each other and the other patrons as the night continued. A handful of the women were once again drooling at their feet, desperately vying for their attention. There had also been more than one set of eyes on Jadis, as well as a lot of backhanded comments made with purposefully raised voices. It certainly hadn't gone unnoticed by their clan, and she knew they were keeping her surrounded. She heard one group in particular encouraging one of their buddies to approach her.

"Damn, dat be a nice piece of ass ya?" the taller one stated to his group.

"You get dat right. Sha be looking good," stated their bigger buddy.

"I'd take dat ass back to da storeroom if I could git sha alone." Another laughed.

"Ya well—I've got an envie for some boudin," the muscular friend hollered to the growing amusement of his buddies.

"I'd bet ya couldn't gitch yo ass within ten feet of chey," the first to speak replied again, as he let out a belly laugh.

The waiter who had been taking care of the clan's table walked over and interrupted them, "Y'all best ignore sha, dem boys ain't gònn fuck round."

"Sho boy," one of them stated.

"Y'all bout to git fucked up." He laughed before walking away and leaving them to their own poor decisions.

They continued the banter and drinking for an hour or so before the tallest of them chimed in again, "Come on, Boon, whachou waiting for, dat poontang ain't gon wait all night."

"Fordetreal," he answered as he tossed back another shot and stood.

Apparently, that was the all the nudging he needed along with his liquid courage. He made his way through the group and bumped Dante out of the way. He managed to give Jadis's ass a hard smack before copping a feel. He didn't even have the chance to let go of her ass before the brazen idiot fell to the floor, his head having been rotated three-hundred-and-sixty degrees.

"Holy shit!" Jadis exclaimed. She looked up at Silas, who had snapped the drunk's neck. *His eyes have fully turned but not his features. In fact, they're all standing without having 'turned,' but are certainly looking to each other with excited expressions. Apparently, they don't want to let on that we're Nosferatu.*

The hollers from the dead man's pals, having witnessed the brief altercation, thundered throughout the tavern, and a ripple of descent quickly spread. It now appeared as if it would be roughly twenty or so to six.

Their clan moved in unison, following Silas's lead, waiting for the fight to begin. Silas had already moved Jadis to a corner and proceeded to stand between her and the approaching, infuriated mob.

Two of the drunk's friends each broke a pool cue over their knee, assuming they would have the upper hand. She didn't quite understand, other than their alcohol-fueled courage made one of them think they could take on anyone in their group.

The mob rushed at once. Dante quickly snatched the four broken pool cues from the two men and tossed two of the cues to the side. He easily knocked them both unconscious with the remaining two cues he kept. He looked at Jadis and playfully spun a broken cue in each hand like a trained swordsman. He was in a half-crouched, silly stance, which cracked her up.

"Only a fool doesn't know when to hold his tongue!" Dante announced.

"Hell yes. Nothing like a good-old tavern fight!" Eden exclaimed as he grabbed one of the approaching men by his hair and brought his face down onto his bent knee. The blood splattered across the man's face and flowed from his broken nose. As he staggered backward, Eden followed up with a swift front kick sending him crashing into a table five feet away. He already had another by the front of his shirt and landed a headbutt. The attacker stumbled backward before he fell to the floor, unconscious and bleeding profusely from the laceration on his forehead.

The noises rose as the fight continued to grow with intensity. The sounds of the punches and kicks, as well as the breaking furniture and shattering glass, not to mention the increasing moans coming from the beaten and broken attackers, drowned out the music thumping in the background from the old-fashioned jukebox. There was so much mayhem, she didn't know where to look.

As their clan made their way through the crowd, bodies were falling and being tossed in every direction while the angry mob struggled to land a single blow.

Lars and Aiden each grabbed two of the larger men and proceeded to slam their faces into a couple of random tables in unison, breaking the tables as well as the men's faces in the process. They looked to each other and laughed as if they had made that move with each other a hundred times. They flipped the men behind them, and they came down flat on their backs.

Two of the men, who had witnessed Silas snap their friend's neck, had set their sights on Jadis, deciding she was the cause of his death. They headed in her direction, only to come face to face with Silas. They attacked at once, doing their best to throw a punch. Silas easily caught each of their fists in his hands, crushing them with a single squeeze. They let out agonizing screams and dropped to their knees. With a quick front kick to the face, Silas permanently silenced them both.

For the amount of chaos taking place, the fight ended rather quickly. She stood in awe as she watched her clan handle business. *They look as if they've choregraphed the entire scene. They know what the other is doing and thinking. Their movements are swift, precise, and graceful.*

She took the opportunity to stand back and try to control the pull she felt to *turn*. The threats to Silas may have been pulling the change out of her but even so, she was able to control it for the first time ever.

The tavern was suddenly silent except for subtle moans coming from the injured. As soon as the fight had begun, Dante and Bain sealed the tavern, leaving all its cherry-picked guests solely for them to enjoy later.

Silas approached Jadis, took her hand, and spun her around. "I saw what you did, baby. That was amazing. You fully controlled yourself."

Everyone gathered together, laughing as they patted each on the shoulder, grasped each other's forearms, and joked about the aftermath. The entire club was in disarray; bodies both living, and barely conscious littered the floor, and the rest of the customers who had been silenced for the time being, wandered around in a catatonic state of being.

"Well, that made me hungry. I do believe it's feeding time," Bain announced as he slid his foot under one of the bodies and tossed it to the other side of the room.

"I couldn't agree more," Dante replied.

Every one of them already had their sights set on their prospective victims. The atmosphere in the club had returned to normal, except for the bodies, broken furniture, and glass strew all about. The music was once again heavy in the background, and the patrons laughed at the chaotic scene. They set up their tables and chairs as if it had been nothing more than a regular bar fight.

Curiously, they don't seem to notice the dead bodies all around. She looked at Silas and cocked her head inquisitively.

"They only see what we allow them to see," Silas answered.

"Good to know." She nodded.

As the night resumed, their drinking, feeding, and conversation was so much more than words. It was the smiles, the laughter, and the kinship; they savored each other's company.

Jadis held her current victim by the hair, facing Silas as he, Bain, and Dante fed from their victims. Eden, Aiden, and Lars had set up a non-broken table and a couple of chairs in the center for themselves, and were sipping their bourbon, having finished their meals already.

Silas walked to Jadis and stopped in front of her, wondering why she was still holding her dead feeder and chuckling. "You going to hold onto her all night?" he asked as he raised an eyebrow in amusement.

"Shit, I don't know?" She shrugged her shoulders and continued to look at her mummified face studying her.

The air suddenly moved all around them, and chairs and tables were shoved out of the way. They were all down on one knee in front of her, with their heads bowed.

"What the hell are you all doing?" she cracked up. "Have you all lost you minds? Get up," she demanded playfully as she pushed Silas's shoulder with her foot.

Although no one answered, she heard Silas calling to her. The blood was so heavy in her mind and body, she failed to catch on. She felt a cool breeze move in behind her. She dropped the body and took a step back, only to run into something solid. She turned around and found herself standing face to chest with someone. She slowly looked up and realized she was looking at a taller, much older version of Silas.

"What the hell?" she stated. She turned back to Silas, looking for an explanation. "My feeder must have bad blood or have had a lot of bad alcohol!"

It was either her laughter or her comment, she wasn't sure, but whatever it was, it caused everyone to laugh under their breath.

"I swear to the Gods, Silas, for a minute, I thought you had moved. Stop playing with me."

"Oh, Jadis," Aiden mumbled.

Eden could barely contain himself, which she found rather odd. *He was never the one laughing, not from a submissive position anyway.* She stared at him, trying to figure out what he was doing when Silas reached out and grabbed her.

She was suddenly on one knee between Silas's legs, with him holding her head in a bowed position.

"I think now would be a good time to fill me in, Silas. Who was I not bowing to?" she demanded silently.

"My father."

"Holy shit!" Her stomach lurched, and she thought she might vomit right at his feet. *"You're kidding me. If it's Santiago, I'm going to kill you."* She kicked Silas in the crotch with the heel of her foot, trying to do it as subtly as possible. He let out a huge belt of air but didn't move or speak a word. That told her more than she needed to know.

"No need to kill Silas, my dear. Do stand." Santiago now stood over her and Silas.

Great! Just someone else reading my thoughts, not that it's even a surprise anymore.

"I must meet the cause of so much chaos," Santiago stated.

Jadis didn't move a muscle, other than having backed up at least six inches into Silas.

"Is he talking to me? He can't be talking to me—please tell me he isn't," she muttered telepathically.

"Who else would chaos be?" Eden answered, doing his best to hold his composure in front of his uncle, and not laugh at Jadis's petrified, drunken state of being any more than he already was.

"Not now, Eden. This isn't funny at all!" she snapped back.

"I see you all are well acquainted. My boys, you're having trouble keeping your thoughts to yourself?" Santiago didn't need to raise his voice to command respect; it was unquestionable.

"We meant no disrespect, milord," Eden answered.

Oh God, anyone with the power to make them bow and apologize isn't who I want to contend with.

"I'm headed to the guillotine, aren't I?" she stated telepathically to Silas.

"We haven't used those in hundreds of years, my dear. We find the sword quicker and a bit more entertaining," Santiago responded.

I need to be anywhere but here.

"Stand now, my dear," Santiago ordered.

Silas gently nudged her forward

She was so nervous, she tripped on her own foot getting up and fell onto her other knee, feeling like a complete moron, which of course brought out another bellow of laughter from the kneeling crowd behind her.

She finally made it to her feet, feeling like she had been struck dumb. She stared at who was now her father as well, studying him as much as he studied her. The power emanated from him, and his energy was like nothing she had ever felt before.

He slowly circled her before finally stopping in front of Silas. Santiago placed his hand on the back of Silas's bent head. *Damn, the legionary Prince Vladislav himself may as well be the one circling me.*

"Well, in case you're wondering, Vladislav and I are well acquainted."

Kill me now. If ever there was a time to shut off my thoughts, now would be great!

Santiago looked at her and cocked his head to the side. "If you would like to meet him, I'm happy to arrange an introduction."

"No, thank you, sir," she replied in a hushed whisper.

"Call him milord," Silas requested.

"You're dead when this is over!"

Santiago stepped in front of Silas. "Stand, bairn."

Silas stood next to Jadis, and he reached for her trembling hand and held it steady.

"You could have at least shown me a picture of your father! At least I wouldn't be standing here, looking like an idiot."

"Shhh—" Was all she got from Silas, and she shushed.

"Silas, don't shush the poor girl. Let her have her say. I find her fascinating."

Santiago stepped in front of her and gently grabbed ahold of her chin. He moved her head from side to side and up and down before letting go. She was sure everyone could hear the frantic beat drumming behind her breast as well as she could.

"So, beautiful girl, I assume you're none other than Jadis?" He robotically cocked his head, waiting for an answer.

She felt Silas urging her to speak. "Yes, milord," she replied.

He turned his attention back to Silas. "No wonder the Gods bestowed her to you; she's your match in every way."

"Yes, she is," Silas agreed, the pride gleaming in his eyes as he peered down at her.

"Needless to say, I'm impressed. This beauty has managed to turn all of you into born-again hunters. You're all pack feeding again," he stated.

All she felt she could do in that moment was hold her breath, close her eyes, and wait for the sword to strike.

"What? Nothing to say? Well, that's a first," Lars blurted out. Jadis, however, found nothing funny about it.

"I'm going to kill you all—" she began when a calm voice suddenly interrupted her.

"Stop, darling. You're scaring the poor girl half to death."

Jadis looked up to see the most regal, stunning woman she had ever laid eyes on. She swore she was looking at a goddess as she approached them. She laid her arms softly over Santiago's shoulders and rested her chin on her forearm.

She's staring right into my soul. Don't look—don't look. She lowered her eyes, not wanting to stare or be disrespectful. She didn't know how to act right now; she felt as if she was in front of a firing squad.

"And this would be?" Jadis asked Silas, trying her best to cloak her question.

"My mother," Silas replied aloud.

"Mhmm—even better." She tried to side-eye Silas in her mind since she couldn't do it physically.

Silas's mother laughed and covered her mouth with the back of her hand.

"It looks like a pack of hungry Dire Wolves came through here." His father walked the room, studying the destruction and death surrounding them.

Santiago bent down over one of her victims and studied the mummified corpse. He looked back to Silas and Jadis, who currently had their backs to him. Even so, Jadis felt him looking at them.

"Well, this is interesting to say the least. Jadis, I assume this is your doing since it's the first time we're seeing mummified corpses after having been drained?"

Again, Silas silently urged her to speak.

"Yes, milord," she replied quietly.

Lars cocked his head towards Jadis. "She can speak, can't she?"

Jadis shot him a searing look with squinted eyes, which only forced their amusement into hushed hysterics.

Santiago picked at the body and rubbed some of the ash between his fingers. He smelled it and proceeded to wipe it off on a napkin he had grabbed off the floor as he stood. As he made his way back to Jadis and Silas, he lifted his hand and flicked his wrist. The bodies blew into a cloud of ash and dissipated while the living quietly saw their way out.

"Tell me, my dear, how did you convince this group into killing again for pleasure?"

She looked at him, but she was at a complete loss for words. *This isn't my doing,* was all she could think of but didn't dare speak it aloud for fear of angering him. She dug her fingernails into the palm of Silas's hand, silently demanding him to do something.

"He can't help you, dear. I would expect Silas to feed with you, but I'm surprised at Eden's behavior. You were the last one I thought would follow suit," he scolded, looking directly at Eden.

Jadis looked to his mother, who now sat in a chair behind Santiago, with a drink in her hand. Her legs were crossed, while her arm rested on the arm of the chair. She looked fully amused as she lifted the glass to her perfect, rosy lips. Her mosaic, black hair hung in soft waves over her breast, almost reaching her stomach, while intricate strands of gems were weaved into the messy, braided side-do. Her low-cut, white dress had gold edging with a long slit that rose up her thigh, baring her perfect legs. *There isn't an unintentional hair out of place. As old as she seems to be, she still looks like she's only in her one* hundred *and thirties. She looks like an Ipheanorian queen sitting there. No wonder Silas and his brothers are so perfect, so gorgeous. Hell, his parents are both stunning.*

"That's enough, dear. Put an end to this," Luciana demanded, motioning with her hand. "Stop teasing the poor thing."

Santiago grabbed Silas, and pulled him in for a tight embrace, along with multiple pats on the back. Silas returned the gesture, leaving Jadis confused.

He patted Silas's cheek and proceeded to walk to everyone else. They all stood and embraced Santiago in the same manner.

"Why is everyone laughing?" she asked Silas privately. His only response was to laugh all the more.

She pulled away, having an unsettling feeling. She quickly realized she was the center of their entertainment once again. However, she didn't dare speak a word. Luciana had also walked over and embraced each of them.

"I've never seen you rendered speechless, Jadis," Dante said through his hysterics.

Jadis went to flip him off and stopped herself, due to their present company, which pushed him over the edge. He and Bain held onto each other, and Aiden had his hand on Eden's shoulder, holding himself up. Eden held his stomach.

"Come," Santiago stated. He pulled her into a loving embrace and picked her up off the ground.

She reluctantly hugged him back and felt the energy surge through his body. *His power is undeniably ancient.*

His mother approached and embraced Jadis as soon as Santiago set her down.

"I believe a formal introduction is in order," Santiago suggested.

"Yes." Silas laughed. "Jadis, this is my father Santiago and my mother Luciana. Father—Mother, this is my mate, Jadis."

"It seems you're a breath of fresh air in my son's darkened life," Santiago added as he gave her another lingering hug.

"Well, Jadis, it's nice to finally put a face to the one we've heard so much about lately," Luciana offered.

Enchantress, Jadis thought.

Luciana heard Jadis's thought. "Yes, my dear, that's correct. My, you're intoxicating." She continued to study Jadis before looking up at Silas and nodding.

"Nice to meet you too," Jadis offered as politely as she could before turning to Silas. "So, you all bowing on one knee? Was that just a joke I wasn't privy to?" she asked.

"Not to begin with," Silas admitted.

"Jadis, we couldn't help ourselves, but the bowing was real," Dante offered.

"As soon as we saw our uncle and aunt appear, we did what's required," Aiden explained. "However, we thought you needed a lesson in *bending the knee.*"

Eden looked directly to Jadis. "Aiden speaks the truth, but you, standing there with your back to them, holding a dead body, was too much for any of us. You were utterly clueless!"

His words brought about another round of laughter, even Silas's parents joined them.

"You've put all of us through the ringer at some point, and more than once I might add. This was just a bit of well-deserved payback." Dante smirked.

"I'm sorry, baby, but we couldn't help ourselves," Silas added.

I may be the butt of everyone's joke, but as least we're not going to die.

"No one else is *dying* tonight, or any other night after this." Santiago scanned the room once again. "Looks like this was one hell of a party, I'm assuming it will be the last?"

Everyone agreed in one way or another, everyone but Jadis anyway.

"My dear, this goes for you too. Am I in any way unclear?" Santiago asked firmly.

So, that's where they get the statement I've heard one to many times. "No, milord."

"Very well. It's time to end the night. You're all headed home. Jadis, address me as Father; milord is so formal." Jadis simply smiled.

They proceeded to follow Santiago and Luciana back to the mansion, who chose to walk home and enjoy what was left of the night. They walked arm in arm, reminiscing about the city they hadn't seen in a couple hundred years.

"Jadis is stunning," Luciana offered.

"She certainly is," Santiago agreed.

"Who called Daddy?" Jadis accused, looking at Eden.

"My thoughts exactly, cousin. Who made the call? Clearly you didn't do it," Silas acknowledged.

A thought crossed Aiden's mind. "It was Maddie, wasn't it?

"If you must know, yes," Eden confessed. "I put his number into her phone in case things went too far. I had a feeling you would drag us all into your feeding frenzy, Jadis." Eden winked at her and smiled coyly.

"You know damn well I didn't drag you in. Silas did, not to mention, I didn't see you protesting."

Dante walked up and wrapped his arm around her neck since Silas had his arm wrapped around her waist. "You do realize we're all going to be punished once back at the mansion," Dante whispered.

"*Punished*? What does that mean?" She felt her face turn ashen as she looked to Silas.

"Don't look at me, my love. I know what's coming," Silas replied as he looked at Dante, seemingly concerned.

"Did you ever explain to her the ways in which our kind are *punished*?" Bain asked.

"No, it hadn't crossed my mind. It's not the kind of conversation you want to have with your newly turned mate."

"Silas, are you being serious right now? If you all are toying with me again, there will be hell to pay—I promise."

They continued to walk in silence for a few agonizing moments. Silas and Dante were on either side of her, and the mere thought of dealing with an angry Santiago told her to run.

"*So, how long should we let her spin?*" Silas asked Dante privately.

"*How long did she have us spinning when she took a leap into the portal?*" he replied.

"That's it. This isn't funny. What's going to happen?" Jadis stopped midstride and pulled away. Her trepidation, not to mention her own disastrous thought pattern, was getting the best of her once again. "I'm not going back to the mansion if what you say is true."

Everyone stopped, and surrounded Jadis.

"One of you had better speak up," she demanded as she waved her finger toward them all.

A voice broke the tension from up ahead. "What's going on back there?"

Santiago and Luciana had stopped and turned to face them. Other than the look Santiago shot their way, the most chilling thing she noticed were the blank stares from the crowd surrounding her.

"Oh shit, is he going to torture us?" she blurted out. She was too busy falling prey to her own mind to notice everyone's growing amusement. Santiago walked toward them, and she took heed and ran off in the opposite direction.

"Good luck," Lars stated as he watched her try to elude his uncle.

She didn't make it but mere inches before Silas had a hold of her. Their guttural laughter permeated the air as she wrenched out of Silas's grip and spun around to face him.

"This—this too, was all a joke?" she vented, not knowing whether or not she should be angry or relieved.

The next thing she knew, Luciana stepped between her and everyone else, Silas included.

"Stop this! You all need to stop scaring her, I will not allow you all continue with this behavior," Luciana stated calmly. She pulled Jadis to her, wrapped one arm around her, and placed a hand on her hip with one raised eyebrow. Santiago stood behind her with his arms crossed, and the jokesters stopped laughing.

Jadis used the moment to flash them a devious smile. *I now have their mother on my side, and I'm going to use it against all of them.* She began a fake cry and let a few tears stream down her face.

Luciana wrapped both arms around her, and Jadis proceeded to wrap her poor, distraught arms around her. She winked at the statuesque crowd with a half-cocked smile.

"My dear, it will be fine—Santiago?"

"I assume you all heard Luciana loud and clear—yes?" Santiago questioned.

"Yes," they answered in one way or another.

Jadis was quite proud of herself for having turned the tables in her favor. She opened a private conversation using her newly discovered *vampiric fuckery*, as they called it. *"If you all want to play games, I can play too."*

Their expressions ranged between various stages of disbelief and shock that she could block out Santiago and Luciana. Amused, she watched as they darted their eyes between each other, looking for answers before they all settled on Silas.

"And how did you manage to block Santiago and Luciana?" Eden questioned as he cocked his head at Jadis.

"Wouldn't you like to know," she replied in jest, still acting as if they had all hurt her feelings.

"Silas, I believe you left a few minor details out. Just how much have her original powers grown?" Eden demanded.

Each of them looked to each other, trying not to laugh at her tucked under Luciana's arms.

"Here we go," replied Dante, to his mother's dismay.

"Excuse me? Bairn, do you have something you would like to say?" Luciana questioned.

"Jadis isn't actually crying, nor is she upset right now. I know she's faking the tears as well," Dante replied, all the while squinting his eyes at Jadis.

She winked back with a devious smile, letting him know she was enjoying every damn minute of the scolding Luciana and Santiago were giving them.

She made a sniffling noise and replied with a disheartened tone, "They're always blaming me for things. I'm not faking, it's upsetting the way they all gang up on me." She sniffled.

She looked up at Luciana with saddened, watery eyes. She then looked back to her jesters and raised an amused eyebrow.

"Jadis, you've got to be kidding me right now! You're so far from being upset or having hurt feelings," Eden scolded.

"Eden, enough, you heard your aunt. Leave her alone and now," Santiago replied in a manner that sent shivers up Jadis's spine.

Eden squinted his eyes at Jadis as he addressed his uncle with a simple nod.

"Don't think you'll get away with this, darling," Dante warned telepathically.

"I don't know exactly what's going on between you all, and I'm quite sure there are games underfoot, but right now, we're ending this," Santiago demanded sternly.

Luciana looked down at her and kissed the top of her head. "Sometimes I just don't know what gets into them." She looked at everyone else as if angry before she turned to walk away. "Let's head home. Shall we, my dear girl?"

"Yes, thank you, Luciana."

"Please, call me Mother, I insist." Jadis smiled warmly as she let her go.

Luciana took Santiago's arm, and they headed for home once again.

Jadis sauntered back to Silas and wrapped her arms around him, waiting for the fallout.

Silas gently pulled back and looked down at her. "You may have pulled that off, but I can assure you, there will be consequences when I get your ass back home."

She was now currently surrounded by the entire group who all moved in closer. She tried to hide under Silas's arms, but he jumped back, leaving her to deal with everyone alone.

"Silas!" She tried to grab his shirt, but he quickly dodged her grasp in a heap of laughter.

"I think you can handle whatever is coming your way."

Everyone quickly surrounded her, blocking her path to Silas.

"Silas, stop!" She demanded as Silas hid behind Bain and Aiden, with one hand on each of their shoulders.

"You want to play games, do you?" Dante stated as he stepped forward, looking less amused than the rest of them.

"Dante, stop!" She laughed nervously. "You all started this."

She placed her palms against his chest to stop him from whatever he was about to do. He gently grabbed her wrists, held them in a tight grip, and looked to the crowd. "What shall we do with her? Any ideas?"

"I have a couple," Eden answered as he stepped closer. "I have a feeling a little someone has just influenced Luciana. I for one want to know how you did it."

"I'm curious as well." Bain eyed everyone before looking at Jadis again. "Influencing an Enchantress is no small feat, not to mention dangerous. I think we should render her powerless again, at least until we see exactly what she's capable of—Silas, your thoughts?"

Silas rubbed his chin, acting as if he were heavy in thought. He dropped his hand from his chin and suddenly held a golden anklet, letting it spin like a globe in his palm.

"Silas!" She stated.

Suddenly, they all held up their hands, holding an exact copy of the golden anklet spinning in each of their palms. Her mouth dropped open, and she failed to speak.

"Holy hell, are you speechless again? Well, that worked in our favor," Lars stated.

Dante wrapped his arm around her waist and pulled her in tight, acting as if he was about to slap his bracelet on her wrist.

"Stop!" She tried to wriggle out of his grasp to no avail.

"Better hurry up. We would all like to attach ours to her," Eden snarled in a joking manner.

She swirled her wrist and disappeared into a cloud of mist, managing to jump into Silas's arms.

"May the powers of Nosferatu help us, I believe we have our hands full," Santiago stated.

"Yes, my love, we do. I felt her powers when I held her while she was teasing them," Luciana admitted.

"You knew she was faking?"

"Of course. I couldn't pass up the opportunity to play along. We've been gone far too long, I've missed this. Plus, I do believe they deserved it."

"How strong do you think she is? From what I've picked up on, I believe she has powers from beyond this realm, not to mention a few others. She's dangerously capable," Santiago offered.

"I agree. I believe it best if we stick around for a while, at least until we get them under control again. The blood lust runs heavy amongst each of them. I also think she's more than capable of enticing them into continuing to feed in their current condition," Luciana stated, the concern in her tone clear.

"Then it has been settled, my dear. We shall stay for the duration. We need to contend with our newly *turned* daughter. She has no idea of the powers she has acquired. I assume however, Silas knows what she's capable of. Nothing gets past that bairn, it never has."

Luciana couldn't agree more. "True, true. I also believe she has blocked us out somehow. I know they were speaking to each other, but I couldn't decipher what was being said. That in itself is more than concerning."

"Yes, I felt it as well. We'll determine what's needed to control her," Santiago agreed.

CHAPTER 9

T hey had been recovering from the blood lust for roughly two weeks, and Jadis was thoroughly bored. Aria and Maddie had now joined them, so she had some company. Silas, along with the rest of their clan, spent most of their time locked up with Santiago, discussing business, all of which the girls weren't privy to.

Jadis lay in bed feeling an innate need to get out of the mansion. She felt a pull, one that she couldn't explain. *What the hell? I need to do something, go somewhere. Anything would be better than hanging around here all day again.*

"It's normal, baby. You're young, wild, and new to all of this. You'll have to deal with a lot of feelings that will seem to randomly take hold of you. The need to roam is one of the greatest pulls of all, other than feeding," Silas explained, having read her thoughts.

His explanation makes sense, but there's also something he's not saying. She rolled over to face him. "I want to go into town. Can we get out of here for a while? Can't they do without you for one evening?"

"I would love to take you out, but it's not that simple. How about we get up and head downstairs for a drink?"

"I guess—it doesn't seem as if I have much of a choice."

"First thing's first, I'm hungry."

There's that sexy, velvety tone I love so much. Shit, I'm hungry as well, and I can never turn down feeding from Silas, so I'll drop the subject, for now anyway.

"Yes." She grabbed the back of his head and pulled him in. He rolled on top of her and parted her legs with his. He turned his head, offering his vein to her with that beautiful, demure look. She greedily took his offering and let the thick, earthly liquid flow from the eight punctures.

His desire increased with every pull, and he moaned in response, desperate to dominate her body.

He pulled his neck away ever so gently, and she released her grip. Her head fell back into the pillow as his blood flowed through her body, satiating her thirst.

He trailed his tongue down the center of her chest, stopping briefly to tease her perfect, plump bud. He kissed his way further down her body, stopping only after his face was between her legs. He pushed her knees a bit further apart with his hands and took her sex into the heat of his mouth. She moaned with pleasure as the twirling of his tongue increased her desire.

Silas let out a throaty, moan, "Mon chéri—you taste amazing." His mouth claimed her swollen nub and his fingers began another assault of their own.

Between the relentlessness of his tongue teasing her sex, and his fingers penetrating her core, her body trembled. Foreplay wasn't on the menu; she wanted it, hard—fast—and now.

"Silas," she moaned, desperate for his rigid, full shaft.

He sucked a bit harder and as he drove his fingers deeper, and he felt her body respond to his dominating assault. Her sex throbbed against his tongue as she climaxed.

"I need you," she whispered as her body flushed with the heated swell.

"I like the sound of that," he replied, with a low, guttural growl.

He slowly kissed his way back up her body, savoring each delicate inch. He took his time, reveling in her desperate need for him. His mouth fell to hers, and he re-positioned her body beneath him. With a hard shove, he found his way deep into her core. He gave her exactly what she wanted, what he wanted. His moans grew as he rode her harder and faster.

"Again, baby," he purred.

He turned her head, exposing her heightened pulse. He felt her inhale and gasp for a deep breath.

The sharp pricks sent a frenzy of electric shockwaves throughout her entire body.

He fed until the need to come inside her rose up. He let go of her neck and began another harsh assault. He thrust his hips harder, each stroke more urgent than the last.

She moaned as the pleasure overtook her body, again. *Silas never ceases to push my body to the extremes of pleasure.*

He felt her tight core squeeze his shaft and pulse around him, bringing his own release to the surface. He let out a heady groan as his body fractured, the warm liquid pumping into her. He slowly rocked back and forth, filling her with his seed. He then collapsed on top of her, both of them feeling sated and slightly breathless.

They finally got out of bed, dressed, and headed downstairs. *Once Silas has had a few drinks and is relaxed, I'll hit him up again to take me out before he goes to work.*

Everyone but Santiago and Luciana were in the parlor, reminiscing. Silas and Jadis took their usual seats, but story time and heading into town had ended. Their nights now consisted of everyone working and the girls hanging out at the pool or goofing off with one another. Santiago and Luciana had full control of each and every one of them, to Jadis's dismay.

She didn't quite understand the need she had to venture out, so she decided if Silas wouldn't agree to take her out, she would just sneak out herself once they went to work. She also assumed after a few drinks, she could convince Maddie and Aria to join her; they too were as bored as she was. She had picked up a few of Silas's mind-bending abilities after turning, and she'd influence them if she had to.

They all had their drinks and were enjoying each other's company as usual, so she decided now would be as good a time as any to ask Silas. "Need another drink, baby?" she asked nervously.

"I do, darling, but if you think we're finishing our earlier conversation, the answer is still no."

"Really? No? Just like that, you're saying no?"

"Unfortunately, love, the answer is still no." Silas raised his eyebrows, waiting for her to continue protesting.

She stood up in a huff and walked over to the bar, and he quickly joined her.

"Baby, you don't get it. I need out of this house. You don't understand. I can't sit here like this anymore," she pleaded.

"Here we go," Eden stated as he sat back, listening to the brewing argument.

"What's going on, baby?" Maddie quietly asked Eden.

"I'm afraid Jadis is bored, and I have a feeling the pull for her to wander is growing."

"What does that mean?" Aria asked.

"I'll explain it all later," Aiden replied.

"If she wants to go out, Aria and I will go with her," Maddie offered politely.

There was a resounding *hell no* from everyone sitting there.

Aria looked to Eden. "Why not? She's not going to do anything if we're with her."

"Aria, you have no idea what that girl will get you involved in. You won't be leaving this house. I won't even entertain the idea," Aiden stated matter-of-factly.

"Eden, I would like to get out as well. I promise everything will be fine. We can just have a few drinks somewhere and be back before dark," Maddie offered.

"The answer is no, end of conversation," Eden stated sternly.

"Excuse me? You do not control me, Eden," Maddie scoffed as she removed herself from his lap.

"Leave it to Jadis to cause three fights in ten minutes." Lars's remark had everyone amused, except for Aiden and Eden.

Aria turned around in Aiden's lap, so he was facing her. "Aiden, you and I are not yet mated. I can, and I will leave with them if I choose to do so."

Santiago and Luciana leaned against the upstairs railing, watching, waiting. They wanted to see what they were dealing with. They were also prepared to deal with Jadis's need to venture out, and this would give them an opportunity to see how powerful she was. The vampirism would surely overtake her reasoning at this stage. Santiago also knew the sudden pull wasn't Jadis's instincts, but something sinister he wasn't sure she could fight.

"How far do you think she'll take this?" Luciana asked.

"We'll soon find out, and I have a daunting feeling if she wants out, she's getting out."

"The girls, think they'll follow along?"

"Most assuredly," Santiago stated.

"You're going to be my mate, so essentially, I do own you, and you'll do as I say," Aiden stated firmly.

Aria quickly got up from his lap and stood next to Maddie with her hands on her hips.

The voices at the bar raised as the argument between Jadis and Silas grew.

"Silas, I will leave. You cannot stop me," she vented, her voice becoming in an inhumane manner.

"My love, I can, and I will stop you. Have you not figured that out yet?"

"We shall see. I feel like a dog in a cage. I can't do this." She pleaded her case again to no avail. Silas stood unwavering.

She stormed back to the group, having quickly realized the girls were on her side. *Maybe the three of us together might be able to reason with them.*

"Here comes trouble," Lars announced.

As soon as she made her way over, Eden and Aiden stood, and it was now a standoff wills. They all stared at each other, waiting on the other to speak.

"If we want to go out, who are they to stop us?" Jadis said, looking only at the girls.

"Agreed." Maddie turned her head and stared at Eden.

Aria dismissed Aiden with a wave of her hand in his direction. "You know I'm in."

"Well, it has been decided. We're going to get a drink elsewhere," Jadis snapped.

The three of them turned to walk out the door, only to be face to face with Silas, Aiden, and Eden.

"Jadis, you never cease to amaze me. I would love to see you try to walk out that door with Maddie and Aria in tow," Dante offered.

Bain filled his glass and tossed Dante the bottle, who then tossed it to Lars.

"Zip it, nanny," she snarked.

Her words did nothing more than to send the three of them into hysterics. Her heart pounded at the mere thought of escaping from Silas.

"We can get out, but I'll have to cloak all three of us. If you both want to do this, you'll need to stand shoulder to shoulder with me, understand?" Jadis stated privately.

"Yes," they answered.

They subtly moved so close to Jadis, their shoulders touched hers.

"Silas, I feel a portal opening," Dante joked.

"As do I. Jadis is about to pull some fuckery. This ought to be good," Bain added.

"We need to be ready." Dante had opened his own conversation with everyone in the parlor. *"You do know what she's about to do?"*

"Yes, let's just see how far she can get," Silas answered.

"Bain and I are ready. Just say the word," Dante replied.

Eden wasn't sure at all if it was a good idea to let them out of their sight. *"I don't want her taking Maddie anywhere, trouble follows her like a dog looking for scraps."*

"Agreed," Aiden stated. *"Aria is stubborn, impulsive, and wild. I don't trust her and Jadis together at all."*

Jadis felt the air change around her and knew right away Silas was prepared to intervene. Dante and Bain were ready as well; their waning energy was undeniable. She decided to act as if she was conceding, hoping they would calm down. She let the girls know they needed to follow her lead.

"Fine, what are we supposed to do then? Sit here like we do day in and day out?" She threw her hands up in exasperation. Whatever it was deep down that had taken hold of her, she was no longer able to fight it, nor did she want to.

"Baby, I fully understand what you're feeling. I'll take you out but right now isn't the time. We have serious business we need to attend to, and you cannot stray from this house alone," Silas said.

"That's fine." Jadis stormed over to the bar with Maddie and Aria following. They stood filled their glasses, trying to ignore the burning stares behind them.

"I'm not sure about this. Eden isn't playing right now," Maddie admitted with a nervous side-eye as she took another drink.

Aria was more angry than worried at this point. "Aiden isn't of the Gods. I'm leaving now just to prove a point."

They stayed at the bar for about fifteen minutes. Silas, Aiden, and Eden had moved away from the door but continued standing.

It's clear they don't trust me in the least, and I know for a fact they're privately communicating with one another as well, Jadis thought.

"There are games afoot, walking to the bar was merely a ploy," Silas rumbled silently to everyone in their group.

"Yep, they're merely planning their escape," Aiden answered.

"We may as well go if we're doing this. By the looks of it, they won't leave us alone. Asking permission was a mistake," Jadis seethed.

"Oh, boy." Maddie stated aloud as she took another drink and moved in close. She rested her arm on the bar and let her elbow touch Jadis'. *"I have knots in my stomach,"* Maddie admitted telepathically.

"I'm scared as well," Jadis agreed.

Aria sat in the bar stool, slightly facing Jadis with her knee touching her thigh. *"Okay, I'm as ready as I'll ever be. I had no idea agreeing to become his mate would give him so much control over me."*

"You have no idea, Aria. Your life is now his, and he owns you and all that you are," Jadis stated.

The look on her face became that of concern. *"What are you saying—exactly?"*

"Forget about it for now. I'll explain it to you later. Right now, we need to go. As soon as I close my eyes, grab ahold of me." Jadis took another drink, set the glass on the bar, and closed her eyes.

The girls disappeared into a haze and materialized in the middle of Vieux Levatou in a heap of nervous laughter.

"I can't believe you pulled that off! How the magic hell did you do it?" Aria asked, in utter disbelief.

"I don't know." Jadis laughed. "It was something I had done once before by accident the night I met Santiago and Luciana. I've been practicing out of sheer boredom for the last couple of weeks."

Maddie had her hand over her heart. "I don't know about either of you, but I need another drink."

Jadis looked around and then pointed across the street. "Well, there's a bar right there."

They walked in and found a table in the back. Their drinks arrived quickly since Jadis simply influenced the bartender.

"Eden is going to be furious!" Maddie laughed. She chugged her entire glass, causing the girls to laugh at her at her.

"When is Eden ever not angry?" Jadis questioned.

"True. Where you're concerned, he always has a migraine," Maddie joked.

"How long do you think we have before they find us?" Aria asked.

"Trust me, it won't be long. I say we finish a couple more drinks and go somewhere else." *I have a place in mind, a certain cemetery we can hang out in,* Jadis thought.

"Where are you thinking?" Maddie asked.

"How about the resting place of Rhiamon Locasta?"

"Hell yes," Aria agreed. "Let's get out of here, that sounds like a hell of a lot of fun. Not to mention I feel like a sitting duck. Forget the drinks; let's go."

"You won't get an argument out of me," Maddie agreed.

They purchased a couple of bottles and headed for the cemetery. Jadis cloaked them just as Silas, Dante, and Bain had taught her to do, knowing their mates were hot on their heels.

"Dammit, that girl!" Silas shouted. "We need their insolent little asses back here."

"I told you to be ready. We all knew she would pull this shit," Dante scolded.

"Never underestimate her. Have we not said that a hundred times," Bain agreed as he set his glass down.

"You're the one who said let's see how far she can get. Well, now we're all going to find out," Aiden growled.

"It seems we have a problem to contend with," Santiago stated. He and Luciana now stood in the parlor.

"Yes. I presume you and Mother witnessed it all?" Silas asked.

"Yes, and Jadis is strong. She's becoming more powerful by the day. We need to prepare. Abigor is aware of her existence. He'll come for her eventually. She needs to be controlled and held steady." Santiago only said what everyone there already knew to be true.

"How well do you think she can cloak herself with Aria and Maddie in tow?" Aiden asked.

"We shall soon find out," Dante rumbled, re-thinking the lessons they had all been giving her. *Yep, that wasn't the best idea. She can probably use her skills to hide for hours.*

The feeling of dread washed over Silas like the waters before a hurricane. His thoughts wandered back to a time not so long ago when he had almost lost her.

Luciana placed her hand on Silas's shoulder. "Calm, my bairn. We won't let anything happen to them. Go get your mate and bring her home. Your father and I'll be awaiting your arrival." Her smile was loving and genuine, her words reassuring.

"I think we're going to need more than an anklet." Dante chuckled to Bain and Lars quietly.

"I swear on all that's Nosferatu, Jadis is going to put me to an early grave," Eden snarled.

"You and I both, brother, and for Aria to follow her, she'll regret that decision," Aiden added.

"I cannot believe Maddie followed suit. What in the hell got into her? I know she can be stubborn, but goddammit, she generally listens to what I say," Eden seethed. Jadis always had a way of stoking his temper.

"You have to ask? I believe Jadis could convince the Gods to follow her." Lars chuckled.

"Let's go. It won't be okay until her ass is back in my hands," Silas snarled.

The girls left the bar and walked to the old cemetery, chatting and drinking along the way. As they passed certain areas, she told Maddie and Aria the same stories Silas, Dante, and Bain had shared with her. She felt alive again, and the closer they got to the bayou, the more it pulled her in. *It feels amazing to be free; however, it feels strange.* She brushed it off thinking it was her need to feel authentic with the wild and all that resided in it once again.

"There it is," Jadis said as she took another drink from the bottle.

They made their way toward the old, worn, wrought-iron gate partially askew, allowing them to easily slip through the small opening. Maddie grabbed Jadis's arm, clearly anxious and a bit afraid to be there now that the sun dipped into the horizon. Jadis, however, reveled in its energy; the cemetery was exactly where they needed to be. Aria was also thrilled to be there. As soon as she slipped her body through the gate, she jogged ahead of the girls, joking around.

"Aria," Maddie called out. "Wait!"

They heard Aria laugh, and Jadis knew she was already headed in the direction of Rhiamon Locasta's crypt.

"Come on!" Aria shouted.

"Well, fuck it," Maddie stated as she ran after Aria

The whitewashed crypt stood before them, gleaming in the moonlight. The sounds of the bayou were alive and filled the night air with an ominous undertone. Jadis took a deep breath; the air was humid and heavy, and the same familiar scent of the rotten foliage and brackish water permeated her senses.

"Jadis, this was the best idea. It's amazing here, you have no idea how much I needed this," Maddie exclaimed.

They wandered, well—stumbled, through the old cemetery, reading the dates and names on the tombstones for the fun of it. Jadis pulled some of the stories from the dead and relayed them to the girls who weren't only intrigued but impressed as hell.

They stopped in front of a cracked, weathered tombstone, and Jadis read the inscription aloud, "'Out of time, out of breath. Barnabé Stockham 1772 – 1796.' Well, damn, he met a painful death."

"What happened?" Aria asked.

"He was bludgeoned to death. He had been drinking on the docks and stumbled into the wrong crowd. A ship of thieves had docked and were selling stolen goods. I can't picture the entire scene, but I know he was beaten and robbed before they killed him."

"How do you do that?" Maddie chuckled.

"It's like an imprint in time, energetic pictures," Jadis explained.

"Impressive," Maddie added. "Do another."

"Okay."

They walked a bit further and stopped in front of another weathered tombstone. "'Claudine Adélaïde 1780 – 1802.' Ohh—damn," Jadis stated.

"Go on," Aria urged.

"What a hell of a way to go. Apparently, she was a young maid, and her lady's house caught fire. Her employer was a hoarder of cats. She demanded she open the door and let them out. Claudine frantically ran toward the flames, and as soon as she opened the door, the cats, who were rabidly trying to escape, lunged. They attacked, having been panic stricken. She fell to the ground near the flames, trying to fight them off. Apparently, she died from an infection caused by all the scratches and bite wounds."

Aria laughed aloud. "Damn, cat scratch fever!" Her statement cracked Jadis and Maddie up.

"As tragic as it was, I can't help but find it funny," Maddie admitted.

They made their way to the water's edge and walked the length of the bayou. Maddie was scared as usual; everything seemed to spook her. Each time she heard a large splash off in the distance, she would jump and let out a yelp to Jadis and Aria's amusement. After an hour or so, the girls finally took a seat next to Rhiamon's crypt. Maddie and Aria were a bit sozzled, and their laugher overtook the sounds of the bayou. They finally felt their first taste of freedom in weeks, and they reveled in it.

It's so nice to be with each other alone for once, well alone outside the mansion's grounds anyway. "I have something else to show you." Jadis stood and pulled Aria and Maddie up.

"What now?" Maddie asked as she stumbled to her feet.

"You'll see." Jadis wanted to take them to the mausoleum Silas had showed her. The three of them drunkenly stumbled backward in a heap of laughter as they stood.

Jadis bumped into something behind her, and she spun around, only find Silas standing there, looking as mad as a wet hornet. She yelped, which caused Aria and Maddie to scream.

As sure as the sun sets, there stood their mates with Dante, Bain, and Lars in tow. The looks on their faces said as much as their silence. Jadis tried to back up, but Maddie and Aria stopped her; they were now hiding behind her with the crypt blocking their only exit.

"Baby, I can explain—" As soon as the words left Jadis's mouth, Silas placed his finger over her lips.

"Not—one—fucking—word," Silas said as he annunciated each and every syllable.

Jadis froze, however, her fear and instincts took over, and she disappeared into another swirling haze. The girls found themselves standing in the middle of what appeared to be a seedy side of town at first glance. It was dark, the neon lights that lit the tourist areas didn't exist and bar after bar lined the dirty streets. The crowds looked as rough as the area itself.

"Jadis, what did you do?" Maddie demanded as her fear turned into amusement.

"I don't even know, honestly. It just happened—I couldn't stop myself."

Aria bent over and placed her hand on her knees to catch her breath. "We better disappear for good this time."

"We can't stand here all night. Run!" Jadis demanded.

Where they had no idea, they just took off down the street. As they rounded the corner, they ran smack into their mates. Jadis, however, ran head on into Silas, bounced off his body, and landed on her ass.

Their mates snatched the girls up without a word spoken. They arrived back at the mansion in minutes, only to be greeted by Santiago and Luciana. They plopped the girls side by side onto the couch.

"Well, this feels familiar," Jadis stated, chuckling.

They looked up, only to see a half circle of frozen, angry, expressions surrounding them. Maddie couldn't help herself and laughed aloud.

"Well shit, looks like you've had your fair share," Eden shouted at Maddie.

"Do not yell at me, Eden. I won't have it!" Maddie shot back.

Eden pushed back his hair with both hands, interlaced his fingers at the back of his head, and stood motionless.

"Well, this has been fun, but I need to go to bed." Aria tried to stand, only to fall back down, causing Maddie and Jadis to burst out in a heap of uncontrollable laughter.

"It's clear they're too drunk to reason with. Maybe we should join them—no?" Lars joked.

"What are we going to do with them?" Dante asked, as he cocked his head in Jadis's direction.

"I haven't a clue right now." Eden had no idea how to contend with Maddie in her intoxicated state.

"The three of you will be dealt with appropriately," a velvety smooth voice said from behind the couch.

Jadis froze, knowing exactly who spoke. Her stomach lurched, and she placed her hands over her chest, trying her best to quell the erratic hammering of her heart.

Santiago was now front and center, kneeling before them with his forearms resting on his knees.

Maddie and Aria's laughter ended, and they practically crawled behind Jadis. The hushed silence was more nerve racking than words could be. Jadis looked to Silas, who stood motionless with his arms crossed.

Santiago captured her attention. "Do not divert your eyes from me, dear girl."

Jadis took heed and looked back at Santiago as painful as it was.

"Jadis, your primal drive runs deep, and your powers are as old as the Gods themselves. You're wild, and impetuous, and ruled by instinct. You have no fear, which I can respect, however, fear is also survival."

I assume this is how scary the Prince of Darkness would look if I were standing in the threshold of purgatory. Santiago's voice was eerily calm, but his words and the intensity in which he stared at her seared through her body like a dragon's flame.

Santiago let out a heavy sigh. "My dear girl, *the threshold of purgatory* is exactly where you'll end up should Abigor get his hands on you. He has no humanity left."

Abigor? Jadis repeated to herself.

Santiago looked directly to Maddie and Aria. "As for the two of you, if he gets his hands on you, you'll be treated no better than pigs or whores. A swift death would be more forgiving. Jadis—Maddie, the two you are mated to my son and nephew. As for you, Aria, you'll soon become Aiden's mate, which puts your lives in greater peril. I gave an order, and the three of you dared to defy me. Where there's defiance, there's punishment." Santiago stood, saying nothing more.

Jadis glanced at her girls but kept her thoughts to herself. *I can't fathom what he means by being punished. All I know is that I wished I could disappear again.*

Silas cocked his head at her. "I dare you to try, my love," he said aloud, which caused everyone to look at her, Santiago included. Jadis said nothing, thought nothing.

"There'll be no freedom," Santiago added before turning back to everyone else. "You know what needs to be done. I expect you all to join me in thirty minutes. We still have business we need to attend to." Santiago and Luciana disappeared as soon as he finished speaking.

The girls looked at each other, not saying a word; they had been silenced.

"Well, I'll be dammed. No words?" Bain asked in jest.

The girls sneered at him but remained silent. They had no idea what would happen after what Santiago had said to them. Their mates approached them for the first time since Santiago entered the room. They stood to meet them face to face, waiting for the anvil to drop.

Jadis placed her palms on Silas's chest, trying once again to quell the beast standing before her. He gently cupped his hands on either side of her face and held her tightly before speaking, "You've only been a fragment of my life, yet your constant defiance is all of my madness!"

"I believe she is everyone's madness," Dante growled.

"And your mine, Dante," Jadis chided.

"Oooh— mockery. She must be angry," Dante replied sounding amused.

"Well, this is one hell of a night already," Lars interjected.

Jadis ignored Dante's last comment, as well as Lars', and turned her attention back to her bigger issue. "Baby, you know I didn't put myself in danger on purpose. I can't explain it, but there's a pull I feel—"

Silas interrupted her before she could continue, "Are you going to stand here and try to justify your actions right now?"

"I'm not trying to justify anything, and I certainly don't want to fight with you," she said sincerely.

"Nor I you, however you continue to provoke me." Silas suddenly laughed aloud. He walked over to Bain, took the bottle from him, and proceeded to fill his glass as Jadis stood in silence. "You, my love, are guided by forces beyond your control," Silas said before turning to Dante. "Whatever will I do with her?"

"Brother, this is a familiar situation we find ourselves in. Once again, I'm afraid I don't have the answers."

Silas took a seat on the couch. "Come," he stated quietly as he motioned for her to sit with him. She plopped into his lap and curled up as he wrapped his arm tightly around her and stroked her hair.

"I'm sorry, I don't mean to anger you or to cause you any grief," Jadis apologized.

"My love, I know." He grabbed the back of her head, turned her face toward him, and rested his forehead on hers. Once he pulled away, she looked up to see an expression of amusement rather than anger, and it frightened her.

Eden took a seat with Maddie in his lap, as did Aiden with Aria. The girls looked to each other with the same confusion, so Jadis opened the private conversation once again. *"What is going on? Why are they so calm right now?"*

"I have no idea. I'm confused. Normally, Eden would have pulled me to our room to finish this."

"I'm afraid they're up to something big, and I assume Santiago is behind it," Aria replied.

They sat quietly, trying to figure out what was going to happen, too intimidated to ask. They kept looking to each other to see who would be the brave one to speak up.

Dante stood and set his glass on the end table. "This has been fun, but father is waiting."

"Agreed. Get up, baby. We have work to do." Silas patted her thigh, slid her over, and stood.

"You're leaving?" she asked.

"Yes, it's time to get to work," Silas replied.

"I guess I'll see you in a bit?" She tried to get him to let her know something, anything, but he said nothing more.

Silas turned back to her and winked. "I'll be back in few hours. Don't go anywhere, my love."

As soon as their mates were out of sight, the girls let out a heavy sigh of relief, trying to decipher their evasiveness.

"That's not how I thought this would end. There's more to this than meets the eye. I'll be dammed if Silas is just walking away that calmly."

"What should we do?" Maddie asked nervously.

"I don't know about the two of you, but I could use another drink. This whole situation has sobered me up." Aria chuckled.

"Works for me." Jadis stood, and they walked over to the bar and filled their glasses.

"Well, what now?" Maddie asked.

"I have no idea. We should just sit outside and wait to meet our maker. This is far from over," Jadis replied.

They headed for the back door, and a swift breeze stopped them midstride. In an instant, four unknown Nosferatu Warriors appeared as if out of nowhere. They jumped and screamed in unison.

"Shit," Jadis exclaimed as they ran for the stairs, only to be stopped head on by one of the warriors.

Instinctually, Jadis disappeared, however he reached out and had her by the arm. He quickly pulled her from the energetic buzz and dragged her to the couch, where Aria and Maddie had already been placed; they had officially been subdued.

The warrior who grabbed Jadis, having the ability to snatch her out of mid-air, stopped any and all thoughts she had about leaving. The warriors stood at attention as if their commander were in front of them. They were expressionless and fully armed. One of them cocked his head at Jadis as if he were curious.

He's familiar. I've seen him before, Jadis thought, when it suddenly dawned on her. *The valley! Holy hell, that's Sigurd!*

They were statuesque, easily over six feet tall and perfectly built. They looked as if they just stepped off an ancient battlefield. Each had a sword sheathed on their backs, along with a couple of daggers tightly attached to the side of their thighs. Behind the course, dark, closely shaven facial hair, the women saw how ruggedly handsome they were. Their heads were also shaved close to the sides, while the top was a tousled mix of long strands of free hair, mixed with long braids, all of which were intertwined and pulled back into a loose ponytail. Their tunics were partially covered by tight-fitting leather vests, and their trousers were tucked into boots which appeared to be from the old world.

Their mates materialized out of nowhere and stood before them. Silas bent down in front of Jadis with his arms resting on his knees, looking exactly like his father.

"I would like you to meet a few of my Mortem warriors. The three of you will be locked down from here on out, call it imprisoned if you will. You won't so much as step outside without one of us or one of my men with you. IF you step out with one of my men, you'll need our permission of course."

"*Imprisoned*? Silas, you can not be serious right now. I surely won't ask your permission to go outside." She tried to stand, but Silas firmly placed his hand on her shoulder. He held up his other hand ever so slightly with his elbow bent; only two of his fingers were raised, the rest were folded neatly at his palm. What sounded like sliding bolts and clicking locks permeated the silence. The reality they were being caged sank in. The girls looked to each other, stunned and confused.

Silas stood as Eden stepped forward. "You'll also be confined to the parlor. Maddie, Aria, when you feel the need to eat, you'll be escorted to the kitchen." Eden waited for Maddie to protest.

"Eden, you cannot do this!"

"I can, I will, and I have," he stated firmly.

"Aiden, I'll just go home to the oasis. I won't be your prisoner, we have yet to be mated." Aria stood, only to be held in place by Aiden.

"You are mine, Aria. You won't be leaving."

"The discussions are over." Silas turned to Sigurd and placed a hand on his shoulder.

"Milord," he nodded.

"Sigurd, know that Jadis cannot be trusted. Don't let her looks fool you. She's as cunning and devious as the Heks you dealt with in Hadeland."

Sigurd nodded. "Rest assured, milord— she won't stray." He then looked at Jadis. "Will you, lass?"

She subtly shook her head no, and their mates disappeared as quickly as they had appeared.

"There's a lot not being said," Jadis stated aloud, not caring who heard her. "I have a sneaking suspicion this has more to do with the name Santiago mentioned than us sneaking out."

"Who the hell is Abigor?" Maddie questioned.

"Where the hell is Hadeland?" Aria asked.

Maddie, Jadis, and Aria looked at each and then back at the warriors and shrugged their shoulders.

CHAPTER 10

Abigor sat in his stone throne, watching the fighters engaged in hand-to-hand combat. The fights took place in one of several pits situated below him. The whoops, hollers, and cheers from the combative, chaotic crowd, the majority of whom were members of his clan, as well as his warriors, reverberated off the stone walls. He had one of his concubines sitting in his lap, tending to his every whim, however depraved it may be.

His brother Vidar approached to relay his newfound information. He took a seat next to Abigor.

"I have news, brother," Vidar offered.

Abigor motioned his hand in his direction. "Go on."

"The Dhamphyr exists."

"Maĭnata mu, that is good news. Is she as powerful as the legends suggest?"

"From what little I've been told, yes. Our scout from Jabari's clan was there when she was taken by the Baskale. The kuchka actually killed it if what he says is true," Vidar stated.

"Where is the scout now?"

"Dead. Once we extracted the information, I didn't see a need to keep him alive."

"And where is the Dhamphyr?"

"Unfortunately, she is mated to Silas Montiago."

"Well shit, that is a problem." Abigor rubbed his stubble-laden chin, realizing she wasn't an easy target. "Where are they?"

"As far as I know, they may be somewhere in Fréyonne. As of last night, rumor has it Santiago had arrived there a few weeks ago. We can only assume he's there to see his bairns. If Silas is there, the Dhamphyr will be with him," Vidar suggested.

"True, and she'll be heavily protected. He will have his men stationed around her at all times." His mood soured knowing not what, but who he was up against.

Vidar picked up an empty cup. "Kuchka! Where's my fucking ale?"

Another one of their concubines filled his cup from a copper pitcher and stepped back without haste.

"Get the fuck off me, your presence is annoying." Abigor shoved the girl out of his lap and onto the stone floor.

She quickly gathered herself together and sat at his feet with her arms wrapped tightly around her knees, which she had pulled against her chest. Her dress was tattered, torn, covered in dirt, and she was barefoot. She had new, as well as old cuts and bruises covering the majority of her face and body.

Abigor and Vidar's younger brother walked in and took a seat. "What have I missed? You seem to be in a worse mood than when I left an hour ago?" Arkyn raised two fingers, and his cup was filled by a concubine.

"The Dhamphyr is real as the legends themselves. Your brother has suggested she is mated to Silas," Abigor answered with a snarl.

"So, that would explain the mood, but she does exist?" Arkyn asked in disbelief as he finished his ale.

"As real as you or your fucking brother," Vidar replied.

"Where's the fucking ale?" Arkyn shouted. The young girl filled his cup back up as quickly as she could. Arkyn landed a back hand across her face, knocking her to the floor. "Why must I always have to ask for my cup to be filled? You're as useful as a dead feeder," he roared.

She gathered herself and managed to stand quickly. "I'm sorry—m—my, milord. I was filling the pitcher," she stammered.

Arkyn landed a front kick to her stomach knocking her to the ground. She was slightly breathless as the kick had partially knocked the wind out of her. "Did I ask you to fucking speak?" He turned to his brothers. "Shiban kuchka is bezpolezen! Why do you bother to keep that whore around?"

"Abigor likes the way his dick feels in her mouth." Vidar laughed, causing Arkyn to laugh along. "How do you plan to get your hands on the Dhamphyr if she is mated to Silas?" There was silence.

They turned their attention back to the grisly fight. The vampires in the pits were bloody, battered, broken, and one of them was well on his way out. They were warriors and fighters from other clans who had been captured, enslaved, and forced to fight to the death. The last fighter standing would move on to the next round or not, depending on whether or not Abigor approved of his fighting skills. They took prisoners of every race from across his country during their night raids and the ensuing battles that followed.

Just as one of the fighters was about to be put to death. Vidar and Arkin jumped to their feet, yelling, "Death! Death! Death!" The winning fighter shoved his hand into the wounded opponent's chest. He stood and raised his hand, displaying the fighter's heart, which was still slowly pulsing. The crowd roared with approval and chanted life, "Zhivot! Zhivot! Zhivot!"

Abigor stood and held up both of his hands; one thumb was pointed up, the other pointed down. "What shall it be tonight?" he shouted. "Pobeda? Or smŭrt?" Meaning Victory or death.

The cheering crowd chanted in favor of victory, "Pobeda! Pobeda! Pobeda!"

Abigor dropped his hand with the thumb pointing down, and there was another uproar of cheers from the rambunctious, drunken crowd.

"Your reward tonight shall be food and ale!" Abigor shouted.

The winning fighter bowed to Abigor and was escorted back to his iron and stone cell. Vidar and Arkin took their seats, waiting for the next round to begin.

"You failed to answer my question. How do you plan to take the Dhamphyr from Silas?" Arkin asked again.

"I wasn't expecting Silas's clan would be involved with her. It's more than concerning, but it can be done."

"Exactly how do you plan on doing that, brother?" Vidar asked. "Is she even worth it?"

"Worth it? Worth it?" Abigor stood in front of his brother, seething in anger. "Don't tell me you're afraid of that bastard?" He whipped out his dagger and placed the blade against Vidar's throat, which caused a trickle of blood run down his neck.

"No, brother, that's not what I'm saying. What purpose does she serve? I'm just curious as to why you want her in the first place?" Vidar snarled.

"If she is what the legends speak of, with her powers, I'll rule all of Bergelême! Is that reason enough for you?" Abigor roared back.

Vidar held up both hands in front of him. "I admire your ambitions, brother. I wasn't aware of your intentions."

Abigor slowly pulled his dagger away from Vidar's throat. He grabbed his cup and sat back down.

Vidar and Arkin looked at each other but didn't speak.

Abigor grabbed a fist full of the girl's hair that had been cowering at his feet and wrenched her head back. "Now, kuchka," he snarled into her face.

She got up onto her knees, placed her face between his legs, and unlaced his trousers. He kept his hand on the back of her head as she willingly took his dick into her mouth; he was her sire after all.

Abigor didn't look to either of his brothers; he just looked down. "We can't exactly get to the kuchka ourselves, so I'll see that she comes to us."

Vidar and Arkin didn't answer. Vidar snapped his fingers, and two more concubines were at his and Arkin's feet.

"When the fights are over, meet me in the Egregore. Bring the Enchantress and the sacrifice with you," Abigor demanded.

It had been a few weeks since the girls had been put on lockdown and despite Silas's warriors' lethal demeanor, they were genuinely polite, well-mannered, and respectful.

A few days into their lockdown, the undeniable urge for Jadis to get outside for a bit returned; only the pull was more powerful than before. She stood and turned toward the back door, feeling as if she were being summoned. As soon as the thought crossed her mind, Sigurd stood in front of her with his head slightly tilted to the side, as if he were waiting on her to make her move.

"Disobeying a direct order never ends well, lass." Sigurd's tone may have been calm, but the underlying command was clear.

"I wasn't leaving, Sigurd," she huffed.

"Duly noted." He stood stoic and waited for her to walk away from the door.

"You going to stand there and stare at me all night?" she asked, with raised eyebrows.

"If need be," he replied.

"Jadis, come over here and sit with us," Maddie offered.

Jadis rolled her eyes and plopped down next to Maddie and Aria. They had succumbed to their mate's control over them. Jadis, however, had feelings she hid from everyone, Silas included.

For weeks now, they had been working around the clock for the most part. Of course, the girls weren't privy to what they were doing, and their unwillingness to disclose even minor details became more than alarming. They had just filled their glasses when their mates finally returned.

Jadis jumped up and ran directly into Silas's arms the moment he entered. "You're back," she whispered.

"Yes, baby, I am. What do you say we head upstairs?"

"Do you even need to ask?" They made their way to the bedroom, and Silas tossed her onto her back on the bed and crawled over the top her.

"I've missed my vampire."

"And I you, my love. I have every intention of showing you just how much."

After feeding and satisfying other more pressing needs, they slept for a few hours with their bodies intertwined. *Silas seems exhausted. It's so good to have him back, but I can tell he has more on his mind than he is letting on,* Jadis thought as she rolled over so she could face him.

"A penny for your thoughts?" she asked.

Silas remained quiet as he played with her hair, while she lay snuggled on his chest. After a few moments of deafening silence, she raised up onto her elbow.

"Tell me, baby, what's going on? This is serious, isn't it?"

"Yes, love, I'm afraid it is, and I think it's time for you to know. I'll gather everyone together. We can meet them in the parlor."

"You're scaring me."

"There's no need to be scared, it's just time I filled you in on what we've been doing."

He replied sweetly, but his words felt placid. "Bullshit, you're hiding something from me."

He playfully rolled over the top of her and pulled her from the bed. "Get dressed, baby. We'll go have a drink."

"This ought to be good," she snarked under her breath.

"Come here, baby." Silas pulled her into his body and held her.

"I assume it's bad?"

"It's concerning is all, I won't lie to you."

"Fabulous."

He cupped her face in his hands, and she held his forearms. "Have I ever failed you?"

"No, but when you talk like this, I know shit's about to get real."

"Baby, it's fine." He smiled warmly.

As they walked into the parlor, Sigurd stood and greeted Silas. "Milord."

Silas nodded and took a seat with Jadis next to him. "I think it's time to fill them in," Silas stated.

"Great." Jadis sighed.

"What's wrong?" Aria asked.

"Who knows, but I assume we're about to find out," Jadis replied.

Silas and Jadis took a seat, and he told them some of the basics, while Jadis sat nervously, waiting for the punch to the gut. Santiago and Luciana joined shortly thereafter and looked casual enough, but the energy Jadis felt raise beneath Silas's cool, outer demeanor when they entered was undeniable.

"Good—good, you're all here. I'll get right to the point. Syth and Agaeus are heading this way. Jadis, your sisters will be joining us tonight," Santiago admitted.

"Why? Has something happened?" *Why Silas would allow my sisters to join us while I'm on lockdown is beyond me.*

"Nothing has happened. It's just business. Obviously, Syth and Agaeus would bring their mates," Santiago replied.

"That simple? I don't think so." Jadis stood from Silas's lap and looked to everyone but Santiago and Luciana. "One of you better fess up and now," she demanded before turning her attention to Dante and Bain.

"As for the two of you, neither of you has made one smartass comment the entire time we've been sitting here." She felt herself take a couple of steps back, and Silas stood.

"Calm, baby. We're going to explain it all." Silas reached for her arm and pulled her into him. She didn't have to see him nod at his men to know that's what he did.

Santiago took a seat across from where Silas and Jadis had been sitting. "Please sit," Santiago demanded politely.

Silas sat and pulled her into his lap on the love seat.

"Agaeus and Syth will be here momentarily and all will be revealed," Santiago added.

Jadis sat quietly, feeling like the air had been sucked from the room. Agaeus and Syth finally walked in from the back door with Skye and Ivory in tow. She jumped up and ran to greet them. Maddie and Aria followed, just as excited to see them as Jadis was. They hadn't seen them in about a month now, and Jadis couldn't have been happier. They greeted each other with a tight embrace and Mag and Limi jumped all over them.

"I can't believe you're here. I feel there's a storm on the horizon," Jadis whispered.

"Something's up. Agaeus and Syth are being ridiculous. They haven't so much as let us out of their sight. When they're working, we have multiple guards watching our every move," Skye added. "We can't even go outside."

"What the hell is happening?" Ivory questioned.

"They won't tell us shit," Aria stated.

"Believe me, they're being just as evasive here," Jadis replied.

"Exactly what the hell have you done now, Jadis?" Ivory asked accusatorily.

"What? I haven't done anything."

"That's not exactly true," Maddie confessed.

"Jadis did some kind of disappearing shit and snuck us all out of the house after we were told not to go anywhere," Aria chuckled.

"I assume there's a bit more to the story?" Skye questioned.

Jadis rolled her eyes, dropping the subject since they had an audience. "Later."

"By the way, who the fuck are those warriors?" Skye whispered.

"Our bodyguards," Jadis answered.

"Holy shit, you must have pissed off the Gods themselves," Ivory whispered, with a quiet chuckle. "The one sitting across from Silas, is that their father Santiago?"

"Yes," Jadis replied.

"Damn," Ivory and Skye replied together.

"Come, you all will have plenty of time to catch up with one another," Santiago called.

The girls walked over and took a seat, waiting to hear what would be revealed. "There's much to discuss, so I'll get right to the point. Jadis you're, what is known as a Dhamphyr," Santiago blurted out.

She darted her eyes between the girls in confusion. She looked to them but for what reason, she didn't know. They looked as confused as she did.

Santiago continued, "As you know, you're a hybrid. Hecate's blood runs deep within you, which makes you the rarest breed of Nosferatu in existence. We suspect there are maybe a handful more in hiding around the world. However, even if they combined what they possess together, they would still not yield what you have the capability of conjuring. You don't yet know or understand the powers you have the ability to harness. Unfortunately, when one carries power that great, it does not go unnoticed. The threats become just as great, and you have been discovered."

Santiago said it as if he has just ordered lunch. Jadis was in utter shock and disbelief. She didn't know who to look at, and she couldn't bring herself to speak. *The fact that no one is making a joke of my silence confirms my fear is justified.* She felt as if rotten, gnarled roots were growing beneath her feet and pulling her into the depths of a hell-filled pandemonium.

Silas turned her head, so she was directly facing him. "Baby, don't be afraid. You're safe. We're just explaining who and what you are. I know you've had many questions as I have. Until now, we didn't have the answers."

Jadis finally managed to speak. "I assume this isn't the end of it? Exactly who has discovered me and why does it matter?"

Again, no one spoke. She could tell they were speaking, just not on a level she could hear. "Abigor! The sooner you tell me the truth, the sooner I can leave," she stated bluntly.

Silas's eyebrow shot up in shock. "Leave? You'll do no such thing."

She got up from his lap feeling as if she were suffocating. She walked toward the bar to get a much-needed breath of air.

Silas stood, and she felt everyone else shifting in their seats. She had to close her eyes to stop from trembling. She felt as if an unnatural pull was dragging her behind a running stallion. She placed her hands on the edge of the bar, stepped back, and rested her head between her forearms, trying to calm herself.

"Aria, I need to get out of here. I need your help and your oasis," Jadis suggested.

"Yes, absolutely. This shit is freaking me out too, not to mention I owe you one." She got up from Aiden's lap and headed to the bar.

Aiden stood, gently grabbed her arm, and raised a questioning eyebrow. "Just where do you think you're going?"

"Relax, I'm checking on Jadis. Where do you think I'm going?" She looked around, motioning towards Silas's warriors. Reluctantly, he let go of her arm.

"Be ready, son," Santiago stated to Silas. *"The pull has taken hold of her, she'll be beyond reason or rational thinking. The sorcery is dark and powerful."*

"I understand, Father," Silas replied with a heavy sigh.

"This won't be easy. I don't even know if I can pull it off," Jadis admitted telepathically.

"Apparently, you can do whatever you want, given the chance," Aria replied.

"Can I tell you something?"

"Always, what is it?"

"Something's wrong with me, but I don't want Silas to know."

"What is it, maybe I can help?"

"I don't know. I have an unnerving need to run, and I don't even know where I'm supposed to run to." Her sudden admission shocked Aria.

"This is concerning. You should tell Silas. You're making me nervous, especially after what we've just been told."

"Jadis, what's wrong?" Ivory asked. She, Skye, and Maddie had now joined her and Aria.

"Tell us, Jadis," Maddie added.

Once Jadis gathered herself, she stood back up, but she remained facing the bar.

"Something's wrong with her," Aria whispered.

"We're not asking again, what is it?" Skye demanded.

"Honestly, I don't know. Something woke me the other night and ever since, I've felt like I need to be somewhere else." Jadis snarled her words.

"Well, forget the oasis. You need to tell Silas," Aria demanded. Unbeknownst to her, Jadis had now *turned*.

"No," she snarled, shocking everyone in the parlor, herself included. She turned to face the firing squad. Their blank expressions were ones that unfortunately she was very familiar with, and the girls had stepped away from her.

"Apparently, I have the ability to do whatever I want from what you've said," she growled.

Silas moved in, turned her around to face him, and put both hands on her shoulders. She placed her palms on his chest and pushed back.

"Stop, Silas. I can't breathe. Leave me!" she demanded. She looked up into his face and felt terrible. "I'm sorry, baby," she said as she jumped into his arms. "I'm so sorry. You know I didn't mean that. I don't know what came over me!" She felt the tears pool in her eyes.

Silas held her so tight, she couldn't breathe. "Silas," she whispered. He let out a sigh and let loose ever so slightly.

"Shhh—I know, baby. I understand your confusion, but we have more to discuss." He gave her another reassuring squeeze before setting her down.

She looked at her girls and apologized to them as well. They waved it off with a kind smile, however it was one that hid their true concern.

"Come sit back down, my love," Silas urged.

"Jadis, what you're feeling is an unnatural pull, one that comes from blackness," Santiago explained as soon as they took a seat.

"Well, that's just great! Haven't I been pulled into enough blackness for one lifetime?" she snarled back.

"We already have a grasp on it, baby," Silas admitted.

"And you decided to disclose this to me on the night when the moon is waning, a night of bad omens?"

"Dear girl, it is for that very reason we're all here. The very reason we're now telling you all you need to know," Santiago answered.

"Please go on then. I'll just bathe in the pool of venom that shall soon become my life."

"First and foremost, you're safe with us, safe within these walls," Santiago offered.

Silas shifted her partially out of his lap, so she was facing him. "Well, this ought to be good," she stated.

Silas explained the situation, "We briefly informed you and your sisters about a clan ruled by a vampire named Abigor. Father also warned you about him the night you all disappeared. He is his father's successor and is out to conquer and rule all of Bergelême—he always has. Abigor's father took his clan to the underground caverns laying beneath Bergelême. His clan chose to hide there during the Great War we told you about, the war his father's clan chose to abandon. Their only mission was to ensure their own survival. They're known as the rulers of the Sixty Legions of Hades. After hundreds of years living isolated in the underworld, they've become masters in the art of black magic. They're a merciless, rogue clan who've been at war with the rest of the clans for centuries. The only entrance into their world is through the Cavern to Hades which sits in the Radomirov Mountains. Bergelême is still quite primitive in comparison to the modern part of the world. Most of the clans living there choose to live as their ancestors did a thousand years ago. Their cities are more like modern-day villages."

"What does it have to do with me?" Jadis questioned.

"As Silas stated, you're the purest of Dhamphyrs. Your powers reach beyond the realm of both the living and the dead, light and dark. You now possess the powers of the Old Gods as well as Nosferatu," Santiago explained.

"I understand, but what the hell has that to do with Bergelême?"

"Should someone such as Abigor gain control of you, manipulate you to do his bidding, all clans living in the land would be in grave danger. He could conquer all of Bergelême should he—" Santiago began.

Silas interjected and cut his father off for the first time. "Enough," he demanded, as he held up his hand.

Jadis was taken aback; she plopped onto her back on the loveseat and covered her face with both hands.

"This cannot be headed in a good direction." Silas reached for her hands, trying to remove them from her face. "Stop," she demanded, holding up one hand as she covered her face with her arm instead. "Silas, I don't even want to know where this is headed."

"Up," Silas barked. Everyone around them obliged, his father included. They all headed toward the bar to give Jadis some breathing room.

Silas lifted her and pulled her body into his lap. She wrapped her arms tightly around his neck. His warm embrace, his love, his strength, enveloped her like a shroud of protection.

Luciana stood with Santiago. "Darling, I believe she has had enough for one evening. We should let her rest and have some time with Silas. He has been gone many days and nights. They haven't had much time together since you've arrived."

"She has to know everything, this cannot wait any longer. You know as well as we do the danger she faces." He kissed Luciana, and not another word was spoken between them.

"This is fucked up all the way around," Aria said to the girls quietly.

"Yes it is. I feel bad. It's as if the gift Hecate has bestowed upon her are also her curse. Something has been chasing her since before we met. I don't think I could handle it like she has. There has to be something we can do?" Maddie said.

Eden had been listening to their conversation. "You'll do nothing, my love. This is beyond any of the four of you. You'll leave this to us, understand? Skye, Ivory, that goes for the two of you as well. Am I in any way unclear?"

"Aria, you'll also do nothing," Aiden demanded.

"I'm expecting an answer," Eden demanded as he looked at Skye and Ivory.

"We understand." They both nodded in unison, afraid of challenging him.

"You stopped your father from speaking any further, tell me what he was about to say." Jadis sat back and looked at Silas's face. *Here comes the final blow.*

"He'll have to take you as his mate to accomplish his goals," Silas admitted.

"We're mated, Silas. What makes him think I would ever agree to that? There's no way in hell it would ever happen. I think you all have lost your minds!" *This entire situation just keeps spiraling downwards, into an abysmal pool of blackness.*

Everyone had now made their way over to them once again, and the girls looked mortified.

"How?" Jadis demanded. Again, no one spoke, but it didn't take long for their silence to speak for itself.

"Ohhh shit! They'll have to kill you, won't they?" Jadis now stood, her body trembling with the realization they would take Silas's life to get to her.

Aria was in shock. "What you're saying is that Jadis is to be mated to Abigor, and Silas is just standing in his way?"

"Yes, for a simple answer," Santiago answered.

I've never known anyone that could say so little but convey so much. She caught Aria's glance and opened a private conversation.

"The oasis has been hidden since life has existed. No one gets in, no one gets out without permission should Jabari order it sealed. You and Silas could stay there. I don't believe there's anywhere safer. You'll have to convince Silas, but we can leave the moment you say the word. Just not aloud." Aria let out a half-hearted chuckle.

"The oasis it is." Jadis used the opportunity to step closer to Aria, while she turned her attention back to Silas.

"Aria, don't even contemplate whatever the hell the two of you are speaking about." Aiden took hold of her forearm. "I know the two of you are up to something."

"I don't know what you're talking about, Aiden!" Aria tried to pull away to no avail.

Santiago stood. "No one will be leaving, at least not you girls."

"What is that supposed to mean?" Jadis turned to face Santiago directly. *It's time to stop being polite and obeying their every command.*

"Jadis, you and the girls will all be staying put with Silas's warriors, as well as Luciana. The rest of us are heading out tonight."

"Bullshit!" It just popped out of her mouth before she had a chance to think about what she was saying and to whom.

Everyone's face remained stone cold as she had just challenged Santiago. He stepped forward to confront her directly. Jadis, however, chose to stand her ground regardless of how intimidating he was.

"Dear girl, I understand your fear as well as your need to protect your mate, however, that wasn't a question requiring an argument. It has been spoken."

"It has been spoken?" she challenged. "I won't allow Silas's life to be put on the line for me. I'll choose death first," she snarled, bearing her canines at Santiago.

Silas moved in behind her and wrapped a tight arm around her waist. *It's the perfect opportunity to take Silas with us.* "Now!" she stated to Aria.

Aria and Jadis gripped each other's forearms, and the three of them disappeared.

They came crashing down on the lush vegetation covering the ground within the hidden oasis. Within seconds, their clan had them surrounded. The looks on their faces were nothing short of outrage, except for Silas's warriors, whose expressions were calm and unemotional.

Silas was half-crouched over Jadis as was Aiden over Aria.

Seconds later, Jadis felt a gentle breeze, and Jabari had them surrounded, a squad of fully armed warriors with weapons drawn.

"Well, hell," he stated. "I couldn't imagine who had entered my oasis so suddenly. I should have known." He began to laugh before realizing the situation appeared to be quite serious.

"I assume this would be Jadis's doing?" he asked.

"Unfortunately, yes," Silas snarled, not taking his eyes off her.

"Santiago, my old friend, what brings you, other than the obvious?" Jabari asked as he and Santiago formally greeted each other.

"Jabari, good to see you as well. I would love to say this is a friendly visit. Unfortunately, I cannot." Santiago glared in Jadis's direction. "You and I shall give them a minute to gather themselves. You need to know the seriousness of the situation. I assume the oasis is protected based on our conversation a few weeks ago?" Santiago asked as they moved away from the crowd to speak freely.

"Yes, hence the reason I was surprised with the sudden appearance. I'll have it sealed and rest assured, my old friend, all is safe, as is your family."

"It needs to be done now," Santiago added.

Jabari spoke in his native tongue to a few of his warriors, "Aiktab alnasi huna 'ankhbar hurras almaebad bi'iighlaq alwaha." He ordered them to head back to the temple guardians and seal the oasis before turning back to Santiago. "My only concern is how did she manage to escape with all of you in tow?"

"It was a temporary adjustment in security, energetically speaking, when Agaeus and Syth joined us," Santiago explained.

"Say no more." Jabari understood.

"Jadis, goddammit, stand!" Silas pulled her to her feet.

Dante grabbed hold of her other arm and met her face to face. "You continue to run on the edge of darkness, and it's infuriating!" His retort was based more from his emotions than his anger.

Jabari began to walk away with Santiago. "Come," he called before looking to Santiago again. "Given the circumstances, they should finish this in private."

Silas dragged Jadis to the temple, keeping a firm grip on her arm as they made their way through the lush vegetation.

The palm trees gave way, and an expansive courtyard appeared before them. Water fountains, lush gardens, and pools adorned the landscape. Giant lion-like statues lined both sides of the sandstone path leading to the temple itself. Giant sandstone columns rose above them, each having been linked to the next by a perfect archway. The curved ceilings had been inlaid with gold, while painted pictures covered the remaining stone work.

Jabari clapped his hands twice. "Take everyone to the Great Hall." Six beautiful ladies dressed in silk led their group down an open corridor adjacent to a large pool in the center of the temple.

"Silas, if you need a moment of privacy with your mate, head up the stairs. There is a room on the left." He pointed "Feel free to join us when you can," Jabari offered politely.

Silas nodded to Jabari and led her up a long, sandstone staircase, and then down a lengthy hallway. In the absence of flaming torches, the dimness gave way to modern electricity.

They entered another large bedroom chamber, and the door slammed shut behind them. He spun her around, so she was facing him. "Why do you continue to defy me?"

"I won't now, nor will I ever let you put your life on the line for me. You can be as mad as you want for all I care. I'll call upon the powers of the Old Gods if it means keeping you from risking your life!" she yelled.

"You have too much faith in your Gods!" he snarled.

"And you don't have enough!"

"My faith lies in Nosferatu. I was born to be a warrior, it's my life's blood. I'll fight my enemies in the fields but not in my home! Abigor will come for you, and I choose to stand between my enemy and my mate."

"And what am I to do if I lose you? What home do I have then?" she yelled even though she felt the need to cry.

"However heartfelt your intentions are, they are nonetheless danger-ous. After all this time, have I ever failed to come home to you?"

"This is different. I can feel it. As you said, they will kill you to get to me!"

"Once again, I find myself in a futile argument. You're all that I love and hold sacred. I'll return as I always have."

Jadis felt the tears stream down her face. Silas grabbed her and picked her up in his arms.

Jadis did all she could to stop him from leaving, and she had failed miserably. *He's going to leave regardless of how I feel about it.* Her tears became that of sobs.

"Baby, shhh—I'm not mad, darling. Please don't cry. I'll never leave you."

"I can't live my life without you," she sobbed.

"Baby, it'll never come to that. I need you to believe me." Silas held her close and washed her in his warmth to calm her down.

CHAPTER 11

Back in the Great Hall, the meeting was well under way. Jabari sat stoic at the end of the long, wooden table. "We have a major concern. Our warrior is still missing, and we believe him to be a traitor and now an enemy of all our clans. We haven't located him since the night Jadis killed the Baskale."

"I assume he would be the vampire we all smelled in the cave as well as the pit?" Eden asked.

"Yes, without further proof, I would be afraid to assume otherwise," Jabari agreed.

"One less enemy to contend with. I would also assume he's no longer with the living. Once they retrieved the information they wanted, he would no longer serve a purpose," Aiden interjected.

Silas entered and took a seat beside his father, looking forlorn.

"Where's Jadis?" Dante asked, sounding as dreadful as Silas looked.

"She's currently under the watchful eye of Sigurd and his warriors."

Eden spread a map out, and everyone leaned over the table to go over the strategy and positions each clan would assail.

"This will be no easy feat. We'll need to draw Abigor out. He will be well armed and well equipped. He'll come for me first and foremost. Jabari, I'll need a legion waiting in the shadows." Silas pointed to the river on the map. "Here along the extended tree line just beyond the Trigrad River."

"Understood," Jabari replied.

"Father, I'll need you to take the Trigrad Gorge, just north of the Trigrad village, where they'll no doubt have warriors waiting."

"I've got it." Santiago placed his hand on Silas's shoulder as he continued giving the orders.

"Eden, you and I, as well as our brothers and my Legion of Mortem Warriors, will take the valley of Ides, leading directly to the entrance of the cavern."

"Understood," Eden replied.

Silas ran his finger along the map, pointing out each area. "Once your location is secured, we'll all converge at the entrance and make our way into Abigor's lair. They don't use modern-day weapons, but they're nonetheless merciless with the sword. Dante, Bain, as you know, it will be imperative the two of you are ready for whatever black magic they'll surely be yielding. Do not doubt their power or deceptions."

"We are prepared, brother," Dante replied.

"We leave for the Radomirov Mountains tonight. Gather your gear, we head out in an hour," Santiago stated.

Silas turned to Jabari. "I assume the chamber is ready?" he asked, with a heavy heart.

"It is." Jabari nodded, having felt all of Silas's torment.

Silas contemplated whether or not it could hold her and looked to Jabari without speaking.

"Rest assured, we know she's a Dhamphyr. We've done what is needed," Jabari replied, answering his unspoken concern. "I give you my word, she'll be well taken care of, my friend."

"Dante, let's do this." Silas sighed.

Jadis lay on the bed, curled up in a blanket, contemplating all that could go wrong. Once again, Silas is putting his life on the line for her. *This is a perilous mission, one that can rip Silas from my life.* Just as the thought crossed her mind, the door opened, Sigurd stepped aside, and Silas and Dante entered.

"Oh, hell no!" The moment the words left her mouth, Silas took hold of her arm and led her from the room. "Let go, dammit! Where are you taking me?" she snarled, trying to fight her way out of his grip.

Dante took hold of her other arm and together, they led her away. They took her one level below the main entrance. There were a half-dozen guards lining the hallway who fell in behind them. Ahead, she could see what looked like a cell. As soon as the three of them entered, the doors closed behind them with a loud clank.

"Silas, you can't do this, I beg of you. Please stay with me!" Silas pulled her into his body and held her tight. "I have a bad feeling about this. The smell of death surrounds you!" She wept again.

Silas picked her up, and she wrapped her arms and legs around him. "Mon chéri, I won't die by Abigor's blade, that I promise you. I'll return to you as soon as I can. Until then, you'll remain here under guard. We need to go now, my love." He set her down and seized her mouth before pulling away. He cupped her face with his hands and looked into her watery eyes. "I love you with all that I am. I'm sorry it has to be this way," he said as he walked away.

She grabbed Dante's shirt. "Dante. don't let him do this. I beg of you!"

Dante didn't speak. He simply pulled her into him and held her tightly. "I won't let anything happen to my brother. We've stood beside each other in battle for six hundred years." He kissed the top of her head, and he too pulled away.

She had mastered the art of being alone; she had buried herself in a grave of emotional isolation that she languished in for a hundred and fifty years. Silas was the beloved, red rose on her tomb, and now he was leaving her.

The door shut behind them, sealing her in her gilded prison. She fell onto the bed and wept. A few minutes later, she heard the latch on the door, and she jumped to her feet. "Silas?" She was a bit taken aback when she saw Sigurd standing there.

"Silas thought you would need some comfort," Sigurd said with a gentle smile. Just as she cocked her head in confusion, Mag and Limi ran from behind him and bounded toward her. She fell to her knees and held them as the tears continued to flow. Sigurd said nothing more as he shut the door behind him.

Arkyn and Vidar were in the egregore, standing at the altar, wondering why the sorcery hadn't yet worked. "Who wants to tell our brother the Dhamphyr hasn't shown herself yet?" Arkyn asked.

"Let's send a messenger. I don't want to fucking be there when he hears the news." Vidar tossed one of the sour jars across the room out of frustration. The clay pot exploded, releasing the rancid substance which oozed down the uneven stone wall. "Send Havlar. He can deal with Abigor."

"*Havlar,*" Arkyn called telepathically.

"What the fuck do you want?" he replied angrily.

"You'll tell our brother the Dhamphyr is nowhere in sight."

"Po dyavolite if I will."

"Go now! That was a direct order," Vidar interjected.

"Uplashen montradacks!" he seethed as he headed for Abigor.

There was a sudden knock on the door, stirring Abigor awake. "Enter, and you better have good fucking reason for disturbing me."

"Milord, we have yet to encounter the Dhamphyr." Havlar stood motionless.

"I expected the Dhamphyr to be here by now. Where the ebasi is she?"

"Milord, I'm merely the messenger." Havlar's words were shaky and uncertain.

Abigor threw a dagger into the stone wall, nearly striking his shoulder. "Where the hell are my brothers? They didn't have the backbone to come to me themselves?"

"Milord, they're in the egregore."

"Relay this message for me, tell the bastards not to leave, or it will be their heads on a stake."

"Yes, milord." With a slight bow, Havlar left, and headed straight for the egregore.

"I see my brother took the news better than we thought, since you're here." Arkyn sneered when Havlar entered.

"Next time you need someone to do your shetaban bidding, don't come to me," Havlar stated.

Arkyn now stood toe to toe with Havlar. "Since when do you give orders?" Arkyn struck him across the face, and trickles of blood seeped from his mouth.

Havlar retaliated and struck Arkyn across the cheek.

Arkyn wrapped his arms around his waist, flipped his own body over, and landed on top of Havlar, who had crashed onto his back, releasing a belt of air. Arkyn plundered him, but Vidar stepped in and pulled him off. "Stop, brother. He's had enough. He knows his place!"

Abigor was a bit taken aback; he hadn't expected to walk into the midst of a brawl. "What in the fuck is all this?"

"Someone doesn't know where they stand," Arkyn growled.

Havlar managed to gather himself off the floor. "Your brother is a fucking coward!" As soon as the words left his mouth, he knew he made a grave mistake.

Abigor grabbed his jaw in one hand and plunged his dagger into his abdomen. "My brother may be a lot of things but a fucking coward he is not." He let Havlar fall at his feet. "Guards! Take him to the cages. He can heal there for all I fucking care."

"Aye, milord," the warrior stated, as he dragged Havlar from the egregore.

"Now if it pleases the two of you, we need to get back to the business at hand. Where's my goddamn Enchantress?" Abigor demanded.

"I'm here, milord," Evanora answered as she took a seat next to the altar.

"It seems your powers have grown weak. The Dhamphyr is nowhere in sight."

"She's protected by forces beyond this realm. I forewarned you she would be surrounded by powerful sorcery. You think your enemies will let her walk right into your arms?" Evanora stated.

"I thought you were the mistress of all things dark?" Abigor tilted his head, waiting for an explanation.

"My incantation reached her."

"Then where the fuck is she?"

"Protected. She'll no longer be reached using sorcery, nor can she hear my intones."

"Then it seems you've been rendered useless to me," Abigor snarled.

"There's another way, milord, unless I'm still useless?"

"I would advise you to watch your sarcasm—get on with it!"

"I feel danger approaching. If you can't get to the Dhamphyr directly, take what she holds dearest. She'll surely come then."

Abigor silently contemplated what she didn't say. "They have no idea we'll be waiting. If we take Silas, she'll find her true self and move into the darkness. She'll come for her mate."

"Precisely," Evanora agreed.

"Brothers, prepare the army of the fury. It will be an ambush, one they never saw coming. Find Folke, make sure the holding cell for Silas is ready. There can be no mistakes."

"Aye, brother," Arkyn stated as he and Vidar disappeared into a haze.

Abigor turned his attention back to Evanora. "Stand and remove your dress."

Evanora stood and untied the black, corseted dress. She slowly removed it from her shoulders, revealing her soft, amber skin. She pulled the dress a bit further down, teasing Abigor with a glimpse of her perfect, round breasts before letting it fall to the floor in a folded pile at her feet, and stood naked before her lord.

Abigor grabbed her by the back of the head and shoved his tongue into her mouth. He slid his hand between her legs, letting his fingers penetrate her. She moaned into his mouth and dug her fingernails into his back. Trickles of blood dripped from beneath the pointed, black tips of her nails. She slid her hand further down and cupped his ass in a tight grip.

He picked her up and carried her over to a musty bed sitting in the corner of the egregore. He threw her onto the bed before removing his clothes.

She repositioned herself, ready for him to take her. He climbed on top of her and forcefully spread her legs with his.

"I'm going to ravage you. I want to feel your pain," he rumbled.

Evanora reached down and wrapped her fingers tightly around his large dick. She slowly moved her hand up and down, as drops of fluid seeped from the tip.

He wrenched her head to the side and hovered over the heightened beat. She let out a harsh gasp, and the pain seared through her body like fire as she let Abigor feed from her.

"Milord—" she moaned as he released his grip and took her mouth to his once again.

Abigor parted her folds with his fingers and harshly pushed them in and out as he rubbed her nub with his thumb. Her heated wetness increased his need to plunder her body.

"I want to break you." He removed his fingers only to find her breast before shoving himself deep inside her tightness.

Her harsh moans were an invitation for more. Every thrust, harder than the last, forced her to gasp for breath; her painful moans became guttural.

He felt more of the warm trickles of blood as she dug her nails deeper into his flesh, dragging them from his shoulders to his ass.

"Milord, harder—" she begged, as her body shuddered with the relentless assault.

"I need to feel your pain," he rumbled.

He flipped her onto her stomach and raised her hips to meet his. He held her face down into the mattress before he began another harsh assault. He thrust himself so hard, she cried out. One fierce drive after another forced her body to fracture with a pain-filled orgasm.

He felt her core pulse around his vein, and his own release convulsed into her. He raised his head and let out a guttural roar.

The sex was loud and violent just as she wanted, needed. He fell on top of her a bit breathless, while his heart drummed in his chest from the exertion. She lay beneath his large, muscle-laden body, succumbing to the intoxicating ache she felt between her legs.

He rolled over and rested his arm behind his head, and she rolled over and rested her head on his moist chest.

"You ever give yourself to another, don't think I won't torture and behead you both," he rumbled.

"Never, milord. My body is yours." She paused before speaking again. "I have something for you."

"What would that be?"

"I think you could trap Silas shall I choose to conjure the Draugrs."

"*Shall you choose*? Is that your way of thinking you have some kind of control over me, Enchantress?"

"No, milord."

"Good, thinking that way finds death quickly," he threatened. "Now speak."

"The only way to kill a Draugr is to put it back into the grave from whence it came. It would be the perfect trap."

"The reason I keep you around—you're useful for more than just a good fuck. Go, conjure the Draugrs."

She slid out of the bed and walked over to pick up her dress as Abigor watched her every move.

Silas, Eden and their clans were in the heart of Bergelême, and each clan had taken their positions. Jabari and his warriors were hidden in the tree line just beyond the Trigrad River, awaiting their enemy's arrival.

Santiago had taken his position, along with his legion at the rim of the Trigrad Gorge. Silas and Eden, along with their brothers and their battalions, had taken their place at the edge of the Valley of Ides.

They would need to secure all three areas before converging at the entrance of the cavern, which would take them into the heart of the underworld. It was a world long forgotten, buried for centuries beneath the battered landscape. Should they lose this battle and be taken prisoner, it would mean a cruel death or worse—having to live in a nightmarish dystopia beneath the rule of a soulless enemy.

Santiago stepped in front of his warriors. "Let's move, span out along the tree line and head for the ridge. We'll drive them further into the gorge. Kilard, take your regiment and flank them from walls of the gorge. My warriors and I will meet them head on. Ready your swords. The only way death will befall them is by beheading."

"Aye, milord," Kilard answered before moving his squad up the steep cliffs where they would lay in wait.

Santiago watched as they disappeared up the cliffs Soon after he and his warriors had taken their positions, a brisk wind blew through the tree line as a legion of Abigor's warriors appeared before Santiago and his. "Find your enemy!" Santiago ordered.

They rushed into battle with a fury. The clanging and clashing of swords filled the night air beneath a turbulent, blackened sky. Explosive pops rang out before their swords beheaded their wounded enemies. The crush of bone and spray of blood sealed the fates of the fallen within the walls of the gorge.

"Now!" Santiago yelled just as he was hit in the face from the side. He spun around and fired two rounds before being attacked from behind. He disappeared into a haze with his enemies following suit. He manifested himself behind them and spun his blades, taking the heads of both warriors.

Kilard's legion rained down from the cliffs into the heart of the battle. He and his warriors charged the ensuing enemy with raised swords.

Santiago questioned Abigor's warriors appearing as if they were about to concede. After such a quick battle, he knew something was amiss. "It doesn't feel right. Get back!" he called out.

They all moved backward toward the entrance of the gorge, some of whom were already moving back up the steep cliffs. The ground beneath their feet gave way. They moved with precision as the earth rose in a dozen piles before them. The dirt tumbled over itself, like newly forming ant hills.

"Draugrs!" Santiago called out. What remained of Abigor's legion resumed the attack, giving the Draugrs time to rise from the grave.

"You must kill them in the grave!" Kilard shouted.

"Cloak yourselves and head for Jabari. It's a trap, and we shall fight together," Santiago ordered. He telepathically let both Jabari and Silas know the Draugrs were about to rise. The entire squad disappeared into darkness.

Jabari and his warriors lay in wait in the tree line when the air waned, and the invisible enemy approached. "Forward!" Jabari ordered.

"Aru—Aru—Aru!" they shouted in response.

One of Abigor's lieutenants appeared before them, along with his brigade who were mere feet from the tree line. Bodies rushed into the battle from both sides, moving amongst each other in a diaphanous mist. The sounds of clanging metal and gunshots echoed throughout the land as headless bodies fell to the cold, damp ground.

Jabari was flanked from both sides. As he spun around to face the threat, he felt a searing burn as the sword penetrated his shoulder. He whirled his sword behind his head and brought his blade across the chest of his opaque enemy before falling to his knees.

Tagar leapt behind Jabari and removed the blade from his flesh. "Milord?"

"Aiwa, brother!" Jabari answered, as he shot an attacking warrior. Before the wounded enemy could escape, his headless body slumped to the ground, having been severed by another one of Jabari's warriors.

Jabari took a few deep breaths as the warm, crimson liquid flowed from the grievous laceration. Tagar and Lamor grasped either side of his tunic and pulled him to his feet. They remained steadfast and fought at his side until the wound healed enough for him to join back in the fight.

Abigor's warriors moved forward again, attacking with a vengeance. Tagar, along with six of his men, met them head on. They advanced into the center of the attack, breaking the enemy's line.

Each stroke of Jabari's warriors seemed to send the enemy further towards defeat.

"Something is amiss. They aren't so easily defeated!" Jabari called out.

They suddenly felt the earth beneath them rumble just as Santiago spoke to him telepathically. *"Jabari, get back. It's a trap. The have conjured the Dragurs!"*

"Dragurs!" Jabari warned.

Santiago and his men suddenly appeared beside Jabari and his. "Clans together!"

Abigor's troops moved in once again; both squads were now converging together, allowing the Dragurs time to claw their way to the surface. Santiago, Jabari, and their warriors were now surrounded by Abigor's as the Dragurs rose beneath their feet.

"Drive them back," Jabari yelled out.

Swords spun and shots rang out in quick succession, driving Abigor's warriors back into the tree line. As Abigor's warriors made their way through the dense forest, Tagar and his brigade met them from behind, who were waiting to ambush them.

Abigor's warriors were now the ones surrounded; their defeat was eminent. The unrelenting clang of metal and hissing bullets faded. Only a few of Abigor's warriors could escape the slaughter. The calling of orders and the shouting from the wounded faded into the distance.

"We now have another enemy to defeat. Attack the Dragurs!" Jabari ordered.

"Move along the edge. They should know we're coming by now. They'll be waiting," Silas ordered.

"Aye, milord," Sigurd answered as he motioned for his warriors to span out. The air in the valley waned before them as Abigor's legion appeared from the shadows.

Silas stepped in front of his men. "Attack—show no mercy!"

All those who stood with him disappeared into a haze before appearing in the center of the battle, each landing in an easy stance. Abigor's warriors shuffled backward as Silas and his men spanned out in a circle. Loud pops overtook the shouts, orders, and clang of metal. Abigor's warriors tried and failed to ascertain a weak spot amongst Silas's advancing squad. The unrelenting swiftness in which Silas and his Mortem warriors attacked, quickly drove them further into the center of the valley.

A hatchet whirled past Silas's head, and he moved swiftly, evading the blow. He spun around to meet another attacker head on. He drove his sword into the warrior's armpit before recoiling his blade. He spun the bloody metal and slashed at the base of the warrior's neck.

Eden, Aiden, and Lars continued to move methodically, evading blow after blow with cunning tenacity. They finished the wounded enemies using only their ruthless blades as they advanced further into the bloody mayhem.

Dante and Bain felt a sinister, dark energy penetrate the night air.

"Do you feel it?" Dante yelled at Bain as he dismembered another advancing enemy.

"I do! What the fuck it is?" Bain shouted back.

The two of them continued their assaults on the emerging enemy, all the while trying to decipher the energy surrounding them. Silas suddenly heard his father's words of warning. *Dragurs!*

"Dragurs!" Silas announced. "They're rising from the grave. Everyone back!"

Piles of dirt surged upwards from the hardened ground. Santiago, Jabari, and their warriors suddenly appeared in the valley to fight alongside Silas. However, more than a dozen Dragurs followed them, along with the remainder of Abigor's legion. The Dragurs in the valley now clawed their way to the surface, appearing as black, soulless, unforgiving shadows. Chilling battle calls of Abigor's commanders greeted their ghostly silhouettes.

The Dragurs offered no response as they continued to grow in size.

"Finish Abigor's warriors, and get the wounded out of here!" Silas ordered before falling back into obscurity.

Silas's Mortem warriors charged the fleeing enemy as everyone else faced the looming threats growing before them.

The Dragurs continued to grow as did their weight, expanding into the size of a large bull. The unmistakable stench of decay filled the valley with their presence. The undead figures were hideous to look at. They appeared to be rotten and decayed; they were soulless beasts conjured straight from hades itself.

Dante and Bain stood forefront, ready to drive them back into the depths of depravity by any means necessary.

"Iron and lead will injure but not kill. They must be put back into the grave and burned!" Dante shouted.

The fully morphed Dragurs descended onto the warriors. The sounds of tearing flesh, yells of agony, and commands drowned out all other sounds. Nosferatu and Dragurs were clenched in hand-to-hand combat;

bodies were slammed to the ground and engulfed in a cloud of dust and debris. The sound of metal meeting bone, and fists meeting flesh, gave way to the flicker of fire, whose smoke and flame rose from multiple graves, along with searing stench of rotten, burning flesh.

Silas was attacked by six large Dragurs who lunged at once. He was able to fend off the attacks and disappeared before attacking one of the Dragurs from behind. He managed to slam its heavy body into a grave before two more descended upon him. Their heavy weight crushed Silas into the freshly dug dirt. He suddenly found himself crashing a hundred feet down onto a hard, stone floor, knocking the wind out of him.

The Dragurs that followed crashed down around him, nearly crushing him to death. He managed to shove them off and roll out from under their burning bodies before feeling the searing pain of an arrow penetrating his abdomen. Two more penetrated his thigh before he faded into the darkness.

Fire after fire lit up the valley; the smoke from the burning flesh was noxious as it twisted and twirled from each grave before rising into the turbulent night sky. The sounds faded as the warriors defeated the Dragurs. The entire valley was overtaken by ash, dust, smoke, burning flesh, and flickering flame.

"Check the wounded and gather your men!" Santiago ordered.

They all converged to access the injured, the missing, or worse the dead.

"Where's my brother?" Dante yelled. "Silas—Silas?" As many times as he called out, there was no response.

"Where the fuck is Silas?" Agaeus demanded, with labored breathing. They frantically searched the valley, along with each grave.

"Over here," Dante shouted. "He was here; I feel his presence."

Bain dropped to his knees by Dante's side. "Goddammit—they've taken him!" Dante roared. He slammed his fist onto the ground, sending dirt spewing in all directions.

"It was a trap. They took Silas to get to Jadis," Santiago announced

Dante jumped to his feet. "We need to go after him and now!" He headed for the entrance to the cavern, along with Bain, Agaeus, and Syth before Santiago appeared before them.

"Stand down, Dante. They will be lying in wait. We cannot hastily run into another trap in the mouth of the underworld. If they were able to subdue Silas, they've planned this carefully. We need to get to Jadis and plan an attack. I won't let the bastard take the life of one of my bairns, much less his mate. We'll prepare to attack Abigor in the heart of the underworld."

"Santiago is right, we're no good to Silas if we fall prey to this," Eden agreed.

"They won't kill Silas before they have Jadis. He's strong, cunning, and a formidable opponent. He knows how to survive," Aden added, still catching his breath.

"Everyone, back to the temple. Sigurd, you're Silas' first in command. "Santiago stated. "You'll be in charge of the Mortem for the time being—at least until Silas returns. You'll remain here. Keep watch from a distance and report back anything you feel is important or out of place. Scout the entire area and under no circumstances are you to go after him. This needs to be planned carefully to save Silas. Understood?"

"Aye, milord," Sigurd answered before he disappeared with his men back into the shadows.

CHAPTER 12

Whatever Dante and Bain had conjured up, along with Jabari's temple guardians held Jadis in the cell, she couldn't penetrate the barrier, no matter how hard she tried. She lay in bed with Mag and Limi curled up next to her. She suddenly felt a searing pain in the abdomen and wrenched in response. She was stunned and knew instantly Silas had been hurt. She jumped out of bed in nothing more than a t-shirt and a pair of panties and headed for the cell door.

"Kilark, open the goddamn door. Silas is hurt!"

"I'm sorry, lass, I cannot."

"What the hell do you mean, you cannot? Open this goddam door, or I'll tear it apart!" She tried to pull it from its hinges, but it didn't budge. "Goddammit!" she shouted as she kicked the bars multiple times.

Kilark stood ready on the other side. "Men, be prepared," he ordered, shifting his stance.

Jadis *turned* and roared at him in response. She bared her canines and lunged. She reached through the bars and grabbed a hold of his tunic.

He grabbed her hand and tried to release her unrelenting grip, tearing the fabric. He was doing all he could to release her grip without hurting her in the process.

She felt a cold wind blow behind Kilark when Dante's sudden appearance startled her. She let go of Kilark's tunic.

As soon as Dante opened the cell door, she took the chance to escape and disappeared, but Dante caught her in mid-air. She tried to fight her way out of his grip to no avail; he easily wrestled her back into the cell.

"What have they done to Silas?" she demanded as the cell door slammed shut behind them.

"Silas is alive. I'll explain everything," He stated calmly as he held her wrists in a vicelike grip.

"Explain now, wizard!"

"Silas has been captured by Abigor. He has been taken into the underworld, but he's alive."

"Nooo," she screamed. "They'll kill him!" The tears streamed down her face, and she fell to the floor as her knees buckled beneath her. Dante knelt and scooped her up off the floor and into his arms.

"We're preparing to attack as we speak, we will get Silas back."

"Get him back? They won't let him out alive! It's me they want," she wailed.

The door opened again and without thinking, she once again took off. Dante lunged and tackled her to the floor of the expansive hallway.

"Get off," she snarled.

"Jadis, stop! I won't allow you to go after Silas, it's exactly what they want." He rolled her onto her back and pinned her arms above her head. She snarled like a rabid dog in response. "Get off me." Mag and Limi lunged for Dante. He turned his head, and they stopped in their tracks but continued their unrelenting snarling—the large whites of their canines undeniable in the dimly lit hallway.

"Jadis, enough!" Santiago demanded as he stood above her, along with Bain, Eden, and Aiden at his side. The distraction gave Dante enough time to get a firm hold of her body, and he carried her back into the cell.

She now had the five of them standing between herself and her freedom. She looked to Aiden, and he walked over and swept her up into his arms. All she could do was cry as he held her tightly. He gently stroked her hair, trying to calm her down.

"Shhh—I've got you, darling."

Dante paced back and forth behind Aiden and Jadis, ready to pull her from Aiden's arms.

Aiden set her down, and she slowly turned to face the group.

Santiago finally spoke, "Jadis, I know this is an unexpected turn of events—"

She interrupted him, "*An unexpected turn of events?* Are you kidding me right now?"

"I understand your frustration, and I understand you're scared. We'll be returning to the valley as soon as we're prepared. We'll bring my bairn back to you, that goes without saying."

"And how are you going to do that?" she yelled. "They want me, and you know they won't let him go!"

"This is non-negotiable. You'll remain here. I won't put you in harm's way." Santiago stood, unwavering.

She tried to step forward, but Aiden wrapped an arm around her and held her in place.

"You don't have the right to keep me imprisoned!" She wrenched out of Aiden's grip and met Santiago face to face. She felt a low rumble rise from her core. "I'll leave, and you'll stand back, milord." Her words, the undeniable anger in her voice, shocked everyone. The changes in her were frightening; she was turning in a way none of them had ever witnessed.

"Jadis, stand down!" Santiago ordered.

"I'll do no such thing. Now get out of my way," she snarled.

Eden stepped between her and Santiago. She shoved him in the chest, sending him a foot backward. Her reaction, not to mention her strength, was distressing to all. Mag and Limi stood at her side and let out a guttural warning, as the hair raised on their backs and the napes of their necks. They slowly crept forward as if stalking their prey.

Santiago waved his hand, calming the Wolves who were ready to defend her tooth and claw. "You won't be leaving, and until I trust the threat against you no longer exists, you will remain here." Santiago tried to ignore her threats, understanding they were solely based on emotion. He also knew she struggled with the thriving powers she didn't yet understand. He would expect no less of a reaction out of anyone whose mate's life was on the line.

She rubbed her face with both hands; there was no way to explain to them the unrelenting thoughts plaguing her mind. They betrayed any and all logic, as did the sudden onset of the unfamiliar powers.

Dante approached her and wrapped her in his arms. "Leave," he demanded. "I'll stay here."

Aiden looked to Eden and realized for the first time that Dante felt more for her than they ever knew. *"He's in love with her,"* Aiden stated telepathically to Eden.

Eden subtly nodded in agreement. *"When did this happen?"*

"Who knows?" Aiden uncrossed his arms and shifted his weight, not sure what to do with the sudden realization.

Santiago stepped forward. "Jadis, we'll inform you of our every move but right now, we need to get back to business." He knew they weren't leaving for two days but wasn't about to disclose that in this moment. It would only serve to upset her more. He placed a gentle hand on her shoulder and squeezed before looking at Dante. "We're headed back. Join us when you can."

Dante nodded as he picked her up in his arms and walked over to the bed. He sat down next to her and held her in his arms as she sobbed on his chest.

"Dante, you have to let me go. I'd rather die than go on living without him," she begged.

"I gave my word to my brother. I've been your sworn protector since the day he realized who you were. I won't betray him."

When Silas woke, he found himself chained by both hands to the wall of his cell. The fog was heavy in his mind, and he felt as if his brain were digging through the mud as he tried to gather his thoughts together. The cell was damp, dark, and cold; he knew he was now in the hands of Abigor.

He heard the clanging of the cell door and looked over to see Abigor walk in. "Look who's finally awake." He laughed. "I'll make this easy—the Dhamphyr for you and your family's lives."

"*I'll make it easy* for you—you'll never lay your hands on her. I choose death. However, I believe I'll kill you before that happens," Silas threatened.

"You can't even get out of those fucking chains, you moronic fool. How do you plan on fucking killing me?" Abigor grabbed hold of his jaw and laughed in his face before striking him multiple times, sending blood spewing from his mouth and splattering onto the blackened wall.

"I'll enjoy torturing you, eventually you will beg for your life."

Silas laughed in Abigor's face. "Do as you wish, but I will not cower!"

Abigor landed another blow, grabbed a fistful of his hair, and yanked his head back.

"I'm going to fucking enjoy this more than you know," he snarled. He landed multiple blows to Silas's ribs before tossing his head forward.

"This is just the beginning." He turned to leave, but before making his exit, he turned back to Silas. "I thought you would like to know we'll be waiting for her. Eventually, she'll find a way to come for you." He let out a sadistic belly laugh before the guards slammed the iron door shut.

Silas's body fell limp, only to be held up by the binding chains. Abigor would return with his brothers, one of whom would toss a bucket of cold water on him to awaken him, and the other would land blow after blow, all the while Abigor demanded the whereabouts of the Dhamphyr; this carried on all night.

"Stick it to him again," Abigor ordered.

They continued giving Silas just enough of the serum to render him powerless without killing him. Abigor stood and watched as Arkyn gave him another round. *We need him alive to get the answers we're seeking. More importantly, the Dhamphyr will feel her mate's death. As long as she knows he's alive, she'll come*, Abigor thought.

The only thing keeping Silas semi-conscious was the plaguing thoughts he had of Jadis. He knew his family would come for him eventually, however Abigor's words weighed heavy. He knew, given the slightest opportunity, Jadis would indeed come to him.

Once Jadis finally awoke, it was daylight, and Dante was gone. *The bastard put me out*, she thought as she lay on her back, feeling nothing less than panic stricken and helpless. All she could think about was that Silas would never sit still while she was in danger. *Screw this! My mate's in trouble and here I am, incapable of doing anything.*

"*Become what you were meant to be, my child. Your powers are greater than you ever imagined. Call upon thy Old Gods.*" The sudden voice in her head startled her.

"*Mother?*"

"*Yes, dear. Your mate needs you. Go to him.*"

"*How am I supposed to do that?*"

"*Reach deep, you have all you require.*" In that moment, Jadis understood what needed to be done. She closed her eyes, opened her mind, and gave into whatever it was she was to become. She called upon the Old Gods as instructed, to bestow her the powers of two realms.

"Deos testor upoon largiantur mihi lumine umbraque virtutum." Once she finished the chant, she felt an ethereal flame warm her core before being consumed by blackness as she was swept into a celestial realm. Standing before her was Hecate and an ancient Nosferatu lord. It was a world devoid of mortal landscape; only a ghostly haze and blackness surrounded them.

A goat and a bull wandered into sight from the blackness and stood beside Hecate and the lord. The goat meeheed, thrashing its head up and down. The bull angrily dug at the ground with his front hoof, and the moist heat from his nose billowed into a cloud of vapor with every angry, wet breath.

"Come, my child. 'Tis time." Hecate turned to the goat, made a small slit at the base of its neck, and let a trickle of blood flow into an ancient chalice. Jadis reluctantly approached her and stood silent as Hecate held the chalice to her mouth.

"Drink, child."

Jadis wrapped her hands around the chalice and swallowed the thick, warm liquid. The lord bit down on the bull's neck and drank from it. He then turned to Jadis and stretched his arm outward. She reluctantly took his wrist to her mouth and fed from him as the bull and goat trotted off into the darkness. The change was immediate, and she fell into the thick, swirling mist and curled into a ball, reeling from the pain. She faintly heard chanting all around her before she faded back into the darkness.

Kilark heard Jadis moaning, and he called out to her. "Jadis—Jadis?" When he didn't get a response, he reached out to Dante. "Milord, something is wrong with the lass."

Dante arrived swiftly, only to find her lying on the floor, curled up and moaning. Max and Limi stood at her side, licking her face and whining incessantly.

"Darling, what's wrong? Talk to me—tell me what's happening. Kilark, what happened?"

"I'm at a loss. She was sleeping before this happened."

"Did you hear her speak? Anything at all?"

"Nye, milord."

"Jadis, wake up." Dante picked her up and placed her on the bed as he laid his palm on her forehead. "She's burning up. Get a cloth."

Kilark nodded and returned with a cold cloth. Dante placed it across her forehead and continued to try to wake her.

"Bain, I need you in Jadis's cell."

Bain quickly appeared at his side. "What the hell is going on?" He bent down and felt her forehead as well. "She's burning up, but she's not sick. This is something else. We need to cool her off."

Dante lifted her off the bed and held her in the shower under the cold water, calling her name.

She felt a chill and shivered uncontrollably. As she opened her eyes, she realized Dante was holding her in the shower with Bain standing next to them.

"What are you doing?" she muttered.

"You were burning up. We needed to cool you down. Tell me what's happened, darling," Dante requested.

"I'm cold," was all she chose to say. *No way in hell am I going to admit to what I just did. I need to get to Silas, and the less they know the better.*

Dante carried her out of the shower and sat her on the edge of the tub, while Bain wrapped a couple of towels around her.

"We know this is more than you being sick. What did you do?" Dante asked again.

She passed out before answering, so Dante carried her to the bed and laid her down. He discreetly changed her into a dry t-shirt, a pair of shorts, and covered her up.

He looked to Bain, speaking silently. *"She's up to something. I feel the powers swirling within her. She's planning on going after Silas."*

Bain rubbed the side of his face, trying to decipher the unknown energy surrounding her. *"Do you think she can get out?"*

"At this point, I'm not confident at all this cell can hold her. I have that unrelenting feeling creeping up."

"As do I," Bain admitted.

She opened her eyes and looked around, only to find Dante and Bain sitting at the side of her bed. She looked over at Dante, whose expression suddenly went stone cold. They stood so quickly, the backs of their knees sent the chairs scooting across the floor with a loud scrape.

"Dante, what's wrong? Did something happen to Silas?" she demanded.

"No, darling, nothing more has happened to Silas. How do you feel?"

"Actually, I feel like shit! How am I supposed to feel being trapped in a cage while my mate is being held captive?" She sat up and swung her legs over the edge of the bed. "What's up with the two of you, anyway? Shouldn't you be going after Silas?"

"This isn't about Silas right now. What have you done?" Bain demanded.

"What do you mean? And why are the two of you staring at me like that?"

"You know exactly what Bain is asking. What did you do this morning?" Dante demanded.

"I have no idea what you're talking about," she replied with a simple shrug of her shoulders.

"I see where this is heading. Don't even think about it!" Dante grabbed her arm and pulled her to the bureau. "Look into the mirror and tell us you did nothing."

She peered at herself in the mirror and jumped back. "Holy shit," she exclaimed. She chuckled under her breath. *It worked!*

"*What worked?*" Dante demanded.

She didn't answer. She just studied the swirling, oil-like mix of raven black and blood red consuming her corneas. She walked back to the bed, saying nothing more. She lay down, pulled the covers over her body, and turned her back to them.

They stood silently, not knowing what to do or what she had done.

"*Father, I think you should see this,*" Dante stated telepathically.

Jadis felt more than one presence behind her, however, she chose not to acknowledge them.

Dante pulled her out of the bed and stood her before Santiago, accompanied by Aiden and Eden.

As soon as she looked at them, they stood rooted in place, darting their eyes amongst each other. Aiden subtly placed his hand over his mouth and rubbed his jaw. He looked to Eden, not knowing what to say.

"Jadis, what did you do now?" Eden demanded.

Again, her only response was to shrug her shoulders. *If they think they can keep me from going to Silas after what Hecate said to me, they're gravely mistaken.* She stood unwavering, her mind was made up. *The moment the opportunity presents itself, I'll make my escape.*

"Dante, Bain stay here," Santiago said nothing more as he motioned for Aiden and Eden to follow him back to the meeting room.

Santiago took a seat and leaned back. "We have another problem. Jadis has somehow conjured up powers we cannot control should she escape. She has yet to reveal what she has done, and we cannot expect she'll remain in the cell much longer," he explained.

"What has she done now?" Jabari asked, his concern clear.

"She has discovered the Dhamphyr side of herself," Santiago stated bluntly. "Should she feel the slightest of shifts in energy, she'll be able to slip through the veil."

"What are we gong to do? We promised our brother we would keep her safe," Agaeus stated.

Aiden leaned back and crossed one leg over his knee. "Jadis has just drawn a line in the sand. There'll be no room for error."

"I agree. As much as it pains me to say it, I believe we should allow her to accompany us. I'm not confident she can be detained. It will only take one minor mishap and don't be mistaken, she'll take advantage of it. She's a master of trickery," Santiago reasoned.

"She'll be safer with us than on her own. At least we'll know what she's planning and where she is at all times," Aiden added.

"It isn't Abigor's intention to kill her, even if she should be captured, which is more than a possibility. We all know she doesn't tend to follow orders," Eden replied.

"If everyone agrees, the only change to our plans is that she'll be accompanying us. Her powers may be useful as well," Santiago admitted.

"What makes you think anyone can control her when it comes to Silas?" Agaeus questioned.

"Either she comes with us protected, or she leaves on her own," Santiago replied. "Unless of course you have another idea?"

Agaeus held up his hands in frustration and shook his head.

"It has been settled. She'll accompany us tonight. All in agreement?" Jabari asked.

Everyone reluctantly nodded.

"I'll go and inform her. The rest of you meet us in the armory. We head out in an hour." Santiago stood and headed for Jadis.

She was still lying on the bed while Dante and Bain paced back and forth, clearly listening in on the conversation taking place in the meeting room. Santiago made another appearance. She stood to meet him and waited for the fallout.

"It seems you've backed us into a corner. Against my better judgement, you'll be accompanying us on the mission," Santiago said.

"You're letting me go?"

"Yes, however you'll remain with either Dante, Bain, or me. Is that clearly understood?" Santiago tilted his head, awaiting her response. "If you so much as step out of place, I'll personally drag your ass back here by any means necessary."

"I understand. As long as I'm allowed to go, I give you my word on Nosferatu. I'll follow any and all orders. The last thing I want is to do something that could jeopardize Silas's life. I won't go back on my word."

"Your words are sincere. You may follow us to the armory, and I suggest you dress properly." Santiago nodded towards her t-shirt and shorts.

Dante grabbed her arm. "I'm not in agreement!"

"I promise, Dante, I'll do whatever you say." He wrapped his arms around her and held her tightly; his embrace was the wash of calm she needed.

He lifted her chin and looked into her eyes. "He's going to be okay, darling. I promise. This isn't the first time one of us has been captured." He winked, trying to lighten the situation up a bit, and she managed to muster up a gentle smile.

He let out a heavy sigh and kissed her forehead. "Get dressed. I can't even believe I'm agreeing to this shit." She simply rolled her eyes at him in response.

CHAPTER 13

They arrived just beyond the valley in a village known as Shiroka Laka. They re-grouped with the surrounding clans, as well as Silas's Mortem warriors. They had called upon the rest of the Shiroka clans who were prepared, willing, and waiting for their orders back in the village. They would move in three separate waves. Santiago and Eden would be the first in line with the Mortem. Jabari's brigade would move in behind Santiago and Eden, while the Shiroka warriors would be the third wave following Jabari. They remained on the fringes of the village, awaiting the rest of the clan's arrival.

Sigurd appeared from the forest and politely nodded to the numerous lords. "Milords, we've found another entry, but it appears the only way into the cavern is through the main entrance. There's one area on the west side of the mountain. It may have been an entrance before having been sealed hundreds of years ago. It can be penetrated but must be done from the inside. The noise from any outside sorcery would arouse suspicion. We could use the wizard's powers, but I fear the rock will be weak on the inside, should it crumble, it would alert anyone in the vicinity."

Santiago stepped forward and turned to face the clans who had arrived shortly after Sigurd. "We'll send part of our forces, divided into several units, into the mountains and surrounding forest. Sigurd, once the battle commences, we'll need you to penetrate the mouth of the cave. Once you breech the entrance, head straight for the west wall and tear it down so our clans on the outside can enter."

"Aye, milord. Our wizard is ready." Sigurd nodded and stepped back.

"Malnick, you and your men will carry on with the reconnaissance work in the front and the rear, so we aren't attacked by the enemy from either direction."

"Aye, milord," Malnick replied.

Santiago spoke to Radul, lord of the Shiroka Laka region. "When the enemy is pursuing us in great haste, you'll lay in wait in the selected location. Hold steady until Abigor's warriors arrive and proceed with the ambush. The area just beyond the gorge is where you'll remain with your men. The path narrows as it passes through the center. The only way out will be back through the gorge or up the cliffs. Half of your warriors will be cloaked in your position in the gorge. The other half of your warriors will remain cloaked at the top of the cliffs."

"Aye, milord," Radul answered.

"Jabari, my clan will lead the advancement into the valley. When the enemy attacks, we'll retreat. Be ready for Abigor's warriors to withdraw, rather than follow us. You'll need to ascertain whether or not there may be another ambush, or a feigned retreat intended to encircle us from two sides of the valley and report."

"We'll be ready," Jabari replied.

"My family will accompany me into the valley where Silas was taken. They'll surely have the Dragurs located throughout the region as before. Everyone will need to be prepared to meet the dead fist to flesh and fire to bone."

"Aru—Aru—Aru!" they replied with raised swords.

Dante stood behind Jadis with his hands on her shoulders, helping to calm her down. Her breathing became deeper as a battalion of chills crept their way down her spine. Silas was so close she could feel him, as well as his pain, and the anticipation sent her mind into a fury of cluttered emotions.

Santiago looked to her, and his words broke her from her train of thought. "Jadis, you're to remain with Dante and Bain at all times," he demanded again. She nodded in response as he continued, "Don't forget you're the target, and they'll do whatever it takes, understand?"

"I understand."

Dante squeezed her shoulders, and she looked up at him for reassurance. He simply replied with a gentle smile and a wink.

"Everyone, take your positions!" Santiago called out.

Santiago walked over and cupped Jadis's hands in his. "Should you be captured, your only mission is to remain alive. Do not underestimate the threat upon you. Abigor is one to be reckoned with. Don't for one minute underestimate the lengths he'll go to get you to yield. He'll use Silas against you. And rest assured, he won't hesitate to use your body, as well as your mind."

Well, that isn't what I want to hear. Silas and my body? The blunt warning unchained the fear she had been holding down, allowing it to erode her confidence. She couldn't fathom being like that with anyone but Silas. Her stomach was tied in a thousand knots, and the realization he would use her body made her sick. She felt herself tremble as Santiago's words faded into the background. Her mind was also focused on finding any feelings from Silas, that he knew they were there. Darkness engulfed the frail light, diminishing all happiness and bliss she and Silas had enjoyed a few weeks ago.

"Jadis—Jadis?" Santiago tried to get her to hear his words. He could tell she was lost within her anguish and no longer listening.

"Jadis." Dante turned her to face him. He lifted her chin to meet her gaze and break her fixation. "Listen, darling, we won't let anything happen to you. You need to listen to our father. He only speaks the truth, so you're prepared to fight your enemy. You need to understand the depths of his depravity."

She looked into his eyes, only to see the dread and worry he hid behind his black irises.

"Jadis, I need you to hear me," Santiago stated.

She slowly turned her attention back to him. "Don't let your emotions cloud your judgement. You'll need to remain sharp and steadfast. You're cunning and powerful. Don't succumb to his darkness. Their magic is powerful. Don't forget the Lord of Darkness stands at Abigor's side."

"You're talking as if my capture is imminent," she stated nervously.

"Nothing is imminent, however during times of war, you need to be prepared for the worst-case scenario. You cannot rush into a battlefield blind and naïve," Santiago explained. He proceeded to pull a 500 Magnum from the back of his waistband and held it out to her. "I assume you know how to use this?"

"Yes." She slowly took the Magnum and pulled the slide back, loading a round into the chamber. He tucked a couple of fully loaded magazines into the pockets of her cargo pants.

"Aim for the head, nothing less. You'll have warriors with sword to finish the job. Now would be the time to call upon your powers and/or your Old Gods as well."

Evanora appeared from behind Abigor, who sat with his brothers above the pits as usual, watching the fights below them. "Milord, permission to approach."

"Approach, what news is it you carry?" he demanded with a snarl.

Vidar sat at Abigor's side with a concubine in his lap. "Get up," he snarled. He shoved her to the floor, waiting to hear what Evanora had to say. The girl quickly gathered herself off the floor and took a seat against the wall with the other girls who were also battered and beaten.

"The Dhamphyr has arrived," she stated bluntly.

"Well, that is good fucking news." Abigor slowly clapped his hands before he stood and held his cup up. "Brothers, the war is upon us. Ready our warriors!"

"Blow the horns!" Arkyn yelled, as he stood with Vidar and Abigor.

Multiple pillar horns overcame the bellows and cheers from the crowd who had been watching the fights. The crowd quickly turned their attention to their lord who stood above them.

"The fight has come to our door. Prepare for war!" Abigor yelled as he and his brothers raised their swords.

The crowd raised their weapons in response and cheered; the fighters were dragged from the arena and back to their cells.

The rest of the crowd disappeared into various corridors to rise to the surface and meet the oncoming enemy, all hoping to capture the mythical Dhamphyr they had only heard about in legends.

Abigor turned to Evanora. "Go and don't fucking fail me."

"Milord." Evanora gently bowed her head and disappeared into the small, darkened tunnel behind his throne.

They had all taken their positions, waiting for the onslaught of their enemy. As soon as the sun had set into the horizon, an eerie silence and darkness fell upon the valley. The only interruption to the silence was the frantic beating of Jadis's pulse, drumming in her ears. Off in the horizon, what sounded like a stampede of horses grew with intensity.

Abigor's legion approached from all directions. The clanking of steel meeting steel also grew in intensity as their warriors lying in wait in multiple locations met the enemy, just as Santiago had planned.

The loud, rapid cracks of gunfire boomed throughout the valley as the attacking wave moved in their direction. A cool wind blew in from just beyond the valley, penetrating the tree line in front of Jadis, Dante, and Bain. The roars from the approaching enemy drowned out the sounds of battle raging beyond the valley. An entire legion of Abigor's warriors morphed from the darkness, heading their way.

Jadis was in the back of the line between Dante and Bain, while Santiago was on the front line, leading their warriors head on into the onslaught of their enemy.

She stood ready, watching as the warriors plunged their swords into the enemy's armored bodes. Heads fell to the ground, and blood and organs spilled onto the valley floor before her. More of Abigor's warriors joined their fallen comrades as they were met blade for blade.

Another one of Abigor's legions fought their way through the chaotic fray heading in their direction.

"It's the Dhamphyr!" one of the warriors yelled as he pointed his sword at her.

"Now!" Dante called out. Their entire squad ran forward, meeting them head on. All of their warriors ran around Jadis, Dante, and Bain, who stayed toward the back of the line.

A few of Abigor's warriors broke through the line, and Jadis aimed for the head just as Santiago had ordered. The hissing of bullets, the rapid succession of shots, as well as steel meeting flesh was deafening. Dante and Bain never left her side as they charged the enemy. Her bullets found their target, and Dante and Bain finished off every stunned warrior.

In the midst of the battle, the ground rumbled beneath their feet as they made their way further into the valley, pushing Abigor's line back. "Dragurs!" Dante yelled as he grabbed Jadis by the arm.

All around her was a whirlwind of chaos and violence. The ground was discolored and slick from the blood; matted clumps of organs and bodies were scattered throughout the valley. The adrenaline pumped through her veins, and the fear clenched her heart as she watched the ground give way. She looked to Dante and Bain, whose faces and bodies were sprayed with the blood of their enemies.

Black shadows slowly rose from the dirt throughout the valley, taking on a grotesque form. The rotten stench was nauseating. She looked around and noticed they were surrounded by what appeared to be massive ant hills. She scanned the valley looking for Aiden or Eden, who were engaged in their own battles further in the valley.

"Dante!" she yelled. "We're being surrounded!"

Arrows hissed past their bodies; they were able to evade the arrows moments before Dante and Bain surrounded them in an invisible bubble. The slew of arrows bounced in all directions after striking the opaque energy. She tried to make Dante, Bain, and herself disappear just as she had done when she pulled Silas and Aria into the oasis. They came crashing down only feet from where they had been standing, unable to penetrate their barrier. She fell to the ground and landed on her back. Dante and Bain gracefully landed on their feet in a crouched position, hovering over her. She quickly gathered herself off the ground.

Before them, a shadowy figure appeared in the form of a woman. She continued walking their way as if she were invisible to anyone else fighting within the chaos.

"Enchantress," Jadis snarled.

"This is it, Jadis. Don't be fooled by her!" Dante stated.

She raised her hands before her and clapped them together. The 'bubble' surrounding them exploded into a haze.

The Dragurs held steady, keeping them surrounded but not attacking. As a few more warriors approached from behind the Enchantress, something took over Jadis. She didn't know if it was the fear, Hecate, or her own powers rising up. She swirled her hand, and a fiery ball of tar formed in her palm. *Cimruta,* she thought as she looked down. She threw the blackened substance, and it hit one of the warriors in the chest, setting him ablaze. He screamed and spun in circles before falling to the ground in a burning heap. She quickly hit two more in the same way, setting them both ablaze as well, their cries of pain succumbing to the blackened flames.

The remaining warriors retreated from the animal they had awakened in the Dhamphyr. The legends of her powers brought about a fear based solely on the stories that had been instilled in them for centuries. They were all afraid to approach the Dhamphyr, unsure of the powers she truly yielded after having watched her send multiple warriors to the grave with a mere flick of her wrist.

The Enchantress didn't move, and Jadis felt Dante and Bain fall to their knees behind her. She turned, only to notice multiple arrows had penetrated each of them. "Dante—Bain!" she called out, before turning her attention back to the Enchantress.

"Stay put, Jadis!" Dante demanded. He had removed the arrows, healing himself from the powerful concoction.

Bain had been struck two more times as the Enchantress somehow blocked their powers with the poisoned tips.

"Well, look what we have here." She chuckled as she slowly clapped her hands. "It seems the legends of your powers are true. I've been waiting for you for what seems like an eternity. Your wizards are more powerful than I gave them credit for—impressive!" She motioned her hand, and two of the Dragurs attacked Bain and dragged him away.

Jadis heard the commotion behind her and Dante as Bain struggled to fight them off. She begged her Gods to keep him safe.

"You bitch!" Jadis roared. She flung a ball in the Enchantress' direction, only for her to quickly deflect it. "Abigor has big plans for you. I'm merely here to deliver you to my lord."

Jadis felt Dante hold her tighter as he jumped straight up, disappearing into the air. The Enchantress trapped them in a dark web and dragged them back to the ground. A half-dozen Dragurs attacked and wrestled them into a large dirt grave. Dante and Jadis were suddenly sucked into the ground, only to come crashing down into a dark cavern below the surface.

Jadis gasped for breath, having had the wind knocked out of her. The only reason the fall didn't kill her was that she landed on more than one of the Dragur's enormous bodies, cushioning her fall. The Dragurs suddenly whiffed into a cloud of blackened ash that rained down on them. She managed to roll over to Dante who lay, barely conscious. She pulled the arrows from his body before noticing they were surrounded by multiple darkened figures. The Enchantress appeared before them once again.

The Nosferatu front and center looked like an ancient Bergelême warrior who had just stepped off a battlefield; she had only seen the likes of which in books. Their orangish-colored eyes glowed in the darkened corridor. They were all dressed in leather and furs; they were warriors the likes of which she'd only seen a resemblance of in Silas's Mortem.

One of them knelt before her. "It's good of you to grace us with your presence, Dhamphyr," he growled.

The vampire speaking was calm and collected. His energy, however, was nonetheless menacing or evil. Aesthetically, he didn't appear to be the monster she had expected. *From all that I've been told, I expected to see an ugly beast before me. I don't even know if this is Abigor or one of his men?*

"I have big plans for you," he snarled. "Now stand, Dhamphyr!" He grabbed her shirt, and she heard the fabric stretch as he wrenched her to her feet.

"Chain the bastard before he wakes." Dante was chained as she stood as helpless as the prey in a leopard's mouth.

Yep, it's Abigor! She fought every impulse to sprint down the unknown corridor. She stood as frozen as a piece of meat in an ice storm.

The Enchantress circled Abigor and Jadis as if she were studying her. "I can see why Silas mated you—you're a stunning little thing," she calmly stated. "I wonder if you're as good in bed as your mate," she hissed.

"You bitch!" Jadis *turned* and lunged for her, breaking free from Abigor's grip. She took her to the ground and had her throat in her hand, muffling her screams.

Abigor grabbed a fistful of Jadis's hair and ripped her off her before she finished the Enchantress. He tossed her onto the floor on her back, and she quickly stumbled to her feet, only for the Enchantress to land a swift blow, knocking her back to the ground again.

"You beiskaldi!" the Enchantress shouted.

Abigor backhanded the Enchantress, grasped her jaw in his hand, and snarled in her face. "You ungrateful kerling. Don't ever touch what is mine!"

"Milord," she replied, her voice shaky and angry.

"Get the fuck out of my sight!" Abigor shoved her into the corridor, and she disappeared into the dark as quickly as she had appeared.

Abigor turned his attention back to Jadis. "Disobeying me will only cause you and your mate to suffer. I suggest you heed the only warning you're going to get," he snarled.

Jadis didn't answer for fear of angering him. She didn't even know how to respond to the threat.

"Answer me," he demanded.

She tried to speak, but the words became lodged in her throat. He grabbed her shirt in his fist and pulled her toward his face.

"Yes—milord. Speak the words, Dhamphyr."

She instinctively dropped one arm across his forearm, spun in a circle, and her elbow crossed his cheek. The unexpected blow caused him to momentarily release his grip, and she took off sprinting down the corridor.

She felt a strike to her face, which knocked her onto her back where she lay semi-conscious. The world around her spun in an abysmal pit of nauseating, pain-filled darkness. She felt the warm liquid flowing from her nose as she struggled to stay awake. She looked up, and Abigor was hovering over her body.

"You're enticingly more than I had ever imagined, but don't be fooled. Your disobedience will be punished," he threatened.

She put her hands on his chest, doing her best to hold him back. He grabbed her wrists and pinned them down. He peered deep into her swirling, raven, and blood-red eyes. He bent over and licked the blood from her lip. She tried to fight him but was unable to move.

"Fucking hell! I never expected for you to taste so amazing. What is that?" he growled. His eyes blazed with anger, clearly reflecting the fact he was also turned on by either the physical altercation and/or her blood.

"Stand!" He wrenched her to her feet. "Before we finish this in my chamber, there's somewhere we need to be. Bind her wrists." He waved his hand in front of her face and released a sedative-like mist, as his guards chained her arms behind her back.

The concoction took an immediate effect. Her thoughts became fuzzy, and her body felt heavy and weak. She felt herself stumble with each heavy, sluggish step as Abigor dragged her down the corridor.

Silas was still chained to the wall, recovering from the beatings. He heard the door slam open and looked up through his swollen, bloody eyes, only to catch a blurry image of Abigor. He blinked multiple time before trying to wipe the blood away on what little of his shoulder he could reach.

"This might wake you up. Look what I've stumbled across. Your mate has come for you, and now I have her." He laughed sadistically.

He shoved her to the floor in front of Silas, still enraged from having been elbowed in the face. "The little kuchka packs quite the punch. She'll make amends for that in my bed tonight."

"Jadis!" Silas roared. The fury he felt toward Abigor coiled like an inferno in the pit of his stomach.

"Silas, what have they done to you?" She tried her best not to cry in their current situation, but looking at Silas battered, beaten, and chained ripped her heart apart. She felt the tears run down her face.

"A man without honor brings death upon himself," Silas stated with a guttural, animalistic growl.

Abigor laughed aloud. "Well, shit! Seeing your mate did light a spark in your ass, but threatening me in your position is a poor choice." He grabbed Jadis's arm and wrenched her off the floor. He shoved her face into Silas.' "Take a good fucking look, for it just might be the last time you lay eyes on your mate."

She hit the wall and tumbled to the floor. As hard as she tried, she couldn't undo the chains binding her arms behind her back. *The shit he waved in my face must be what they're giving Silas and Dante.* She no longer felt an attachment to her powers in any capacity.

Abigor looked to Silas once more with a sardonic grin. "I have one more surprise for you. Bring him."

Vidar and Arkyn walked in and tossed Dante, who was also chained, beaten, and drugged, to the floor. Abigor turned and with a swift kick, he sent him crashing into the opposite wall. He turned his attention back to Silas once again and stood nose to nose with him. "I've captured, chained, and chastened what you deem most sacred." He let out another decrepit laugh. "The Dhamphyr may fight me for now, but don't think for one fucking minute I won't break her. Not only will she get down on her knees and bow to me, but we'll be mated when the next Dark Moon rises in a month's time."

Neither Silas nor Jadis spoke a word, not even telepathically, for fear of being heard.

"Chain him to the opposite wall. They shall witness each other's pain and suffering before death strikes. They shall witness that as well."

Vidar and Arkyn dragged Dante to the wall and chained him before enacting another beating, so Silas and Jadis could watch.

"Sorry to leave so soon, but I feel another need growing your mate is going to take care of." Abigor grabbed ahold of his crotch and laughed. "Guards!"

"Sire," Draconia nodded. He walked to Jadis and pulled her to her feet.

"Take the Dhamphyr to my chamber."

"Aye, milord."

"To your chamber? That will be a grave mistake," she growled.

Abigor grabbed her jaw in his hand and snarled into her face. "I'll enjoy every fucking minute of breaking you." He let go and shoved her head to the side.

Silas roared in response and wrenched the chains, trying to pull them from the wall. "Leave her be!"

Jadis looked up at Silas and caught his eye. She revealed the swirling black and blood-red color before letting them cool back down. It was enough to let him know they had other plans and weren't alone. As much as he tried to hide it, the shock was evident. His eyebrows shot up in bewilderment, and he went wide eyed.

"With your newfound energy, I believe you're ready for the arena. Give him half the dose." Abigor turned around and dragged Jadis out of the cell.

A group of warriors grabbed Bain and pulled him from the Dragurs clutches. They were able to physically fight them back into their graves, with each Dragur succumbing to a fiery death.

"Dante, Jadis—they have them," Bain muttered, half-conscious.

The ensuing battle had waned now that Abigor's warriors had what they came for. They quickly retreated back into the heart of the underworld.

Santiago was at Bain's side. "Get him back to the village. The tips of the arrows were poisoned. Summon your healers."

"Sigurd, remain here with your men and continue with the reconnaissance. We need a way to get into the cavern through the west entrance and sooner than later."

"Aye, milord."

"Radul, I need you to remain with your men as well. Secure the entire area!" Santiago ordered.

"Understood, milord."

Santiago and Jabari, along with the rest of their family, made their way back to the village. The healers attended to Bain, while Santiago, Eden, Aiden, and Jabari continued to plan their rescue mission. This time, however, it would be in Abigor's lair, deep within the pits of the underworld.

CHAPTER 14

Abigor's guards unbound Jadis's arms and tossed her onto a bed in what she assumed was his personal chambers. They left and slammed shut a large wooden door. She heard the clanks of what sounded like large bolts sliding into a metal latch.

It was dark, lit only by lantern and candlelight. The gentle, spitting flames looked as vulnerable as she felt. The longer she watched the shifting shadows, the more malevolent they appeared. She sat on the edge of the expansive bed, which was indeed carved for a Lord. Plush animal furs covered it in its entirety. It was nauseating to see all the furs, and all she could think about was Mag and Limi.

She stumbled to a chair at the far edge of his chamber, as far from the bed as she could get. She placed her feet on the edge of the chair, pulled her bent legs tightly to her chest, and rested her head on her knees. She sat there in utter dismay; she couldn't stop the racing thoughts. She was plagued by emotions and a fear that coiled around her with blackened mouth and fang. She was consumed with worry, not only for Silas and Dante but Bain as well. Try as she might, she couldn't keep her eyes open. The sudden clanking sounds of the heavy door opening startled her awake.

"I expected to see you in my bed." Abigor walked in, along with four females who appeared to have been beaten on more than one occasion.

"Take her to the showers and clean her up." He threw a pile of clothes to one of the girls. "Dress her in these and if she escapes, your death will be a painful one," he threatened.

They submissively nodded as he took a seat in a chair opposite a large stone slab that appeared to be a desk of sorts. It was littered with maps, a couple of large lanterns, and some sort of swirling amber ball resting in the center of four claw feet. He lifted his cup, only for it to be filled by whom Jadis assumed was a chamber maid, who had also entered shortly after the four girls. She stood against the wall to the side of the stone slab, holding a copper pitcher.

The girls motioned her toward another area that appeared to be a smaller cave off the main chamber. Two warriors stood guard outside the entrance with their backs to them.

"What are you doing here?" Jadis whispered.

Not one of the girls spoke a word, but their eyes pleaded for her to stop speaking to them. One of them held her finger to her lips. She didn't speak again for fear of what Abigor may do to them, or her. *I truly pity them, and here I am in the same situation.*

They motioned for Jadis to undress and clean herself up. They handed her a rag and a bar of soap, while another turned on the water. The politely diverted their eyes, but Jadis caught a glimpse of their pain, their torment, and the sorrow they currently felt for her.

She stepped into the water, which quickly took her breath away. It was tepid at best and chilled her to the bone. She washed as quickly as she could to get out from under the water raining down from the cavern ceiling.

They handed her a large piece of hand-sewn linen to dry off with and a white, form-fitting, sheer silk gown, and nothing else.

She was motioned to sit on a stone seat, and the girls attended to her like they were ladies-in-waiting. They towel dried and loosely braded her hair before motioning for her to stand. Each of them carefully studied her appearance before leading her toward the opening.

"Well shit, I didn't realize the extent of your beauty under all that fucking blood and grime." Abigor stood and approached Jadis. The girls kept their heads lowered before he motioned for them to leave.

"Get out," he snarled. They practically tripped over each other as they headed for the door.

Abigor slowly circled Jadis before finally stopping behind her back. He lifted a handful of her hair to his face and smelled it. He then placed his face in the crook of her neck and inhaled. "Jasmine, you smell like your blood tastes," he whispered into her ear.

She turned her head to the side to fend off his advances. Abigor then moved in front of her. He tugged at the front of her dress and pulled her into his body. He placed his other arm around her lower back and moved in for a kiss.

She instinctively head-butted him and ran for the door, only to find it didn't budge. She reluctantly turned to face the monster she assumed she had enraged once again. She leaned her back against the door, trying to disappear.

Abigor wiped the blood from his nose and let out a devilish laugh. "I see you still have some fight left in you," he snarled as he slowly stepped toward her. "I'm curious if you're this fucking feisty in the bed as well?" He pulled her into his arms, threw her onto his bed, and hovered over her. "You will yield, Dhamphyr. Not only will you yield, but you'll also give your body to me before the next Dark Moon. You're already trying my fucking patience and so far, I have been kind. Do not force me to break you."

"I'll never yield," she replied, in a low rumble, before thinking twice about her reactions. *My defiance only seems to turn him on.*

He lowered his body onto hers, and she felt his hardened groin resting on her stomach. He sat up, straddled her, and pinned her arms above her head.

"What shall I call you other than Dhamphyr?"

Well, this isn't the response I expected, Jadis thought.

"You're known by your clan as Jadis? I feel a more appropriate name would be befitting."

She refused to answer and was taken aback when he bent down and shoved his tongue into her mouth. She bit down without thinking it through.

He pulled back and backhanded her. "You'll quickly learn defiance will not be fucking tolerated!" A sudden knock at the door interrupted their altercation to her relief.

"What the fuck do you want?" he bellowed.

"Milord." Evanora slowly opened the door, only to see Abigor straddling the Dhamphyr in his bed. Jadis saw the jealousy and rage radiate across her face.

"Why the fuck are you bothering me?" Abigor demanded.

"Milord." She politely bowed her head in response. "This is always our time."

Abigor jumped off Jadis and bounded toward Evanora. He grabbed her jaw in his hand. "Our time is done. You know I'll be mating the Dhamphyr, so why do you insist on being such an insolent kuchka?"

"I meant no disrespect, milord," she replied in only a whisper.

"Then be gone!" He shoved her out of the chamber and slammed the door in her face.

Had I not had a seething hatred for her, I would feel sorry for her. It's clear she's in love with him. How she can love such a monster is beyond reason.

"Fucking interruptions, can I ever just get an ounce of solitude?"

Jadis sat up and scooted against the headboard, with her knees tucked against her chest.

"Guard!"

"Sire?" answered a voice from the other side of the door.

"No more interruptions regardless of who the fuck it is."

"Aye, Sire."

Abigor turned his attention back to Jadis. "I believe I'll call you Petra as your bravery seems to be forged of stone. No one has ever had the will to defy me as you have."

He headed to the shower, and she remained in place, contemplating her next move. After what seemed like an eternity, he walked back into the room and was completely naked. She quickly diverted her eyes, fearing the worst. He crawled under the skins and lay on his back with one arm behind his head.

"I had the skins brought in for your sake. I could care less about the modern comforts of your breed. Don't make me regret my kindness. Now get into this bed properly."

"No, I won't lie with you." She tried to slowly crawl out of the bed.

He grabbed her arm. "You think you have a choice?"

She tried to yank her arm from his grip, but he flipped over and once again pinned her body beneath his.

"Not only will you lay in my bed, but you'll also remove that fucking gown."

"The hell I will!"

"Where in the fuck do you get your stamina? Either you remove that gown, or I will."

The fear and nervousness besieged her mind and body. *To be naked in his bed feels like the ultimate betrayal to Silas.* The next thing she knew, he ripped the gown over her head and tossed it to the floor. She now lay pinned beneath him, naked.

"Either sleep, or I'll make you so fucking tired, you'll have no choice," he threatened.

The underlying tone brought up the words of warning Santiago had spoken. *'He will use your body.'* In that moment, she chose to not push him any further. She relaxed, letting him know she wouldn't continue to fight him. He too relaxed.

"Now sleep before I decide otherwise, Petra."

She slipped out from underneath his body and slid as far to the edge of the bed she could get. After what seemed like an hour, based on his heavy breathing, she hoped he was asleep and silently cried to herself. Regardless of her current situation, she was provided some sort of comforts while Silas and Dante were beaten, drugged, and chained in a dungeon. She vowed to do whatever it took to save Silas and Dante. *Whatever it takes,* she told herself. She decided to try to reach out to Silas.

"Baby, can you hear me?" She waited. *"Silas—can you hear me?"*

"Try as you might, he cannot hear you I've seen to it." Abigor's voice startled her, and she went rigid.

"I assume you're not tired yet? Maybe I should find another way to release that energy of yours." He rolled on top of her.

"Get off me!"

"Grant me permission and now. I need to scratch a certain itch," he growled.

"I'll never give myself to you willingly," she snarled.

"Well shit, I guess we find ourselves in a predicament. I do like to toy with my prey. You'll give yourself to me tonight, or it will be at Silas's expense." She froze at the threat.

"So be it." Abigor jumped out of the bed and pulled on a pair of old-world trousers that laced up the crotch. She managed to grab the sheer gown and put it on, not knowing what was about to happen.

He grabbed her by the arm and dragged her out the door. She knew they were headed for Silas as they made their way down the expansive, winding, stone tunnels.

"Abigor, stop! You can't do this," she demanded. She grabbed his forearm and tried to stop him from pulling her down the corridor.

"You'll learn your lesson, you insolent kuchka."

"Abigor, stop!" she begged.

"Open the door." The guard unlocked the door and shoved it open.

Silas and Dante snapped their heads in her direction, and Silas appeared more alert than the last time she saw him, and some of his injuries had slowly healed. Abigor still had a tight grip on her arm, and he swung her forward. "It seems your mate chooses not to obey, and she has a desperate need to try my fucking patience."

Dante and Silas's physical response, as well and the look in their eyes, conveyed more than words. Silas morphed into the monster she had come to know.

Abigor's knuckles split the skin over Silas's cheekbone, and the force of the blow sent blood splattering onto the stained wall.

"Stop!" Jadis yelled. She lunged for Abigor and took his throat into her mouth. He wrenched her off as his fist connected with her cheek, driving her body to the ground.

"Jadis," Silas snarled, his tone animalistic. "Don't yield to him no matter what he does or threatens to do to me!"

"I won't yield to him now or ever!" she raged.

"Shut your fucking mouth, Dhamphyr!" Abigor demanded. "Your mate is now to be called Petra."

Pure rage crossed Silas and Dante's faces.

The air exploded from Silas's lungs, and fresh ripples of pain radiated through his torso from the blow of Abigor's foot.

"Face me fist to fist," Silas demanded.

Abigor's guards turned their attention to Silas and Abigor.

The concoction Abigor had given Jadis earlier had begun to slightly wear off. Her eyes were now the swirling, oiled mixture, and her pupils had become an obsidian diamond, just as Silas' had when he fed. She felt her body take on an entirely different essence as she slowly rose up behind Abigor. She cautiously backed into Dante and stood on her tiptoes.

He knew exactly what she was doing and subtly bent down. He took as much of her blood as he could while Silas kept Abigor's attention. *"Don't be so brazen, Jadis,"* Dante demanded telepathically before he released his grip.

She slowly stepped forward with a deep rumble. She slit her wrist open with one of her newly grown, sable, pointed nails. Abigor spun around and saw the blood spewing from the gash. His expression was one of utter disbelief.

"Touch my mate or Dante again, and I will end my own life," she snarled.

Abigor lunged for her, slit his own wrist, and shoved it into her mouth to heal her. The blood dripped into her mouth, but the gash continued to pool at her feet.

"What the sorðinn?" Abigor snarled.

"I am a Dhamphyr. You are not my mate, therefore your blood will not heal me. Should you choose to raise one more hand to either Silas or Dante, I shall choose death," she snarled in an inhuman tone as the blood ran down her fingers, splattering onto the ground at her feet.

"You're stubborn to a fault, Petra. I'll fucking deal with you accordingly!" He grabbed a fistful of her hair and without any other immediate alternative, he shoved her face into Silas's neck.

She took his vein as Silas gently rested his head on hers. She spoke privately as she wrapped her arms around his battered body. *"Silas, what are we going to do? I can't stand to see you like this."*

"Be still, baby. That was a dangerous move but brilliant. I believe you may have just bought us the time we need, but I don't want you to push him any further."

"I had no choice—I won't let him take you from me."

"Whatever you do, do not yield to him. Play his game as long as it takes, no matter what it takes. Understand what I'm saying to you? Don't challenge him any more than you already have." Once again, Silas and Jadis were connected through their mutual torment.

"What exactly did you do to yourself? How is his blood not healing you?" Silas asked.

"It's a long story," she replied, and Silas almost let out a chuckle.

"Enough!" Abigor saw her wound healing and ripped her from Silas.

"You play a dangerous game, Petra. The more you fight me, the bigger of a challenge you become, and I love a fiendish challenge!" He still held a fistful of her hair as he snarled in her face.

She felt her body weaken, and she staggered on her feet. Abigor let out another seething laugh. "Not only have you taken his blood, but you've also consumed the sedative." He tossed her over his shoulder and left.

Jadis awoke and was still in Abigor's bed; it had been this way for what she assumed was about a week now. She prayed her blood could help heal Dante as she hadn't seen them again. She had no idea how long she had been asleep this time; the concoction kept her sated.

"It's about time you joined me. It's time to introduce you to my clan."

"Good luck," she stated as she rubbed her face.

Abigor let out a chuckle as he stood at the edge of the bed. "Get up, the games begin soon."

"Games? What are you jabbering on about?" she mumbled.

Abigor grabbed her ankle and yanked her toward him. "You'll need to dress appropriately. Tonight, I'll be introducing my soon to be mate," he stated.

She sat up on the edge of the bed, pulled a skin up to cover her body, and watched as he headed for the door and opened it.

"Enter." The same four young women that were there on the first night walked in, two of whom seemed to have fresh cuts and bruises.

"Milord," they stated as they bowed their heads.

"Take her to the shower."

They nodded without speaking and motioned for Jadis to follow.

"I'm in no mood for your bullshit, Abigor," Jadis mumbled.

The look of shock that shot across each of the girls' faces rippled through Jadis. Abigor grabbed her arm, and the girls quickly moved aside, cowering at his feet.

"Get up! I won't tell you again. Either they can shower you, or I will."

Jadis didn't speak as she was focused on the girls' petrified reactions.

"Have it your way." Abigor proceeded to yank her off the bed and dragged her to the shower. She barely managed to hang on to one of the skins. As they entered the bathing area, he turned on the water and shoved her under the spray, ripping the fur from her grip.

The girls followed behind, not knowing what to do or how to respond.

Abigor removed his pants and stood under the water with her. She quickly covered what little of her body she could. He grabbed her wrist and slapped the bar of soap into her hand.

"Now wash your fucking body, or I'll take pleasure in washing you myself."

"Wash your own ass," she replied as she threw the soap at his face, only for him to catch it. She didn't know if it was her *turning* or the fact she threw the soap at Abigor, but the girls ran and cowered at the opposite end of the shower area.

The hard smack of the back of his hand split her cheek. She watched as the blood slowly swirled down the drain. The clear water became a reddened, spiraling mixture at her feet.

The wound failed to heal once again. "Streð mik—now look what you fucking made me do! Get my trousers," he demanded.

One of the girls quickly ran from the area and returned with a pair of dry trousers. He put them on without lacing them up and tossed Jadis over his shoulder.

"Put me down!" She tried to fight, but it was useless. Her powers had succumbed to the concoction as well as the powerful, dark magic residing within his underworld.

"I cannot introduce the most powerful Dhamphyr in existence to my clan if she can't even fucking heal herself," he roared.

As he carried her naked, she managed to get off his shoulder, but he swung her around and carried her in his arms instead.

"The more you fight me, the worse things will be for you," he threatened.

"Put me down!" She managed to wrap her legs in his, and he fell to his knees and landed on top of her.

His men reached down to pull them both up. "Stand down," he demanded. "Ebasi, Petra! You're pushing your fucking luck," he yelled. "Have it your way." He settled himself between her legs and pinned her arms down. He bent down and seductively bit her bottom lip with his canines before he trailed his tongue up her cheek and licked the blood from her face. "I love it when they put up a goddamn fight. Now you can lay there naked beneath me, or you can do as your fucking told!"

"Get off me!" she demanded again.

Silas and Dante heard the commotion outside the door and the muffled sounds of Jadis and Abigor's angry voices.

"What the hell is going on?" Silas snarled to Dante.

The door slammed open, and Abigor tossed Jadis into Silas before he could comprehend what was happening.

Jadis wrapped her arms around Silas and clung on for dear life. *"What's happening, my love?"* Silas demanded.

"Abigor," Dante snarled. "Face me, you fucking coward!"

Abigor ignored Dante, grabbed Silas by the jaw, and seethed into his face, pressing Jadis's naked body between them. "First of all, she is known as Petra, and you'll address my mate to be accordingly."

"Jadis is mine! You will never fucking have her," Silas snarled.

Abigor landed a hard blow to his face. "I already have her, but it seems I have a bigger problem to contend with. Petra can't heal herself without your blood, and tonight is the night of her introduction as my queen. Now feed Petra before I slit your mate's throat myself."

She slowly removed one of her arms from around Silas's body, and he realized what she was doing. He bent his head, offering her his neck. She slipped her wrist to his mouth as she stood on her tiptoes, allowing him to feed from her at the same time.

"I need you to stop taunting him. You managed to buy us some time, but I can't stand the sight of him hurting you."

Only when she fed from him could they speak on their own level. She figured that out when she fed Dante, and he was able to speak to her, unbeknownst to Abigor.

"I love you with my life, vampire," Jadis replied.

"And I you, mon chéri. *Fear not, this will be over soon. I promise you on all that I am."*

"Enough." Abigor wrenched her from Silas, and she hid her wrist until she felt it was healed. Silas also controlled his reaction to having just fed from her.

Abigor grabbed her arm and dragged her out of the cell.

"The next time we meet, you'll be in the arena," Abigor hissed telepathically to Silas before slamming the door shut.

CHAPTER 15

"**D**ante, we need to get the out of these goddamn chains and get Jadis out sooner than later," Silas raged.

"You don't have to tell me anything I don't already know," Dante replied with a guttural growl. "I don't think our clan will make it in before the Dark Moon has risen. Did Jadis feed you?"

"Yes, and her blood is different, more powerful. There's something dark. Her eyes? What did she do?"

"We don't know. The night you were taken, something happened to her back at the temple. Do we ever know what that girl does? The only thing I do know is that she conjured up something deep, something dark," Dante rumbled.

"Leave it to my mate. Her healing only from me—that's new."

"Whatever she has done, it bought us some time. They can't kill you if she can't heal without your blood."

"Dante, they'll use you against her instead."

"Yes." Dante nodded his head and said nothing more.

"I'm hoping when she sees me in the arena, she can keep it together and not do anything rash." Silas let out a heavy sigh, knowing she would react in one way or another.

"Good luck with that, brother. Unfortunately, we both know better."

Abigor slammed his door open, and the girls were still sitting in the same spot. He carried Jadis into the shower and left. *Apparently, we aren't showering together, thank the Gods.* She assumed the only reason was that he wasn't sure he could control himself, and he knew he couldn't have her before the Dark Moon, at least not without her permission.

"Make sure I don't see one spot on Petra."

"Yes, milord," the girls replied softly.

"You come with me," he demanded as he pointed to one of them.

She reluctantly followed him out, and Jadis knew exactly what he wanted. She heard the door in the main chamber slam shut as he left with her. *It's her or me. He chose the safer alternative; screwing me would be disastrous. Even though I pity the poor thing, I am relieved.*

After she had showered, they took their time making sure her hair was perfectly braided in multiple layers on top of her head. Loose strands gently hung around her face and over the top of her head. The longs strands also softly flowed down the back of her neck and shoulders. It was clear looking at herself in the foggy, cracked mirror, Abigor wanted her to look like a Bergelême princess, mirroring his own appearance. *The only difference in our hair is that his head is shaved on the sides.*

The girls placed a gold and silver tiara on her forehead and weaved the ends into her hair on the side of her head. The front had a large, swirling black Musgravite stone in the center, surrounded by what looked like long branches carved in silver. Eight long, thin stygian pendulums hung loosely around her face and the sides of her head.

"Leave me," Abigor demanded as he got out of bed to dress.

"Milord," the girl replied. She slipped out of the bed and quickly dressed before leaving Abigor.

He headed for the cells to inform Dante and Silas which one of them would be in the arena for the night.

Once again, the cell door opened, and Abigor walked in. "Dante, you'll be fighting tonight, and you'll have quite the audience. I had planned on it being Silas, but it seems we have a bit of a problem where Petra is concerned, as you know."

"I'll be the one to see you draw your last breath," Dante threatened.

Abigor dismissed the threat. "The guards will escort you to the arena. I would love to honor you with my presence, but Petra is awaiting me. She's in my chamber, dressing as we speak. As for you, Silas, you'll be the one to watch his brother's death tonight." He laughed sadistically.

Abigor turned to his guards. "Take Silas to the cage closest to the arena."

Abigor left, and six of his warriors grabbed Silas and Dante. They escorted Silas down the long corridor behind Dante, both of whom were chained by hands and feet. They heard the crowd going wild the closer they got to the arena. The vibrations from the chaos and excitement of the fights vibrated through the uneven stones at their feet. Dante felt the heavy, fast-paced thumping of his heart. Small droplets of sweat dripped from his face and body, and his muscles went stiff. He began to *turn* as the threats grew with the anticipation of having to fight in his weakened state.

They stopped at the main entrance, and Silas was thrown into a cage facing the arena. Dante stood on the other side of the bars facing the arena's entrance. Silas stood in front of the bars and looked to Dante, who stared back at him as if for the last time.

Dante spoke aloud regardless of who could hear, "Take care of our girl should things not go my way."

"Don't think like that. We've faced far worse. Hell, back in the day, this would have been our choice. Don't forget who you are, brother," Silas demanded.

They nodded to each other while Dante waited to be ushered into the arena.

The girls led Jadis out of the shower area and to her relief, Abigor hadn't returned. The girl he had left with was back, fumbling with her clothes. Jadis hurried over to the girl and pulled the hair away from her face. "Are you okay?" Jadis asked.

She gave her a subtle smile and gently shrugged her shoulders. "It's not what you think," she whispered.

Whatever pull Abigor has is beyond me. First the Enchantress and now her? However, she didn't question it further as she had bigger problems to contend with.

They dressed Jadis in a dark-green, linen dress, trimmed with gold lace. The green and gold braided belt was perfectly knotted at her hip and hung loosely around her waist, with the ends hanging unevenly down her thigh, almost reaching her knee. The dress was cut with a very low neckline extending down the front and partially exposed her breasts and stomach, as well as most of her back. The slits rose up both sides of the dress and bared her thighs. The knee-high gladiator flats were an exact match of the dress. The green and gold braded laces tied just below her knees.

She was standing at the edge of the bed when the door swung open. The girls jumped and looked to the floor, making sure they didn't make eye contact with Abigor. Jadis, however, nervously turned around to face him.

He stood in bewilderment. He couldn't believe the sight before his eyes. *She's more than stunning; she's magnificent, and she is mine.* He walked in a circle around her body and studied her.

"Po dyavolite, you are a vision to behold. Your duplicity is simply intoxicating." He motioned for the girls to leave.

Jadis stood looking back at Abigor, whose trousers, tunic, and boots matched her dress perfectly. For whatever reason, it did more than offend her. "We may look alike, but don't be fooled. I do not belong to you," she snarled.

Abigor let out a noxious laugh. "You belong to me now, and the sooner you figure that out, the better off you'll be." He stood chest to chest with her, lifted her hair to his face, and took a deep breath. "In less than a month, your body will also belong to me."

He placed his hand on her lower back and motioned her toward the door. They walked down multiple stone corridors and winding stairs with a half-dozen warriors following. As the sounds of a cheering crowd grew with intensity, Jadis felt her pulse quicken, which sent her stomach churning in a hundred ways. Normally, she had Silas at her side to calm her racing thoughts. Now, she was on her own. She stopped walking to catch her breath.

Abigor stopped and looked at her curiously. She leaned against the stone wall and was bent over, holding her stomach. "I can't do this. Take me back to your chamber," she demanded softly.

"I'll do no such thing. The crowd awaits your arrival. They're all expecting to finally lay their eyes on the mythical Dhamphyr—now move!"

The rambunctious sounds grew with intensity the further they went. She did everything she could to not vomit at his feet. They walked through a tunnel and from what she could see, a ledge appeared and seemed to be about twenty feet above an enormous arena. Only a short stone wall separated the edge from the arena below, and a large stone throne stood before her.

"Hold her," Abigor ordered.

"Aye, milord." The guards each took ahold of one of her biceps but didn't take their eyes off her. Their blank, transfixed expressions, and the way in which they studied her, only ramped up her heightened, anxiety-ridden state of mind.

Abigor entered the cavern alone and stood before the stone thrones. The cheers of the crowd at his appearance erupted into a deafening roar of whoops and hollers.

She noticed two vampires who looked exactly like Abigor, turn to catch a glimpse of her as they took their places next to Abigor and raised their wooden cups.

A hushed silence fell over the arena below as Abigor lifted his hand with only two fingers raised. "Tonight, you shall meet the elusive Dhamphyr!" Once again, their rambunctious, deafening cheers drowned out all other sounds.

"Our Dark Lord has bestowed us a divine gift. We shall stain the land with the blood of our enemies," he shouted.

The thundering cheers of approval vibrated up through the floor beneath Jadis's feet. Abigor turned toward her and held out his hand. The guards let go and motioned for her to enter. She backed up, only for the warriors who had followed them in to stop her, blocking her only exit. She managed to take a deep breath and quickly get her shit together. *Tonight, I'll show no fear.* She lifted her head, straightened her back, and walked toward Abigor. The roars of the crowd became that of gasps. She held onto the sides of her dress, trying to avoid taking his hand. He didn't waver and based solely on the look on his face, she heeded the warning and took his hand.

"The Dhamphyr exists, and she belongs to me!" The crowd went wild before quieting down to hear what else he had to say.

"Bow to them," he snarled under his breath.

"Never," she shot back. She noticed the look of shock crossing the face of the two other vampires standing next to them, in regard to her having challenged Abigor in front of his entire clan. *Screw them too.*

"The Dhamphyr bows to no one!" she roared to the hushed, gaping crowd. They erupted into another frenzy of roars, and fist pounding. She looked to Abigor and cocked her head to the side, waiting for a response.

"Let the fights commence!" Abigor announced; the crowd once again erupted.

Abigor turned to face his brothers. "She's impetuous to a fault. I would like you to meet my brothers, Vidar and Arkyn."

They nodded in her direction with fixed expressions and a cold, unforgiving gaze that moved up and down her body.

The way they stared chilled her to the bone. *There's an unforgiving cruelty behind their eyes.*

Vidar stepped forward, grabbed a long lock of her hair in his hand, and bent over to smell it. She slapped his hand away and snarled, "Do—not—touch—me—again," she stated, annunciating each word.

"What did you fucking say to me?" Vidar grabbed her hair at the base of her neck and wrenched her head back.

Abigor grabbed his arm in response. "Remove your fucking hand from what is mine!"

Arkyn stepped back, but the confusion and rage in his eyes is clear. He had likely never been spoken to like that either.

"I see why she tries your fucking patience, brother. Have you not broken the kuchka yet?" he snarled.

"Take you seats," Abigor demanded. They obliged and sat in smaller thrones on either side of Abigor's. A couple of maidens appeared, filled each of their cups, and stood behind Arkyn and Vidar.

"I have a surprise for you tonight, Petra. Now sit."

"And where am I to sit, exactly?" She looked around to find the only other seats were a small stone slab next to either Arkyn or Vidar. She opted to be as far from Abigor as she could get, so she walked in the direction of one of the seats on the other side of Vidar.

Abigor grabbed her hand. "You can choose to sit in my lap, or at my feet on the floor like a common whore."

"Then I choose the floor." Abigor's brothers' eyes widened with raised eyebrows; her defiance stunned them both.

She turned to sit on the floor, but Abigor grabbed both sides of her waist and pulled her into his lap.

"What are you doing? Let go of me!" she demanded.

"I asked which you would prefer, but I never said you had a choice. Now be still."

She tried to get out of his lap to no avail. *It's clear his only motivation is to show the crowd I belong to him.* "Get your hands off me," she seethed.

Abigor simply held her tighter, and pulled her further into his lap. *Fighting him right now is futile,* she thought, having decided to give in. It seemed the more she fought, the more he enjoyed it.

"At least you could scoot the hell over," she snarled.

Abigor let out a devilish laugh and re-positioned his body to allow her a bit more room on the stone seat.

"Bring Petra an ale," he demanded.

A young gal seeing to Abigor's needs filled a wooden cup and handed it to her. Jadis gave her a gentle smile and chugged the entire cup to Abigor, Arkyn, and Vidar's amusement.

"What are you waiting for? Fill it again," he demanded, seemingly amused.

The gal filled her cup with shaky hands, and Jadis chugged it as well; it was the only solace she had to calm her nerves.

The three of them laughed aloud. "Well, apparently, the Dhamphyr can drink. Who knew?" Arkyn stated.

The cheers of the crowd below them grew with intensity as the winner of the last round was brought back into the arena.

"Milord," a voice spoke from behind them.

Jadis turned around only to see Evanora approaching. *The hatred she feels for me is more than evident. Although I feel the same. If it hadn't been for that bitch, I wouldn't be sitting here, and Silas and Dante wouldn't be chained and beaten. I will make her suffer.*

"What is it?" Abigor asked without looking at her.

"I was coming to watch the fights, milord."

"Do as you wish."

Evanora took a seat next to Arkyn, and Jadis heard her mumble under her breath.

"If you have something to say, say it, bitch," Jadis snarled.

"Dare not challenge me, Dhamphyr!" Evanora seethed, as she stood and faced her.

Jadis jumped up from Abigor's lap and stood face to face with her. She reached out and grabbed Evanora by the throat. "I have no problem meeting you hand to hand if you choose to threaten me!"

Evanora grabbed her wrist and raised her other hand, only for Abigor to grab hold of it. He forced Jadis to release her grip. "Don't think I won't cage you like a worthless whore should you lay one hand on Petra. Either take a seat or get the fuck out of my sight."

"She's nothing more than a fucking worm, and you're the apple! What is it she possesses that pulls your desire?" Evanora screamed.

"She possesses everything you don't!" Evanora's head snapped to the side, and Jadis cringed from the sound of the blow. "Do not challenge me. Your presence has become an annoyance!"

"Dobre dyavolite, tonight just gets better and better," Arkyn shouted.

"I say we put those two in the arena together," Vidar suggested.

"How about I take you to the arena, Vidar," Jadis snarled.

Arkyn spat out his drink and bellowed in laughter. "This is turning out to be one hell of a night."

"Talk to me like that again, Petra —" Vidar began.

Jadis cut him off mid-sentence, "Or what?"

"You're a brazen kuchka. I would heed the only warning you're going to get. I may have to cut that fucking tongue out of your mouth," Vidar roared.

Jadis rolled her eyes as Abigor sat and pulled her back into his lap as he ordered Arkyn to sit. "Arkyn, take a seat." He then turned to Jadis. "Petra, I think you're going to enjoy the main event," he suggested.

His laugh was nothing short of sinister, and she knew it had to be Silas or Dante who would be fighting next. Her heart lurched and drummed like a hammer against her breast.

Another opponent appeared from the main entrance. As soon as the warrior walked in, Jadis tried to jump to her feet. However, Abigor grabbed her. She swung her arm around, and her elbow met his face. The blow was enough for him to release her. She ran to the edge of the ledge, grabbed hold of the stone wall, and leaned as far over as she could.

Abigor grabbed her from behind, slid his hands around her waist, and harshly pulled her body to his. "I would punish you for that, but it seems this will be punishment enough. You shall watch your wizard meet his fate. Trust me, if you ever lay a hand on me again, I'll make you regret it without killing you. You'll beg for mercy should you push me any further," he threatened.

She knew it wasn't an idle threat and she stood frozen in place at the mere thought of what might happen to Dante. She felt the tears cascading down her cheeks. She scanned the entire arena and noticed Silas in a cage on the opposite side. He too was watching. Silas looked up, and their eyes met. As soon as he saw her, she saw the rage crossing his face. She gave him a half-hearted smile, and he responded with a wink and a nod. The simple gesture meant more than words ever could in that moment; they both turned their attention back to Dante.

Dante managed to gather himself together as he picked up the heavy sword that had been tossed at his feet.

Abigor stood next to Jadis and held up his hand. The entire crowd as well as Dante turned their attention to him.

"Tonight, you will all witness one of our most formidable enemies fall to their knees!" The crowd erupted.

Dante thought to himself that this wouldn't just be another spectacle. *I'll need to end the fight quickly if I have a chance at surviving without the use of my powers. Tonight, will be the beginning of our reckoning.* He looked at Jadis and gave her a quick wink. He then spun the sword in his hand just as he had done in the bar with the pool cue, letting her know he had this. She smiled sincerely and winked back.

"May the fight commence!" Abigor shouted.

When Dante's opponent charged him, he was able to evade the initial blow by lunging to the side. The resounding clang of blade meeting blade rang throughout the arena. Their demeanor was beyond that of anxiousness; a look of hunger filled both of their eyes as they fought for their lives.

Dante's adrenaline pumped so fast, it was hard for him to control his breathing. Between the adrenaline and the drugs, he grunted with every swing of the heavy sword. He spun around and slashed at his opponent's back, and the tip seared through his flesh. As his opponent spun around to evade the full blow, the tip of his blade sliced through Dante's arm as they leapt around each other.

Jadis gasped for breath every time their blades glanced off each other. Each of them evaded blow after blow before the tip of Dante's opponent's blade crossed his bicep. She covered her mouth with both hands and held her breath as she watched the blood run down Dante's arm.

Dante slipped around his opponent and spun his sword around his head before swinging it toward his opponent's neck. However, the fighter bent backward, avoiding the deadly blow.

Dante met his opponent's sword with his and knocked it from his grip. His opponent lunged and wrapped his arms around his waist, plummeting Dante to the ground. The air exploded from his lungs as he landed on his back.

Dante lost his grip from the force of the blow, and his sword flew from his hand and slid through the dirt before resting beyond his reach. They were now locked in each other's arms on the ground, both struggling to gain the upper hand. They traded blow after blow and struggled to hold onto one another as their bodies became slick from the blood flowing from their wounds.

Dante looped his left arm around his opponent's right arm and pinned his elbow against his side. He threw his weight against his opponent in a desperate attempt to overwhelm him and regain control of the grapple. Dante twisted his body around as he swept his right leg back. There was a bone-snapping crunch as his opponent's elbow twisted too far in the wrong direction and the warrior bellowed in pain. As Dante regained control he saw his sword was just out of his reach. He tried with all the energy he could gather to wrestle his enormous opponent closer to it.

The moment Dante released his grip to grab for the sword, his opponent flipped his body over and, using his own momentum, he also lunged for the sword. Dante crawled across the dirt arena on his knees, and with his good arm, he grabbed the sword.

They both struggled to their feet and spun around to face each other. Dante lunged toward his opponent, who moved to the side in one fluid motion, evading Dante's blade.

Dante was breathing heavily as the sweat and blood dripped down his body. He gasped for a fresh breath. The hatred he felt for Abigor for having involved Jadis in all of this, and the thought of her being taken as Abigor's mate, gave him the will he needed to continue fighting. He wanted to unleash all of his rage and hatred on Abigor but for now, he would take it out on his opponent. He swiveled in his opponent's direction, jumped forward, and landed a well-placed kick to his chest, which sent the warrior crashing to the ground once again.

His opponent tumbled backward head over heels; dirt and dust swirled around his broken body. He rolled over, jumped to his feet, and thrust his sword forward, only to meet Dante's.

As their swords met, all Jadis could do was pray to her Gods to give Dante the strength he needed to hold his own.

Dante took a deep breath. *This is just another enemy, just one of countless I've faced in my lifetime, and it ends now.* He lunged for his opponent, wrapped his arms around his large body, and took him to the ground. He landed blow after blow into his opponent's face, rendering him powerless. His opponent could no longer fight back against his relentless assault. Dante boldly stood above the fallen warrior, placed the tip of his blade against his chest, and shoved. His opponent's eyes widened as he gasped for breath before his battered and broken body went limp.

The crowd erupted in cheers and chanted life, "Zhivot! Zhivot! Zhivot!"

As Jadis watched Dante end the fight, she let out the breath she had been holding in before tears of relief trickled down her face.

Evanora moved to her side. "I see your mate across the arena," she whispered close enough to Jadis's face, she felt the venomous warmth of her breath.

She snapped her head in Evanora's direction, and her emotions were undeniably raw. Evanora laughed and spewed her hate. "It seems you hold the wizard close to your heart, that's a grave mistake!"

"You're nothing more than Abigor's decrepit, used-up wench," Jadis growled.

"And you'll soon know exactly what Abigor is capable of," Evanora seethed.

Abigor, Arkin, and Vidar stood at the ledge, just on the other side of Jadis and Evanora. They were too busy deciding whether or not to spare Dante's life to notice the fight brewing between them and Evanora took full advantage, in order to taunt Jadis.

"I believe I'll see to your mate after he's taken back to his cell. You took what was mine and tonight, you'll feel the darkness as it descends around you like a storm, when I take his life."

Dante pointed his sword at Abigor. "Soon, you too shall meet my blade!" he bellowed through the noise of the chanting crowd, as he stumbled further backward. Unable to hold the heavy sword any longer, he tossed it to the ground and fell to his knees. He looked to Jadis, only to see her face to face with the Enchantress.

Abigor stood in disbelief. He hadn't expected Dante to be the winner, but he had no choice but to oblige the crowd. He held up both hands, one thumb facing up, the other facing down. He dropped the thumb facing down, sparing Dante's life.

Jadis landed one hard blow to Evanora's face, and she gasped in utter shock. "I'll put you to the grave!" Jadis roared.

Evanora grabbed hold of her face. "I'm going to kill you and your mate. Fucking whore!"

Jadis grabbed her body and threw her over the ledge. Evanora disappeared into the air as Jadis jumped after her.

"Kakvo sorðinn?" Abigor yelled as he and his brothers followed them over the ledge.

Evanora and Jadis came crashing down into the arena to the utter disbelief of the cheering crowd. Dante was in shock as he watched Jadis throw her over the ledge, hot on her heels, and he jumped to his feet.

"Jadis!" Dante yelled. He began to run to her, only to be subdued by multiple guards as they filled the arena on Abigor's orders. He was quickly subdued, chained, and drugged.

"Jadis!" Silas roared.

The dust and debris swirled at their feet as the cheers quickly became that of stunned gasps at the sight before them. Evanora began to disappear into a twirling plume, but Jadis grabbed her before she fully vanished. She had her by her throat and picked her up off the ground with one hand.

Evanora let out a muffled scream and chanted in old world Bergelême. Jadis dropped to the ground on one knee, brought Evanora's body down, and across her other knee, breaking her back. She lunged on top of Evanora's broken body and took her throat to her mouth.

Through the roars of the crowd, Jadis faintly heard both Silas and Dante yelling her name.

Abigor grabbed her from behind and ripped her off Evanora.

Dante's vision blurred, and the ground spun beneath him. He felt himself lose consciousness as the vision of Jadis faded, and the blackness consumed him.

Jadis tried to wrench herself from Abigor's grip, but he took full control of the situation. "You've now seen the powers of the Dhamphyr," he shouted. "Take the Enchantress away," he demanded before looking at Jadis. "If you move from my side or make one false step, I'll kill Dante before your fucking eyes," he snarled.

Jadis gathered her composure and stood at his side as if she belonged to him, knowing his words weren't a mere threat.

"She yields the power to defeat the Enchantress. Now we shall defeat our enemies!" The crowd cheered once again as their shock and fear settled.

"Meet your queen—Petra!" The crowd all took a knee and bowed their heads.

"Tonight is a night of great celebration!" The crowd stood once again and roared.

Abigor placed his hand on her lower back and led her out of the arena, followed by Arkin and Vidar, who were too shocked at the sight of her taking on the Enchantress to do anything other than follow Abigor's lead.

As soon as they were out of sight, Abigor grabbed her by the throat and slammed her body into the wall. "Tonight worked in your favor as well as mine. But do not think for one minute I'll tolerate any more of you fucking insolence."

They made it back to Abigor's chamber. He threw her onto the bed and hovered over her body. "We can remain enemies or become bedmates. You can either suffer and witness those you hold most precious suffer a worse fate, or we can rule the sixty Legions of Hades together. You have until dawn to choose, or I'll choose for you."

As soon as he left, all she could do was curl into a ball and weep. She could no longer handle the emotional torment.

CHAPTER 16

The cell door opened, and Abigor entered. Dante was chained to the wall, hanging unconscious. He raised his hand, and his guard tossed a bucket of cold water on him. Dante gasped for breath and struggled to open his eyes.

"Take them both down and chain them to the floor." They were tossed onto the stone slabs as his warriors chained their ankles and wrists.

Abigor paced the floor between them before speaking. "Your performance was a fucking surprise, which is the only reason you're still with the living. I've made a decision—Dante, shall you survive the night, you'll continue fighting in the arena. As long as you perform as you did, you'll continue on. I'll fight you until you lie in the dust and refuse to go on."

Abigor turned back to Silas. "I never expected for Petra to take on the Enchantress, however, her actions in front of my entire clan has shown them the powers of the Dhamphyr. They now fear her beyond all. She's lucky, tonight worked in my favor. I thought you would like to know I've given her a choice to make before dawn. If she chooses to remain my enemy, I'll make her life so fucking unbearable and pain filled, she'll either beg for my pity, or she will willingly become my bedmate. Either way, I'll enjoy ravaging her body from dusk till dawn."

"You harm one fucking hair on her head, I'll end your life before you take another breath," Silas roared. Abigor let out a belly laugh, ignoring the threat.

"By the looks of your brother, I assume you'll witness his death tonight. I believe that will be punishment enough for now."

Before Abigor left, Silas heard the rattling of chain before he felt the pain radiating across his body and the warmth of the liquid as it ran down his waist. He let out a gut-wrenching roar and covered the gash with both hands.

"Don't go anywhere," Abigor snarled as he left.

"Dante, speak to me, brother. I need you to stay with me," he pleaded through the pain.

"I'm okay, brother," Dante replied with a raspy whisper. "Jadis fed me as well, and I feel my body healing."

"And just when were you going to fill me in?" Silas asked. He pulled his blood-soaked hands away and watched as the wound slowly closed.

"It hadn't crossed my mind until now. Whatever she has done has made her blood all the more powerful. I too feel the darkness swirling within it," Dante admitted.

Silas and Dante were relieved to be resting on the stone slab, on their backs, after having been chained on their feet for weeks now.

Dante turned his head and looked at Silas. "What's on your mind, brother? I can feel it, but I'm too tired to decipher your thoughts."

"I need you to do something for me," Silas replied with a heavy sigh.

"You know my life is yours, what is it?"

"If I should meet my death, I need you to take Jadis as your mate."

Dante was shocked, and not quite sure how to respond. "You're talking crazy, brother. We'll all get out of here alive, don't fail me now."

"You know as well as I do, he'll kill me the night of the Dark Moon should we not escape. Nothing will stop him from taking her as his mate. Her life will be nothing less than misery and torture, and I cannot bear it. I won't go to the grave with that being my last thought."

"Stop, Silas. You talk as if you're already dead. Not only will our clan be here, but rest assured you and I will find a way out of these fucking chains. If we can get to Jadis again, we can make sure she knows what to do."

"Dante, I need you to promise me on the word of Nosferatu. Shall it come to that, I need you do this—I won't surrender her to that monster."

"You're thinking is irrational, and your emotions are clouding your judgement."

"I know you're in love with her. I see it in the way you look at her. I saw it the night you were dancing with her in the club. I feel the tormented thoughts that weigh heavy on your mind. I need you to give me your word. It's the only way Abigor won't possess her."

After a few moments of silence, Dante finally spoke. "If it eases your torment even for a moment, I give you my word on Nosferatu. Shall you meet your death, I'll take her as my mate."

"Your words are sincere," Silas replied. Another brief silence followed.

"Should I take her as my mate and you live, then what? You know I'll no longer be able to control my need to possess and dominate her in every way. What then, brother?" Dante asked, genuinely concerned.

"Should that happen, we will have a lifetime to figure out our bullshit. At least she survives, that's all I care about."

"It seems you've thought about little else. Exactly how long have you been contemplating this?"

"Since the night I was captured. I knew without a doubt she would come for me."

"You know damn good and well she'll never agree. She's as loyal to you as they come."

"You'll have to do whatever it takes to convince her."

"Apparently, the drugs have clouded your memory. You seem to forget who we're talking about. And should you live, the bond between Jadis and me will never be broken. The jealousy will quickly pit us against each other with her stuck in the middle. What are your plans then?"

"You and I shall become bonded as well. We'll feed from each other before death finds me."

"Talk to me when you're thinking rationally. If we feed from each other we may as well be in the same bed together for the rest of our existence."

"Promise me, Dante," Silas pleaded.

After a long pause, Dante spoke the words his brother needed to hear, "On my honor as your brother, I'll do as you ask."

Neither spoke another word.

Jadis heard the door open, sat up, and wiped the tears from her face. The four girls who had been attending to her slowly entered the chamber.

"Milady, we're here to dress you for the night," one of them whispered.

"Get out!" *I'm in no mood to shower and dress again for Abigor's sake. I've had enough, and I'm too emotionally drained to deal with anyone or anything.* She lay back down, refusing to move.

"Please, milady, you have to get up," the young gal pleaded, her voice nervous.

"I don't have to do a goddamn thing, leave me!"

"Milady, don't let him break you. It's what he wants," another whispered.

"Tell me your name," Jadis demanded.

"Iva, milady."

"And the others?"

Iva pointed to each of the girls as she spoke their names for the first time, "Mirela, Ivet, and Rayna," she whispered.

"How long have you all been here?"

"Years, milady. We've learned how to survive and so shall you. I was given to him in exchange for my father's life. You're a Dhamphyr after all, are you not?"

Her words weighed heavy. *Here I am curled up in a ball, crying myself to sleep. One of the most powerful beings on the planet, and these young ladies with nothing, have figured out how to survive. They could only be in their early twenties, and I was a hundred and seventy-plus years old.* It was all she needed to get her shit together.

"Yes, I'm a Dhamphyr." She stood and headed to the shower. *If they can survive all this time, I can certainly figure out how to put an end to Abigor.*

She showered and let the girls attend to her as needed. Once they were done, she crawled into the bed and cried herself to sleep again.

The clanking of the heavy door startled her awake, but she remained still with her back to the door, hoping Abigor would leave her alone for the rest of the night. She heard him showering and as soon as the water stopped, she bunched part of the fur in her fist.

Abigor crawled into the bed next to her. "I'm awaiting your answer, Petra. I know you aren't sleeping."

She rolled over to face the monster beside her. "I've made my decision; I'll never willingly agree to be your mate," she replied in only a whisper.

She gently cupped his jaw in her hand, and she felt his pulse quicken beneath her touch. He rolled on top of her and held her wrists tightly.

"Cornered animals are the most dangerous of their kind," she hissed.

"You're fucking stubborn, Petra. I met an Enchantress who had your iron will, and now she begs at my feet for a pittance of attention."

"Touch either Silas or Dante again, there are a hundred ways I can and will take my own life," she threatened. "Neither will end up in the arena again."

Abigor let out a nefarious laugh that chilled her to the bone. "You will yield, Petra."

"Try as you might, it won't be before the night of the Dark Moon," she stated defiantly.

"Hold your tongue! Why must you continue to challenge me?"

"I'll willingly give you my body, but it will be when and only when I choose to do so," she said softly.

Abigor looked shocked at her sudden admission and took her mouth to his. She responded and allowed his tongue to meet hers. *Give him just enough of a taste to leave him desperate for more.* He rubbed his hands up her waist and cupped her breast in his hand as he continued dominating her mouth.

"Give me your body and now, Petra," he moaned against her lips.

"Not tonight, but soon enough, you shall have all of me. I'll give myself to you before the Dark Moon."

He took her mouth once again, and she willing gave him *a pittance of attention* before she gently pulled away.

Everywhere Abigor went, he made sure Jadis was at his side. He took pleasure in showing her off in front of anyone crossing their path. She continued to give him just enough of what he needed to satiate his unrelenting demands.

Abigor learned that Jadis challenging him was a way to get to Silas and Dante. His punishments generally ended with beatings that now failed to draw blood or cause any serious injury. She was no longer able to hurt herself either; he had promised to torture Silas and Dante as she watched, or worse, kill Dante altogether. His warning was absolute, and she took the searing words to heart. The two of them were now in a standoff of wills. They had checkmated each other, and she had everything to lose should she move the pawn one step in the wrong direction.

Abigor and Jadis were in the great hall, along with the most prominent members of his clan, which was now a nightly ritual. She leaned back in her large wooden chair, with her legs crossed, and one arm resting on the armrest, while she sipped her ale. Abigor was at her side of course, sitting at the head of the table. It would be another long night of drinking, feeding, and raucous debauchery.

They didn't take mates, not like her clan did; they kept feeders and concubines in every corner of the room. Their loud, boisterous voices, vulgarity, laughter, and general behavior was obnoxious, crude, and demeaning. She hated every nauseating moment of it. They spoke of rumors floating around the clans, slanderous tales were told, wages were made for almost any reason, and reputations of those that had crossed the wrong path were assassinated.

"How's Petra doing?" Arkyn asked. He loved nothing more than to taunt her, and it had quickly become his favorite pastime.

She flipped him off in response, and he laughed aloud, as did everyone else. She held her tongue for the most part. Abigor's threats always came before his clan made an appearance.

"You're sour tonight, Petra," Abigor stated.

"What I am is bored."

Abigor cupped her jaw in his hand. "If you're bored, I'm sure I can entertain you in other ways." He glanced down at her cleavage peering out from beneath another low-cut gown, along with a slight head nod.

"I have a headache."

"You continue to test my patience."

"And you mine," she replied, with furrowed eyebrows.

He leaned in closely. "I've waited long enough. Give me your body tonight, and I'll see to it you have all you desire. With a few exceptions, of course."

She rolled her eyes, and he reached around to the back of her head and pulled her in. She accepted his desperate kiss, however it lingered on too long, and she gently pulled back. He held her head in a tight grip and stared her dead in the face.

"Everyone is watching," she whispered. It was her excuse for him to stop before he took it further.

"What the fuck does it matter to me who watches? I own you. I can do whatever I want."

"I care! I won't be looked down upon like I'm another concubine," she growled.

"Why don't you finish what you started, brother," Arkyn yelled, interrupting Abigor and Jadis.

"Why don't you stop talking out your ass," Jadis snarled.

"I do believe I'm sitting on my ass." He smirked.

"Then your ass is smarter. It can do two things at once," she retorted. Roars of laughter followed her snide comment.

Arkyn laughed aloud. "Seems you've swallowed another wasp, Petra."

"The whore has a sharp tongue. You should put the kuchka in her fucking place," Padrick barked. He was another one of their highest ranking warriors who always made her skin crawl.

Abigor disappeared and appeared only after having hold of his throat. "Shall I show you what the Dhamphyr you refer to as a *whore* can do?" Abigor roared. "Petra!"

Everyone quietly moved aside as she sauntered her way over.

"You think of me as a whore?" she rumbled into his ear. "Let's see if a *whore* can do this." She slammed the palm of her hand into his face and latched on. The cimruta seeped from her palms as she *turned*.

He choked and coughed as the thick substance oozed in, filling his mouth. The smell rose into the air, followed by the searing, crackling of burning flesh.

He released a muffled roar and grabbed for her hand. "Call me a whore again, and I'll consume you," she snarled into his face.

Abigor laughed aloud and slowly clapped his hands as the rest of the clan stood in stunned silence.

"I believe you're the one who has been *put in his place*," Abigor snarled. "Take him!"

Padrick was dragged away as he choked and coughed, which sent the liquid spewing from his mouth. Everyone stood in awe as Abigor led her out of the large hall, headed for the fights.

Abigor stopped in the hallway and quickly waved his hand across her face, to stop her from using the powers he'd just witnessed. He allowed her access to them only when he wanted to show them off. Each time, she only managed to conjure them momentarily at best.

Every night brought about an anxiety-ridden reaction in her body. She always expected to see Dante thrown into the arena. She sat for hours with a knot in the pit of her stomach as she was forced to sit in Abigor's lap.

Jadis looked to Abigor's brothers deep in thought. *Arkyn and Vidar are always loud and argumentative. They constantly banter back and forth, all the while roaring with the cheering crowd. They're cruel to the concubines, and it seems nothing the girls do ever pleases them.*

"You look nervous, Petra. Waiting for your wizard?" Vidar asked.

"Why do you always have to be so goddamn annoying?" Her reply only increased his amusement.

"Why do you choose to react so?" He laughed.

She rolled her eyes and did her best to ignore his taunting.

"Kuchka, get over here," Arkyn demanded.

One of the concubines rushed to his side and climbed into his lap. Another made her way around and filled all their cups with fresh ale.

For Jadis, drinking had become the only way to stop her body's unrelenting reactions until the fights had concluded for the night.

Vidar and Arkyn bantered back and forth but stopped momentarily to bellow with the crowd. Vidar jumped to his feet when one of the fighters was knocked to the ground after having been struck with his opponent's blade. After hours of anticipation, the fights ended and once again, Dante was spared. The heaviness always set back in not knowing the reason he wasn't fighting. At times, she didn't know which was worse.

The following day, they wandered arm in arm down another expansive hallway headed in a direction Jadis hadn't yet been. Arkyn, Vidar, and a few of Abigor's warriors were in tow as well. They were engaged in conversation she was uninterested in; it was mostly rumblings about their clans and what was taking place in the underworld. She always held out hope they would say something, anything, about her clan attacking.

She saw the faint glow of what looked like sunlight creeping in from an opening before them. The closer they got to the entrance, the brighter the light became. Her heart pounded at the mere thought that they were leaving her underground hell.

She heard the faintest sounds of what she thought were birds chirping, so she listened intently. *Sure enough, birds are indeed singing.*

"This is a glimpse of what your freedom can look like should you give yourself to me, Petra," Abigor stated as he let go of her arm.

In front of her was a large cavern lit by an unnatural sunlight. As beautiful as it was, she was disappointed they were still underground. Abigor, his brothers, and his men followed her into the light.

"How is it your asses aren't burning?" she asked. Abigor chuckled but didn't respond. She held out her hand to feel the light's warmth as they walked through the expansive gardens. There were waterfalls, trees, plants, and flowers. A multitude of birds and insects fluttered around the cavern, some of which seemed to be conjured right out of a fairy tale.

"How can so much beauty exist in such a decrepit place?" she asked.

An unwanted voice answered, "I thought I smelled the stench. What is the beiskaldi doing in my garden?" Evanora demanded.

"Well, fuck," Jadis growled.

Evanora slowly approached them, dead set on putting Jadis in her place beneath her wrath.

"Answer me, milord. Why is she here—this is mine!"

Abigor grabbed her face and threw her to the ground. "Nothing is yours!"

She scrambled to her feet. "I'll destroy the gardens as easily as I created them," she screamed.

Abigor latched onto her throat with a tight grip. "You have served your purpose, Enchantress. I no longer see the need to keep you around. Take her and chain her with the whores. You're no longer what I desire," he roared. "You'll now serve another purpose, Enchantress. You'll be the one laying beneath my warriors."

"I'll fucking kill you!" Evanora ripped her arms loose and lunged at Jadis.

Abigor held up his hand, stopping anyone from interfering. "I want to know what else the Dhamphyr's hiding."

Jadis dodged her, spun around, grabbed a fistful of her hair, and yanked her back. Evanora stumbled backward before a blackened net consumed Jadis.

"You shall die at my feet, beiskaldi!" Evanora fumed.

Jadis swirled her hands and threw her arms to the side, and the blackness exploded. She had morphed, her eyes now the oily pools of swirling color. She lunged and snatched Evanora by the throat with one hand and seized her arm with the other.

Evanora roared words in another language, and the energy hit Jadis in the chest, taking her breath away. It knocked her backward and off her feet. Even so, she held her grip and took Evanora to the ground with her.

Whatever it was Evanora conjured, Jadis's body seemed to absorb it. The cimruta oozed from her palms as she rolled Evanora over and pinned her body to the dirt floor.

"You're dead inside! You'll forever be caged in your own prison of hatred," Jadis roared.

Evanora's pain-inflicted screams echoed throughout the cavern, and her broken sobs pierced the air as her skin melted from her shoulder and throat.

Abigor separated them, and his guards dragged Evanora her away as she wailed. Her fermenting hatred and inconsolable sobs were that of someone drained of all hope.

Jadis woke to the sounds of voices. Arkyn and Vidar sat opposite the stone-slab desk. She heard the rustling of the maps, and she listened intently for any details. They were talking about an ensuing battle coming to them from the west.

Her pulse quickened with the only thought that crossed her mind, *they're coming.*

Arkyn cleared his throat, and the three of them looked at her.

"I know you're awake, Petra—speak," Abigor stated.

"I have nothing to say." She rolled over to face them, only to realize she was naked.

Abigor heard her thoughts. "You may dress if you like, but I'd rather look at you naked."

"How am I to dress with your brothers staring at me?"

"I'm sure you'll figure it out," he rumbled.

"You're an ass," she stated, to his brother's amusement. She pulled the furs around her body and walked to her gown sitting on a chair across the room. She headed for the shower area and dressed. She turned around, only to see Abigor standing there, and she jumped back.

"What the hell are you doing?" she snapped.

"Admiring what is mine," he replied. He stepped forward, pulled her toward him, and bent down, claiming her mouth. "I think it's time you give yourself to me. I don't feel the need to wait any longer."

She put her hands on his chest and gently held him back. "You know the consequences as well as I do," she whispered. She noticed the defiance cross his face as she grabbed the back of his head and pulled him in for another kiss.

He pulled back, took her hand, and walked back to his desk. "I won't wait any longer, Petra," he added.

They continued with their conversation as if it were business as usual as soon as Abigor took his seat. She walked around the desk and stood between Arkyn and Vidar. She rested her palms on the desk and leaned over to see what they were doing. To her surprise, Abigor leaned back in his chair, watching her.

She flipped up the corner of one of the maps. "You're expecting someone?" she asked with a coy smile.

"It seems your clan has other plans. We're just preparing to put an end to them once and for all. Soon enough, they too will be your enemies," he replied smugly.

She took in every detail in its entirety. *I have to get to Silas and Dante. The pain I'm about to feel will be well worth it.* She stood and casually leaned her body into Arkyn's shoulder and rested her butt against it.

Abigor's demeanor changed. "Don't touch another," he snarled.

"And if I do?" She crawled on top of his desk and rose up on her knees. Abigor stood in response to the challenge.

Her head snapped to the side from the blow, and Arkyn and Vidar jumped to their feet, sending the chairs sliding backward.

"Ohhh—that hurt," she seethed. "What else are you going to do? You can't break me, you can't fuck me, and you certainly can't make me bleed." She let out a deep-throated snarl.

He *turned* with her taunting, grabbed both of her shoulders, and slammed her onto her back on the desk. He jumped on top of her, and she felt the stinging sensation radiate across her cheekbone.

"I can *break you*, I can *fuck you*, and I can make you bleed should I choose to do so!" he growled sadistically.

She grasped his tunic in both hands, pulled his face to hers, and snarled, "Then do it, you fucking coward!"

The next thing she knew, he had her throat in his mouth and drank from her. She grabbed the large orb off his desk and tried to hit him in the head.

Arkyn lunged and grabbed it from her hand. "Enough, brother!"

He and Vidar grabbed him and pulled him off her. "You can't fucking take her blood!" Vidar roared.

Abigor released her throat, jumped off her, and tossed her into the wall. She hit the wall and heard a loud pop. She screamed as the blow had broken her wrist and split her forehead open. *My mission is complete. It looks as if the injuries are his doing.*

"What did you do?" she cried out, trying to act innocent.

"Po dyavolite, Petra, why do you continue to insult me!"

She lay on the floor, crying, and rolled over, holding her wrist against her chest.

"Get up," Abigor demanded.

She couldn't stand. Everything was fuzzy and fading in and out in blurry succession. He grabbed her up and with no other choice, headed for Silas with her in his arms.

CHAPTER 17

"If we can connect with Jadis and get her to feed us again, we can break these chains," Silas stated.

"As much as we've been reaching out so far, she hasn't heard us. There has to be another way," Dante replied.

"The Moon will rise tomorrow night, and I expect you to honor your word, brother."

"I won't go back on my word, Silas."

A cool breeze wafted through the cell, and they sat up and looked around.

"Jadis?" Silas called quietly.

A slow-moving mist filled the cell between them and twirled like a small water spout. The Enchantress suddenly appeared from within the mist. They jumped to their feet, ready to meet their enemy, but she held up her hands in a gesture of peace.

"What the fuck are you doing here?" Silas growled.

"Your mate has become my problem," she seethed. "I believe I have a way to get us both what we want."

"What are you saying, Enchantress?" Silas questioned.

"It seems we now have the same enemy," she replied calmly.

Silas and Dante glanced at each other, utterly confused.

"Get on with it," Dante demanded.

"I'll release you from your chains, but first, you'll both give me your word, on your honor, you will spare my life should we meet again."

They tried to comprehend what she was offering.

"If this is another trick, don't think we can be so easily fooled," Silas replied.

"There is no deception. Agree to my offer, and I'll see you are released before the Dark Moon rises."

"Go on," Dante stated.

"I want you to kill Abigor, it is that simple."

Silas and Dante went wide eyed in bewilderment, not believing what they were hearing.

"If Abigor thinks he can toss me aside so easily, without consequence, then he has made a grave mistake!"

"What has caused you such distress, and why are you coming to us to do your bidding?" Dante asked.

"The Dhamphyr! Who the fuck else would it be? She may look like a rose, but her thorns are poison. If I had a fucking choice, do you think I'd be standing here with the two of you?"

"We agree to your offering," Silas stated without hesitation.

"The poison I've created that has been running through your veins will cease tonight. Now give me your word."

"On the word of Nosferatu, we will kill Abigor should you release us," Silas agreed.

"Then so it shall be but do not be fooled—should I get to the beiskaldi first, I will kill her," Evanora admitted. "Your powers will be useless down here. Dante, take heed," she added before disappearing.

They stood frozen, looking at each other in disbelief. "What in the hell has Jadis done?" Silas growled.

"Who knows, but whatever it was, she has angered the wrong enemy. The Enchantress will kill her given the chance."

"Yes, but now we have a fighting chance. Once we're free of these chains, it will be Abigor's death," Silas stated.

They suddenly heard the clanking of bolts, and they snapped their heads in its direction.

Abigor entered with Jadis in his arms. She was bleeding profusely from her forehead, and they saw her holding her wrist.

"What the fuck have you done to her?" Silas raged.

Abigor stood momentarily as a thought swept across his mind before speaking it aloud. "I'm curious, just how close are the three of you?" He carried Jadis to Dante and tossed her to him.

Dante caught her and wrapped her protectively in his arms.

"Feed her," Abigor demanded.

"Jadis, look at me, darling. I've got you," Dante whispered.

She touched his face and was able to connect telepathically, *"You can't heal me, Dante."*

"My blood will heal you," he admitted

She looked up at him, not understanding. *"If you can heal me, then they will kill Silas!"*

"Feed her!" Abigor demanded again.

"My blood will heal you. I'll explain another time. Take what you need and trust me when I say Silas and I are not dying tonight." He lifted her head to his neck. The sharp sensation caused reactions in his body he wasn't prepared for. It took all he had to not respond physically; the harder she sucked at his vein, the more his body yearned for something more.

"Kakvo sorðinn? It seems my suspicions are true. I no longer have a reason to spare your mate's life, Petra."

She stood from Dante's lap and faced Abigor.

"Do not challenge him," Silas demanded.

She ignored Silas and approached Abigor until they were face to face. "You're the evil, nefarious shadows lurking in the dead of night. You're the evocative whispers in darkened woods and empty rooms, a cesspool of depravity. Your reckoning will soon be upon you," she seethed.

Abigor backhanded her in front of Silas and Dante, who both let out a gut-wrenching roar that vibrated the entire cell.

"You want to play kitten? Then show me your claws," Abigor snarled.

She'd never been struck in such a manner until having been captured by Abigor. The blow crossed her temple, and the pain radiated across her face. *I've been slapped before, but this—Abigor knows how to hit,* she thought as she let her sable-colored claws slide from her fingertips as she snarled, "I'll never be your chained, obedient bedmate, nor a kitten lapping milk at your feet!" She swung her hand across his throat and ripped it open. The blood splattered across the room onto the wall and floor like speckles of paint on a canvas. Small, red droplets fell from the tips of her nails, staining the floor at her feet.

Silas and Dante continued to struggle, unable to break their chains.

Abigor took a deep, liquid-filled breath, only to choke on his own blood. She began to lunge but was suddenly attacked and held back by two of his warriors, one of whom waved the poisonous mist across her face.

Another cough sent blood spewing onto the floor. Unfortunately, Abigor's wound was already healing. He let out a gut-wrenching, soul-stealing laugh as he wiped the blood from his mouth. He slowly, meticulously clapped his hands.

"The anger, the power seething inside you, waiting to unleash itself, is unimaginable! Beasts shall feed, and terror shall rein. Now ask yourself, my dear, how valuable is their life to you? You'll choose the one that will meet his death tonight." His words ripped through her like shattering glass.

"This is between you and me. Jadis has nothing to do with this! Leave her be," Silas demanded.

"Petra will spend the rest of her life spreading her legs for me. Together, we shall rule the sixty Legions of Hades."

"Let's give you both a little taste of what's coming, shall we?" He pulled her body to his and shoved his mouth to hers in front of Silas, who roared with the fury of the Gods. The entire cell trembled as rock and dust rained down from the ceiling.

She put both her hands on his chest and tried to push him away. She felt the excitement in his groin rise, as her body was pressed against his. He released her mouth and looked into her swirling eyes.

Abigor snarled, and looked at Silas. "I fully understand your lust for her."

He grabbed her ass and pulled her body tighter into his, inches from Silas who at this moment could do nothing but watch. He kissed her again as he reached up and grabbed her breast and kneaded it in his hand. She clamped down on his tongue, and he reeled back.

"You fucking celice," he snapped with a guttural roar as he spat the blood onto the floor at her feet.

"That was a big fucking mistake," he warned.

"I'll never yield to you," she snarled. The blow landed so hard against her cheek, her knees buckled beneath her.

He looked at Silas. "You're lucky she's worth the fucking trouble. He spat a mouthful of blood at Silas's feet. I'll give her that. It might take a week, a month, maybe longer. She may be stubborn to the core, but I'll have her purring in my fucking lap. I'm going to render your brightest day into the darkest of night when I take the only thing you've ever loved. Petra will become mine tomorrow night."

He knelt and softly brushed her bruised, swollen cheek with the palm of his hand. He took a firm hold of her jaw and turned her face from side to side, intently studying her. He slid his thumb across her bottom lip, slightly pulling it to the side before letting go. "You and I know full well she has yet to bloom. Her powers have been lying dormant deep inside her since turning. I suppose you wanted her to grow on her own. I see that now, however, I'm unwilling to wait. I'll be the one to witness her true powers unfold," he snarled.

"Chain her to the fucking floor. Make your decision, Petra, or I'll choose for you." They left, slamming the door behind them.

Jadis cried, unable to control it any longer. It was all too much to handle.

"I promise you, we will get out of here, baby," Silas stated.

"Such a thought is naïve, Silas," she cried. "I'm dammed. I have been my whole life. Death follows me and everyone I hold dear. I can't do this anymore!"

"You aren't dammed, baby. You have been bestowed a divine gift. Your powers won't fail you, neither will Dante or me. I love you beyond measure and right now, I need you. Stay with us for a little longer."

Silas is my dark vessel, my power, my anchor, she thought, however fleeting it was.

"Baby, I'll be there with you side by side, chained or not," Silas added.

"Listen to Silas. We will not fail you," Dante agreed.

"What dupery it is, the false beliefs we tell ourselves. He will take you from me," she cried. She felt it in her core. *Silas's life is in jeopardy, even so his words, how he speaks to me always seems to soothe my torment.*

"Shall we meet them tooth for claw, baby?" Silas asked.

"We shall." She smiled sincerely at her vampire, knowing he wouldn't let them be separated.

"Awe—don't swoon on me now, my dear. Save that for later," Silas answered with a wink, followed by his beautiful, lascivious grin which caused her to chuckle.

"Jadis, you've seen the maps. Santiago, our clan is attacking tonight?" Dante asked, having had enough of the lovey-dovey bullshit. He had also pulled her thoughts when she fed from him, what little he could manage.

"The reason for your injuries, you chose your pain to relay the information?" Silas asked with a heavy heart.

"Yes." She sat up against the wall, pulled her knees to her chest, and re-adjusted the chains binding her ankle.

"I love you, Silas, and I'm sorry I've been the reason for both of you suffering."

"Our hearts will always be as one, and you are not the reason we're in this position," Silas replied.

"What have you done to the Enchantress, other than break her back?" Dante joked, trying to calm her down.

"What do you mean?"

"She came to us tonight before Abigor brought you," he admitted.

"What the hell did she want?"

"To make a deal with the Devil," Silas replied.

"What are the two of you talking about?"

"She came to make us an offer—her life and ours for Abigor's," Dante added.

"Silas, she wants you dead," she replied.

"Maybe—but apparently, she wants Abigor's death more than mine," Silas stated.

"What happened?" Dante asked again.

She simply waved her hand as the story was too complicated. "We had a fight. I took her lover, almost killed her, and she was dragged away." She tried to give a short explanation to a long story.

Silas and Dante let out a light-heated chuckle, which in turn forced her to laugh as well.

"Guess what, darling," Dante stated.

"What?"

"When we get out of here, I believe I'm going to take you horseback riding."

"What? Horseback riding? That's the most random thing I've ever heard you say. We're about to die, and you're talking about riding horses?"

"Dante does love his horses." Silas smiled. "He had a stunning black Stallion when we were young. Mystic was his prize possession."

"Mystic, that was his name?" she asked.

"Yes, he was a beauty, no doubt about it. He was a gift from father. He was wild beyond measure, his stubbornness forged in iron. He was magnificent, and nothing, no one, would ever break him, and I admired that," Dante stated with a coy smile.

"Reminds me of someone we know," Silas added.

"He would never be *broken*, huh?" *They're speaking to me about having strength to go on without saying it.*

She looked at them both and their sincerity meant more to her than they could ever imagine. She felt more for Dante in this moment than she ever thought possible, and she realized for the first time, his feelings for her ran about as deep as they could get.

"Have I told the two of you lately how much you truly mean to me?" She couldn't wrap her mind around the thought of losing either of them.

"We feel the same, darling," Silas stated.

"Mon amour, no one will ever hold my heart the way you do," Dante finally admitted.

The look they just gave each other tells me there's more to their words than they're letting on. The dread quickly set back in. "Tomorrow night, the Dark Moon will rise." She sighed.

"Don't worry, baby. We'll be free tonight," Silas admitted.

She was stunned to hear the words. *It's just too good to be true.*

"Baby, we need you to hide before the moon rises. Is there someplace you manage to get to until we can find you? No matter what, you have to remain hidden. Should Abigor get a hold of you, you will become his mate." Silas's words brought about another wave of fear and panic.

"The gardens," she stated.

"Gardens?" Dante asked.

"Yes, there's a small cave behind the smaller of the waterfalls. I noticed it the day it was shown to me. I know Abigor doesn't know it's there, but Evanora does"

"No matter what it takes, I need you to hide. You have to get to the cave. We'll come for you. I need you to listen, Jadis. He won't be stopped should he get his hands on you, understand?" Silas asked sternly.

"I understand."

They spoke to each other for what seemed like hours, planning their escape, when the door once again banged open. Abigor stood front and center. His guards picked her up from the floor and unchained her.

"Who shall it be, Petra?" Abigor asked as he spun a strange-looking dagger in his hand. "You mate—or your wizard?"

She suddenly felt as if Abigor had just shoved her head under the water while she fought for a breath of air.

"Abigor, don't do this," she begged. "I'll give myself to you if you spare them both!"

"No, Jadis, do not yield!" Silas demanded.

"It seems you cannot make up your mind, so I shall make the decision for you," Abigor stated as he pointed the tip of the dagger to Silas. "Your mate?" He then pointed the dagger to Dante. "Your wizard?"

"Abigor, I'll willingly become your mate. Don't do this," she begged.

He pointed the dagger towards Dante. "I think I'll spare your life—for now anyway. You'll be the one to fight in the arena tonight after I take Petra as my mate."

Abigor moved so quickly, she didn't even see him before he appeared in front of Silas. He gripped Silas by the shoulder as one hand plunged the dagger into his abdomen multiple times. Silas fell to his knees with a guttural roar.

"For as long as we've walked the earth, your clans have looked down upon us. Now I look down upon you, on your knees as you watch me take the only thing you hold in your heart. You shall meet your death knowing Petra will be mine!"

"Silas—! Nooo! What have you fucking done?" she screamed.

Dante roared so loud, the entire cell shook. Silas's blood pooled onto the floor and seeped outwardly toward her feet. She spun around in a fury and swiped her nails at the base of one of the warrior's neck and ripped his throat open.

Abigor lunged for her and dragged her from the cell as she watched Silas slump to the floor. She fought, wailed, and screamed for Silas. "You bastard! I'll fucking kill you—Silas—Silas!" she screamed, as Abigor dragged her away.

Abigor threw Jadis across the chamber. She landed on the floor, and her body tumbled across the room. She quickly jumped to her feet and lunged for him, but the force of the blow sent her spiraling to the floor once again.

"Chain the kuchka and drug her. Don't leave her unattended for any reason!" he ordered.

Jadis was rushed by his guards. They dragged her to the bed, threw her onto her back, chained her arms to the wall, and drugged her again.

She continued to wail. "I'll fucking kill you!" she screamed through her tears and cries of gut-wrenching heartache.

Dante continued to talk to and beg Silas to stay with him. Silas only managed to speak a few words between his moans; he faded in and out of consciousness as the toxins flowed through his veins. After what seemed like hours, the chains rumbled and clanked. The sounds from them crashing onto the stones rang through the air. Dante broke free and rushed to Silas.

"Brother—get up!" He picked Silas up and laid him on his back on the slab. "Don't fail me—stay with me!" he demanded.

"Feed from me, brother. The dagger was poisoned. I need you to honor me now more than ever before," Silas begged with a rugged whisper.

"You won't die—now fight, goddammit!" Dante begged.

"Feed from me!" Silas demanded again.

Dante bit down on his neck and took Silas's blood. "Feed from me now, brother." Dante slit his wrist and placed it against Silas's mouth, and he swallowed what he could before he coughed, sending blood splattering from his mouth.

Dante felt the poison seep into his body along with Silas's blood. He forced more of his life-giving blood into his mouth before the toxins soured it.

"Jadis—she's all—that matters. Get to her—now," Silas demanded, with another breathless, raspy whisper.

"I won't leave you!"

"Brother—don't let her weep for me. Let her know my last thought when I closed my eyes was her smile. The way in which she looked at me took my breath away. When her eyes are filled with tears, I—I need you to wipe them away. Whatever y—you do, don't let my death shatter her insatiable lust for life." His words were broken and discordant.

"You won't die. I promise, now stay with me!"

"Find Jadis!" Silas begged.

"Death won't find you tonight. I'll come back for you!"

There was a loud commotion in the corridor outside the cell door. What sounded like hollers, orders, and the clang of metal, along with the sounds of rapid of gunfire grew in intensity. The cell door suddenly blew off its hinges, slamming into the far wall with an explosion of metal meeting stone.

Dante crouched beside his brother, ready to fight anyone who entered. A group of warriors rushed into the cell and surrounded them. Santiago, Eden, Aiden, and Bain were suddenly standing before Dante.

"Get Silas the fuck out of here. He's dying!" Dante ordered, in a state of shock, his tears turning to rage.

"What have they done?" Bain yelled.

"The dagger was poisoned. Take him!" Dante roared.

Bain and a few of their warriors grabbed Silas and pulled him to his feet.

"Jadis, where is she?" Aiden demanded.

"With Abigor," Dante yelled.

They rushed from the cell, following Dante as he headed for Jadis while Bain took Silas.

An onslaught of Abigor's warriors met them in the hallway; they were no match for the fury Dante and his family yielded. They managed to clear a path for Bain and the warriors so they could make their escape with Silas.

"Aiden, go after Arkyn and Vidar. They'll seize Jadis and take her directly to Abigor should they find her," Dante ordered.

She tried for what seemed like hours to break free, so intent of escaping she hadn't even realized the clanging sounds and pops of gunfire filling the corridor on the other side of the door was their clan.

She heard someone softly speaking, even though the drugs had already taken their toll. *"Now is thy time, my dear. Unleash what you truly are."*

Hecate! She tried to calm down enough to draw on her powers. It seemed each time she tried to reach out, she was blocked. Her powers were useless; her emotional turmoil was more than she could control. She continued to cry hysterically; she was completely panic stricken, not knowing if Silas were still alive. She yanked at the chains, trying to pull them from the wall.

"Calm your emotions, my child—use them, draw from them. Now take my hand," Hecate whispered.

Jadis closed her eyes and tried to relax. She took multiple deep breaths before concentrating again. She reached out and felt an ethereal sensation around her fists. "Mother," she cried aloud.

She suddenly felt the cimruta release, and she wrapped her palms around the chains. The metal melted beneath her grip.

The guards focused their attention on the unrelenting chaos and commotion beyond the door and hadn't realized she had broken free. She slowly rose to her feet behind them.

They suddenly felt the air behind them chill and spun in its direction. Before them stood the Dhamphyr, the rage in her eyes, the colored pools swirling within them took their breath away. They jumped back and raised their swords in her direction.

She swung her hand and sent them crashing into the wall on the opposite side of the chamber covered in cimruta. She flicked her wrist and lit one of them on fire. He spun around the room, howling in pain. The other dove behind the desk.

Jadis sprinted to the door, ripped it open, and ran as fast as she could with the remaining warrior in hot pursuit.

She had to leap over the bodies of beheaded warriors who lay on the floor of every corridor. Blood and body fluid splattered the walls and dripped from the ceiling, splattering onto her face as she ran. The slick floor caused her to slip more than once. She recognized some of the fallen and realized her clan had made it into the cavern.

She ran through the chaos, not recognizing the warriors who rushed in every direction, having to dodge the ones attempting to grab her. She instinctually found the corridor leading to the gardens. To her relief, the closer she got to the gardens, the corridors became empty, and the sounds of the unrelenting chaos faded into the background behind her. She followed the light as it grew brighter with each frantic step she took in its direction. She ran amongst the trees and plants and leapt to the ledge leading into the cave. As soon as she made it through the waterfall, she heard multiple warriors rushing in. She stood with her back to the cool, damp wall and held her breath. She dared not move or breathe. She covered her mouth with her hands to muffle her gasps for breath. She heard the warriors frantically searching the gardens.

"The Dhamphyr isn't here. Search the halls!" someone yelled out.

She stood frozen as their voices faded. After what seemed like an eternity, the water splashed against her body. The warrior stopped and stood right in front of her, scaring her to death. He looked like a canvas, soaked in a mixture of blood and water running down his body, obscuring his face. She *turned*, bared her canines, and snarled, ready to face the threat but to her utter relief, it was Dante.

She leapt into his arms. He caught her and squeezed her so tightly, she thought he would crush her. "Where's Silas?" she cried.

"There's no time to explain, and I know this isn't what you want to hear, but you must take me as your mate," Dante blurted out.

"What?" She couldn't comprehend what he was saying.

"I don't have time, darling. The Moon is rising," Dante growled.

"Dante, I won't take you as my mate. I belong to Silas!" she cried. The next thing she knew, she was on her back in the dirt with Dante on top, holding her down. He quickly grabbed the bottom of her dress and wiped the blood from his face, so he didn't look so menacing.

"What are you doing? Get off me!" She tried to fight Dante, but it was no use. He had her pinned beneath his powerful body.

"Listen to me, darling, I don't have time to explain, and I know you're beyond confused. Silas—this was Silas. He made me give him my word I would take you as my mate should things go wrong."

"Where's Silas?" she demanded again. "Don't tell me—nooo!" She sobbed uncontrollably, realizing the only reason this was happening was that he must be dead. She tried to get out from under Dante to no avail.

"Silas isn't dead, but death is near. I won't lie to you, nor will I deceive you. I'm begging you to trust me. I gave my brother my word," he admitted as he held her steady.

The chaos running through her mind was tantamount to the battle raging in the corridors.

"We don't have time for a discussion or an argument. Abigor isn't far behind. Jadis, agree to be my mate and now. Speak the words, darling."

She had no reason to believe Dante's words weren't truthful and sincere. *They must have a plan. Silas would never ask Dante to take me if he hadn't thought this through.*

"Speak the words, mon amour," Dante gently urged.

"I'll take you as my mate," she sobbed.

Dante gently placed his mouth on hers and claimed her. He partially removed their clothes and settled between her legs.

She tried to relax and let him take her, but her mind and body were in a state of shock and panic. She took a deep breath and wrapped her arms around his neck and gave in.

Dante slipped his hardened shaft into her body, slowly at first, allowing her body to accommodate him.

"It's okay, darling—I promise all will be okay," Dante whispered as he rocked his hips.

She felt the sensation rising to the surface. She could no longer hold it back or control it. Her body responded, and Dante was now becoming her mate.

He thrust himself into her a bit harder and felt his orgasm quickly rise to the surface. He didn't have time to take it slow. "Give me your vein, darling," he whispered.

She turned her head, allowing him to feed from her, which would bind them together for the rest of their lives. The harsh stab of his canines puncturing her flesh seared through her body, and the pain between her legs gave way to pleasure.

As he fed on her blood, the sensations of feeling her body responding to his rocked him to his core. He was taken aback by the sudden surge of power he felt within her blood. *Her blood is unique, dark, and other-worldly.* He took what was needed and released his grip.

"You're mine now—say it," he growled.

"I'm yours, Dante," she cried.

"Then take my vein and become my mate, darling."

Her canines penetrated his flesh, and she pulled the liquid from the punctures. His blood was intoxicating and hit her. *It's potent, magical, beyond anything I've ever tasted or felt before.* Her mind swirled into a dizzying pool of pain, pleasure, and emotional torment. The pull she now felt for Dante was as powerful as her feelings that she was betraying Silas.

Jadis feeding from his vein brought about his orgasm, and he felt hers rise to the surface. Her body trembled beneath his as her sex throbbed against his shaft.

"Together, baby—the bond will be complete," he moaned.

They climaxed together, and she felt the heat of him filling her core. She continued to cry, and he lovingly wrapped her in his arms, feeling every emotion racing through her mind and heart. They became mated under the Dark Blood Moon on the floor of the cave. She felt her emotions attach themselves to Dante; the bond was undeniable.

"Shhh—it's okay, mon amour. You are now mine, and my life is yours. I love you, Jadis. I've loved you from the moment I first laid eyes on you, but I need you to know, I would never betray my brother, so don't think one for one more minute you are betraying him."

"I know, Dante, and it doesn't matter now. You are mine."

"Get up, mon amour. We don't have time to cuddle." He winked, trying to comfort her.

Had she not been so emotionally distraught, the unexpected joke would have made her laugh. She felt her body calm, and reason and determination took over the emotional agony. She knew Dante would never let anyone touch her, especially now.

"I promise you, I will destroy Abigor to honor not only you, but Silas as well."

They snuck out of the cave and as soon as they made it out from under the waterfall and stood on the ledge, they were met by Abigor and at least fifteen of his clan members standing below. Half of them lunged and took Dante to the ground below the ledge.

Abigor leapt toward Jadis and tackled her to the floor. "The time has come, Petra!" He pinned her beneath his body and realized Dante had mated her by the look of the swirling, amber liquid around her pupils. He roared with such force, she assumed the Gods heard him.

"It's too late, you fucking bastard!" she screamed.

"You took her as your mate? You fucking imbecile," he roared.

"Get off me!" she demanded as she tried to get out from underneath him. She felt Dante's blood strengthening her body. She was able to wrench her arm free and landed a blow to his cheek with her elbow.

He grabbed her wrist and forced her to release the grip she had on his throat. He yanked her off the floor by the front of her dress and tossed her out of the cave. Her body splashed through the waterfall, and she barely managed to grab the ledge with her hands and one leg.

Abigor stood above her, lifted her up by her throat, and spun her around so she faced Dante, who was surrounded below. "She will now witness your death. She will become my mate one way or another!" he roared.

"Then face me alone, you fucking coward," Dante roared from below.

Abigor leapt from the ledge with her and landed face to face with Dante as he slammed her body onto the ground.

"Release the bastard. He's mine!" Abigor demanded.

They shoved Dante in his direction and dragged Jadis by her leg to get her out of the way.

Dante managed to grab a sword from one of the warriors as he snapped his neck and met Abigor blade for blade.

Two of Abigor's warriors lunged for her as the rest watched the fight between Abigor and Dante, keeping them both surrounded.

She was able to quickly roll over, get to her feet, and evade their grasp.

The thundering sounds of heavy boots and the shouts from the ensuing warriors grew with intensity as they rushed into the gardens.

She was knocked down after being hit in the face with the butt of one of the warrior's swords when she looked toward the oncoming commotion.

She rolled over to face another onslaught. *Dante and I are going to be captured again, this time our fates will be sealed.* Her heart pounded as the adrenaline filled her body with a ravenous anticipation of what was about to happen.

"Jadis!" She heard. As she looked up, Aiden and Eden were rushing her way. Their swords took down two warriors in the process. Aiden grabbed her arm and pulled her into his body. She watched breathless as their clan met Abigor's with an explosion of fury and brutality.

The fight ended quickly, and Abigor's men fell, bloody, broken, and dismembered; not one of whom was left breathing.

Dante had Abigor pinned to the ground, and he was bleeding profusely from the gaping wound where his arm had been separated from his body by Dante's wrath.

Dante roared, "Your death is in honor of my brother and Jadis!" He twisted his head and ripped it from his body. He looked up and released a gut-wrenching roar. He was still holding Abigor's head in his hand as the blood pooled at his feet. He finally tossed it aside and grabbed for Jadis, ripping her from Aiden's grip.

She wrapped her arms and legs around his body and clung to him. Once again, she cried uncontrollably.

"Silas?" she asked hysterically.

"We have Silas, and he's alive. Bain and a few of our warriors have taken him to the village," Eden replied, still catching his breath.

"Take me to him," she begged.

CHAPTER 18

Silas was lying in bed in Tagar's wizard's quarters. His breathing was labored, but he was still alive. Jadis rushed to his side, grabbed his hand, and cupped it in hers. Dante stood behind her, along with the rest of their family who stood in hushed silence.

"Don't leave me—talk to me, baby," she pleaded softly.

Eden approached her and placed his hands on her shoulders. "He's sedated, but he's strong, his body is fighting, but he needs your blood. Feed him, baby girl."

She slit her wrist and let the blood drip into his mouth. After Dante let her know he had had enough, she crawled onto the bed next to him and wrapped her arm over his bare chest and cried. Dante proceeded to give Silas his blood as well.

It had been two days, and Jadis and Dante hadn't left his side. Dante remained in the room, sitting in a chair next to them, and Jadis stayed in the bed. She felt Silas move next to her, and her eyes shot open. Dante felt it as well and sat up.

"Silas," she whispered.

He slowly opened his eyes and looked into hers. "You're here, my love," he replied, his voice barely audible.

"Yes, baby. I'm here. I haven't left your side."

"I'll be okay, darling."

She lay on his chest, and he wrapped one arm around her body before he fell back to sleep. This time, her tears were that of relief.

She looked to Dante, and he gently smiled with watery eyes. He stood and sat on the edge of the bed with Jadis and rubbed her back. "He's going to be okay, my love. Between the two of us and our blood combined, death won't find him."

A week later, they entered the main temple, and their clan, along with Jabari, had been anxiously awaiting their return. They stood with bated breath, witnessing their arrival. Maddie, Aria, Skye, and Ivory rushed to their mates' side with cries of relief.

Mag and Limi barked, growled, and jumped with uncontrollable excitement as Jadis entered.

"Mag—Limi," she stated, elated to see them again. She dropped to her knees on the stairs so she could greet them. Silas and Dante bent down on one knee and greeted them as well.

"Idvam," Silas called to Mag and Limi as they proceeded up the expansive stairway, too tired to acknowledge anyone else. They headed straight for the bedroom in silence.

"What's going on with them," Maddie asked as she clung to Eden. "Are they seriously going up to bed together?"

"It appears so. They've been through hell and back, in the literal sense. We have no idea what they've had to deal with over the last month," Eden answered.

"They're okay, aren't they?" Aria asked with tears in her eyes. She kept her arms wrapped tightly around Aiden, genuinely concerned for sister.

"Yes, physically, but until they're ready to face everyone, we won't know what took place. I can only imagine the torment and pain they've suffered," Aiden replied sadly.

"Why is Dante going with them?" Skye asked quietly.

"Who knows. They're probably not ready to leave each other. Silas and Dante have always had an unbreakable bond. They just need time," Syth replied.

Santiago looked to Luciana. *I know what they've done. I can feel it,* he stated privately.

Yes, I can't imagine what our bairns must have endured for that to happen. The tears filled her eyes, and Santiago wrapped her lovingly in his arms.

"They're alive, home, and with us. That's all that matters. Silas and Dante will be fine. It's our daughter I'm most concerned with," Santiago admitted aloud. "After what I witnessed, we may need to take the memories from her."

The rest of the clan looked at Santiago and then at each other with the same look of sadness and concern.

"The horrors that poor girl must have endured are unimaginable," Luciana stated.

"Silas will heal her in time, but until they're ready to make an appearance, we will allow them their privacy." He gently kissed Luciana. "Calm, my love, your bairns are home and safe."

Silas and Jadis stood on the plush rug, while Dante turned on the water in the shower. They undressed and tossed their clothes into a pile on the floor. The three of them stood under the warmth of the spray for about a half hour. They headed straight for bed and crawled under the amazingly warm, plush covers, and Silas and Dante slid into bed on either side of her.

Mag and Limi jumped on the bed and greeted them with excited kisses and wagging tails.

"It seems they've missed you," Silas stated as he pulled Mag's face to his.

"I can't believe we're actually home," she replied as Limi continuously tried licking her face.

"They do love you," Dante replied as he messed with Limi. After a short time, they settled down at their feet.

Silas and Dante rolled over, now both facing her. She lay on her back, not knowing who to look at. She felt an overwhelming pull in both directions.

"Dante, I'm sorry you had no choice but to take me as your mate. Silas, I know I betrayed you, and I'm sorry." She rubbed her face with both hands, trying to keep herself from crying.

"Look at me, darling." Dante gently turned her head toward him and sat up on his elbow.

"I chose you willingly. Do not question my love or desire for you. I would take you as my mate a hundred lifetimes over, regardless of the situation."

Silas was also up on one elbow, looking down at her. "My love, I made this decision, and I haven't regretted it for one minute. Don't ever feel like you've betrayed me. If anyone owes anyone an apology, Dante and I owe it to you. We—forced this upon you," he stated with a heartfelt smile.

"So what now?" she questioned.

"The three of us are now bonded for an eternity. You'll choose to take who you want, when you want. The choice will always be yours. There will be no jealousy, no judgement, no anger. Dante and I will always love you, and nothing—nothing has changed between you and me," he stated adamantly.

She rolled over to face Silas and gently cupped his face in her hand.

"I thought I lost you." The tears streamed down her face.

Silas pulled her body onto his and claimed her mouth. After a long-heated kiss, he gently pulled away.

"I love you with all that I am, mon chéri. Now I believe your mate is waiting for you." He nodded in Dante's direction with a genuine smile.

She nervously rolled off Silas and over to Dante. She had no words, but the love and pull she felt for him was undeniable.

"Come, mon amour." Dante reached over and pulled her body beneath his. His mouth met hers, and their kiss was one of desperation and love. It was the first time they had touched each other as lovers, as mates, and without the looming threat of death hanging over their heads. The genuine passion reflected in his kiss said it all.

"I also *love you with all that I am, darling*. Silas speaks the truth. The choice of lovers will always be yours without repercussions. Silas will always have the final say when it comes to you and rest assured, he and I are as bonded to each other as we are to you. Just not in the sexual kind of way," he teased, with a wink. The off-handed comment forced the three of them to laugh.

"So, how does this work exactly?" she asked, her voice shaky.

"What do you mean, baby?" Silas asked.

"I'm tired and just need to sleep. Who do I cuddle?"

"Both." Dante chuckled. "Make yourself comfortable. We'll do the rest." Instinctively, she rolled onto her side and rested her head on Silas's shoulder, with one leg bent over his groin, and her arm resting over his chest. Silas wrapped his opposite arm around her and placed the one facing Dante behind his head. Dante scooted closely behind her and draped his arm and leg around her naked body.

"Are we safe?" she mumbled.

"Yes," they answered in unison.

They remained in the room for a week, sleeping off the emotional and physical torment, not to mention the drugs. Jadis woke many a day and night, calling out or fighting off an invisible enemy. Silas and Dante were always there to comfort her.

After a few days, she realized it didn't matter who she slept on. They both found a way to accommodate her as well as themselves. She fed from them as needed, and they fed from her as needed. The rest of the time, all they had the energy to do was sleep.

Jadis stirred, feeling like she was awake for the first time since having arrived home. Silas and Dante were already awake, quietly lying beside her.

"Good morning, baby. You slept quiet last night," Silas said.

"Feel better, darling?" Dante added.

She kissed them both before responding. "Yes, I finally feel okay. How are my mates?"

"Baby, we've been through shit like this for hundreds of years. To us, it's nothing more than another battle behind us," Silas replied.

"You're the one we're worried about," Dante responded.

"I feel good and having the two of you at my side seems to have drowned out the demons."

Silas rolled on top of her and looked down at her. "You have no idea how much I needed to hear that," he mumbled. "Since you're feeling better, I'm going to shower. We should see the family today. They're worried sick about you and would love to see you." He stole another heated kiss before rolling out of bed. "I'll leave you to your mate." He winked. He got up and made his way into the bathroom. As he closed the door, she rolled over to face Dante.

He wrapped her in his arms, and she felt an urge creep up from deep down. He rolled on top of her and laid his heavy, perfect body on hers, and took her mouth to his.

"This time, I'll have you the way I've only envisioned." He moved one of his legs between hers and pushed them apart. He dragged his canines down the vein on her neck, forcing her heart to skip a beat. He slid his hand up her thigh and gently massaged it.

He slowly moved back and forth, rubbing his hardened erection against her nub.

Damn, I want him. She wrapped her arms around his body and ran her hands over the muscles on his back.

"You feel amazing," she whispered.

"You have no idea how long I've desired to be with you like this," he admitted.

His hand made its way up her waist, across her ribs, and up to her breast. He ran his thumb over her hard, pink bud.

She wrapped her arms around his neck and moaned beneath him, yearning for every thick, hard inch.

He wrapped his hand around the back of her head and pulled her face to his. The warmth of her tongue and the subtle taste of Jasmine only served to ramp up his need to possess her in every way. With each gentle touch of his, her moans grew with nervous anticipation.

He pulled away and peered into his new mate's eyes. "I need you to know how much I truly love you," he whispered. He also felt how nervous she was, which made him desire her all the more.

"I know, baby, and I love you more than words can ever express," she replied.

He kissed her neck and slid his tongue across her throat and over her hammering pulse. He trailed gentle kisses down her neck, moving down to her perfect breasts. He suckled the hard, pink nipple he had only seen beneath her silk top. He teased it with his tongue as he had so many times in his mind. He slid his hand between her legs and let his fingers find their way into her wet, anxious core. She responded, sending his body into desperate need to fuck her like he had in his dreams.

She gasped and arched her back, needing more. He continued to relentlessly rub her sex with his thumb as he slowly slid his fingers in and out. He licked his way down her stomach, and her body quivered beneath his touch.

He moved far enough down to place his face between her legs. After he pushed her knees further apart, he swirled his tongue around her sex.

Her moans grew in intensity, and the sensation overtook her as he suckled the soft flesh. She grabbed the back of his head in one hand and bunched the sheet in the other.

"Dante," she whispered. "I need you inside me."

With each taste, each twirl of his tongue, he felt her tremble. Her sex pulsed beneath his mouth.

"Dante," she moaned with a raspy whisper. "I want you—now." The climax rose, and her body convulsed with its release. He stayed put and continued to tease her body until she was consumed with the heated orgasm.

Moving from between her legs, he suckled her nipple again, satiating a long, pent-up desire. He moved up her body and shoved his tongue in her mouth. With a hard thrust, he was inside the heat of her desperate core. He gently turned her head, exposing her neck before he pierced the soft, scented flesh.

Her blood flowed over his tongue, and every swallow brought about his need to come inside her. He let go of her throat before allowing himself to come and offered his vein to her.

He felt amazing as he rocked back and forth. With each forceful shove, he penetrated deeper. *Holy hell.*

"Drink, baby," he groaned. He repositioned his neck to her mouth. Her canines pierced deep into his musky, flesh and she savored every drop of his powerful, archaic blood.

He responded to her thoughts as she fed from him and thrust his hips so hard, she released her grip with a guttural, pain-filled growl, bringing his orgasm to surface.

"Dante—" she growled as the sensation took hold of her body again.

"Take it, baby," he whispered.

She let out another heated moan as her orgasm shattered. He also let out a guttural groan with his own release. His body shook, and his shaft throbbed as his liquid flowed into his beautiful mate's body.

"Ah shit, you have no idea how bad I needed that," he whispered. "I can't believe how amazing you feel."

He lay on top of her, breathless as their chests rose and fell together. He finally pulled out and rolled over, taking her with him.

"You're finally mine—say it," he stated.

"I'm yours, wizard, now and forever. Promise me you'll never leave me."

"I'll never leave you, baby. Why do you even think such a thing?" he asked, a bit surprised.

"I don't know. Things have been a bit crazy lately, in case you haven't noticed," she replied. "Maybe I'm being paranoid, I'm sorry," she whispered. "You have no idea how scared I was when I saw you in the arena. If something would have happened to you—" The tears gently pooled in her eyes.

"Look at me, baby." Dante gazed into her eyes. "I knew exactly how you felt, and don't ever apologize. What you've endured is more than most could have survived. You're more than I ever dreamed of, and I'm beyond honored to be your mate. I've held you in my mind and heart for so long, it's hard to believe I now hold you in my arms."

"You taking me as your mate means more to me than my words can ever express. Don't you ever forget that."

He took her mouth to his once again before rolling over with her. She lay in his arms and dozed off.

She woke with her head resting on Silas's chest. His arm was wrapped around her, and Dante was draped over her from behind.

"Hi, baby," she stated, looking at Silas smiling.

"Hi back." Silas smiled as Dante rolled onto his back.

"You slept well today," Silas whispered.

"There's a good reason for that," Dante teased.

"Dante," she barked as she landed a backhand on his stomach. He grabbed her hand and laughed.

"Better watch out, brother. She's quick with the smack," Silas chuckled.

"The two of you better not start that shit," she demanded, to their amusement.

"What else is on your mind, darling?" Dante asked.

"How are we going to tell everyone we're also mated?"

Silas and Dante shrugged their shoulders. "We just tell them," Silas replied.

"We just walk downstairs and be like hey, we're all in bed together," she joked.

"I say we have a party and let everyone know we have *an announcement* to make," Dante teased as he and Silas laughed aloud.

"Great idea, wizard. It worked out so well the last time." Their chuckles grew into full-on laughter.

"Let's get up. I think we could all use a stiff drink," Dante offered.

They dressed and headed out the door. Silas had his arm wrapped around her neck, and Dante had his arm around her waist. She had one arm around each of them but as soon as they stepped out of the doorway, she could hear everyone's voices downstairs. She trembled and stopped in mid-stride.

"What's wrong, baby?" Silas asked.

"I don't think I can face everyone. They're probably angry I'm the reason they were all dragged into that situation." She backed up into the bedroom, but Dante cupped her hands in his.

"Let's get one thing straight—none of this was your fault. Don't you for one minute think that. This is the life we've always lived and the threats to our kind are nothing new," Dante stated.

"Baby, Dante is right. Our clans have faced Abigor for eight hundred years. This wasn't your doing. The only reason you were in that situation is because of us." Silas lifted her chin and gave her a passionate kiss.

She wrapped her arms around him and squeezed before he gently pulled away. Dante pulled her into his body and wrapped his arms around her. He kissed the top of her head and patted her butt.

"Come, baby, it's okay." Dante started.

She let out a heavy breath and clung to their arms as they headed downstairs.

As soon as everyone saw them, a hush crossed the room, and the silence sent her spiraling.

"Well, I'll be damned," Eden stated, breaking the awkward tension. The entire family swooped in, and Skye and Ivory cried as they hugged Jadis.

"Hmhmm—think I can squeeze in here?"

Jadis let go of Skye and Ivory and grabbed onto Aria, who gave her a tight embrace.

"Move it," Maddie stated playfully to Aria, as she wrapped her arms around Jadis.

"I'm not sure if the three of you are feeling up to it, but maybe we can celebrate?" Aiden suggested as he swept Jadis off her feet.

She wrapped her arms and legs around his body and clung to him. She felt Silas go stiff, and Dante growled under his breath.

Everyone went wide eyed, and Aiden was taken aback. He slowly set her down.

"What the hell's with Dante?" Maddie questioned Eden telepathically.

"I don't know what that was about?" Eden replied.

Jabari broke the tension-filled room with a huge belly laugh, and his arms stretched outward. "Come—let us celebrate! Our clans have been reunited." He moved in and greeted Silas and Dante with a forearm grasp and a heavy pat on the back, as well as a hug. They returned the gesture in kind before he pulled Jadis in for a tight embrace.

Eden pulled her from Jabari and wrapped his arms around her. "You don't know how good it is to see you, baby girl."

She looked up and genuinely smiled. They kissed each other's cheeks with a warm greeting.

"I'm so happy to see you too. Thank you for everything." Eden gave her another suffocating squeeze, and she returned the heartfelt gesture.

From behind, someone cleared their throat. She turned only to see Bain standing there. "Bain!" He moved in and swept her into his arms. "I haven't had a chance to tell how worried I was about you," she stated.

"You have no idea how *worried I was about you*." He gently set her down after giving her another tight squeeze.

The attendants moved around the room, handing out drinks to everyone as they moved into the main parlor.

Silas, Dante, and Jadis held onto each other as they walked with their clan. The casual glances in their direction were undeniable. *They're all trying to decipher what's going on with the three of us,* Jadis thought.

"Well, hell," Santiago stated as he entered with Luciana. "It appears our bairns are all back under one roof." He and Luciana hugged Silas, Dante, and Jadis for what seemed like an eternity.

Although they were beyond curious, no one brought up Bergelême, nor did anyone ask about what actually happened, to Jadis's relief. She wasn't ready to talk about it, much less relive any of it.

She stood with her girls while they filled her in on some of what had been taking place at the temple while they were gone. They were careful not to go into too much detail. They also filled her in on everything everyone had done to make sure Mag and Limi were well cared for, doing their best to avoid any serious subjects.

She heard Silas and Dante laughing along with everyone else. Their conversations however, went into greater detail. *As they said, all that had happened was just another battle won to them. It doesn't seem to faze them at all. I refuse to fall prey to Abigor's torture. He will no longer control me or my emotions, especially from beyond the grave.*

"I know you all are dying to know what happened, so ask. It's okay—really," Jadis offered.

They hit her with so many questions in unison, she couldn't help but laugh aloud. Silas and Dante looked to her, and she winked back. They grinned ear to ear and turned their attention back to their conversations.

Silas patted Dante on the shoulder. "It seems our girl is going to be fine," he stated aloud.

"It seems so," Dante agreed, smiling from ear to ear.

"Their girl?" Aiden repeated to Eden and Bain. The two of them shrugged their shoulders, just as confused.

Santiago's loud voice brought the attention to him. "I think a toast is in order."

Everyone shouted in agreement. Silas and Dante moved in next to Jadis, and she stood between them.

Everyone in the room held up their glasses.

"Often times, it is not the strongest that win the battle, but those who push forward with tenacity and determination. Not every dark cloud brings the storm. Your journeys have been challenging and ominous, May you never turn back. This celebration shall be in honor of your triumph and all you have accomplished." Santiago raised his glass and nodded.

They all hollered and clinked their glasses together before moving about, while the girls remained seated at the bar.

"I see you're still acting as Jadis's nanny," Bain joked, fishing for information.

"I believe I've recently acquired a different title," Dante replied as he placed a couple of hard pats on Silas's shoulder.

"What was Abigor like, if I may ask?" Aria asked politely and with caution.

"He was a monster." Jadis stated. "He beat the shit out of me so many times, I lost count."

"Oh Jadis, are you sure you want to talk about all this?" Maddie asked.

"Absolutely, the bastard is more than dead, thanks to Dante."

"Okay, tell us everything," Ivory stated. They moved around and took a seat at the corner of the bar so they could face each other as Jadis told the tales.

"I also fought the Enchantress a couple of times, not to mention I broke her back the night Abigor put Dante in the arena to fight."

"No—you didn't." Skye said it so loud, it drew the attention of half the family.

"I did. She was actually in love with Abigor, which was the main reason we got into more than one altercation."

"No way," Aria stated, sounding shocked.

"She was sooo jealous. If it weren't such a terrifying situation, I would have enjoyed it."

They laughed, drank, and listened intently as Jadis told them as much as she could. She was truly having fun with her girls again and hadn't noticed the huge storm that had appeared sometime during the night, at least not until a crack of thunder caught her attention. The wind howled, and the palms outside bent with its relentless power. The rain beat against the expansive windows, and the thunder and flickering lightning continued to grow with intensity, as did her anxiety. She tried to push it aside, but the relentless storm was getting the better of her, for what reason she didn't know.

Silas and Dante looked at each other and turned to their mate. "I feel her anxiety as the storm grows closer," Silas stated.

"As do I. We should make sure she's okay," Dante replied. "Those memories are going to plague her for quite some time."

Jadis felt Silas and Dante move in behind her, and she reached up with both hands. Each of them took a hand as she swiveled around in the bar stool to face them. "Is everything okay?" she asked.

"Yes, we just wanted to check in. You seem to be enjoying yourself." Silas replied with a wink.

"I am. I'm okay, baby." She beamed at them.

"Is the storm bothering you, darling?" Dante asked.

"Sort of, not sure why," she admitted.

The girls all sat quietly, but their inquisitiveness was unquestionable. They were trying to figure out what was going on between Silas, Dante, and Jadis.

"We just wanted to make sure you didn't need anything," Dante said. He bent over and took her mouth to his. Their tongues met, and they kissed as if no one else was in the room.

The girls slid from their bar stools, waiting for Silas to take him down, but the opposite happened. As soon as Dante pulled away, Silas took her mouth to his.

"What the fuck?" Bain stated aloud.

"It seems everyone has questions," Silas said telepathically. He and Dante looked at Jadis, waiting for her response.

"Why not." She shrugged. *"They're all going to find out soon enough."* She finished her drink, and Dante re-filled it.

The three of them clinked their glasses together and took a drink. Silas and Dante pulled a bar stool next to her and took a seat. She swiveled her bar stool toward Silas and leaned into his body as he wrapped his arm around her back.

Dante pulled her leg over his and held onto her thigh, while she wrapped her arm in his and held onto his forearm.

The stunned looks on everyone's faces said as much as their silence. *"How long should we let them stand there like that?"* Jadis asked silently.

"Maybe all night," Dante joked.

"Since no one else dares ask, what the hell is going on?" Eden asked as he rubbed his temples, which caused Jadis to laugh aloud.

"Eden, don't tell me you feel a migraine coming on?" she joked.

His head snapped up in her direction, and Jadis, Silas, and Dante could no longer contain themselves.

Lars let out a belly laugh after seeing Eden's reaction to her quip. "Jadis is baacck."

"What's the matter, Bain? Cat got your tongue?" Dante questioned.

"Fess up. What is going on with the three of you?" Skye demanded.

Silas, Dante, and Jadis looked to each other, and she nodded to Silas.

"Jadis and Dante are now mated, and my brother and I are bonded," Silas blurted out.

Everyone was shocked with the sudden admission. The reactions went on and on. Everyone looked to each other as well as the three of them.

"Would one of you care to explain?" Eden politely asked.

Silas and Dante looked at Jadis. With a slight side-to-side motion, she moved her head and furrowed her eyebrows, telling them no. They knew exactly what she meant. *The three of us are the only ones who understood the dire circumstances it took for me to agree to mate Dante. Not that it makes a difference now, but I'm not comfortable telling everyone the intimate or not so* intimate *details just yet.*

"That will remain between the three of us," replied Silas. No one dared ask another question. They all respected their decision.

Jadis looked at Aiden and felt a wave of anguish wash over him. She and Aiden captured each other's gaze, both of which were filled with unspoken emotions and shared understanding. There was a sadness lingering behind Aiden's stoic expression and Jadis's empathetic smile. She noticed how Aria glance up at him, studying his reaction. Finding himself at a loss for words, Aiden looked down at Aria with a forced a smile, one he hoped would provide her with a sense of reassurance regarding the two of them. He couldn't believe this was happening. He felt as if his world were spinning, and a slow coil wrapped itself around his body, constricting his breath.

Aria lowered her head, discretely rolled her eyes, and let out a heavy sigh.

Aiden kissed her head and calmly took a sip of his drink, trying to hide his genuine feelings. *This is the result of me being an idiot. Instead of killing Vidar, I should have gone after Jadis. She is truly lost to me. There's no question now I'll have to stand on the outside looking in for the rest of my existence. Any hope I had was just put to the grave.*

"I believe this is cause for a celebration," Santiago announced as he stepped forward with Luciana at his side. Santiago placed a hand on both Silas and Dante's shoulders.

"Mountains do not rise without earthquakes. Some bonds are lost in the fire, while others are forged in them. Anyone can love when the sun is shining. Only in the darkest of storms do you find the heart that truly loves. The three of you have conquered true darkness. May you walk many a lifetime side by side with the fierceness of a dragon. Your bonds are ones that shall forever be revered."

Santiago pulled Jadis in and wrapped his arms around her. He kissed the top of her head and stepped back, holding her hands in his. "As Nosferatu, our greatest gift in life is to find a mate. Not one in need of saving, but one who will stand by our side in battle without wavering. You have proven your loyalty and strength beyond measure. We are proud to call you our daughter."

His words were so sincere, she felt the water pool in her eyes. "Thank you, you have no idea how much that means to me," she replied, a bit choked up.

Everyone in the room broke the silence with a shout of some sort as they clapped their hands. To her relief, they were genuinely happy for them.

The party resumed without further questions, and the energy was the lightest it had been all night now that all was revealed.

"Darling," Dante called from across the room.

Jadis turned to face him, and he and Silas sauntered her way with a coy smile, darting their eyes between each other.

"What are the two of you up to?" She asked, the curiosity killing her.

Dante kissed her and stole a little tongue in the process. "I have a little mating gift for you." His smile radiated across his face.

"Really?" she asked, shocked. *How did he find time for that?*

Dante turned and nodded toward Jabari, who laughed aloud. "Ohhh—he has a gift for you all right."

Zach entered through the main temple entrance, carrying what appeared to be two cats, one tucked gently under each arm. She jumped to her feet and stood between her mates. They each reached out and took one of the kittens from him and turned to her.

"Two leopards? Are you kidding me?" she stated, sounding elated.

"Yes, baby. I figured if anyone could care for them properly, it would be you," Dante replied.

"I love them. How did you get them?" she asked as they handed her the cubs.

"Unfortunately, their mother was taken by a crock at the edge of the Sacré River. One of our groundskeepers found them," Dante explained, as she and the girls swooned over them.

"That's terrible," she stated as she handed Aria and Maddie the cubs before leaping into Dante's arms.

"Thank you, baby. By the way, have I told you how much I love you lately?"

"Yes, mon amour, and I you."

She looked to her mates. "What should we name them?"

"Not sure?" Dante looked to Silas and held up one of the cubs in the air. "How about we call this little girl Sindri?"

"I love it, and we'll call this little guy Badru," Jadis stated.

"Badru, meaning one born during the Full Moon, perfect." Dante smiled.

"Sindri and Badru—perfect names," Silas agreed. He took Badru from Jadis and held him up.

Everyone walked over to see and hold the cubs. Mag and Limi jumped around, trying to smell and see their new companions. Dante and Silas bent down and introduced their newest family members to each other.

Jokes, laughter, and lighthearted banter filled the room for hours. Jadis continued telling her girls stories of the underworld to their shock and amazement as they played with the cubs.

A large clap of thunder echoed through the parlor, and Jadis yelped and ducked as if she were about to be struck. Her reaction caused each of the girls to jump and flinch.

Silas and Dante's heads snapped in her direction and they exchanged a quick glance. Feeling her embarrassment, and not wanting to over react for her sake, they casually strolled over to her.

"Are you okay?" Maddie asked, as she gently rubbed her arm.

"I'm okay. I don't know why I reacted like that," Jadis replied a bit embarrassed. Even though her heart was racing, she tried to play it off.

"We should go to bed, baby. It's been a long night, and you look tired," Silas offered as he squeezed her hand.

"I am tired. I'll go to bed. The two of you stay here and enjoy yourselves." She smiled.

"Nonsense, when have you ever gone to bed without me?" Silas asked.

"You want me to answer that?" She joked. *Silas had put me to bed alone many a night when I had angered and/or defied him.*

He and Dante laughed aloud, having heard her afterthoughts.

"Shall we?" Silas bowed slightly and held out his hand. She chuckled, grasped his hand, and turned to Dante.

Dante swept her into his arms and took her mouth to his. "I'll be up shortly. I want to sit with Bain for a bit."

"Promise you won't be long."

"I promise, darling. I'll be up soon," he replied with a wink.

"By the way, I love my gifts, in case I haven't said it."

"And I love you. Go, I won't be long."

Silas and Jadis politely excused themselves and headed up to bed with Mag, Limi, Sindri, and Badru.

Dante and Bain took a seat on a couple of plush chairs, away from everyone else. Dante sat back and crossed one leg over the other. Bain handed him the bottle of Sanotri Hibori after having filled his glass and sat back listening to Dante as he explained all that had happened.

"So, what are we going to do about the Enchantress?" Bain asked.

"I don't know, but rest assured, we won't stop until we destroy her."

"Count me in. I want to see the bitch in her grave as much as the three of you do. She's still a threat to Jadis," Bain huffed.

"Yes, and she won't be leaving our sight anytime soon," Dante stated.

"Count me in. I'll remain by your sides until the bitch is ash beneath our boots."

"Don't reveal anything we've spoken about to anyone else."

"You have my word," Bain agreed.

"By the way, you have no idea how worried she was about you."

Bain let out another heavy sigh. "I was just as worried. I knew you and Silas could handle yourselves. I wasn't so sure about Jadis, to be honest. Tell me, how is the mating?" Bain asked, trying to lighten up the conversation.

"Everything I had ever dreamed of or could ask for," Dante admitted.

Silas and Jadis entered the shower and stood under the warmth of the water. She turned to him, knelt, and took his sex into her mouth as she held onto his taunt ass with one hand and gently stroked his shaft with the other.

He replied with a heavy groan and planted both hands on the shower wall as her tongue made its way around his tip before consuming him again. He grabbed the back of her head and wrapped her wet hair around his fist, forcing her to take him deeper.

She could taste the salty liquid seep onto her tongue as she took her time savoring every pulsing inch, at least as much of it that would fit.

He let out a low, guttural curse, and the sensations overtook his body. "You keep that up, and I'm going to fill your mouth."

She squeezed his shaft in response to his low growling, and twisted and moved her hand up and down with a tighter grip, massaging what her mouth couldn't.

The heat of her mouth and the strength of her hand, forced a wave of arousal crashing to the surface, and he could barely hold it back.

"Ahh damn—" He lifted her up into his arms and placed her firmly onto his vein. "I'm going to ravage you," he groaned.

She wrapped her legs around his body and reveled in the feeling as his hardened muscle slid in. "I need you," she moaned.

His arms enveloped her, and his warmth washed over her like a wave, unfurling all of her senses. She moved up and down, slowly taking him all in as he held her ass in a tight grip. "My God, you feel amazing—exactly what I need." She let out a throaty groan. "Take me to bed."

He carried her out of the shower and fell into bed on top of her. She wrapped her arms under his and around his back before sliding her hand down, gripping his perfect ass and pulling him further between her legs.

He slid his hand behind her head and claimed her mouth. She pushed her tongue past his fully extended canines, and their tongues met in a desperate, long-awaited reunion. His touch was exactly what she needed. *I need to feel him, to make love to him, and to be desired by him.*

"You own all of me, my love," Silas whispered, responding to her thoughts. "You feel amazing, by the way. You have no idea how bad I want you again—and again." He smiled, his voice raspy with need.

"Mmm—sounds perfect," she replied softly.

Silas let out another low growl. "I'll forever love you softly but right now, I need to fuck you hard." He pulled her thigh up over his waist, gently settling himself further between her legs. He rubbed his tip against her tight opening. He slowly rocked back and forth as he moved his hand up her thigh and over her hip. He then traced the back of his fingers across her ribs before caressing her breast and teasing her nipple with his thumb.

He felt her squirm beneath him, begging him to be inside her again. He slithered his tongue down her neck as he dragged his upper canines across her throat, lingering over her pulsing skin.

She moaned with every touch, every kiss, every breath. "You feel amazing." She slid her hands over his shoulders, down his arms, and around his back, feeling his muscles flex and ripple with every move he made. She moaned as she trailed her tongue over his throat. She gently nipped his neck just above his vein, and she felt the jolt shoot through his body.

"Take what you want, darling."

She pulled the blood from his vein, sending a shockwave of need through her own body. She finally released his neck. "Give it to me," she moaned, practically begging him to take her all the more.

He repositioned her body under his and gave a hard shove. She flung her head back into the pillow and moaned with each powerful thrust. She turned her head, baring her neck for him.

As he fed, he forced his erection deeper into her body. "You're mine—say it, baby," he demanded softly.

"I'm yours, vampire." She let out a breathless moan, and her body trembled, and her sex pulsed. "Holy shit—" she groaned.

He felt her release and drove himself deeper. He was rough, forceful, and desperate to feel her in every way. He let out a low, throaty growl that vibrated her body as he pulsed inside her. They were drowning inside each other's orgasms. After all that had happened, they needed to feel alive, together. They lay breathless as his body consumed hers.

After a few moments, Silas lifted his head and peered into her eyes. He moved the hairs off her forehead before kissing her again.

"You have no idea how much I needed you." She began to quietly cry. "I thought I had lost you, and I hate him for what he did to you!"

"Don't cry, baby. I'll never leave you. I have no words to describe the rage I felt toward him." He gently wiped the tears from her cheeks, feeling every ounce of her heartache and pain. "We're home now. Abigor is dead, and you're safe. Don't let the thoughts plague your mind, baby."

"I love you, Silas."

"And I you, mon chéri."

The love they felt for each other was never greater than in this moment.

Jadis awoke when she heard the shower turn on. Shortly thereafter, Dante slipped under the covers. She rolled over, and he wrapped his arms around her and took her mouth to his.

"I love you, wizard."

"And I you, my mate."

She laid her head back on his chest and draped her leg over his crotch. She reached for Silas, who had already moved in behind her. He wrapped his body around hers, and she reached for his forearm and tucked it under her breast.

CHAPTER 19

Santiago decided it would be best for his clan to stay in the oasis for the duration, at least until the Enchantress was located and dealt with appropriately.

The girls found themselves once again on a complete lockdown while their mates conducted whatever business they needed to attend to, more specifically, locating Evanora.

After a month or so, Santiago decided to have Silas pull the warriors back to allow Jadis some space. Silas and Dante's arguments went unheard as Santiago wouldn't waver. Jadis, however, was completely relieved.

Santiago had also decided to bestow Dante and Aiden the honor of becoming a lord after all they had done. The ceremony would take place in a month's time under the light of the full Wolf's Bane Moon. Jadis was elated for them both. If anyone deserved the very honor of becoming a lord, it was Dante and Aiden. Silas and Eden couldn't be happier for their brothers, and they would be the ones to title them. The ceremony was all anyone in the oasis, Nosferatu or bruja, spoke about. Everyone wanted to be a part of it or at least witness it. The vast majority of whom had never seen anyone bestowed such an honor. The excitement surrounding it all also drew a lot of unwanted attention to Silas, Dante, Eden, and Aiden to their mates' dismay.

The girls sat at the natural pool in the middle of the expansive gardens just as they did almost every day. The girls were finishing lunch, while Jadis sipped her drink.

"What are you going to do now that you'll be mated to not just one but two lords?" Aria laughed.

"I don't know, but not like you're one to talk. Your mate will now be a lord as well," she teased back.

"But we only have to deal with one," Maddie added.

"All I know is you better reel in some of you brujas. They keep looking at my wizard like they do, we're going to have a serious problem," Jadis stated.

Aria laughed, knowing she was serious. "Believe me, they've been forewarned. The two of them are no longer allowed on the temple grounds. One more side eye, and they'll be out of the coven as well. I got your back, sister."

Jadis tilted her glass to her in appreciation. "I say you get rid of them permanently before I do."

"If you wish it on a serious note, they'll be gone by morning," Aria offered.

"Then tell them to start packing. No one looks at one of my mates like they do, not to mention the looks they give me. So far, I've brushed it off per Silas and Dante's orders."

Aria rolled her eyes. "Jadis, the last thing any of us want is for you to take care of it. We all know you don't follow their orders." She called Jabari telepathically. *"Father—"*

"What is it, love?" Jabari answered.

"I want—well, Jadis wants Mercia and Aisley gone, tonight."

"What's the problem?"

"Dante." She replied.

"Say no more."

"Now that that's been settled, want to go down to the river?" Aria asked.

Ivory set her glass down and looked between the girls. "You know our mates will never agree to that."

"Who says we have to ask permission?" Aria stated. "I'm so bored, I don't even know what to do anymore." Aria was as wild as they come and had never known constraints. Abigor loved her as if she were his own flesh and blood, however, he chose to raise her to be a warrior, not a daughter. She was willing to defy Aiden anytime she felt like it.

"I couldn't agree more. Maybe we should just cross the line again. We can suffer the consequences later, but at least we can have some time to ourselves," Jadis suggested.

"As always, you know we're game. I don't care what Syth has to say, and I'm tired of asking permission." Skye looked to Ivory, who nodded in agreement.

"And how are you going to get away from Silas and Dante?" Maddie joked.

Jadis winked at her. "I have a plan."

"Oh shit," Ivory stated.

"I feel an anklet already." Skye lifted her leg in a joking manner, which caused them all to laugh aloud.

Maddie suddenly went stiff and stopped laughing. They looked over to see what scared her and sure enough, Eden and Aiden were walking over. Skye quickly pulled her leg to her chest and rested her foot on the chair.

Jadis cleared her throat and spoke telepathically, *"Relax, they don't know anything. Don't act suspicious. Eden will smell it a mile away."*

"Well, hello there." Aria reached out for Aiden's hand, trying to act as normal as possible.

Eden bent down and kissed Maddie. "What are you girls up to?"

"Nothing, my love. We just finished lunch. What are the two of you doing out here?" Maddie asked, as she pushed her plate to the side.

Jadis sensed Maddie's trepidation and knew Eden would certainly sniff it out, so she quickly cloaked her.

"I wanted to see my mate before we headed to our meeting," Eden stated.

Once again, he's studying us with his incessant inquisitiveness, Jadis thought.

He looked to each of them more than once as if he were trying to pick up on something. It made Jadis nervous as always, so she took a moment to call Silas telepathically before speaking to Eden. "I'm going to see Silas and say hi before you bind his time again." She winked at Eden, who smiled warmly but still cocked his head in a questioning manner.

Silas was already waiting for her in the main temple. "Hi love, everything okay?" he asked.

"Yes, I just wanted to see my vampire before they steal you from me for the remainder of the day," she stated, as she leapt into his arms.

He gave her a heated kiss before speaking, "What are you all doing this afternoon?"

"The same thing as always, nothing," she joked.

Silas is looking at me just like Eden did. He doesn't trust me at all. She quickly interrupted his train of thought, "Where's Dante?"

"He's with Bain in the weapons room, messing around."

"I'm going to say hi before he's taken away also." She kissed Silas again before he set her down.

Eden and Aiden walked in. "Well, I guess that's it. I won't keep Dante too long." She smiled.

Silas smiled warmly as he patted her butt. "Go find your mate." He held her hand until their arms had stretched all the way out, before yanking her back for another heated kiss.

She chuckled and ran her hand over his perfect ass. "You sure you need to go to the meeting?"

He looked at Aiden and Eden, who were waiting on him. "Unfortunately, yes." He gave an over-dramatic eyeroll.

She laughed at the mocking gesture. "So be it."

She headed for Dante while Silas walked away with Eden and Aiden. She entered the weapons room, and Dante was with Bain, going through a large cache of weapons. "Hi, baby. Hey, Bain."

"Hey there, Jadis," Bain replied with a warm smile.

"Come," Dante stated as he held out his hand.

She jumped into his arms and squeezed him. "I miss my wizard. I wanted to say hi before you meet with everyone for who knows how long."

"Is that all you wanted?" He pulled her head back so he could look into her eyes.

"Yes, what else could there be?"

"Darling, with you, anything is possible."

She interrupted him before he prodded her mind. "Where's Silas?"

"With Aiden and Eden. They should be in their meeting already. We'll be joining them soon. What do you have planned?"

"Nothing, we're just hanging out, as usual. The girls are finishing lunch, so I wanted to come see you."

Dante kissed her again and set her down. After a pause, he called to her, "Darling, you sure you're not up to something else?"

"Like what?" She tried her best to sound innocent, which forced Bain to laugh to himself. She left and appeared back at the table by the pool. "Okay, I think we're safe. Let's do this now. We can go to the river for a swim."

"Jadis, how do you know Dante and Silas aren't already on to you?" Maddie asked nervously.

"I influenced them, a little something I picked up from Silas. I made it so they wouldn't want to communicate until they're in each other's presence. They both seemed to be casual enough. I don't feel like they felt any reason to question my motives. I also cloaked Eden. Maddie, you are a terrible liar."

Unless she was with the girls, she listened to Eden and did what he said when he said it. They loved to tease her and knew how much she enjoyed being a rebel with them. However, she was always nervous, which was all the more entertaining.

"The river is quite far." Maddie took a drink and looked at Aria nervously.

"It's not that far. Plus, I have a lot I can show you all on the way. I'm sure Jadis can get us there and back in no time, but I'd rather walk," Aria suggested.

Jadis motioned to the girls with her hand. "Well, let's go before Silas and Dante meet up, or we're good as caged."

They headed to the private swimming area that had been used as a bath house at one time. They knew it was off limits to everyone else as long as they were there. They took hold of Mag, Limi, Sindri, and Badru and then held hands with Jadis. She took them out of the temple grounds in a haze, so no one saw them physically leave. The girls landed in the dense landscape about a mile from the temple, making sure they were far enough away from prying eyes. They stood nervously and waited a few anxious moments for their mates or guards, but none of them appeared. They headed to the edge of the river and jumped in. They leapt off the palms into the clear, cool water, jumped off the rocks, and enjoyed their newfound freedom. After playing around in the water for quite a while, they sat on the edge of the river. Jadis had also conjured up a few bottles of Glendeon MaCru for them to enjoy.

"Want to see something cool?" Aria asked.

"What do you have in mind?" Jadis was genuinely curious. *Aria's world is fascinating, and she's as fun loving and adventurous as one can be.*

Ivory looked at Skye and Maddie to see if they agreed. They shrugged their shoulders. "We're in."

"Well, this place is beyond the oasis. We have to head into the desert." Aria looked at Jadis, wanting to judge her reaction, not knowing whether or not she was ready to head out on her own again. She wasn't sure she felt safe enough to venture out without Silas and Dante in tow.

Everyone sat in silence for a few moments, waiting on Jadis to answer. "Why not, I can't be afraid of lurking monsters the rest of my life."

"Then it has been decided. Jadis, do your thing. Take us two miles west," Aria demanded. "Shit, having you around is like having a personal driver."

They were discussing the Enchantress and what their next move would be when Dante and Bain appeared.

"It's about time the two of you joined us." Eden looked at the two of them, who were three hours late.

"How's our mate?" Silas was curious why he and Bain had both arrived at the same time. He felt an immediate shift in the air and quickly realized there was a strange energy around himself and Dante that began to wane.

Dante shot an angry look Silas's way with their combined realization. "I was going to ask you the same thing. Jadis was supposed to be with you," Dante stated.

"She said she was with you," Silas replied.

Lars laughed aloud. "Well, I'll be dammed. You should see the looks on your faces right now."

Jabari once again found himself thoroughly entertained as Dante and Silas shot an angry look Lar's way, which only ramped up his and Jabari's laughter.

"Essentially, they've been gone for three hours now?" Silas rumbled.

Eden and Aiden quickly stood, while Agaeus and Syth shoved their chairs back in a huff.

"Aria's defiance is beginning to match that of Jadis," Aiden stated.

Jabari smirked at Aiden's remark. "I warned you she was self-willed and wild. I did not raise her to be timid."

"Maddie will have her wings clipped the moment I get her ass back here," Eden stated as he headed for the door.

Santiago stood and faced Silas and Dante. "The two of you need to give Jadis some space. You've been hovering over her since the day you returned like a couple of wolves protecting their pup. Even they know when it's time to learn to walk on their own without fear or protection. Jadis is no different. She needs to find her strength again. She can no longer fear the world around her, nor can the two of you keep her isolated. She's more than capable of handling herself."

"Father, have you not met her? That girl gets into more situations than anyone I have ever met," Silas fumed.

"Jadis has always been a traveler between two worlds. Allow her to find her footing again," Santiago scolded sternly.

Ignoring his father, Silas called Sigurd telepathically while Dante listened. *"Where's Jadis?"*

"Milord?" Sigurd answered.

Silas looked at Dante with a dreadful feeling. *"Where is Jadis? She's at least in the oasis—yes?"*

"I haven't seen her since earlier. We were instructed to stand back on your orders. Last we saw, she was heading into the private bath house with her girls."

"Yes, you were," Silas replied, as he and Dante glared in their father's direction.

"This is exactly what happens when you leave her alone for one fucking minute," Silas snapped.

"Hence the reason she isn't allowed her freedom, nor left up to her own devices." Dante turned to Silas. "Let's get going," he huffed.

Silas motioned with his hand. "Only the Gods know where the five of them are right now."

"They could be anywhere by now. If Jadis chooses to use even an ounce of the abilities the two of you've been teaching her, she can probably hide from us for hours. I told you both it was a bad idea. She's continuously pulling Maddie in, and the more they're together, the more Maddie infuriates me," Eden seethed.

"Don't blame this on Jadis. Maddie doesn't have to go anywhere. It's obvious she makes her own choices," Silas retorted, defending his mate, even though he understood exactly where Eden was coming from.

"I don't have time to go back and forth with you," Eden replied.

Dante gave Eden a cautionary side eye. "Don't put this all on my mate."

"Don't put this on Jadis? Shit, that girl has been running since the night I met her, and now she's got Aria pulled in." Aiden walked with Eden, ignoring the burning glares Dante and Silas shot his way.

"Looks to us like Aria doesn't listen to you for shit, regardless of whether or not Jadis is around," Dante shot back.

Aiden ignored the comment and followed Eden

"Those girls just caused an entire roomful of grief." Jabari couldn't be more amused at the ensuing altercation taking place.

Luciana spoke to Santiago from the gardens, where she lay resting in the shade of a large palm tree. *"What's going on, my love?"*

"The girls have disappeared again." Santiago chuckled.

"She's going to be the death of those boys. Come, my love, join me outside while they hunt down their mates." Her amusement grew when she saw the angry looks on the faces of her sons and nephews as they appeared from the temple.

Aria took them to a triangular temple that was well hidden amongst the others, and led them through long tunnels and down various stairways. They wandered into a few of the smaller chambers, admiring the ancient hieroglyphs and carvings before making their way down another small set of stairs. Appearing before them was a large chamber where a small freshwater pool sat front and center. It was fed by a natural underground spring and was quite large. The water was crystal clear and stood still as glass. Sunlight lit the darkened chamber from a large, hidden opening at the top. Jadis looked up to see where the light was coming from, and she had no idea how the light got in as the opening wasn't visible from the outside.

"Who would have ever thought this was even here." Maddie was quite impressed. "It's beautiful."

"Damn, who would have thought?" Jadis looked at Ivory and Skye, who also stood in awe.

"Shit, Jadis, we should hang with Aria more often. You've become pretty boring since mating Silas and Dante," Ivory joked.

Skye joined in on her amusement. "I agree. Aria, can we move in with you?"

Jadis laughed along in a mocking manner before shoving both Skye and Ivory into the pool.

"Jadis!" They yelped before splashing into the crystal-clear water.

Maddie bent over, placed her hands on her knees, and laughed aloud. Ivory and Skye popped out of the water, laughing.

"Let's join them," Aria suggested as she shoved Jadis into the pool before she and Maddie jumped in, followed by Mag, Limi, Sindri, and Badru.

They sat on the edge of the pool, sipping their drinks, teasing one another, talking about their mates and how mad they probably were.

"I bet Silas and Dante are losing their minds about now." Jadis chuckled. "I kind of feel bad," she admitted.

"What did you just say?" Aria questioned.

Jadis rolled her eyes in response and shoved her backward into the pool.

Aria rose from the water. "I'll remember that!" She hopped onto the edge and pulled the water from her hair.

"How have they not found us yet? What exactly did you do?" Maddie asked.

"I learned pretty quickly how to cloak myself, very well in fact. My mates have been teaching me," Jadis explained.

Maddie let out a belly laugh. "I can only imagine what Eden is thinking. Until meeting you all, I haven't disobeyed him like this in a hundred years."

"I'm sure Aiden isn't very happy, to say the least," Aria replied.

"You think Aiden is upset now, wait until you pull this shit once you're mated," Skye said.

"I can't even imagine, but he has no idea. He won't control me like that."

"Oh, Aria." Ivory rolled her eyes mocking her. "You have no idea. He can, and he will control you."

"Really? I don't think we've been controlled at all." Jadis laughed, remembering back to all the times she, Skye, and Ivory had taken off on their mates.

"You do realize Silas and Dante will find us soon? I feel them. I'm actually surprised it's taken so long. I'm impressed with myself," she joked.

Maddie looked at Jadis a bit worried. "What time is it?"

"It's only like ten p.m.?"

"Maybe we should head back. I'm sure Eden is wanting to kill me right about now."

"Let's go. I'm hungry anyway." Aria stood and wiped the dirt off her butt.

They headed out of the temple and into the cool, desert evening. The silver beam of the moon lit the barren landscape, devouring its darkness.

They took ahold of Jadis's hands, ready to head back, when a rush of wind hit them. They jumped back, and Ivory, of course, could always be counted on to let out a scream that scared the hell out of them all.

"Holy shit," Maddie yelled, along with a scream of her own.

"Well, this is a very familiar situation," Eden snarled.

Maddie couldn't muster a word; she stood frozen in place, based solely on Eden's hardened expression.

"This will be the last time, mon chéri." Silas slowly approached her with Dante at his side.

"Jadis, I am now your mate. You will not defy me again. Silas is correct, *this is the last time.*"

"The two of you don't own me. Nor do you have the right to keep me locked up. Father said I could leave—well, sort of." She placed her hands on her hips and stood her ground.

The ensuing arguments lasted about ten minutes before their mates tired of it. They grabbed the girls up and appeared as an angry mob back in the main temple.

Santiago and Luciana sat with Bain, Lars, and Jabari, sipping their drinks in the parlor when their sudden appearance interrupted them.

"Ohhh—my lords!" Luciana joked, with a hearty laugh.

"They sure have their hands full," Santiago replied.

"The two of you can come at me with tongues aflame, but do not think I'll get down on my knees before either of you." Silas and Dante's eyebrows shot up at Jadis's statement.

She quickly side-eyed Bain when she heard him choke on his drink from across the expansive room. She stood with one raised eyebrow, waiting for the fallout. The way in which they stood menacingly quiet intimidated her. She backed up one cautious step at a time, ready to run to their room. With each step back, they took one step forward in unison. The only break in the silence were the angry voices and multiple arguments taking place all around them.

She took one more step back and tripped on the bottom step. She spun around to run, but Silas and Dante each had a hold of one of her biceps. They escorted her to their room and plopped her down on the edge of the bed.

Dante crossed his arms and looked at Silas. "Exactly how are we going to punish our mate for her continued defiance?"

Silas rubbed his chin and thought for a moment. "I say we punish her the old way."

"What does that mean?" She slowly stood up, but Silas met her chest to chest.

"I believe we're going to show you exactly how we're going to punish you." He grabbed her bikini top, pulled it over her head, and tossed it to the floor, along with his own shirt. He picked her up and positioned her body in the middle of the bed and hovered over her.

She placed her hands on his chest to hold him back, and he let out a growl that vibrated through her hands and into her gut. Dante tossed his own shirt to the side and crawled onto the bed next to them.

"We're going to show you exactly how much control we have." Silas moved off her, and Dante bent down and took her mouth.

Her heart thumped against her breast with the sudden realization of what they were talking about.

Silas and Dante re-positioned themselves, and Silas took her mouth while Dante pulled her shorts and bikini bottoms off. "Wait—" she began.

"*Wait* for what, love? You certainly don't *wait* to do what you want," Silas rumbled. He forced his mouth to hers once again before Dante moved back in.

Dante's tongue met hers, and he cupped her breast in his hand while Silas moved in next to him after removing his own pants.

Dante moved down and teased her nipple with his tongue as he moved his hands further down and rubbed her sex. He felt her body respond to his touch, and she let out a gentle, nervous moan as her pulse quickened.

Silas rubbed his face up the side of her and whispered, "Tonight, we shall *punish* you together."

They were side by side doing, whatever they wanted to her, to her body. The nervousness, the anticipation only seemed to ramp up her desire for them both.

They know exactly what they're doing, as if they're seasoned profession-als, she thought, as they moved around each other, solely focusing all their attention on her.

Dante moved further down and pushed her legs apart. He felt her trembling and heard her nervous thoughts, which only heightened his arousal. He nipped her sex and teased it with his tongue. Slowly, he slid his fingers into her heated, wet core. He began a relentless assault between her legs.

Silas took her mouth before he moved down, cupped her breast, and teased her nipple with his tongue.

She tried to breathe calmly, but her body had other ideas. *They're surely putting me in my place. They control everything about me, but they can do what they want, when they want, and how they want. I'm utterly powerless.*

"Don't forget it. We own all of you," Silas whispered. He moved off the top of her and rolled onto his back while Dante grabbed her legs and flipped her over. She now lay on top of Silas, while his tongue danced with hers. Dante inserted his fingers, and she pulled away from Silas's mouth and gasped.

Dante lifted her hips, so her butt met his crotch. "Wait—not like that, Dante." She found herself stuttering the words.

"Shhh—" was all Dante said.

Silas placed his hands on either shoulder and pushed her down. She stopped to suck both his nipples before licking and kissing her way further down, knowing what he wanted. She wrapped his hard shaft in her hand and moved it up and down, teasing him with her tongue.

Dante moved his fingers in and out of her heated core, reveling in her anxious, nervous anticipation. He placed his hand on her back and slid it up to her shoulder. He grasped hold, ready to dominate her from behind.

She slid Silas's shaft into the warmth of her mouth and twirled her tongue around the tip.

Silas let out a guttural moan and grabbed the back of her head, moving it up and down as she took as much of him as she could into the heat of her mouth. "Ahhh quod os vestrum," he moaned. She tightly gripped his shaft in her hand and followed the motion of her mouth, nearly undoing him.

Dante suddenly shoved himself so hard into her core, she let go of Silas's shaft and let out a guttural, painful moan along with a belt of air.

Silas pushed her head back down, and she took him into her mouth again.

At least Dante's not doing what I thought he was going to do.

Dante rumbled, "Well, now I know exactly *what to do* the next time you need to be punished."

He moaned with each hard thrust and rubbed her sex as he rocked his hips back and forth. He felt her core shudder as she pulsed all around his shaft, bringing forth his own desperate need to come.

She let go of Silas once again as the sensation cracked opened. Her body released like never before. As soon as she was finished, Silas and Dante re-positioned themselves.

She was suddenly face down on top of Dante with Silas behind her, ready to take her for himself. "Jesus, you feel amazing," Silas groaned as he thrust himself inside.

Dante placed his hand on the back of her head and pushed it down as she let out another belt of air. She licked his tip before taking his shaft into her mouth. He felt the tips of her whites scrape along the sides. "Be careful, mon amour," he said, with a moan.

She nipped the tip with her canines, and he flinched in response. He squeezed the back of her head before wrapping her hair in his fist. She had to place her hand on his hip to stop him from shoving himself so far down her throat, she choked.

Silas continued to thrust himself and felt the swell of his own orgasm rising to the surface.

Another wave hit her, and her body trembled, along with Dantes. His shaft pulsed, and the thick, warm liquid filled her mouth. She swallowed and sucked harder, bringing about a large guttural snarl from him as he released himself.

"Irrumabo me, eo cum infantem est ita," Dante growled, as the ecstasy overtook his entire body.

Silas let out a guttural groan as the three of them orgasmed together. They fell into a heap on the bed, breathless and moist from the hour or so of them relentlessly punishing her. It was a nervous mix of ecstasy and pleasure; one she'd never experienced. *If this is punishment, then I'll defy them every chance I get.*

"Don't even think about it," Silas said, as he landed a hard smack on her ass.

"Oww—what the hell, Silas?"

"Baby, this was just one of many punishments we have in store should you push your luck again," Dante threatened.

"Sounds intriguing," she teased.

"*Intriguing*? Darling, this was just a soft punishment," Dante replied.

"From what I felt, it wasn't soft at all." Her statement caused Dante and Silas to laugh with her.

"After all that's happened, it feels so amazing to be in bed with the two of two," she stated.

"I couldn't agree more. After our little adventure, there's nowhere else we'd rather be," Silas replied.

"If you call that a *little adventure*, I don't even want to know what you all would call a grand adventure."

"If you behave yourself, maybe Silas and I will take you on a *grand adventure*," Dante teased.

"That's a hard pass," she stated adamantly.

"Where's your spirit and sense of adventure, baby?" Silas winked.

"Don't you all think I've been on enough *adventures* for one lifetime?"

"Maybe we'll just take you horseback riding then." Dante laughed.

Silas and Jadis laughed as well, remembering back to Dante's random story about his Stallion.

"Petra!" a voice called out.

The three of them shot straight up in bed and stared at each other with looks of shock.

"What the fuck?" Jadis stated as the color drained from her face.

They didn't know if what they had all heard was real or not as they darted their eyes amongst each other. She looked to Silas and Dante, and they simply stared at each other, trying to hide their expressions.

"It's okay, baby. It was just a shared dream," Silas stated, trying to calm her racing pulse.

"We are mated and bonded. What one dreams as will the others," Dante added as he moved the messy hair off her forehead.

"Sleep, baby, we've got you. It's just a dream." Silas lay back down and wrapped his arm around her. She laid her leg over his crotch and rested her head on his shoulder.

Dante slid in closely, placing his heavy leg over hers, and draped his arm over her lower back in a protective wrap.

They lay there quietly, contemplating whether or not they heard the name being called out.

"I don't think I'll leave the temple after that," Jadis stated, truly scared.

"It's okay, baby. It was just a dream," Silas offered, again.

"From painful experience, the two of you have a funny way of not telling me the truth."

"You're safe, baby. We've got you. Now sleep, darling," Dante added before gently caressing her head and putting her to sleep.

Continue reading with

The Legend of Mortem Book 3 | Beyond the Veil